Whispers Across Time

To Granpa with my best wishes

J. R. Whittle

J. Robert Whittle

and Joyce Sandilands

By J. Robert Whittle

The Lizzie Series
Lizzie: Lethal Innocence
Lizzie Lethal Innocence - *Audio Book (CD, MP3)*
Narrated by J. Robert Whittle
Lizzie's Secret Angels
Streets of Hope
Lizzie's Legacy

Victoria Chronicles
Bound by Loyalty
Loyalty's Reward
Loyalty's Haven
Paperback and Hardcover Editions

Laughing Through Life: Tales of a Yorkshireman (CD)
(Autobiographical vignettes of Robert's own life)

By J. Robert Whittle and Joyce Sandilands

Whispers Across Time

Moonbeam Series
Leprechaun Magic
by J Robert Whittle and Joyce Sandilands
Leprechaun Magic - *Audio Book (CD)*
Narrated by Joyce Sandilands

3 On A Moonbeam
by Joyce Sandilands
3 On A Moonbeam - *Audio Book (CD)*
Narrated by Joyce Sandilands

Whispers Across Time

J. Robert Whittle
and Joyce Sandilands

Publisher's note: This book is a work of fiction set in the City of Victoria, BC and the Washington State cities of Seattle and Everett. To enhance the story, real places and people's names have sometimes been used, although the characters are fictional and are in no way intended to represent any person living or dead.

First Printing: 2007
Second Printing: 2008

Whitlands Publishing Ltd.
4444 Tremblay Drive, Victoria, BC
Canada V8N 4W5
Tel: 250-477-0192
www.bestsellingbooks.ca
Whitlands@shaw.ca

Cover photo and design by Joyce Sandilands
Cover design, text and layout by Jim Bisakowski, Desktop Publishing
Back cover photo by Tara Poilievre

Library and Archives Canada Cataloguing in Publication

Whittle, J. Robert (John Robert), 1933-
Whispers across time / J. Robert Whittle, Joyce Sandilands.

ISBN 978-0-9685061-9-6

I. Sandilands, Joyce, 1945- II. Title.

PS8595.H4985W44 2007 C813'.54 C2007-903891-3

Printed in Canada by Friesens, Altona, MB

To our four wonderful children,
Robert, Carol, James, and Christine,
our five grandchildren, Jamie, Courtney, Michael, Shayla and Alef,
and two great grandchildren, Kintia and Jaxon.
We love you all.

Acknowledgements

Winners of a Gold Medal IPPY Award … how sweet to hear those words in May 2007! The year has seen many changes to our lives and careers but perhaps the most exciting was finding out we'd won this Independent Publisher Book Award. The winning book was, *Loyalty's Haven,* our 7th full-length novel. It was a wonderful feeling to know our work was being recognized by the industry and our peers. In the early days of this 11-year old contest before they had shortlists, we were unofficially told *Lizzie: Lethal Innocence* had done very well. Having only series books, we didn't enter again until 2007. We're glad we did.

It's hard to believe, my wife Joyce, and I have been producing these books for eight years. *Whispers Across Time* is our 10th book (8th full-length novel, 1st non-series book and 2nd author collaboration).

I actually wrote *Whispers* between 2001 and 2003 as a diversion from more serious writing with no intention to publish. When I told Joyce what I was writing, she was surprised, especially knowing I had never read a book or seen a movie of this genre. I think she commented, "Where on earth did you get the idea of a time travelling mortal angel? I think I'll want to publish this one!" So, with the last of the Victoria books now out, it was time.

Joyce always adds her own touches to my books during the editing process and we decided it was time her writing was recognized. She's done a marvellous job once again, especially helping me with the romance scenes although we did have an issue about how 'modern' it could be!

She particularly enjoyed adding some extra historical items to the Everett portions of the story as her maternal grandparents (Joyce) settled there for a few years in the '20s with their six children attending school. Two of her uncles married and settled in Everett.

As usual with my books featuring local history, some of the characters are somewhat real and *Whispers* is no exception. A heartfelt thanks goes to one character who, to enable some privacy, shall remain nameless!

Thanks again to all of you who have encouraged and cajoled us over the years, buying and reading our books, giving them as gifts and reading library copies. You are always asking for more and no words can express our gratitude. We hope you have as much fun reading this book as we had writing it.

Thanks again to our team of Tara Poilievre (Office Assistant), Deborah Wright (final proofreading) and Jim Bisakowski (cover titles and layout). We couldn't do it without you and Joyce is more aware of that fact than I.

Thank you also to local archives, bookstores, the supportive public in general and Joyce (of course) who produces all our books as well as covering a myriad of other tasks. In addition to editing, marketing, websites etc., she also designs our posters and this time, to her credit, is the fantastic *Whispers* cover—utilizing a picture she took, appropriately you will discover, in Ross Bay Cemetery. Joyce wanted this cover to match our book and be different—with a little help from Jim, our graphic designer, she has achieved just that!

If you wish to receive notice of new books, newsworthy events, and craft shows we're attending in your area, we'll be happy to add you to our exclusive email list which we promise to share with no one. Go to our website and click on 'contact us,' give us a phone call or use my email address below. If you don't use the internet, we would be happy to put you on our phone list, by special request.

We depend more and more on the internet so we can reach our far-flung fans. The books are not available in bookstores outside of our home area (Victoria, BC and Southern Vancouver Island), however, we're always happy to hear from you by phone; and yes, we also sell books from our home and out of our car—we never leave home without them!

Our labour of love has continued much longer than we had ever thought possible. We will continue bringing you great, family friendly reading via markets and Christmas craft shows, however, time marches on and it's not only an issue of expense but also weight—as we get older, we often wish our books were lighter! However, readers tell us our books make great entertainment for all ages and knowing they not only bring enjoyment to adults but, are responsible for increasing the number of youthful readers in our troubled world, this makes it all worthwhile.

J. Robert Whittle and Joyce Sandilands
August 2007
robert@jrobertwhittle.com
250-477-0192 PST (Victoria, BC)

www.jrobertwhittle.com
www.bestsellingbooks.ca

Main Characters (in order of appearance)

Oliver Ryan – Seattle newspaper reporter in 1916
Tom Watson – Oliver's guardian angel
Bertha and Jane Bentley – mother and young daughter in 1916
Harry Jenson – Oliver's editor at Seattle *Observer*
Jack Marquette – Seattle rum runner
Ben Olson – Seattle police detective
Peter – Jorgenson chauffeur
Gus and Beth Jorgenson – Seattle businessman and wife
Nancy Wilson – Victoria singer
Mary Beth Janick – teacher at Everett High School in 2000
Egger Brothers – rum runners from Seattle area
Jake Mendell – Port Angeles sheriff
Constable Harry Gray – Victoria Provincial policeman
William Pendray – ghost of Victoria businessman
Kathy – receptionist at the Gatsby
Albert Lane – a major shareholder of Seattle *Observer*
Margo Lane – daughter of Albert Lane and future activist
Rev. Charles McLough – minister on Interurban train
Alice Jones – wife of gold miner
Helga Lieberman – housekeeper at hotel in Everett
Rev. Allen McDuff – Everett minister
Joanie – disabled waitress at Everett diner
Charlie & Belle Evans – Everett pioneers
Yana Mikolovich – ghost of 14-year-old violinist
William Rushmore – Chief Angel of the Americas
May Brown – a rebellious angel from San Francisco

(contd)

Main Characters (continued)

Gordon and Janice Janick – Mary's parents
Kate Reardon – Everett newspaper reporter
Capt. Jonas Longbow – evil spirit
Todd Harper – PE teacher at Everett High School
Butler Family – ghosts of an Everett family
Archibald Grimwold – lawyer in defence of native boys
William Russell – Victoria dentist
Agnes Millington – ghost of actress/activist
Gertrude Tuttle – widow of Victoria soldier
John Blakey – thief and murderer
Sergeant McTavish – Victoria policeman
Jebediah and Meg – Nancy Wilson's adopted parents
Ruth – University of Victoria student
Judy – waitress at The Charming Inn, Oak Bay
Phoebe Kitson – manager at The Charming Inn, Oak Bay
Elizabeth Button – student at Everett High School
Jack Thornton – Everett barber
Sam and Molly Logan – Victoria couple in 1917

Whispers Across Time

Chapter 1

Oliver Ryan was a mediocre court reporter with a flair for embellishments to his daily column of facts. An American from Seattle, his regular although often boring assignments, in British Columbia's capital city, often found him following one criminal or another through the Canadian courts as they fought extradition.

With time on his hands between assignments, he often returned to the courthouse experiencing some of the interesting court cases that did not involve American citizens or, he wandered the streets of Victoria, and that fateful night of December 5th, 1916 was no exception.

A storm, with its relentless rain and biting winds had, for the past 24 hours, raged down the Strait of Juan de Fuca blowing in from the Pacific, permeating every nook and cranny. Now deserted, the city streets became small rivers making travel, even on those which were paved, precarious.

Moving from bar to bar and trying to keep dry in his travels, by midnight Oliver found himself in the Brown Jug Saloon on Government Street. Not seeking conversation, he made his way to a small empty table in the shadowy corner. A soft-spoken loner, Oliver didn't make friends easily and usually drank alone.

Half an hour later, struck with an impulsive thought, he gulped down the rest of his drink and left the saloon. Pulling his hat down hard on his head, he stepped out into the storm. With his coat collar buttoned tightly against his stubbly chin, he fought his way south along Government Street, his diminutive height making the distance a greater challenge. Walking purposely and, as quickly as humanly possible despite oft-concealed puddles, he passed the Empress Hotel and cut through the trees near the old Douglas House leaving the street lights behind. Now on Douglas Street, it took only minutes to reach Beacon Hill Park, its stark darkness appearing on his left while, to his right, several lighted houses gave him some measure of comfort. Listening for the sound of the waves, he soon found himself on a gravel surface—the main coastal thoroughfare, Dallas Road. Turning eastward he struggled on, unaware he was wet through, but blatantly aware of the crashing sound of angry waves pounding the shoreline only feet away.

Walking for what seemed like hours and having no idea where he was going or why, a single strike of lightning suddenly flashed before him, illuminating the wrought-iron gates of Ross Bay Cemetery. Instantly, he knew this was his destination.

He pushed the heavy gate open and moved cautiously through the darkness. Sober now and, his senses heightened, he was even more aware of the noises as the wind roared through the trees combining with the rumble of the sea.

A chill ran up his spine when a shaft of moonlight appeared lighting the graveyard and displaying an amazing array of monuments—granite crosses of all sizes, religious statues, and even a mausoleum—making his heart thud in his chest. Sitting gratefully on a flat-topped gravestone, he experienced a moment of lucidity.

What on earth am I doing here? he thought.

Imagination pushed logic to one side when he thought he heard his name being called. Looking around, he was not prepared for what happened next. From behind him, in the moonlight's dim light, a ghost-like figure materialized. He tried to run away, to scream, anything, but terror held him rooted to his seat. He could only watch helplessly as the ghostly figure came closer. Eyes wide and teeth beginning to chatter, he smelled a hint of tobacco as a rush of cold air brushed his cheek, and a firm hand clamped onto his shoulder. It was the last thing Oliver remembered before his life changed forever.

Feeling a strange sensation, he became aware that he was no longer sitting on the hard surface; flailing his arms about, he felt tree branches pull at his clothes. In seconds, the darkness gave way to moonlight. *I'm above the clouds and it's not rainy! I can't believe this,* his thoughts screamed. And then he noticed he was not alone.

For the first time since feeling that strange sensation, he became aware of his ghostly chaperone beside him. Looking down, he saw lights and they were coming closer. He rubbed his eyes sure he must be dreaming, but then he saw the rooftops … too late. Wincing, he closed his eyes and waited for the crash of a landing, but he felt nothing. Opening his eyes, he realized he had landed on his feet and he was back in his flea-bitten hotel room.

I'll wake up in a minute, the 28-year-old reporter told himself as his eyes met the ghostly stare of the apparition-like figure of a man dressed in period costume and wearing a beaver skin top hat. Voice quaking, Oliver asked, "A-a-are y-you a g-ghost? A-am I dead?"

"No, son, you're not dead," the figure chuckled. "Actually, you're none the worse for wear. I'm an angel and you've been chosen for a special mission. I have to leave you now but I will return very soon."

The wispy apparition quickly melted away and Oliver hurried over to the gas lamp, turned it on and looked around the room. Finding nothing unusual, he looked out of the window onto Langley Street.

I know someone was here, he talked to me but where has he gone?

Confused and a bit frightened, he slipped off his overcoat and hung it behind the door. His fingers touched the cloth, aware of the dry fabric and when examined for tears, he realized it was also surprisingly unharmed by the trip through the trees. Rushing back to the window, he assured himself that rain was indeed still falling as it bounced under the street lamp. A moan of anguish escaped his trembling lips. Staring down at his shoes, he noted they were also clean and dry; no mud or water stained their shiny surface.

Too exhausted to care and, beginning to tremble, he turned down the lamp and lay down on the bed pulling the covers over him. But his mind refused to sleep. No dreams had ever disturbed Oliver's slumber before this night. No thoughts of life's injustices had ever troubled him, nor any harsh unfair sentence from a bad-tempered judge ever kept him awake, but tonight his thoughts churned with restless emotion. *Did I really meet an angel?*

Trying desperately to unscramble the puzzle surrounding the night's events, he eventually lapsed into a fitful slumber. Waking to the light of day and realizing it was morning, he took out his pocket watch—surprisingly visible in the limited light. He groaned at the thought of being late for work and sat up, swinging his legs over the side of the bed.

"Blast, I'm not going to have time for breakfast," he muttered, getting up and lighting the lamp. Then, as realization struck, he groaned again. "I can't go to court in a suit I've slept in!"

He looked down and saw the creases in his pant legs and gasped. They were smooth, sharp and looked freshly pressed. *How can that be?* Oliver combed his hair and rushed to the door, grabbing his coat, hat and briefcase. As he did so, he was positive he heard a chuckle which unmistakeably belonged to that—angel!

Cases came and went quickly in the Bastion Street courtroom that morning. The judge's gavel banged often as he passed the usual stern sentences and the day wore its own familiar boredom for the court reporter. After a welcome lunch, Oliver had the sudden urge to take particular notice of the afternoon session, even that which he did not have to report. He was surprised when his mind twisted in pain when an old man in the prisoner's box searched the court with his eyes, seemingly screaming for help as the judge berated him.

"You're a vagrant, sir, and I shall lock you away!" the judge cried haughtily from his lofty perch. "No respectable citizen would vouch for a man like you."

Oliver's hair prickled on the back of his neck and he distinctly heard a voice speaking in his head.

Go on, Oliver, it urged. *You will, you will!*

Completely out of character, the court reporter leapt to his feet, startling the whole courtroom.

"I will, I will, your honour!" he called out.

The judge glowered over his dark, horn-rimmed spectacles and his lips twisted grotesquely as his gavel crashed onto the desk.

"Case dismissed!"

The open door allowed a gust of wind into the courtroom and, for a fleeting moment, Oliver again heard the familiar chuckle. After paying the man's small fine and signing an official-looking document, the two men stepped outside into the pouring rain.

"Why did you do that, son? You don't even know me," said the old man.

"You've a young grandson in Vancouver who needs you," Oliver replied, though he'd no idea where the thought had come from. "He's sickly and desperately needs you." Oliver heard the man's gasp and wondered to himself how he knew these things about the stranger.

They ate a meal at a Broad Street café in almost total silence, a meal Oliver knew he was going to pay for, and then walked down to the Hudson Bay Company dock. Oliver bought the stranger a ticket on one of the coastal vessels leaving immediately for the mainland, slipped some money into the old man's hand and pushed him gently toward the gangway. The man turned to say 'thank you' but Oliver had already hurried away. When the man reached the ship's deck, he walked toward the bow, peering out into the growing darkness to see if he could catch a glimpse of the kind stranger.

"Who was that old man?" a dockworker inquired of Oliver as he walked away from the ship.

The hair on Oliver's neck prickled uncomfortably when he heard himself say, "That's Ned Jones, just an old man down on his luck, going home for Christmas to make his little grandson happy."

Turning to go, light rain splashed onto Oliver's face and he stopped at the end of the jetty and took one more look back at the ship. He couldn't see the figure of the old man due to the shadows but he waved anyway. With nothing else to do, he walked down to the harbour, his mind working overtime in an effort to supply answers, but nothing made sense. There were no hard facts to support his actions, no real connection to Ned Jones and, totally out of character, he'd spent his own hard-earned money on someone else's welfare.

Under a streetlamp on the causeway across from the Empress Hotel, he checked his billfold and, as his wet fingers counted the money, the voice spoke to him again.

Don't worry, Oliver, it's all there.

I'm losing my mind, he told himself. *This has to be some kind of a crazy dream.*

The lights of the Brown Jug Saloon seemed an even more welcoming place than usual so he entered and ordered a drink, gratefully taking a long swig as the frowning bartender watched. The tables were full so he moved to the end of the bar, standing alone. He knew immediately that despite the bad weather he would again follow his urge to go to Ross Bay Cemetery. *Will I find an answer there?*

Retracing his steps of the previous night and making better time, within half an hour he was again standing before the cemetery gate. *This is silly,* he thought, but he pushed the gate open and stepped through. Instantly, moonlight illuminated the pathway between the gravestones.

You performed well, Oliver, mission completed! said the familiar voice, mixing eerily with the wind.

Suddenly, the cemetery was awash with bright sunshine. The rain stopped and, among the gravestones, flowers bloomed. First, he recognized the voice and, as the man materialized, wearing the same black suit, waistcoat and long, flowing black cape as the night before, but was he really an angel?

"Am I dreaming?" asked Oliver.

"No, son, you're not, you have been directed to this place. Come through the gate to the Afterworld. You're one of us now."

"But I'm a mortal," Oliver argued. "I'm not dead!"

A sudden cold wind swirled through the cemetery. Apparitions popped out of gravestones materializing into mortal forms. As each new arrival waved a greeting, a few more drops of cold sweat formed under his hat until they began to trickle down his temple.

Wiping his hand quickly across his face to make the scene go away, Oliver watched the curious shapes of the apparitions as they gathered around the smiling figure of—his angel. For the first time, he was able to clearly see the man as he sat cross-legged on the edge of a large stone monument. From under his beaver skin top hat, silver-white wisps of hair peeked—hair which matched his mutton-chop whiskers. His face was round and friendly and he had the unmistakeable look of a city gent, although his white shirt and stiff collar gave him a distinctly uncomfortable appearance.

"You, my boy," he said, "have the best of both worlds. You're a mortal angel now and I'm your guardian." When he spoke, his voice was strong but in keeping with his friendly countenance.

"Bu-but how … who are you, sir?" Oliver stammered.

"The name is Tom Watson," the figure chuckled. "I don't suppose you noticed the name on that gravestone you sat on last night?"

Oliver shook his head numbly and turned to look for the gravestone. Finding it easily, he read the inscription: *Thomas E.*

Watson 1757 – 1816. Amazed, he turned quickly back to talk to the man but, in that moment, the sunlight faded and Tom Watson, along with the other apparitions, had disappeared in the darkness.

Oliver found himself standing alone on the cemetery pathway.

"My guardian angel?" he whispered. "Me a mortal angel? This is ridiculous, what is happening to me? I must be losing my mind."

It was a long, lonely walk back to the city as his mind pondered the madness of his thoughts. Rain dripped from his hat, blowing into his face. He couldn't be an angel. He was a man, a mortal like everyone else, yet strangely, his footsteps now passed the saloons of James Bay and Government Street with no thoughts of entering.

Entering his room he took off his coat—again surprised to find it dry. He removed his shoes, sighing resignedly as he noted their dry, shiny surfaces. He picked up his briefcase. He had work to do; his courtroom notes had to be written up for his employer, the *Seattle Courier*. He fully expected his editor would have his usual reaction, laughing at his story and using his heavy lead pencil to cross out whole sections. Sighing again, he glanced at the note he had pinned to the back of his door reminding him the boat left for Seattle at midnight, knowing he would have to work quickly to get it done.

Sliding his hand into his briefcase, he was shocked to find it empty, totally bare of its earlier contents. Panic engulfed him and he rushed over to the little table. His papers were gone. There would be no report for the newspaper after all. His heart beating out of control, he hesitated as something caught his eye and he stared in disbelief at the neat stack of papers on the other side of the table. His notebook and fountain pen lay beside them.

Hands shaking, he picked up the first page and read the perfectly written report … written in his own hand. Oliver's knees began to buckle and he sank down on the wooden chair. This was proof he wasn't dreaming, but did it prove he was a mortal angel?

Chapter 2

Unusually bad weather continued to lash Victoria's harbour as Oliver boarded the CPR steamship *Prince Rupert* for Seattle. Packed into one of the small draughty passenger cabins with at least a dozen others, he pulled his coat around his legs. He looked around, casually observing the people sitting opposite him, tipping his hat back slightly on his head to have a clearer view. Knowing they were in for a rough ride tonight, he settled back in his seat, feet wide apart flat on the floor, and folded his arms across his chest.

In the dim light, his eyes strayed to his left where a little girl of about four years old stood in front of a young woman in her late 20s. The child began to cry, pulling at her mother's arm.

"Can't you keep that kid quiet, lady!" a middle-aged heavy-set man with a large growth of beard, growled irritably.

Oliver's heckles rose at the unfeeling intrusion. He flicked his eyes onto the bearded passenger and smiled inwardly when he heard himself speak. "Please, sir, mind your manners." He was well aware he looked younger than his 28 years but he seemed to have more courage than normal and it quieted the man. Normally, he would never have interfered but he felt his heart go out to the little girl and her mother, who just stared straight ahead.

He looked at the child and winked as a tear fell from her cheek onto her coat lapel. The little girl looked shyly away, burying her face in her mother's lap. He eased himself over a few inches in the limited space to give them more room. The woman looked up at him with sad but grateful eyes and then turned away as her daughter tugged on her sleeve again. Oliver wasn't able to hear their whispered conversation over the din of the engine.

She said something back to the child gently touching her cheek and the little girl went to stand beside Oliver. He pulled his coat aside, patted the seat beside him and winked. She looked over at her mother again but her eyes were closed.

With her lower lip beginning to quiver, the child looked back at Oliver. He held out his arms and, with a new brightness in her eyes, allowed him to lift her onto the high seat. Sandwiched between this stranger and her mother, she grasped her mother's arm and shyly looked up at him. Oliver smiled and gave her another of his happy winks. The little girl grinned through her tears and almost giggled.

Billy Yashob watched the interlude and glared across the cabin in the semi-darkness. He was a big man with a vicious temper, feared by all who knew him, but Oliver's words had seemed to hold a quiet warning. He had an uneasy feeling about this young man with the wire-framed spectacles. There was an unusual strength and confidence surrounding him and the gentle reprimand had left Billy with a slight feeling of guilt—an emotion he had never experienced before—at least, not that he could remember.

As expected, once the ship left the protection of the harbour, a brisk wind and rough seas buffeted the ship as they made their way across the strait and down the Puget Sound to Seattle. Few passengers risked leaving their seats as they watched others stagger about when they got up to take a walk. Most of the passengers tried to sleep but a few brought out sandwiches. Oliver noticed many were put away uneaten. The little girl slept most of the journey, slumped over her usually dozing, mother's lap.

Most of the passengers hurriedly disembarked when they reached the city pier some hours later, scurrying through the rain seeking shelter or transportation. Several others dashed into the tiny wharfside café for a hot coffee or breakfast.

Oliver, not being in a great hurry, was one of the last to reach the top of the gangway. He stopped and looked behind him for the child and her mother, knowing he had left them in the cabin. He knew he should hurry, his schedule was rather tight, but he seemed to have developed an unusual interest in this child.

When they caught up to him, he asked, "Do you live in Seattle? Is someone coming to meet you?"

In the dim light, Oliver watched as the woman put down her suitcase and picked up the sleepy child. Struggling to balance herself on the sloping walkway, she bent slowly to pick up the suitcase but Oliver's hand reached it first.

"Thank you, sir," she said, almost in a whisper then, grasping the rail with her free hand, she cautiously began to descend.

Watching them go, it brought memories back that Oliver had tried very hard to suppress. Abandoned as a child and raised in a Seattle boys' home for orphans, he had no family or ties of any sort. *Why should I care what happened to these people?* Suddenly his mind turned back to the old man in Victoria whose gravestone he'd sat on and he remembered Tom Watson's explanation.

If I'm a mortal angel, he thought, *I can do anything I want. Didn't my money come back when I spent it on the vagrant?* He smiled as the sad-eyed woman reached the firm, flat boards of the dock and turned to take her suitcase.

Careful lad, careful now! came the voice in his head.

Not sure why he was being given such a warning, he ignored the voice and pointed the way to a little dockside diner a short distance ahead. He had often partaken of a meal here and knew they were hearty and the price was right. The woman looked reluctant and when they reached the door, she asked for her suitcase again.

"Ma'am, my name is Oliver Ryan. I have some business here in Seattle but I would be honoured if you and your little girl would be my guests for breakfast." Not sure where these words had come from, yet fully aware he had uttered them, he took advantage of her confusion and led them to a table by the window. Laying his briefcase on the bench, he removed his hat, shaking it gently, sending a spray of water onto the floor as the little girl woke up.

"Hello, Mr. Ryan, nice to see ya again!" He recognized the middle-aged waitress as Alice, whom he'd spoken to on several previous occasions. "What can I get ya, folks?"

After a brief discussion with his companions, who had noticeably relaxed after sitting down, he ordered them meals and drinks.

"What about yourself, Mr. Ryan?" asked Alice.

"I'll not be eating right now but you can give me the bill for my guests' meals and I'll pay you before I leave," he said quietly.

She threw him a questioning glance, quickly writing out a slip and handing it to him. He took some coins from his pocket and handed them to her.

"Keep the change, Alice," he mumbled, as she walked away. He picked up his hat and stood up. "I must go and attend to my business. I would like you to wait here for me. I'll be back within two hours."

Looking up at him, the young woman reached across the table and let her hand rest on his. "God bless you, mister," she whispered, and her childish voice burned deep into his heart.

Oliver pulled his briefcase toward him and said goodbye, winking at the little girl who smiled. Moving quickly to the door, he put his hat on and stepped out into the rain. He looked back and, seeing the child's face pressed to the window, waved briefly before pulling his hat down over his eyes and heading toward the road.

Realizing how wet it was, he grumbled under his breath that he would be soaked to the skin long before he walked the mile to the newspaper office. As he walked, his mind wandered. *Something strange is happening today,* he thought. *I seem to have an unusual compassion for my fellow man. Everywhere I turn someone seems to need me.* He closed his eyes for a moment and thought of the pending reaction of his editor, no doubt, fuming at his tardiness. A rush of cool air touched his face and he heard the sound of a door clicking behind him. His eyes snapped open and he realized he was standing in the outer foyer of the newspaper office.

"He's waiting for you, Oliver," said the receptionist, sniggering as she thought of the usual reception the editor gave this reporter.

As he walked slowly along the corridor, he suddenly thought of his clothes and looked down. *They're dry again!* Then other thoughts raced through his brain … thoughts too wild to be true. *Did I travel across town on a mere thought? Was this one of the benefits of being a mortal angel? What is going to happen next?*

His editor and boss, the grossly overweight Harry Jenson, glowered at the back of the court reporter as Oliver scooped the papers from his briefcase and handed them to him. As he looked them over, Harry's eyes blinked in obvious surprise although he tried to conceal it.

"This …," he began, stopping as if frozen in time when Oliver moved his hand casually through the air. Grinning to himself, Oliver waved his hand again and things immediately returned to normal.

Oh, you're learning fast, my boy! Tom Watson's voice whispered.

This is interesting, thought Oliver. *Old Harry hasn't a clue and I'm getting used to hearing my guardian angel's voice.*

In fact, Oliver was so used to hearing it by now, he was beginning to expect it. He realized that, as an angel, he was still an amateur with powers that needed exploring although he would no doubt need some guidance. As a mortal, he'd never really enjoyed his own life, often feeling quite sorry for himself. Possessing no sense of humour or concern for others, he'd never experienced a real belly laugh or the joy of someone's arms around him. Christmas, only about two weeks away, was just another day in a long boring year.

Teased constantly about his glasses as a child at the boys' home, he had retreated into himself. As he grew into adulthood, he had become even more reclusive, brooding over his loneliness. Now everything seemed to be changing. He was realizing that from the moment he'd stumbled into the Afterworld, his mind had become more alive and inquiring. He'd spoken up in the courtroom, saving a vagrant from an undeserved prison sentence and offered to help a mother and child who, at this very moment, awaited his return. Uncharacteristically, he smiled. *Is this, the role of a mortal angel?*

Waving his hand, he made time stand still again. He had not really been listening as Harry issued a stream of compliments. *So out of character!* Oliver thought, grinning. His urge was to leave the newspaper office and return to the diner immediately but he needed his next assignment and Harry always had it ready. Running his gaze across Harry's desk, he saw the file with his name on it; he opened it and read the handwritten note inside:

Find and interview Jack Marquette, the big-time rum runner.

Committing the information to memory, he returned the file to the desk and left the room, flicking his hand. With Harry's voice in his ears, Oliver went outside and whisked himself back to the waterfront diner on a thought.

Bertha Bentley sighed with relief when she saw the bespectacled figure of the kind stranger threading his way through the tables toward them. She gently shook her sleeping daughter.

"Janie, the man is back, wake up," she whispered.

Little Jane opened her eyes and sat up, looking sleepily at Oliver.

"Are you an angel, mister?" she asked, through squinted eyes.

Oliver felt the colour leave his cheeks.

"He certainly is Jane," said her mother. With a touch of pink brushing her cheeks, she added, "I wasn't sure you'd come back, Mr. Ryan. You said you would be a couple of hours!" She looked over at the clock on the wall.

Smiling, he shrugged out of his coat, folded it, then tossed it onto the bench beside him before sitting down. "My business took less time than I had anticipated," he said briefly, as Alice arrived.

"I'll have an egg sandwich and a coffee now, please Alice." Looking over at the young woman, he raised his eyebrow. "Make that two coffees!" Then, as an afterthought, he added, "What flavours of ice cream do you have today, Alice?" Watching Jane out of the corner of his eye, he saw her smile excitedly when the waitress mentioned 'strawberry.' "And a dish of strawberry ice cream for the young lady!" he laughed. His eyes followed the waitress as she hurried toward the kitchen. "Don't forget the cherry on top, Alice!" he called.

"Not a chance, Mr. Ryan!" she replied with a grin, giving the swinging door a push.

Toying with her spoon, Jane grinned shyly as she watched the man fold his arms on the table and look at her mother, now with a serious expression on his face.

"Well, I now know this is Jane, but what is her mother's name?" Oliver asked uncertainly, not accustomed to asking women for personal information.

"I'm sorry, Mr. Ryan," she began.

"Oliver," he corrected her.

"My name is Bertha … Bertha Bentley. We live in Victoria. My husband is a Canadian soldier," her voice dropped to a whisper, "that is, until the war took him from us six months ago." As she spoke, her voice caught and he watched a single teardrop slip from her eye onto her cheek, twinkling as its moisture reflected the light as it moved slowly downward. He could almost feel the pain of her loss in that single teardrop before Bertha wiped it away.

The waitress returned, placing a large dish containing three mounds of ice cream, each with its own cherry on top, in front of the wide-eyed youngster. Then, she pushed the sandwich under his hand and placed two cups of steaming black coffee in the centre of the table. Muttering something unintelligible, she turned and walked away.

"I have some family here," Bertha continued.

"You'll be staying with them? Where do they live?" he asked, between bites.

"I'm intending to find my cousin Ben Olson, but I really don't know where to start."

"And in the meantime?"

"A rooming house," Bertha sighed. "I have a little money."

Fumbling in her handbag, several coins rolled onto the table. Oliver's heart felt like fingers were squeezing it so tight he could barely breathe. A cold draught hit the back of his neck and he felt the invisible hand on his shoulder.

Now what are you going to do, son? asked his angel.

He had never been able to make quick decisions but Oliver made this one instantly. "You can stay at my place," he said reassuringly, "and tomorrow we'll look for your cousin."

Chapter 3

As the taxi sped them to his apartment at Washington and First Street, Oliver absorbed Bertha's story of worry and hardship. There was a moment of uncertainty in his mind as the elevator took them up to the fifth floor to the one-bedroom apartment he called home. He didn't know how he was going to accommodate these people but somehow he knew it was going to be all right.

When he unlocked the door and swung it open, he caught his breath. Something was wrong, this couldn't be his apartment. There were carpets on the floor, new paint on the tattered walls, and the furnishings appeared to be new. Unknown doors opened to left and right down an unfamiliar hallway. He took a deep breath.

My key did open it, he thought.

With Bertha watching him curiously, he stepped back into the hallway and double-checked the brass plate on the wall. He sighed when he saw the numbers *502*.

Ah, this must be more of my angel's work! Fumbling for words to explain his strange behaviour, he mumbled, "I forgot the manager was having it painted while I was away!"

He moved down the hall, opening doors but Jane was already ahead of them having spied a rocking chair in the living room. Two of the three bedrooms were delicately decorated in blue-flowered wallpaper and matching quilts for his guests. The third housed his familiar old bed along with his well-worn, but cozy bedspread. The bathroom was now slightly larger and the newly painted kitchen had a bigger table and unfamiliar curtains over the sink. There seemed to be bright new linoleum everywhere and the living room had mainly unfamiliar-looking upholstered chairs which matched a new couch and area rug. With his heart beating like a steam engine gone wild, he shook his head and looked up at the ceiling.

Tom Watson's whispered words caught his ear. *Accept your destiny, son, you're an angel now!*

"I'd better check my larder," he mumbled, opening one of the kitchen cupboards. By now, he wasn't at all surprised when he found it rather full of cans and boxes of food. He opened other cupboards and found them all neatly set out with new china, glassware, and serving bowls. He seemed to know instinctively where things were located. The sink caught his attention and he realized the ever-present dirty dishes he usually left in the sink were absent and even the coffee pot was primed and waiting on the stove.

"My, you have a lovely place and so neat and tidy," Bertha complimented him, interrupting his thoughts. "Are you sure we won't be imposing, Mr ... Oliver?"

He felt the warmth of Jane's tinkling laughter as she ran from room to room coming back to the kitchen to join them and slipping her little hand in his.

"Not at all, it's rather pleasant to have company," he heard himself say. "It doesn't happen very often."

Awhile later, when they were sitting in the living room, Jane suddenly came running into the room.

"I hear music, Mommy. Can we go listen? Please? Please?" she pleaded, pulling her mother's hand as she talked to Oliver.

Bertha went over to the balcony door and opened it a crack.

"Good gracious! She's right. There are people down on the street singing Christmas songs, Oliver. Let's put our coats on and go out on the balcony."

Reluctantly, he agreed to join them. *Bunkum!* an inner voice snapped, suppressing the urge to join in the song as they looked over the railing at the street buskers. He'd always spent Christmas alone thinking others were stupid for bothering to waste their time observing the festive season. This year would be no different, he assured himself. His conviction wavered slightly when he felt the tiny hand squeeze his fingers again and Jane handed him his jacket. Eyes wide with excitement, she looked up at him and pulled him outside, peering through the wrought-iron railing at the handsomely-dressed singers below.

"Does Santa Claus come to your house, mister?" she inquired as they came back inside to get warm about ten minutes later.

Oliver squirmed under the barrage of thoughts jumbling his brain as he tried to escape the child's pleading eyes. "I have to go out for a while," he suddenly announced, "make yourselves comfortable. I won't be very long." He picked up his briefcase and left before either of them could ask any questions.

Standing in the hallway outside his apartment, he took a deep breath and checked the space between his doorway and the next apartment. He was still unsure how all those rooms seemed to fit into the limited space.

Moving toward the elevator, he noticed one of his elderly neighbours hurry to get in before he could reach it. Ignoring him, she allowed the door to close. Cocking an eyebrow in annoyance, he decided to test his angel power. Quickly sending a thought wave down five floors to the front door, he was there in the blink of an eye. He watched the old lady exit the elevator and walk across the foyer toward him.

The wicked grin slipped from her face when she saw him holding the main door open. She muttered to herself and staggered sideways, flopping into a nearby chair. Staring mesmerized at the space between her feet, she muttered, "Impossible, impossible!"

Snowflakes were falling as Oliver went outside, smiling to himself as he buttoned his coat.

Well done, lad! said the voice with a jolly chuckle. *However, you don't want to give someone a heart attack merely for your pleasure!*

Rolling his eyes, he set out for the Forth Street police station, a few blocks away, moving quickly through bustling groups of Christmas shoppers, arms laden with packages. Stamping the snow from his feet at the door, he met the stern, inquiring stare of the desk sergeant. Producing his billfold he extracted his press card with nervous fingers. He didn't like this place of harsh authority where men carried guns on their hips and prisoners stood cowed in handcuffs, though the role of court reporter often brought him here.

"And what do you want?" the desk sergeant growled irritably.

"Information," Oliver replied timidly. "I wondered if you might know a man by the name of Ben Olson?"

The innocent request had a startling effect on the officer who suddenly snapped to attention, his hand banging the call bell in front of him. Two more policemen hurried to join him.

"Who did you say you wanted?" the desk sergeant demanded, cocking his head to one side as the reporter repeated himself.

There was a moment of silence before a voice, not far away, called out gruffly, "Send him in!"

Grinning wickedly, the desk sergeant pointed toward the room from where the voice had come. Oliver followed the direction of the sergeant's finger and suddenly became aware of another of his angel abilities. *I can see right through that wall!* Startled, he glanced back at the sergeant and wiped a trickle of sweat from his forehead with his handkerchief.

"Go on, lad," the sergeant chuckled at the reporter's seemingly obvious reluctance. "I guarantee he won't bite you!"

He took a few steps forward casting his eyes back to the wall. He concentrated harder and again the wall disappeared, revealing a balding, middle-aged man in uniform sitting at his desk. He was frowning as he stroked the stubble on his chin and watched the open doorway.

Moving across the hall, Oliver summoned all his courage and walked through the door. Politely offering his hand, he felt only mildly rejected when ignored. Suspicious eyes raked his body but he moved toward a chair, quickly jerking upright as the policeman commanded, "Stand!"

Normally, the court reporter would have accepted this treatment without a whimper, but this was no ordinary day. He had the powers of an angel and an impish desire to teach this arrogant bully a lesson. Thoughts flashed through his head as he remembered his mission and Bertha's plight. He wondered again, why he cared so much.

"I'm inquiring for a Mr. Ben Olson," Oliver said softly.

"I'm Sergeant Olson! What about it?"

The admission came with a long hard stare from the detective, one that sent a momentary shudder down the reporter's backbone, although he was amazed with his luck at finding the man so easily. He could feel no kindness or caring in this man, as his penetrating eyes bore through him.

"Your cousin, Bertha Bentley, and her daughter are here in Seattle from Victoria and need your help," he heard himself say with a firmness that made the staring eyes blink at him. He then lowered his eyes onto the desk. The uncharitable thoughts running through the detective's brain became clearly readable to the court reporter. *My word,* Oliver thought to himself. *I can actually hear what he's thinking. He's going to lie to me.*

"I don't have any relatives named Bentley," Olson growled.

Indignation chewed at the young reporter's conscience and he felt personally insulted. This man's family needed a helping hand and he was totally lacking any sense of compassion. Furthermore, he was actually lying to an angel! As a mortal, Oliver would have accepted the answer and walked away, but the angel in him now took control.

With a flick of his hand, time stood still. Reaching across the desk, he pulled a file out from under the sergeant's now rigid hand. Opening it and glancing over one of the reports, he noticed Olson had made notes about conflicting testimonies of witnesses to a mysterious robbery.

Staring at the names of the suspects, Oliver's mind searched for their souls and soon the form of a guilt-ridden man came clearly to him as a vision. Quickly closing the file and turning it over, he wrote the man's name, his whereabouts, and location of the stolen property on the outside of the file, scrawling his signature below.

Suddenly, Tom Watson's voice whispered an urgent warning. *No, no, son, angels can't sign their name!*

Too late! As Tom's voice faded, Oliver watched the letters of his signature disintegrate into a waft of smoky vapour, slowly burning the shape of an angel onto the paper.

"Explain that to your superiors!" he softly chuckled before leaving the office. Passing the now silent and unmoving policemen he had seen earlier, he left the building. Cold winter air caused him to breathe deeply and he felt snowflakes on his face as the door banged shut behind him. Flicking his hand to start time again, he hurried away.

At the police station, Sergeant Olson stared in disbelief at the file under his hand. His finger slowly traced the scorched outline of the angel as he read the notes Oliver had written.

"Who's been in here?" he bellowed.

"Nobody's been in your office except you, why?" came the grouchy desk sergeant's reply, unaware that the memory of the past few minutes had been wiped clean by Tom Watson as he watched over his new protégé.

Detective Ben Olson neglected to answer the query. Instead, he gazed in fascinated wonder at the file in front of him. He could hardly take his fingers off the angel-like scorch mark on the paper enjoying the strange calming tingle that ran through his fingertips.

Frowning, he stared at the wall as thoughts of his cousin Bertha popped into his mind. They'd been playmates as children in Seattle but, over the years, he'd lost touch with her. Family had said she was married to a Canadian from Victoria, an army man. Shaking his head, a growing curiosity now began to fester in his brain. *I wonder what happened to her?*

A drop in temperature made the sidewalk slick as Oliver wandered into the warmth of a diner just a few doors from the newspaper office. The waitress greeted him by name and he ordered coffee and asked for the phone book. *I had better look for Bertha's other relatives,* he thought but, finding column after column of Bentleys, he groaned inwardly. *My word, this is going to be a daunting exercise.*

Back out on the street, he shivered, noting the snowflakes were now much larger. He hurried for the streetcar rumbling along Fourth Avenue toward the neighbourhood known as Denny Regrade, cautious of the slippery sidewalk. *I'll stop in at the Methodist Meeting Hall; perhaps the minister will be able to offer some advice.*

Jumping off at the next corner, he slipped and found himself on the ground. Groaning, he tried to right himself, but his shoes kept sliding out from under him. Out of the corner of his eye, he suddenly noticed a large black automobile skidding toward him. He made a valiant effort to reach the sidewalk and almost made it before the car roughly nudged him in the back, sending him careening again, arms and legs flailing, before he landed softly in the deeper snow alongside the curb.

"Are you all right?" asked the uniformed man who jumped out of the driver's seat, coming cautiously toward him holding onto the car for support.

In the back seat, the passenger also opened his door and anxiously repeated the inquiry as the chauffeur helped Oliver to his feet. Although protesting, he allowed the man to assist him into the back seat assuring them he was all right. As they slowly drove away, Oliver turned to his benefactor and realized the hazy features of the well-dressed gentleman were slightly familiar. Squinting, he reached up to his face.

"My spectacles!" he groaned. "I must have lost them when I fell."

The man beside him reacted immediately.

"Peter, can you go back to the corner? It seems our passenger ...?" he said, turning to Oliver.

"Oliver Ryan," offered the squinting reporter.

"It seems our Mr. Ryan has lost his glasses."

"No problem, Mr. Jorgensen," Peter replied, already turning the car around in a driveway.

"Thank you, Mr. Jorgensen," said Oliver repeating thc name and realizing why the man looked somewhat familiar through his hazy vision. Jorgensen was a well-known Seattle shipping magnate whose picture he had seen many times. "I appreciate your help, sir."

"Don't even mention it, Mr. Ryan. It's the least we can do after almost running over you!" Gus Jorgensen replied in a jovial manner.

Arriving back to the site of the mishap stopped further conversation as Peter got out of the car to search the area.

"It appears he has found them, Mr. Ryan!" Jorgensen announced jubilantly as Peter returned to the automobile holding the glasses in his hand.

"I'm afraid you won't be able to wear these, sir," said the chauffeur, handing several pieces into his boss' outstretched hand.

"The lenses still appear sound," commented Jorgensen, handing the pieces to Oliver. "We'll go straight over to the opticians on Virginia, Peter. Sam will solve our problem and quickly, I dare say," he assured Oliver, who was now looking woefully at the broken pieces of frame.

Somewhere a clock struck four as the Jorgensen car drew up outside the opticians and Peter came around to open the door, taking Oliver by the elbow until he was safely inside.

Oliver was pleased to see several racks of spectacle frames displayed on the counter. Mr. Jorgensen explained the problem to the optician, whom he obviously knew and, in no time, Sam had Oliver trying on pair after pair of frames before settling on one he referred to as his 'English wire-framed eyeglasses with deep-hooking earpieces.'

Eager to please, the optician gathered up the broken pieces and hurried into a back room. Within ten minutes, he returned with the new glasses in hand. Using a white cloth, he polished them briskly.

"There," he said proudly, slipping the spectacles onto Oliver's face. "These should be exactly like the ones you broke, how do they feel? We want them to fit correctly."

After a couple of minor adjustments, Oliver turned to look at his benefactor. "You're Gus Jorgensen, the shipping magnate, aren't you, sir?" he asked quietly.

"Yes, I am. Forgive me, in the excitement I neglected to introduce myself," Gus chuckled, not surprised in the least at being recognized. "I'm afraid you have me at a disadvantage as I only know your name, Mr. Ryan."

Oliver quickly explained his occupation mainly as a court reporter and mentioned his regular visits to Victoria. He saw the light of interest flash in the ship owner's eyes and wondered what chord he'd inadvertently struck.

"I'll call it even, Mr. Jorgensen," Sam interrupted, grinning again as he waved his account in the air, "if you give me two tickets to Nancy Wilson's concert on the 15th!"

The shipping magnate's hand flashed into his pocket and immediately produced two tickets, laying them on the counter. Looking up and, with a serious note in his voice, Jorgensen murmured, "Remember to give generously, Sam. It's for a good cause."

"By all means, Mr. Jorgensen, that girl is a true angel and to be admired for the work she's doing … and such a beautiful voice," his voice trailed off as the men made their way to the door.

Urged on by curiosity, Oliver tried his angel power focussing his thoughts on Jorgensen's mind. Instead, all he heard was Tom Watson's chuckle.

You can only read minds under certain conditions, Oliver, and those conditions are for you to discover!

As the shop door banged behind them, Gus announced, "I need to call at the theatre, then we'll drive you home, if that doesn't inconvenience you too much."

"Not at all, Mr. Jorgensen," Oliver replied.

The snow was coming down much more thickly as Peter slowly manoeuvred the large black car to a stop in front of the James Moore Theatre.

"Come inside with me, Oliver," Gus invited as he climbed out of the car. "I'll introduce you to Jim. We might be able to find you a couple of tickets for the show, if you'd like them."

"Three tickets would be appreciated, if you don't mind, sir," Oliver called after him as they manoeuvred the slippery sidewalk.

"Three?"

"Yes, sir, I have two young ladies I'd like to bring, if that's all right."

Inside, James Moore, the theatre's owner, welcomed them heartily, shaking Oliver's hand. With him was a young man, arms laden with flowers, and the most beautiful redheaded young woman Oliver had ever seen. She let out a scream of delight when she saw Gus, flinging herself into his arms.

Oliver felt humbled by the open show of affection between these two people and remembered seeing this girl's face on posters and in newspaper reports. This was Nancy Wilson, Seattle's adopted sweetheart of song from Victoria. Introductions were warm and the redhead took him by the arm, tugging him along behind the others, toward the restaurant where she explained they would have coffee.

Ghostly fingers prodded Oliver's back. *Go on lad, tell her about Bertha and Jane.*

Goaded into action, while they were waiting for their coffee, Oliver told his attentive audience of Bertha Bentley's predicament. He explained how he had met her, his desire to help, and the reason he was wandering Seattle's streets in a snowstorm.

"I think we'll be able to help you, Oliver," the red-head responded. "We'll get you your tickets, and Gus ...," she smiled coyly, "you know Ben better than anyone. He would listen to you."

Later, with three tickets in his hand and Nancy's assurance everything would work out, Oliver rose to go.

"I really must be going," he mumbled.

"Tell Peter where you live and he'll see you home, son," Gus murmured, shaking the reporter's hand. "I'll stop here a while."

"Come and see us again," Nancy added. "You're an angel, Oliver, and it's been a delight meeting you."

Oliver smiled and thanked them again.

The wind had come up and snow was drifting across the sidewalk in a thick fluffy blanket. Oliver stepped cautiously out onto the street and saw the Jorgensen car at the curb.

Inside the car, Peter glanced up from his book and noticed Oliver just as the reporter's thoughts went to the hallway outside his apartment building. Oliver smiled when he found he had arrived at that very spot, unaware he had left behind a very confused driver staring at the unfinished stride of his snowy footprints.

Using his key to open the door, he stepped inside. Sniffing the air, the delightful and unfamiliar aroma of home cooking teased his nostrils. He felt the warmth of Jane's greeting as she ran to meet him, leading him into the kitchen. Bertha motioned to the table, set neatly with plates, cutlery and pretty napkins.

"We were waiting for you, Oliver. Dinner is ready."

Taking their seats, he sat in stunned silence as the child said Grace before picking up her fork. Ecstasy brushed his taste buds when he took his first mouthful—palatable home-cooked meals being exceedingly rare. His expression of approval produced a smile of gratitude from the cook as he heard the soft eerie whisper.

Now you know what you've been missing, son, all because you offered the hand of friendship to someone less fortunate.

Later, lying in the quiet darkness of his room, Oliver spent some time thinking about his new role as an angel. Still learning and not quite sure of his powers, he struggled between being a mortal and an agent of the ghostly Afterworld.

On Saturday, he took his houseguests shopping in Seattle's well-stocked department stores *Frederick and Nelson* in the Rialto Building, and *The Bon Marché* at Second and Pike, ending at *Rhodes'* huge store. While eating dinner in a restaurant, they talked about Victoria's premier stores.

"The *Hudson's Bay Company* built a new store on Douglas Street," Bertha began with a sigh, "but instead of opening, it's gone to a wreck, windows are broken and they had to board it up against vandals. Victoria is experiencing some hard times because of the war but we still have *David Spencer*'s and *Woolworth's*." Bertha's face turned sad. "Shops are no good, Oliver, if you don't have any money to spend."

Back in the apartment, Saturday evening passed quietly and Oliver felt the thrill of reading to a child as she snuggled up beside him in the rocking chair. Outside, that afternoon, they had studied the wonder of snowflakes melting into droplets of water on the palms of their hands as she giggled. The spectacles resting firmly on his nose seemed to mist over when each new experience tugged at his heartstrings and he knew that little by little his crusty uncaring character was changing. Bertha's insistence, however, on a visit to church that Sunday evening would prove to be more than an ordinary experience.

She wants to give thanks for what? he thought, *for being destitute and lonely?* Jane came over and stood by his knee, looking up at him with such a cherubic expression, he weakly agreed.

Due to the bad weather, very few of the faithful attended that evening service at the First Methodist Church on Second and Columbia. There were no crowds inside the hallow'ed walls and Oliver felt completely out of place, yet strangely at peace. Music from the organ droned mournfully on, almost drowning out the singing as Bertha sang her often off-key rendition of the hymn.

Jane tapped his hand and whispered impatiently. "Sing, Mr. Ryan, sing!"

Raising his eyes to the great wooden rafters, he made an effort to join in. Feeling one of those now-familiar sensations when something extraordinary was about to happen, he raised his eyes. In the limited light, he was shocked to see a host of angelic apparitions floating effortlessly beneath the dark-stained beams. Their voices, all in perfect tune, gently soothed his ears. Unafraid of his new-found abilities, he glanced over at the minister before taking a cautious look around the congregation—obviously unaware of their cherubic visitors.

Walking home after the service, they braved the cold to window shop on Second Street, enjoying Jane's squeals of delight as she ran from window to window looking at the many festive Christmas displays. One of the larger stores had Santa and his helpers surrounded by wrapped presents and a myriad of toys, jingling bells and moving lights. Even Santa's sleigh, with several large reindeer, appeared ready to fly! Jane's face pressed against the window as she excitedly described what she was seeing; they practically had to drag her away.

At last, past the stores and with Jane between them, they were able to walk faster, their breath making wispy clouds in the cold night air. Returning to the welcoming warmth of the apartment, as he hung up their coats, Oliver realized just how much he enjoyed having their company. *Is this what family life is like?* he wondered.

Chapter 4

Routine and the need to find Jack Marquette for his newspaper interview, took the court reporter all over the city for the first two days of the following week, finally tracking his quarry down to a café close to one of Seattle's busy jetties.

Oliver grimaced when he saw Marquette's companion and felt the unfriendly, suspicious eyes of Detective Sergeant Ben Olson frowning at him as he approached the table.

"Don't I know you?" he heard Ben ask.

Ignoring the question, Oliver responded to Jack's greeting and found him to be a man of impeccable manners, as he rose and held out his hand.

"May I interview you for my newspaper, sir?" the reporter inquired, showing his press card and expecting an instant refusal.

"Sure you can," Marquette replied, grinning with obvious amusement, "but not today, son. How about Thursday at one o'clock, right here at this table. Bring your family along and I'll buy you lunch."

Stunned by the unexpected reply, Oliver thanked him and turned to leave when he heard his angel whisper. *Stop worrying about that policeman, I wiped his memory clean. He won't remember your visit to the police station; instead I've planted a thought about Bertha Bentley in his mind.*

Leaving the café, Oliver pulled his hat down and made his way over to the jetty, his head full of questions.

"Are you always there, Mr. Watson?" he muttered softly.

Only until Christmas, was the reply.

"Then what?"

You're on your own after that, my boy!

"But I don't know what powers you've given me," Oliver whined, "I'm too new at this angel stuff." The reporter's mind began twisting and turning, his brain sifting through the things he had learned. *I can stop and start time, transport myself across town on a thought, read minds, see through walls and, the money I need always seems to be there. But what else can I do? Maybe I can hover over the city or sit on a cloud?* he thought, allowing himself a frivolous moment, and chuckling as he considered other possibilities.

Darkness was just falling when he arrived at the corner of Washington and First and decided to try his first hovering. Concentrating harder than ever before, low and behold, he felt himself lifting from the ground. He was both shocked and delighted to find himself looking down at the street lamp. He looked around to make sure he was alone and, leaning forward, immediately found himself moving. He was so involved in his actions he didn't notice the streetcar come around the corner and stop, letting off an old lady who looked up and screamed when she saw him.

Disaster struck and he felt himself falling. Barely managing to control his descent, he fell into the snow not far away from the frightened woman. The streetcar had moved off, but she was still screaming and pointing her umbrella at him. Fortunately, there was no one else around and, unhurt but wiser, he whisked himself home, commanding her memory to erase, and hoping it worked.

Dusting the snow off his coat, he opened the door to his building. "That's going to take practice," he muttered as he waited for the elevator.

In the evening, he played games with Jane and quietly perfected the art of moving objects with his mind when no one was looking. For the first time in his life, Oliver was having some fun.

He wished he could help bring Bertha some hope and contentment in life, without realizing the mere thought did so. As bedtime came around, he almost fell asleep himself as he quietly rocked Jane, lulling her into a peaceful slumber.

Thursday arrived and, excited by the invitation for lunch with Jack Marquette, Bertha and Jane put on their coats and shoes and waited for him at the door. The reporter was now feeling more confident with his angel abilities, although he was a little surprised when he again found Sgt. Olson sitting with his friend. Introductions were made and cautious smiles exchanged as Ben and Bertha were reunited. Chatting quietly, the cousins seemed oblivious to the others as Oliver conducted his interview.

Marquette was a rum runner with an impish sense of humour and he truthfully answered question after question with the nonchalant indifference of a man confident in his abilities. The interview ended 45 minutes later and Oliver extended his hand to thank the man.

Bertha shyly hugged her cousin and thanked Marquette for lunch. Jane, who was playing with the last of her ice cream, jumped up and, grabbing Oliver's hand, pulled him to the door.

That evening Oliver wrote his report. There was no condemnation for the rum runner in the silky smooth prose of this reporter. Instead, Oliver found himself depicting Jack Marquette as a man of honour with an infectious sense of humour, easy laughter and a generous manner—a gentleman who flaunted the fractured liquor laws of Seattle. Staring at the finished paper in disbelief, he knew these were not his words, nonetheless he shrugged in resignation.

The next afternoon as he stood in front of Harry Jenson, he heard the editor grudgingly admit his work was first class. The next words, however, were not what he had hoped for—his new assignment would take him back to the tiresome law courts in Victoria for Monday morning.

Outside, he kicked at the snow in frustration and trudged back to the apartment grumbling to himself. He was ready for more exciting assignments and hated the thought of spending hours in court listening to bad-tempered judges and pompous lawyers. Almost home, he turned into the biting wind whipping up Washington Street from the harbour and thought he felt a hand on his shoulder.

Don't fret, son, your life is going to see plenty of excitement. Have patience and, just a warning, we'll need you at Ross Bay for your inauguration on Christmas Eve. I'll come for you just prior to midnight.

Those words haunted Oliver as he watched Bertha lovingly prepare her daughter for the Nancy Wilson concert that evening. Leaving at 5:30, they walked through the snow to his favourite eating place two blocks away. He carried Jane part of the way and her tiny arms encircled his neck providing a comforting feeling of trust, something Oliver had never experienced before.

They enjoyed their meal and, afterwards, caught a taxi to the theatre. Arriving, as several groups of well-dressed theatregoers, alighted from their fancy autos, Bertha watched them enviably. As the crowd pushed them through the entrance, a uniformed female usher took their tickets and led them to their seats. They found themselves in a little balcony box which had a perfect view of the stage. Several others quietly joined them, looking at them questioningly and whispering among themselves.

Oliver noticed Bertha looking around at the opulent decor and watching the extravagantly dressed patrons arrive—women in beautiful floor-length dresses and fur coats and men wearing fancy dark suits, bowler hats and fur-trimmed coats. To Oliver, who never usually noticed this sort of thing, they were greatly overdressed and he leaned over and said this to Bertha. Her awe-struck expression turned into a smile and she covered her mouth with her hand and giggled.

Jane reached over and took Oliver's hand as the orchestra finished their warmup and the stillness of expectation settled over the theatre. "Mummy says this lady lives in Victoria," Jane said softly.

"Your mother is right," he whispered back.

At that moment, Gus Jorgensen and his wife arrived with two other people. The shipping magnate silently greeted Oliver as they hurriedly took their seats.

Oliver looked over at his guests and smiled in the low light. *Already their happiness is worth coming,* he thought.

The conductor entered to rousing applause, bowing toward the audience. He turned around and, raising his arms as spotlights focussed on the curtain, the orchestra began to play. Slowly, the great purple wall opened revealing the beautiful young woman Oliver had met just days before. The theatre erupted with cheering and applause and Oliver again watched the faces of his guests. Jane's mouth was open, revealing such delight he thought she must be thinking that Nancy was the angel!

Indeed, Nancy did look quite heavenly tonight with her lovely red hair cascading about her slim shoulders. The lights created an aurora around her and her hair and peach-coloured dress sparkled as she walked slowly toward the shiny black grand piano at centre stage, where Nellie Cornish waited. The applause died down as the orchestra began the introduction to the first song and Nancy's lovely soprano voice filled the theatre.

The time went so quickly it was hard to believe it was already intermission when the curtain closed and the lights came on. Jane asked to go to the bathroom and Bertha excused themselves. The Jorgensens and their party also left the box leaving Oliver to look around him for the first time. He had heard so much about the James Moore Theatre but had never been inside before this week's events. He was amazed at how much he had enjoyed the performance and vowed to come more often.

When the concert was over and Nancy was taking the last of her many curtain calls, Oliver went over and quickly murmured his thanks to Gus for the tickets. Bertha picked up her daughter, who had fallen asleep in her chair and they slipped quietly away. The lobby was nearly empty as Oliver took little Jane from her mother and they left the theatre. Making their way to the first streetcar stop, they were grateful when the tram arrived minutes later. As they sat down, Jane suddenly raised her head and looked at him.

"Was that lady an angel, Mr. Ryan?" she asked rubbing her eyes.

Slow to answer, Oliver glanced down at the innocent face as the girl's eyes fluttered closed once again, and he sighed. In that brief moment he experienced the first thrill of love he'd ever felt. It surged through his body and a feeling of warmth engulfed him causing him to tighten his arms around the little girl.

Arriving at his apartment, they found a note tucked underneath the door. It was from Ben Olson and, without reading it, Oliver had a feeling of foreboding. *Has that hard-nosed detective experienced a change of heart?* Silently, he handed the note to Bertha and their eyes met. As he made tea, he thought about the note again and a deep feeling of disappointment crept over him. He knew his houseguests would be leaving. He'd grown fond of the brave Canadians and he knew he would miss them. Twenty minutes later with Jane settled into bed, Bertha came into the living room. Her expression told him he was right.

"Oliver," she whispered, hesitating in the doorway. In her hand, she held the note. "Ben is coming for us in the morning at eleven o'clock. He has a little cottage that has become vacant and he says we can live there for as long as we want."

Oliver knew he should have been excited and relieved for receiving such good news but instead he felt sadness. Knowing she must be relieved, he congratulated her and made light of the situation until they were laughing about her future plans. As if reading his mind, she played along but, at 11:30, when they mutually agreed it was time to retire, she went over to him and kissed his cheek.

"Don't be sad, Oliver, you can come and visit us any time you like. You're our dearest friend, you know. I-I don't know how Janie and I would have managed w-without you … thank you," she said haltingly, and quickly left the room.

Lying in bed that night, he stared out of the window and watched as silver clouds touched by the cold fingers of a winter moon, passed above. He thought of the lessons he had learned since that first day in Ross Bay Cemetery and wondered if this was also part of the training for his role as an angel. His quiet unmeaningful life had been turned upside down and would never quite be the same, and yet he realized he was happier than he had ever been. It was a strange and foreign feeling.

On the point of sleep, his mentor slipped into the room, materializing slowly as he settled silently onto the chair. Removing his beaver skin hat, the ghostly apparition grinned at the sleepy reporter who had raised himself onto his elbows.

"I've popped in to give you a little advice, son," he whispered with a twinkle in his voice. "You've already found out you can stop and start time and now I want to tell you it's just as easy to go backwards or forwards."

Forcing his tired eyes to focus, Oliver sat bolt upright.

"You mean I can see the future," he gasped, "things that will have changed 50 years from now?"

"Yes Oliver, you can, but you must use your power wisely."

"I could change the bad things that have happened," he mused.

"No, you can't," the angel objected. "You mustn't attempt to tamper with the past, history cannot be changed."

Falling back onto his pillow, Oliver closed his eyes for a moment and, when he looked again, Tom Watson had disappeared. Tossing and turning in tormented sleep, his eyelids snapped open when daylight streamed through the curtains.

Have I been dreaming? he wondered. Rising, in thoughtful contemplation of Tom Watson's words, he began to dress. *That wasn't a dream, it was real, but what did it mean?*

Through breakfast, he patiently listened to Bertha's hopes and plans for her and Jane's future. Now that she had a home, she was bubbling with expectation and rightly so. He was tempted to take a peek into the future but dispelled the thought when he remembered his disastrous experience of hovering. A gentle touch brushed his fingers and he snapped back to the present to find Jane looking at him with sad eyes.

"What's the matter, honey?" he asked, lifting her onto his knee.

"I want my daddy to come home for Christmas," she whispered looking up at him with pleading eyes. "Do you think he will, Oliver?"

"I don't know honey," he replied, his eyes meeting Bertha's as Jane left the table and ran into the living room.

His reporter's instinct quickened. Should he use his powers and investigate the whereabouts of Corporal Jim Bentley?

"There's been no word from Jim for so long," Bertha whispered emotionally. "The army lists him missing in action; he's just disappeared." She got a faraway look in her eyes and they glistened with tears. "Now I'm worried that if he did come home, he won't be able to find us."

Frowning, Oliver posed a solution for her suggesting she write to her former neighbours giving them her new address. Then he extracted the last date and place when Bertha knew her husband was alive. Bertha changed the subject by offering to do the dishes so he could have a last visit with Jane and soon they were playing on the floor, chattering about Santa Claus and Christmas.

At exactly eleven o'clock the next morning, a knock sounded on the door and Oliver went to open it. Their bags were ready and Ben mumbled that he'd take them down to the car. As if in a daze, Oliver helped them on with their coats and went down the elevator with them. They shyly hugged goodbye and he carried Jane to the car and closed the door.

As Ben started the engine, Oliver stood on the curb trying not to look sad and waved as the car whisked them away. Seeing Jane blow a kiss to him through the back window, Oliver felt a pang of regret and would have returned it but they turned the corner. He wiped a tear from his eye and shivered, suddenly realizing he was without a coat and hurried inside.

He was once again alone in life and, alone with his thoughts; for the first time in memory it saddened him. As he opened the door to his apartment, he blinked … gone was the long hallway with the extra doors and the colours … everything was as it had been before Bertha and Jane's visit. He took a deep breath and let it out slowly. *I really do need to redecorate this place,* he thought, but a smile now brushed his lips—a plan was beginning to take shape in his head on a more pressing matter. Finding a pencil and notepad, he sat down and wrote out his thoughts.

A few minutes later he was repacking his suitcase, then collecting his briefcase, he went to put on his coat. Looking around the apartment to be sure he hadn't forgotten anything, he closed his eyes and sent his thoughts to the Empress Hotel in Victoria. A moment later, he was standing on the walkway looking up at the elegant hotel as the sound of a clanking streetcar passed over the James Bay Bridge behind him. He was quick to note that these streets were dry with no sign of snow and the grass in front of the hotel was green.

Walking across the bridge and heading toward town, Oliver called in at the post office on the first floor of the Dominion Government building, acquiring stamps and posting a note to his editor. He chuckled inwardly when he realized he could deliver it faster himself.

Going outside, he stared back across the harbour at the hospital liner tied up at the CPR dock and he could almost feel the pain of each wounded soldier as he walked or was carried down the gangway. He shuddered and continued up Government Street, noticing many sad-faced women and wondering how many of them were waiting for news of loved ones or husbands.

He stopped to look in the Burns Meat Shop at the corner of Courtney and shook his head at the high price of beef compared to Seattle. Across the street, the Windsor Hotel spilled its arguing drunks onto the sidewalk and two bonneted ladies stepped from an automobile in front of Rogers' Chocolates.

He paused as a heavily loaded dray pulled by four snorting horses came up the incline of Broughton Street and crossed Government in front of him. Their harassed driver cursed loudly as he cracked his whip just above the horses' ears. Squeals of women and children sounded as pedestrians scattered, leaping for safety.

Entering Victoria Book and Stationery, the bell above the door announced his presence. Oliver easily found the supplies he needed to replenish his briefcase and handed the friendly clerk the necessary coins. Going back outside, the bell tinkled in his wake.

He turned toward the *Victoria Times* newspaper office on Fort Street, and realized that the gnawing feeling in his stomach was telling him it was lunchtime. Wanting to finish his business before stopping for something to eat, he entered the reception area receiving a glare from the girl behind the desk.

Flashing his press card to impress her, he asked for a list of Victorians missing in the war. Eyebrows raised, she pointed to a table in the corner where two old people were reading some printed lists. Half an hour passed before he found Jim Bentley's name, listed as missing in action on October the 10th, 1915 at the second battle of Ypres.

Scribbling the information on his pad, Oliver left and made his way to the Carlton Café over on Broad Street. Taking the only empty table, he ordered a sandwich and coffee, eating in silence as he planned his next move.

Staring at the once-white table cover, his eyes involuntarily became glowing orbs as a picture took shape on the tablecloth. Sweating profusely, he watched a battle scene unfold—shells rained down and men choked helplessly in the trenches. Unable to tear his eyes away, Oliver moaned as one soldier stood out from the rest. He knew instantly he was watching Bertha's husband. Leaping from his trench, rifle in hand, Jim Bentley faced the enemy, his body sagging grotesquely into the battlefield mud as bullets tore through his flesh.

"Are you all right, sir?" the waitress whispered, concern in her eyes as she gently touched his shoulder. "You look like you've seen a ghost!"

Smiling ruefully, even as a shiver went down his spine, he looked up at the young woman and weakly nodded. Paying his bill, he quickly left, hoping the chilly air would clear his head. Reaching his hotel room, he felt ill and hurried up the hallway to the bathroom, throwing up into the toilet. Feeling slightly better, he took his key out of his pocket and walked down the hallway to his door, opening it with trembling fingers. Turning up the gas lamp, he watched flickering shapes dance about on the walls. Drawn like a magnet to the writing table, his eyes settled on the clean surface and, uncontrollably, the battle scene continued.

"No more, no more," he begged, covering his eyes as the images tormented him. Finally managing to drag his eyes away, he slumped to the floor.

Sunday morning church bells woke him and, with no recollection of undressing or climbing into bed, he stared at the stains on the ceiling. Had he really seen the demise of Jim Bentley in that war-torn field in France or had he been dreaming?

Glancing around the room, he saw his suit, clean and pressed on a hanger, a shirt folded neatly, and his shined boots beside the chair. His briefcase stood open on the table as if he'd been writing a report. He knew these signs, his ghostly mentor was close at hand.

"Mr. Watson," he began, talking quietly to the empty space. "I'm not sure I can handle this role, sir."

"You don't have any choice, son, you have been chosen and so it must be."

Oliver shook his head helplessly. *It makes no sense to be arguing with a ghost ... or guardian angel ... or whatever you are! Nothing makes sense any more.*

Over the past few years, he'd read several volumes on witchcraft particularly after interviewing a man who claimed to be a clairvoyant. He had also attended a performance at the Royal Theatre where a medium craftily made things happen for a gullible audience. But this was real and, for the first time, it frightened him.

Moving around the room in his ghostly form, although invisible to his protégé, Tom Watson's telltale tobacco smell gave him away.

"I know you're still here," Oliver muttered angrily.

"Oliver, we didn't send you to find Jim Bentley," Tom reminded him, "you chose to go there."

"That was horrible."

"War is horrible, son, but men never learn. They'll do it again in 1939."

"Y-you've b-been there?" Oliver stammered incredulously but he received no answer. His mind suddenly alive, he thought of escaping to a happier time.

All afternoon he thought about it and by the time he went to bed that night he'd made his decision. Tomorrow he'd travel on to the end of the century. He could be there and back in the blink of an eye. The words of his guardian angel helped him make up his mind. *Remember, son, time stands still while you're gone.*

In the morning he awoke, eager to put his plan into motion. Setting his mind once again on the front entrance of the Empress Hotel, he thought of Monday morning in the year 2000.

Chapter 5

Oliver stared in disbelief at the large, red doubledecker bus standing on the smooth, black pavement in front of the Empress Hotel. The hotel looked almost the same as he knew it, except its ivy covering was gone and there was an addition on the north end which, by its circular driveway, he guessed was the new entrance. Walking closer, he watched fascinated as remarkably fancy and large automobiles expelled their curiously dressed passengers, who were welcomed by uniformed attendants.

The ladies aren't wearing long skirts any more, he noted, but as soon as this thought went through his mind, a very long car pulled into the circle taking his attention. Gaping at its length, he watched open-mouthed as a number of beautiful young women with long hair and very short skirts climbed out and hurried into the hotel. Counting how many were leaving the car took his attention at first and then it struck him. *Good heavens, they're hardly wearing any clothes at all! The year 2000 is going to be more interesting than I imagined.*

He looked out at the street and, because it was winter and most women were wearing long coats, he wasn't aware of the drastic style change, but he was actually more interested in the unusual automobiles. These colourful cars raced along at seemingly breakneck speeds with only a whisper of noise and Oliver stood on the sidewalk and gawked as they passed.

People stared at him as he stood rigidly near the doorway. Hardly daring to move, his eyes roamed up and down the wide street and across the harbour. He couldn't believe the changes around the causeway—new odd-looking buildings that were tall and light-coloured and people in colourful clothing. He felt a surge of newfound interest and adventure charge through his veins.

"Are you an actor, sir?" asked a female voice at his elbow.

Startled, Oliver turned to face an attractive blonde woman, of about his own age. She was also colourfully dressed, but did not seem to be wearing one of those little skirts, and her long coat and matching hat were the most extraordinary colour of purple he had ever seen. Around her neck, she wore a long silk scarf which had tones of purple and green mixed together. Quite unused to seeing such colourful clothes he was mesmerized, but smiled and awkwardly tipped his hat. Coupled with his confusion, he felt rather ridiculous finding he was unable to speak and, merely shook his head, self-consciously touching his hat again.

She smiled and her eyes twinkled with merriment as she watched him. "I'm so sorry to disturb you, sir," she apologized, suddenly thinking she should take a picture of this unusual little man who reminded her of Charlie Chaplin.

She has the most beautiful green eyes, thought Oliver.

"Would you mind if I take a video of you standing in front of the Empress?" she asked.

Not understanding either why she found him of such interest, or what a video was, although he assumed it was the unusual-looking box in her hand, he nodded politely.

Moving back a few steps, Oliver watched as she stepped onto the driveway and put the box-like contraption up to her face. She seemed to be looking through it, much like a camera but, as he watched, a little red light appeared and she moved the box sideways for a few seconds. The light went out and she came back to him, displaying a puzzled expression.

"That's strange, you're not visible in my viewfinder," she announced, examining the camera and shaking her head in astonishment. "It was working fine a moment ago."

She backed up a couple of steps and looked at Oliver again, feeling there was something not quite right about this man who was dressed in period costume. When he took a step toward her, she backed up.

"I'm sure your camera is all right, Miss. Let me introduce myself, my name is Oliver Ryan, I'm a newspaper reporter from Seattle. Would you allow me to buy you a coffee?"

Feeling somewhat relieved that she knew a bit more about him, she offered no resistance as he indicated the little pathway through the garden to Government Street. As they walked, she introduced herself.

"My name is Mary Beth Janick, Mr. Ryan … Mary is fine. I'm a high school teacher from Everett. I love to visit Victoria but until now my trips have been rather short. This time I've come for the entire week, mainly to do some family research while I'm on Christmas Break. Do you know the city well, Mr. Ryan?" she asked, watching the good-looking, yet serious young man, out of the corner of her eye as she pulled her gloves back on and put her video camera in her bag. *He seems somewhat younger than I am,* she thought warming to his company as he unmistakeably moved to her left side. *His unusual style of clothes could be confusing my judgement but his old-fashioned manners are quite delightful.*

"Well, I used to many years ago," he replied, forcing a grin, "but everything has changed so much."

Icy fingers touched the hairs on Mary's neck as she felt the pressure of his hand on her elbow as they crossed the street. An unusual sensation surged down her arm which moved quickly through her body stopping immediately when they reached the other sidewalk and he let go. This totally unnerved her for a moment and she told herself she was imagining it.

Mixing with Christmas shoppers, they threaded their way up Government Street, past the many souvenir shops which seemed to hold a fascination for Oliver. Each time they crossed a street, he took her elbow and the same sensation tingled through her body. When they came to Rogers' Chocolates, Oliver stopped to look in the window and then peeked quickly through the door.

"Some things never change!" he whispered to himself, when he saw the distinctive chandelier was still there.

Continuing up the street, Mary allowed him to go ahead of her, and she watched his every move. At the corner of Broughton Street, he waited, again taking her arm before crossing the street and again the feeling returned.

This is crazy, who is this guy? she thought as he stopped in front of the China Shop.

Oliver stared at the building he remembered as the Windsor Hotel, quickly realizing it had gone through substantial alterations. The veranda was gone and its batwing doors were no longer evident. The echoes of rowdy, drunken laughter sounded only in his memory. Now, the windows displayed beautiful china, glassware and other interesting items. Farther up the street, he noticed the Brown Jug Saloon was now a linen store and he grinned at his memories from a week ago.

Mary listened as he gave fascinating descriptions of the buildings that used to be and the changes that had taken place. *He must be a historian*, she thought. *It seems we have something in common.*

"How quaint, I wonder what is down there?" she asked, pointing to a cobbled courtyard area running between some older-looking buildings. The street sign read, 'Bastion Square.'

"The Law Courts and Courthouse," he replied absentmindedly.

Glancing across the street, he noticed Trounce Alley remained, but 'Wilson the Tailor's,' was now a glass-fronted building nicely accented with wood—a large sign read 'W & J Wilson.'

"Wilson's men's wear," he informed her. "It's been there for a very long time and it's my favourite clothing shop."

As they continued to the next block, she thought about what he had said. *Wilson's is a high-class store, he couldn't possibly have bought his clothes there.*

He stopped suddenly, causing people to go around him, and a puzzled expression crossed his face.

"What is that green sign?" he murmured, more to himself.

"You mean Starbuck's?"

What has happened to the bank? he thought to himself.

"You've never had a Starbuck's coffee? Come on I'll treat you," she insisted, taking his arm and leading him across Yates Street.

They entered what seemed to be a café which smelled heavily of coffee. He looked up at the menu on the wall, seeing a long list of flavours and names that were totally foreign to him. Recognizing his understandable confusion, she asked if he liked milk in his coffee. He shrugged and she went ahead and ordered. Planning to pay, he looked in his billfold concerned his old money would give him away, but thankfully it had been updated … or so he surmised seeing that it looked quite different.

"Go ahead and get a table, Mr. Ryan, I'll bring it over," Mary told him. Wincing when he heard the amount the cashier needed—a five-cent coffee was now more than three dollars and Mary had already paid the cashier before he'd recovered. Shaking his head in disbelief, he went to find an empty table.

"You look surprised," she whispered when she joined him, putting the tall mugs on the table. "What's wrong, Mr. Ryan?"

Oliver's mind was not on the coffee as he stared trancelike into space. He'd jumped into the end of the 20th century without any preparation and now felt grossly out of place. With his mind whirling, he settled on a new course of action. *If you don't help me Tom, I'll simply have to tell this girl and hope she'll understand.* Looking around, he neither saw Tom nor heard any whispered words of comfort or direction. He knew he was on his own. He took a sip of his coffee and smiled.

"This is different but very nice!" he commented.

"You like it," she said pleased with his reaction. "It's called a latté, they're very popular."

And atrociously expensive! he thought. "Do you believe in angels, Mary?" he said aloud, placing his hand over hers.

"I'm not sure," she whispered, feeling the colour rise in her cheeks and realizing that unusual sensation returned when he touched her.

"We'll finish our cof … latté, and then I have a surprise for you," he said, feeling proud of himself for taking the first step in his new plan. Quickly changing the subject, they talked about the décor of the room and Mary told him she was a history teacher with an interest in the history of Victoria and its architecture. This set him off on a tangent they both enjoyed until he began to notice the strange looks they were receiving from other customers.

"Why are people looking at us like that?" he whispered.

"I don't know," she lied not knowing quite how to tell him. "We're finished anyway; you said you had a surprise for me."

"Yes, I did. Close your eyes, Mary I'm going to take you on a trip—to 1916!"

Puzzled and not sure if she had heard his words correctly, Mary's eyelids flickered shut. She felt his fingers grip her arm and a rush of cold air on her face. She was wondering why she was trusting this man who was virtually a stranger, when she experienced another odd feeling … one of great calmness.

"Tell me about Victoria in 1916, Oliver," she whispered, leaning toward him but keeping her eyes tightly shut.

"Open your eyes, Mary," he replied. "We're here."

Her eyelids fluttered open and she gasped. She guessed that this very small room was in an old hotel, but how was it possible to be here? Were they still in Victoria? What kind of man was he to bring her to this dive? And then she remembered he had said '1916.' Hearing a loud clanking noise outside, she went quickly to the window and drew back the flimsy curtains. Her heart was beating wildly.

"That's a streetcar over on Fort Street," he said casually.

So we are still in Victoria, she thought with relief, unable to pull herself away from the unusual scene. She realized they were probably on the third floor and, below, horses came into view pulling large carts. "Oh my gosh, we are in 1916," she said aloud. "Those are drays aren't they?"

Despite the closed window, she could hear the driver cursing as the crack of his whip rent the air. Mary's thoughts were going almost as fast as her heart, which she thought was going to burst any second. *His suit!* She suddenly realized why it looked so out of place. *This is impossible, it just can't be happening.* She had come to Victoria trying to find her family roots and, instead, had stumbled into an unbelievable adventure with a man from another era. "Am I dreaming?" she asked, tearing her gaze away from the window and turning to look at the stranger with a new curiosity.

"No Mary, you're not, but I think you need an explanation." He pulled the chair away from the desk and offered it to her. She gratefully sat down and he sat on the bed across from her. For a while, they just stared at each other as Oliver tried to work out what he was going to say.

"We're in my room in the Temperance Hotel on Langley Street," he began slowly. "It's not much but it's all my boss will pay for when I work here. I can assure you I am a sane and honourable man, for what it's worth, although I'm sure you're having some doubts right now, Mary. I'm a mortal angel. I'm able to travel on thought waves, but I live in 1916."

"You're kidding me, right?" she exclaimed, but before he could answer she had a horrible thought … her face went white and her hand flew to her mouth. "Does this mean I'm stuck here in 1916?"

"No," he said gently. "I can take you back any time you want."

She sighed audibly, although staring straight ahead; then she sighed again as if to shake herself back to reality. Silently, she desperately tried to regain her composure and relax. *I have to be able to think clearly,* she thought, standing up and going to the window. "I suppose this is why my video camera didn't take your picture. Do you think I would be able to use it here in 1916? Without waiting for him to answer, she rambled on, her thoughts spilling out one after the other. "I arrived in Victoria yesterday with the intent of searching for some of my ancestors who used to live here. I planned to spend the rest of the week here as a holiday. I have some time off from school until it starts again in January." She stopped to take a breath.

"I might be able to help you trace your family," he stated. "I'm a court reporter; I have access to records unavailable to you."

"Oh! 1916 records? That would be just around the right time. Could you really, Oliver?" she asked, now feeling slightly better, then her expression changed again. "I'm feeling quite hungry all of a sudden," she said timidly. "Is there somewhere we could go to eat?"

"Not dressed like that you can't," Oliver declared, looking at her with squinting eyes. "We'd better find you some 1916 apparel. I'll give you my coat for now, leave yours here!"

Again taken by surprise, Mary nodded, vaguely aware of her actions as she took off her coat and donned his. He led her downstairs to the street and moving as if in a trance, confused thoughts galloped through her head. *Should I trust him? What choice do I have? What if I want to go back, would he really let me go?*

At this point, they came to a busy Government Street bustling with shoppers. Oliver took her hand and linked it through his arm. He had heard part of her thoughts and realized he had understandably confused her. With so many people around, coupled with traffic noises, he found himself unable to hear her any more but silently promised she had nothing to fear, unaware that even his thoughts gave her a measure of comfort.

All the shops they passed were busy so he took her up Douglas where she gawked, fascinated by the trams and old cars. Suddenly, she realized what a grand adventure this could be and started to relax, telling herself she would have to be cautious and find out more about this unusual man. Stopping at Percy Scurrah's Ladies' Store at 728 Yates, they went inside. Oliver told her to look around and pick out what she needed.

Thrilled with the choice of long dresses she had only seen in magazines and the internet, she soon had various pieces of clothing hanging over her arm. A clerk led her to a little cubby hole with a curtain. *Hmm, not unlike some of our older shops at home,* she thought, closing the curtain behind her then peeking out to see where Oliver had gone. Finding himself embarrassed to be in a women's shop, he stood near the door staring out at the street. Within half an hour, she had made her selection of a dress, petticoat, cardigan, coat, hat and scarf deciding she quite liked the styles of 1916. Bundling her own clothes together to hide them, she went out to the cashier.

"Make sure you have enough to last for a few days," Oliver quietly suggested, seeing she was only purchasing one dress.

She went back to the rack and selected a dark green calf-length wool dress she had tried on. He smiled his approval as he paid the bill and the clerk watched them with curiosity as they left the store.

Beginning to feel she was in some kind of a period movie, Mary giggled to herself. *What a story I'm going to have to tell my students ... oh heck, they'll never believe me!* Thank you for the clothes, Oliver. I could have paid for them myself, though," she told him.

"No you couldn't have, you don't have the right currency and besides you're my guest. It's all right, come on," he added, "let's get something to eat. I'll introduce you to my favourite restaurant."

Holding tightly to his arm and almost having forgotten how hungry she was, she showed more interest in her surroundings as they headed over to Johnson Street. He pointed to a bank on the corner that looked vaguely familiar.

"That's where we had our latté; it's Starbuck's in your world!" he informed her and he finally heard her laugh.

They continued along Government for another block as he told her briefly about some of the buildings they were passing. They turned left at the next corner and walked toward the railway station.

"It all looks so different. I was just looking at a tourist brochure of Market Square on the ferry this morning, I believe it was in this block—it's a group of old buildings they've turned into a sort of old-fashioned shopping mall with an area in the middle where they hold concerts and events. This is amazing!" she exclaimed as she looked up and read 'Occidental Hotel.' She distinctly got the feeling that this imposing structure had been replaced by a modern building in her time. She decided she'd have to make some notes.

Two E & N trains sat at the station, steam spewing into the cold December air. The American teacher stared at the dull-looking Johnson Street trestle in fascination, noting that the tracks crossed the harbour even back in 1916. *It certainly has acquired a new, larger design and a nice paint job by the year 2000,* she thought, remembering its modern-day vibrant blue colour. Oliver cut into her thoughts by opening the door of the hotel and following her inside.

"I believe that train station is still there today, Oliver, I mean in my day. It looks smaller, perhaps because the bridge is larger," she whispered as they waited to be shown a table.

"The bridge is larger?"

"Yes, it's a new design that cars use and it raises when tall boats need to go underneath. It's painted very spiffy now, too!" She laughed, seeing his surprised expression. "What's wrong?"

"That's an old expression, it's still in use?"

"Oh sure, I got it from my grandmother!" Mary laughed.

Oliver watched delighted as his companion looked all around them at the unfamiliar furnishings. They heard snatches of conversation from two men at the next table and she made a face nodding in their direction. Their voices were getting louder and it soon became apparent to everyone they were arguing about the provincial election and a change of government from Conservative to the Liberal Party.

She turned her attention back to the menu. "Cripes, a full steak dinner for $2.10!" she hissed, reaching into her handbag to retrieve her notebook and pen. Realizing her video camera was still in her bag, she silently decided not to complicate the situation any more … she would leave it in her suitcase for the rest of this holiday.

Oliver watched her curiously hearing some of her thoughts then she began to write brief notes in her notebook about the menu and its prices, adding other notations about the bridge and nearby buildings.

"What kind of a fountain pen is that?" he asked, holding out his hand.

Smiling impishly, she handed him her cheap ballpoint pen.

"The nib is too pointed," he observed. "How do you fill it?"

"Try it," she encouraged him, pushing her notebook toward him.

He proceeded to write his name, occupation and address. "Smooth," he whispered almost inaudibly. "Where can I get one?"

"You can have that one, Oliver," she replied, beginning to feel quite comfortable with this man who said he was a mortal angel, "but it's not a fountain pen, it's called a ballpoint pen."

"A new invention," he whispered reverently, seeing her take a bright green coloured one from her bag.

When they'd finished eating, he led her along Wharf Street past the dockside warehouses of Rithet, McQuade and Hudson Bay, then back on the other side of the street to Yates. Mary was obviously excited at the fascinating array of unique shops, offices and stores they were passing on the harbour. She watched as two gentlemen dressed in long, fur-trimmed coats and bowler hats pushed through the doors of the fashionable Hotel St. Francis then she squealed excitedly when her companion pointed out the Majestic Theatre, opposite Langley Street near his hotel.

"Please take me there," she begged, squeezing his arm.

"Oh, all right," he replied, "but I'm not much of a theatre-goer."

"We open at six, guv'nor," the cleaning lady told them through a partly opened door, as they read the billboard announcement.

Tipping his hat and receiving a smile from the woman, Oliver turned, took Mary's hand and led her across the street to Langley, passing the Sign Works on the corner and arriving at his hotel opposite the police station at the corner of Bastion Street.

He held the door open for her, then took her elbow to climb the two flights of dark stairs. Going inside, he dropped the parcel of clothes onto the bed while Mary watched him closely. In every way, he was acting the gentleman. This man who'd whisked her back in time obviously did not intend to send her back to the year 2000 just yet, but where would he expect her to sleep? Relief flooded her mind when Oliver turned from the window, grinning mischievously as he heard snatches of her thoughts and felt her discomfort.

"Let me show you to your room," he announced, surprised at how much he was enjoying himself.

Taking her out into the hallway to the next door, using a key, he showed her a room which was the duplicate of his own. He turned on the lamp before going over to the clothes closet and drawing back the curtain. This revealed a connecting door between the rooms.

"Toilet's at the end of the hall," he explained over his shoulder, as he drew back the bolts on the hidden door. It opened and he stepped through into his own closet.

"It's chilly in here," Mary complained, hugging herself as she watched him disappear. *How did he do that, he must have unlocked the door in his room when I wasn't looking, but when did he get the key—he's been with me all along?* She shivered momentarily and then he was in the doorway again.

"I think you'll need this," he said, handing her the parcel of clothes, neatly wrapped in brown paper and tied with string.

She took it over to the bed, pulled off the string and began to unwrap it. As she did so, she heard a sound and turned to look at the washbasin in the corner, its single cold-water tap dripping monotonously. She sat down on the bed and looked all around her. The window curtains, although clean, were faded and flimsy from too many washings. She wrinkled her nose realizing the pungent smell was from the gas lamp.

"Who are those ancestors you're trying to find?" he called.

"My grandmother, Jane Sprott, and her mother, Bertha Bentley."

Oliver stopped and jerked around to face the open door.

"Who did you say?" his raised voice echoed between the rooms.

Chapter 6

There was an uncanny silence from the other room as a cold hand seemed to reach out and touch her. Mary stepped through the closet and realized he'd gone to his desk and was hurriedly writing something on his notepad. Curious, she went to stand behind him and looked over his shoulder. She was shocked to see splotches of dampness staining the paper; his body trembled with emotion. Oliver was crying. Her curiosity now intense, she leaned over his shoulder and read his words. Instantly she understood.

Jim Bentley, your great grandfather,
was killed in France October 10, 1915.
Your great-grandmother, Bertha,
left Victoria with Jane, your grandmother,
as a 4-year-old, at the beginning of December 1916.

Mary's hand grasped Oliver's shoulder in astonishment.

I know them. They're living with a relative
in Seattle; his name is Ben Olson.

Shoulders hunched, he let the ballpoint pen slip from his fingers and wiped a tear from his cheek. His face had gone deathly white.

"Can you take me to see them?" she whispered impulsively.

Conflict raged in Oliver's mind considering the strange situation in which he now found himself. Should he, could he, really take a person from the future and transport her back in time to meet her own grandmother as a child? *Why not, Mary is already here in 1916,* he reasoned, visibly trying to collect his wits as he made up his mind. "Yes, we'll do it, but first we have an errand to do," he decided aloud. "Get your coat, it's snowing in Seattle."

Dashing back to her room, she hurriedly put on her new coat, hat and scarf, locked the door, grabbed her gloves and handbag and returned through the closet to Oliver's room.

"Ready?" he asked reaching for her hand. "Close your eyes."

The whisper of cold air again brushed Mary's face, then a familar sensation, as snowflakes kissed her skin melting into tiny droplets.

Oliver's voice cut through her concentration. "We're here."

"My goodness," she gasped, staring at the sign which read 'Police Station.' "This is Seattle's old Forth Street Station. Did my grandmother live near here?"

Without answering, he tugged her through the door, to the amusement of the desk sergeant. Stamping snow from their shoes, Oliver boldly inquired for Sgt. Ben Olson.

"I can assist you," the policeman snapped.

The reporter's eyes turned toward the wall of Olson's office. Behind it, he could see Ben was alone and sitting at his desk.

"Ben!" Oliver called past the startled sergeant. "I need to talk to Bertha."

The detective ground his teeth then came to his feet, grating his chair along the floor as he did so. A bad day had left his temper frayed and he was in no mood to be yelled at. Mary glanced over at her companion while the desk sergeant, smirking gleefully, cautiously moved off to one side. Oliver's eyes became tiny orbs of fire directed at the wall across the hall. This was the first time Mary had experienced this phenomenon and it terrified her. *What is happening?* she thought frantically. Suddenly, he was normal again, smiling as the detective came out of his office and sauntered toward them.

"Well, hello Oliver," he murmured. "Bertha and Jane are well looked after. They're living in a house I own on Prospect, just off Sixth up on Lake Union. They'll be happy to see you."

"He was very helpful," Mary commented when they were outside again. "How do we get to Prospect?"

"Hush woman, close your eyes and hang on."

Hardly a moment had passed when she heard his chuckle.

"Open your eyes."

When she did so, she was surprised to find they were standing in the midst of a toy department.

"We need to get Jane and Bertha Christmas presents," he said, going straight to a collection of dolls.

It didn't take long before they had picked out two dolls and several other toys and paid for them. Going next to ladies' wear, Mary found a nice sweater and skirt for Bertha and they hurried outside with their parcels. Seconds later, they arrived at the little cottage.

Mary gasped as she opened her eyes and stared at the dilapidated building with its cracked and broken windows, peeling paint, broken chimney and missing shingles.

"Oh Oliver," she said sadly, not letting go of his arm, "it's a dump! I'm afraid to see what it's like inside."

Two faces appeared at the window and Mary heard a child scream Oliver's name. Almost at the same time, the door flew open and the little girl ran toward him. Mary's heart was thumping wildly and she feared she might faint. Taking two deep breaths, she watched as the child she knew to be her grandmother, ran into Oliver's arms, while a young woman, no doubt her great-grandmother, Bertha Bentley, stood smiling in the doorway.

When Oliver released the child, he flicked his hand and time stood still for the Bentleys. Mary gasped when she saw the now-familiar expression on Oliver's face and his amazing eyes ....

"You're frightening me," she exclaimed, wrapping her arms around her body as tears welled in her eyes.

"Keep still, Mary Janick," he whispered. "You're going to be privileged to watch an angel at work. Come a bit closer."

Moving carefully around the child, they stood at the open doorway. First, he pointed to the fireplace and Mary stared in disbelief as she heard the crackle of fire and burning logs appeared. Next, pieces of wallpaper hanging loose about the room crept back into place, their colour rejuvenated; paint freshened and windows repaired themselves, as if by magic. Carpets and furniture materialized from nowhere and light bulbs that were dead and blackened from age suddenly sprang into life throwing a warm, cozy light over the comfortable scene. Waving his hand again, an evergreen tree materialized and an array of old-fashioned decorations distributed themselves about the branches. The bag with their presents flew through the air landing already beautifully wrapped with festive paper and ribbons, on the bare floor below the tree. Meanwhile outside, the roof, chimney and fence repaired themselves.

Pulse racing, Mary's body shook with emotion. "This is a miracle," she whispered, stealing a glance at him.

Slowly, the tension seemed to ease from Oliver's frame and his shoulders slumped as if this work had sapped all his strength; the burning light in his eyes dulled to their normal blue colour and he flicked his hand to release time. Jane ran past them into the house, her excited chatter filling the room again as she saw the tree and presents.

Making careful introductions, he gave no indication who Mary really was. Sipping tea at the kitchen table soon after, Oliver gently broke the sad news to Bertha that Jim wouldn't be returning home.

"My daddy's in heaven now," Jane announced with child-like innocence after her mother had explained Oliver's message.

With tears streaming down her face, Bertha wrapped her arms around her little daughter and rocked her. Mary felt like an intruder as the poignant scene played itself out. She got up to look around the room hoping to find some personal mementoes of their family. She was puzzled why they hadn't noticed the changes to their home, then realized Oliver would have had something to do with that, too.

Knowing this opportunity may never come again, she waited until it was appropriate and began questioning Bertha on family matters, learning things about distant relatives in England that no amount of research could have unearthed. Awed by this unusual experience, Mary found Bertha to be a fascinating subject, very happy to have a willing audience even though she had no idea Mary *was* her family.

When Bertha asked if they would stay for dinner, Oliver looked at his pocket watch and realized how late it was. They quickly made their excuses and Jane went to get their coats. Darkness was closing in around the Prospect Street residence as they said their goodbyes. After putting her coat on, Mary experienced a moment of deep emotion when she sadly said goodbye to her grandmothers. Silently, she gave Jane a hug and a kiss on the cheek, as a huge lump grew in her throat.

"It's strange," Bertha whispered, holding Mary for an extra moment. "It feels like a part of me is going with you. Please come and visit us again."

"Thank you, it's been wonderful meeting you," Mary replied, drawing away and desperately trying not to cry.

Putting on their hats and gloves, they stepped outside waving to the Bentleys before walking off through the snow toward Sixth Avenue. Turning the corner, Oliver stopped and pulled Mary closer.

"Just a minute, I've forgotten something." Focussing his mind on the back wall of the little house, he caused a neatly cut and stacked woodpile to form. "There, now we're ready. Close your eyes, we're going back to Victoria, Mary."

Weeping softly, Mary lay her head on Oliver's shoulder, her thoughts overwhelming her. Her ancestors were real to her now, not just names in a book. She had actually talked to them and touched them, such a priceless memory.

Feeling Oliver's arm release her, she opened her eyes and found she was back in his hotel room. She stared up at him and for a brief moment in time their eyes met and neither seemed to be able to look away. Gas lights flickered out on the street throwing eerie shadows around the room and a clock struck five o'clock somewhere out on Victoria's darkened streets. Oliver blinked and gently touched her shoulder.

"Are you all right?" he asked, his voice displaying his concern.

She nodded and searched in her bag for a tissue, wiping her eyes.

"We'd better go find something to eat," he said.

"You know, I'm really not very hungry yet," she replied, speaking very softly. She suddenly felt exhausted and a bit embarrassed wanting to be alone to collect her thoughts. "I need to write down some notes about my family before I forget, and then I think I'm going to have a little nap."

"Good idea," he agreed. You've had a rather busy and unsettling day and forgive me, Mary, for not thinking. I've got some writing to do anyway, so why don't you come get me when you're ready."

"I don't want to keep you from dinner, Oliver. Please go ahead without me," she suggested.

"I wouldn't think of it, my dear. You go have your rest."

Mary finally gave in and went through the adjoining door to her room. Quietly locking one of the bolts, she hung up her coat and removed her dress before climbing exhausted into bed. It took all of her energy to write down some brief notes before turning off the light and falling back onto the pillow. Thinking of her grandmothers and everything that had happened, in seconds, she was asleep.

In the next room, Oliver smiled as he worked at his table. Two hours later, lying on his bed, he was startled awake. Sitting up in a daze, he heard sounds from next door and realized Mary was awake.

I must have fallen asleep, he thought. Getting up and splashing some cold water on his face, he quickly combed his hair, straightened his room and put on his shoes. *That's odd, why am I so concerned about neatness all of a sudden?*

Hearing a light knock and the click of the bolt being released, he looked up to see Mary as she poked her head through the closet.

"Hello," she called merrily, "are you decent?"

"Come in, come in," he replied, grinning when he saw she had her coat on.

"I'm sorry I kept you waiting so long, I'm famished!" she apologized.

"Perfect timing, I just finished," he lied, his stomach had been complaining even before he lay down.

"Oliver, is there somewhere I can buy a toothbrush and some necessities? In all the excitement, I completely forgot my suitcase is over at the Gatsby in the year 2000."

"Oh that's no problem for an angel. Did you have time to unpack the suitcase?" he asked.

"No, I just left my bags inside the door."

"That's easy then, I'll simply go there and get them for you!" he replied, his eyes sparkling mischievously.

Getting the information he needed, he concentrated and quickly found himself in another hotel room. This one was very different from his and much larger with flowered wallpaper. He spotted the suitcase and a smaller bag, picked them up and sent himself back to 1916. Seeing him suddenly materialize only seconds later, holding her suitcases, Mary burst out laughing and had to sit down.

"I wouldn't have believed that if I hadn't seen it myself! You're a lifesaver, Oliver."

He took the bags into her room and she followed, telling him to give her five minutes and he went back through the closet.

"Would you like me to take you out for a beer—experience something a bit less civilized?" he called. Hearing her affirmative reply, he continued. "The Brown Jug Saloon is not as noisy as some of the drinking establishments and I promise you'll enjoy the architecture."

"I'm game," she called, "as long as they serve quick meals!"

A biting wind whipped up from the harbour as they stepped from the protection of the hotel into the dark street. Oliver offered his arm and, with heads down against the wind, they headed up Bastion Street. Turning the corner, piano music, laughter and shouting was heard, obviously coming from several different saloons. Groups of people, all men as far as she could tell, were also milling about on the street. Mary was surprised to see so many out on such a horrible night.

Ahead of them, a drunk cursed viciously when he fell against a wall and stumbled into their path, causing her to tighten her grip on Oliver's arm. Thankfully, they soon arrived at the saloon and Oliver pushed through the swinging doors ahead of her. Voices instantly lowered to a rumbling murmur when they saw the couple enter—rarely were females seen in these sacred male establishments. Soldiers, many with bandaged limbs and heads and some on crutches, mixed with sailors and on-strike miners, all showing an eagerness to get a view of the attractive young woman.

Pushing his way through the heckling crowd, Oliver led her over to the long, highly polished bar which already sported a row of boisterous and obviously inebriated customers. He acquired two beers, slopping much of the froth onto the floor as they forced their way through the crowd to a space at the wall.

Feeling a bit more unnerved than she expected, she forgot about food and her eyes moved back and forth about the room taking in every detail of the notorious, dimly lit tavern. Looking around at the gawking faces, she clutched her beer glass and took a tentative sip. *Not bad,* she thought, taking another as an argument started in the centre of the room. Settled with a swift kick from another patron, the crowd was obviously growing restless.

"Can we go somewhere else, Oliver?" Mary shouted into his ear, tugging on his arm 15 minutes later.

Dropping their glasses on the bar as they went by, they hastily pushed their way through the crowd to the door. When they stepped out into the freezing air, amidst loud comments from the men inside, they now found only a few hardy souls huddled in doorways drinking from bottles and talking noisily. Darkened shop windows added to the blackness, broken only by widely scattered electric street lights.

Mary took his arm again and he led her four doors up the street to the White Lunch Café. As they entered, the waitress informed them they were closing in five minutes. They were able to purchase a beef sandwich and some delicious-looking apple cake and the woman offered to fill a jar with coffee for them, asking if they needed cups.

Tightening the lid, she wrapped brown paper around it and handed Mary the two cups. Securing their promise to return the jar and cups the next day, they hurried outside laughing all the way back to the hotel. Putting down the hot jug as he opened the door, they went inside and he helped her remove her coat. He poured them each a steaming cup of coffee and unwrapped the sandwich.

"I'm sorry if that was too much for you tonight, Mary, and we missed a proper meal," Oliver murmured. "Oldtime saloons are not what you thought they'd be then?"

"That place is evil," Mary exclaimed through her mouthful. "I'm not surprised the government banned them."

"Banned them?" Oliver retorted, staring at his guest from the year 2000 and watching her mouth bend into a smile.

"You have no knowledge of history beyond your own time, have you, Oliver?" she asked playfully.

"No I don't; it hasn't happened yet!"

"But you'd travelled into the future when you met me?"

"That's true, but I'd arrived only minutes before you saw me. I really didn't know what my capabilities were; actually, this is all very new to me and I'm still learning."

Sitting on either end of the bed propped on pillows, they talked about their lives and the times they lived in, steering consciously away from subjects that were too personal. Mary grinned as a sudden thought came to her.

Oliver may be a mortal angel from the past but I'm his angel of the future! "Let's try an experiment," she said aloud. "I'm going to go outside. I'll bet you can send me back to 2000 just by thinking it!"

"I don't know," he replied, as a feeling of unmistakable dread came over him. "No, I have to touch you. I brought you here to 1916 and, anyway, it's almost midnight Mary, you'll freeze out there."

"It wasn't as cold in 2000; come on, humour me I'm not ready to go to sleep anyway. Try it with me, please," she pleaded, jumping to her feet, "and, if it works, you have to promise you'll come and get me. Remember, it's December 18th, 2000 in front of the Empress."

"Of course I'll come and get you, but how will I find you?" he asked, helping her back into her coat. "Remember, I'm new at this."

"I'll go outside and you send me to the Empress when you're ready. I'll start walking and cut up to Government at Courtney. You come meet me—it'll only take me ten minutes to walk all the way if it doesn't work; otherwise I'll be in 2000 on December 18th!"

With a sinking feeling, Oliver watched her leave the room. What if something went terribly wrong? How would she get back? He found himself inordinately concerned. He'd never felt this way about anyone before; it was even different than his feelings for Bertha and Jane. Taking out his pocket watch, he noted the time as ten minutes to twelve. Concentrating, his mind sent her to the Empress. He left the hotel trying to act naturally although his heart was ready to explode.

She has to be wrong about my capabilities, he thought. Wanting to run, but walking quickly so he had time to look for her, he went over to Courtney Street then up to Government, doubts flashing through his brain. *Was this merely a ploy to escape? Surely, she couldn't walk back into the year 2000 without touching him? H*e could easily see it was still 1916.

Crossing the bridge at the causeway, he scanned the front of the Empress as a clock in the distance stuck midnight. Panic clutched at his throat—she wasn't there. His glasses steamed up with the heat from his face as he struggled to remember what she had said.

Four minutes had passed when a realization struck him. *If Mary is in the year 2000, the Empress should look different ... holy smokes, I have to go to 2000!* he thought frantically. Sending his thoughts flying to the end of the century, he breathed a sigh of relief when the updated entrance of the hotel appeared. As he looked around for Mary, he thought what a lovely day it was as the cold winter sun reflected off the harbour waters. *But where is Mary?*

Shoulders slumping in disappointment, he frantically ran from one door to the other not even aware of the curious stares of pedestrians. He'd lost her and could hardly bear the thought. At that moment, he heard a snatch of urgent conversation between two people.

"It's lunchtime and I'm hungry," a lady said to her companion.

Lunchtime? thought Oliver. *You idiot, it should be nighttime!* He closed his eyes, made the adjustment and heard Mary's voice.

"Where on earth have you been?" she demanded from behind him, obviously frantic. "I thought you'd abandoned me!"

"Actually, I thought you had!" he exclaimed, so relieved to see her he embraced her emotionally. Uncaring of watchful eyes, she tightly held onto him. Moments passed and still locked together, he murmured in her ear, "Close your eyes, we're going home!"

Their lips met in a first kiss just before Mary felt the rush of cold wind on her face. She knew they were going back to 1916 but she felt as if she were in heaven.

Despite the late hour, they sat up for awhile sharing the last cup of cold coffee and the cake. When tiredness finally overtook them, they kissed goodnight like shy lovers in Oliver's closet and finally ended a full day which had seemed like a lifetime.

Chapter 7

Oliver lay on his back and stared into the darkness, his mind running over the changes in his once-boring existence. First, there was Tom Watson who had invested the powers of a mortal angel on him, and then there was Mary, a wonderful girl from the year 2000, who'd stumbled into his life. His thoughts had turned from uncaring and selfish into a deep feeling for the welfare of others, now strangely aware of their pain and suffering and willing to help. He drifted into a fitful sleep with Mary Beth Janick still in his thoughts.

Sleep well, my boy, Tom Watson's ghostly voice whispered as he appeared by Oliver's bed. Oliver's body relaxed and he slipped into a deep slumber.

Amazingly, they both felt fully rested when daylight woke them giving promise of a more pleasant winter day. Eager to venture into the city, Mary splashed icy cold tap water on her face and went to the small, cracked mirror to apply her makeup. Thinking she saw something in the glass, she turned to look behind her expecting to see Oliver, but no one was there and she turned back to the mirror.

Immediately, the image of a smiling, top-hatted gentleman with snow-white hair and mutton-chop whiskers appeared. Her fingers, gripped the edge of the sink, turning white as goose bumps rose on her arms and a chill shot down her back. Her eyes never wavered and finally the image faded away.

"Oliver!" she croaked trying to call him but knowing she was hardly making a sound. She heard his footsteps and sagged into his arms trembling.

"What is it, Mary?" he whispered. "You look like you've seen a ghost."

"I think I have; do you have a friend who is a ghost, by any chance? He looked friendly enough," she replied, trying to describe the older man.

“I think you’ve just had a visit from my guardian angel, Tom Watson,” he informed her. “There’s no need to be concerned, he’s merely looking after me and often comes to talk to me.”

She looked at him with a bewildered expression; he thought she might faint, so he sat her down on the bed. He looked around the room but Tom was not revealing himself so Oliver decided not to tell her any more. She’d been frightened enough already for one day.

“You mean he can just pop in whenever he feels like it?” she asked, with a visible shudder, and Oliver sat down beside her and took her hand trying to reassure her.

“He’s a nice person, Mary, and is always available if I need him. This is an unusual job I seem to have been given,” he said.

“I’ll try not to be frightened but what a strange sensation that was. Will I ever meet him—I mean to talk to?”

“I don’t really know, Mary, it’s all so new to me. I feel like a baby angel learning to walk, and around every corner is a surprise. What I do know is we both need a proper meal, so let’s go get some breakfast. It will help you feel better.”

On the way to the Baltimore Lunch Room, they dropped the cups and jar into the White Lunch Café, thanking the girls profusely, and continued up Government arm-in-arm. As they walked, Mary consciously studied the couples she saw and suddenly remembered that customs until the middle of the 20th century were such that it was deemed bad manners to publicly display affection.

Now I remember ... my grandmother used to be quite disgusted with people who kissed in public or put their arms around each other as they walked—no wonder he gives me his arm all the time, she thought. *Customs certainly changed by the 21st century!*

Oliver broke into her thoughts by bringing up the subject of Tom Watson. “Tom must have had a reason for showing himself to you and I’m sure he’ll mention it in time. Meanwhile, we’re going to court this morning,” he told her. “It’s Monday and I have some work to do immediately after breakfast.”

The dark dismal courtroom in Bastion Street emanated a strange, unfriendly feeling to the girl as they took their seats in the area reserved for the press. The wooden seats were hard adding to the dismal atmosphere. As Mary let her eyes explore every nook and cranny, she squeezed closer to her companion.

There was a picture of King George V of England behind the judge's chair and nearby were the tables used by the councillors, similar to modern-day courts. She shuddered when she saw the empty prisoner's box with its chest-high rail and knew this was a place of tears and sorrow. Two court clerks with long, sad faces shuffled papers and it wasn't long before three lawyers wearing long black robes and comical white wigs appeared.

Suddenly, the deep rattling voice of the clerk sternly announced, "All rise for Judge Austin!"

Feet scraped the bare wooden floor and two latecomers tiptoed awkwardly into the public observation benches as Judge Austin swished into the court and glared out at the tiny assembly.

"Bring in the prisoner!" the clerk announced loudly.

Writing fiercely, Mary took down every detail in her notebook. *This is the stuff from which history lessons are made,* she thought. She couldn't wait to astound her students with her knowledge of this old-time English court procedure.

Three cases passed in front of the crotchety judge and Oliver's ballpoint pen hadn't written a word. In no time, recess was called and the courtroom emptied.

"They'll be back at two," Oliver informed her, "we'll go get some lunch."

"You haven't taken any notes," she commented, looking at him quizzically.

"Don't need to, my editor's not interested in this petty stuff, he wants only the details on the Egger boy."

"Who's he?"

"He killed a man in Seattle and thought he could escape up here. He has two brothers who are notorious rum runners and, no doubt, he was involved with them when this crime was perpetrated."

They walked silently the rest of the way along Wharf Street before turning into the restaurant at the Occidental Hotel.

"Hello Oliver," an acquaintance greeted the reporter as they passed in the doorway.

"Who was that?" Mary asked, reaching for her notebook when they sat down at a vacant table.

"That was Waldo Skillings, a local haulage contractor," he replied, "and a really fine man."

"Skillings … Skillings …," she muttered, "that name rings a bell."

Interrupted by a waitress, they ordered poached salmon and coffee. Suddenly, a confrontation began at a neighbouring table and a chair went crashing to the floor. Everyone watched as the man who was standing shouted abuse at the occupants of a nearby table. Arms waving, his voice rose to a deafening crescendo, urged on by his smiling lady companion. Cutlery clattered noisily on plates of half-eaten food as the object of the man's attention hurriedly departed.

"I wonder why he's so angry. Do you know him, Oliver?" Pen ready, Mary waited for his answer.

"That's Joe North and those men were Victoria City Council officials. They're disputing some issue about Broad Street."

After lunch, they walked slowly back to the courtroom but, hearing a commotion, they saw a man run behind the building chased at a distance by two brown-uniformed policemen shouting at him to 'Stop.' Hurrying to the courthouse, they arrived as another policeman ran past them.

"The prisoner has escaped!" he yelled.

"Well, there goes my story, it seems," complained Oliver. "We might as well go and see what has happened."

Inside, pandemonium had erupted as several officials ran into the courtroom from nearby offices. Judge Austin marched up to the bench and banged his gavel sending shock waves through the court.

"Court adjourned!" he snarled, his face twisting into violent contortions.

"Wow, this is exciting," Mary chuckled as the courtroom cleared. "Now what happens?"

Out on Langley Street, the reporter stopped to talk to a policeman, Constable Harry Gray, whom Oliver knew fairly well. After being introduced to Mary, he supplied more details of the prisoner's escape.

"He had help that is for sure. We won't catch Egger this time," the lawman predicted. "It looks like one of his brothers sprung him. They were seen running down to a waiting boat and it'll be a fast one."

"Are you not going after him?" she asked.

"Only two boats have any chance of catching them, Miss; the harbour patrol is down with engine trouble, and the other one is out at Gordon Head, too far away." The policeman's face radiated a sort of reverence when he mentioned this second boat. "Now there's a boat that could catch the devil himself, especially with that redhead at the helm!" he exclaimed, shaking his head.

Intrigued by the obvious enthusiasm of the lawman, Mary continued her questioning.

"Who's the redhead and where is Gordon Head?"

"Easy Miss, one at a time," Harry chuckled. "Nancy Wilson is the redhead and Gordon Head is over on the east side of town a few miles out. Her boat is the *Stockholm*. They have an office on Wharf Street. I have to go now—enjoy your stay, miss." Harry left them and Oliver looked out at the harbour.

"I have an idea, Mary, hang onto me and close your eyes," her companion urged, focussing on the jetty at Port Angeles.

Putting her arm around his waist, she closed her eyes and waited for the telltale cold wind on her face.

"We're here," he whispered, his lips lightly brushing her cheek. He felt her arms tighten about him not letting go as she opened her eyes and saw they were on an unfamiliar jetty.

Hank and Charlie Jeffs, two brothers and longtime Port Angeles fishermen, were sitting on crab traps repairing their equipment when they heard footsteps behind them on the old jetty's rough planking.

"Where the hell did you come from?" Charlie growled, spitting a stream of tobacco juice across the boards.

"That incoming boat," Oliver began, ignoring his question, "whose is it?"

"They came out of Victoria, we watched 'em all the way but don't know who it be," Hank explained.

"Mind if we watch?" Oliver asked.

"Suit yerself," Charlie replied, not taking his eyes off his work.

Twenty minutes later the incoming craft cut its engine and bumped against the pilings. Three wild-looking young men scrambled onto the dock. Mary noticed one had an angry red scar tracing a line from ear to jaw, taking her attention as he extracted a gun from his pocket, waving it in the air.

"Where's yer law, old man?" Milo Egger shouted, pointing his gun right at them. Mary grabbed Oliver and they backed away a couple of steps. The other two men, now also holding guns, came forward to join him.

Oliver reacted quickly. Moving his head slightly, time stopped and he winked at Mary, releasing her hold on him. She frowned, hugging herself as he walked over to the Eggers. Taking their guns, he calmly dropped them into the water. A ray of sunlight shone through the clouds and something caught his attention down at the end of the jetty. He turned to look and saw a building some distance away. Standing in the doorway, also frozen in time, stood the sheriff; it was his badge Oliver had seen.

The young angel's pulse raced. *Wow, I'm getting good!* "Now we're ready to deal with these hooligans," he said to Mary, jerking his head again as he came back to stand with her.

Appearing confused, the Eggers looked down at their empty hands and desperately looked from one to the other. One of them noticed the lawman now moving toward them and cursed, causing great confusion as they began yelling at each other. Urgently searching their pockets but finding nothing, they looked desperately at each other.

"Let's get outa here, boys, I don't wanna go back to jail," Milo shouted, taking off for the boat with the others close behind.

Suddenly, dark thunder clouds which had been gathering over the past hour or so, sent a sharp crackling bolt of lightning into the swelling sea not far away. The three men yelped, jumping into their boat. The engine roared and they pulled quickly away from the jetty.

"They're getting away!" Mary cried, grabbing his arm.

Oliver heard Tom Watson's voice and smiled.

Well done, son, their punishment will be delivered from a higher authority than ours.

"Hold on," Oliver instructed her, "we're leaving."

Arms around his waist and her head resting on his back, she closed her eyes, now unafraid of their unusual mode of travel.

Sheriff Jake Mendell blinked with surprise as he neared the fishermen, looking around for the young couple he'd seen.

"Where'd that couple go, Charlie?" he growled.

"What couple?"

"The couple you were talking to?"

"Ain't talked to nobody," Charlie muttered shooting an extra long stream of tobacco juice toward the lawman's boots. "Yer seein ghosts now, are yer, sheriff?"

Turning away, Jake shook his head. To say the least, his association with these two local characters was abrasive and downright strange at times, and now they'd added a couple of ghosts to their repertoire. Shaking his head as he walked away, he had no way of knowing that an angel had forgotten to wipe his memory clean, as had been done to the fishermen.

Back in Victoria, Mary released her grip on Oliver and sat down on the bed, immediately jumping back up.

"My handbag!" she groaned. "I must have put it down while we waited for the boat."

"Hold on, we'll go back for it," he muttered, grabbing her arm.

In the minute they'd been away, Charlie Jeffs noticed the bag with the handles and yelled after the departing sheriff.

With several quick strides, the lawman had it in hand and, even as he returned to his office, his eager fingers examined the contents finding a large billfold containing many odd-looking cards.

"Could I have my handbag, please?" Mary asked, her voice obviously startling the officer as she and Oliver appeared behind him.

"Where'd you come from?" he retorted, the hairs on his neck bristling as he stared at the couple. In his hand, he held something rather extraordinary—a card-like identification that said 'Driver's License'—something he'd never seen before. On it was a woman's photograph. His eyes flicked up to Mary's face, instantly noticing the similarity. He moved his thumb and noted the date of her birth. "This is a joke ain't it, ma'am?" he croaked as a sickly sensation bit at his stomach.

"Could we go to your office, sheriff?" Oliver interrupted, realizing the situation wasn't going to be as easily remedied as he had hoped. "You'll want an explanation, I imagine."

"I certainly will!" Sheriff Mendell replied. Putting the card and billfold back into the bag, he tucked it under his arm.

Watched closely by the two old fishermen, Mendell struggled with his self control as he led the way back to his office, looking back often to make sure the couple were following.

As they walked, Oliver tried to make conversation by commenting on her handbag which reminded him of the carpetbags people used for travelling.

"What would you know," she began defensively, "girls have to carry a lot of important things around with them!"

"Yes, but when it becomes too heavy to carry …," he shot back caustically, receiving a jab in the ribs.

Arriving at the sheriff's office, he ushered them into the sparsely furnished room and pointed to two wooden chairs. Removing his hat, he hung it on a nearby hook, still keeping the handbag under his arm. Oliver watched the sheriff's every move as he stood in front of his desk. His face was a mask of doubt and suspicion, but he wasn't watching them any more. He moved Mary's handbag to the desk and then unexpectedly turned it upside down.

"Don't do that, you have no right!" Oliver snapped. "Put those things back and give us the bag. You know it belongs to Mary and she has committed no crime."

"Don't give me any trouble, son," the sheriff growled. "I'm trying to understand, but I have to admit this is as strange as it comes." Feeling a need to assert his authority, he took his revolver from its holster and lay it on the desk next to the contents of the handbag.

Mary began to shake but, at that moment, she was very glad she had left her video camera at the hotel. She was about to grab Oliver's arm when she realized his eyes had glazed over. *Oh no, it's happening again,* she thought, pulling her hand away and watching him expectantly.

Suddenly, as if in slow motion, the sheriff and his chair began to lift into the air.

"What the hell?" Mendell gasped, looking down at the desk. He clamped his hands tightly to the arms of the chair, whimpering as he floated toward the door passing through the wall as though it weren't even there. On down the alley between some buildings he floated close to the ground then, without warning, the chair set down in a muddy puddle!

Naturally brave and resourceful, the lawman stared down at his now muddy boots, which he had shined so carefully only hours before. Never a believer in the supernatural, his thoughts were foreign to him. He'd been very aware of his flight but struggled to believe it and tried to get off the chair.

"Blast!" he muttered as the chair lifted once more and more slowly made its way back to his office. His eyes clamped shut when he saw the wall rushing toward him. Opening them again, he levitated over his desk, then slowly settled to the floor.

"Now will you let me explain?" Oliver asked calmly.

Wide-eyed, the sheriff nodded. As he listened to the strange tale the reporter told, he tried his best to understand.

"A-A m-mortal angel and y-you wish me no harm!" he stammered.

"None at all, I'll even help you," Oliver said calmly.

"How?"

"Those men in the boat," Oliver continued, "I can tell you who they are and where they are."

"Who are they?"

"Milo Egger, an escaped prisoner wanted for murder in Seattle and his two brothers who executed his escape from the Victoria courthouse this afternoon."

"I know about them, are you sure?" Mendell asked. His breathing settled back to normal and he quickly scooped Mary's possessions back into her bag, handing it nervously over to her.

"Yes, I'm sure, sheriff," the reporter replied calmly. "I'll go and locate them for you."

"Don't leave me here, Oliver," Mary begged, grabbing his arm.

"It's all right, Mary dear, I won't leave you," he murmured, kissing her hand, surprising even himself with his actions.

Watching carefully, Jake saw Oliver stiffen as if in a trance. Observing a wisp-like haze, Mary and Jake both wondered what was happening but, before they could digest the thought, Oliver's eyes popped open again and his body relaxed.

"They're marooned on a rock two miles down the coast. They can't swim and their boat's been smashed to pieces," he chuckled. "I wouldn't rush out to get them just yet, sheriff. By morning they'll be darn cold and grateful to be rescued!"

"Are-are you going now?" the sheriff asked. "Will I see you again?"

"If your thoughts are loud enough, I'll hear your cry for help."

"My cry for help?"

"There may come a time when you'll need my help again," Oliver replied with a rueful smile.

The two men shook hands then Oliver put his arms around Mary. "Take me home, my dear."

Blinking, Sheriff Mendell stared at the empty space where the unusual couple had just stood. He briefly wondered if his mind had been playing tricks on him until he looked down at his mud-caked boots. Having no family, he was a lonely man in a far-flung outpost often with time on his hands, but at this moment, he remembered he had a secret to guard. He banged his fist on the desk and chuckled.

Chapter 8

Arriving back at Oliver's hotel room, Mary let out a sigh, enjoying the feeling of Oliver's arms around her and not wanting to let go.

"What's wrong?" he asked as they separated.

So confused were her feelings, she didn't want to admit to him what she was thinking; she barely wanted to admit it to herself, so she merely shrugged her shoulders.

"Come on, Mary, I know there is something bothering you." As soon as he said it, he wanted to bite his tongue. *This is so out of character for me!* he thought, but he found himself taking her hand and sitting her down on the bed.

The action did seem to loosen her tongue and she began talking so fast, he could hardly keep up with her. "Oliver, since I met you I've had the most exciting time of my life. You're such an interesting and kind man. Even though I've only known you for a few days, I feel like it's been forever and I don't want anything to change."

"I can't see how that can be possible, Mary," Oliver replied. "We're from two different worlds and you have to go back to your work at school."

"I know," she said pulling her hand away. Clenching her hands in her lap, she stared at them, not knowing what else she could say—she didn't want to scare him away. *You're an angel, Oliver, you can make the unexpected happen; I believe you could find a way to do anything, if you wanted it badly enough,* she thought, her head spinning.

He liked Mary too and hearing snatches of her thoughts, he reckoned she just may be right. *When am I going to send her home, when she goes back to school? We may never see each other again. I'm not sure I want that to happen either.* This thought startled him. *Am I falling in love ... how ridiculous! I don't even know what that means or feels like. Maybe Tom can help me. I'll have to think about that later*. Feeling awkward, he abruptly changed the subject. "When do you have to be back in Everett?"

"For Christmas Day dinner at my parents' house, I moved back with them recently; it saves me a lot of rent. I'd really like to buy a townhouse one day—that's like a smaller house," she explained. She felt she was babbling, not sure of how much to tell him. "Please come with me."

Conflict tugged at Oliver's brain. Did he want to meet her parents? Did he really want to go and spend time in the year 2000 and see what awaited him there? He also knew he had an appointment at Ross Bay Cemetery on Christmas Eve. All his life, Christmas had meant nothing but loneliness and now things were changing almost too quickly. Then suddenly, he felt an unfamiliar need for company with friendly people and a yearning for a seat beside a Yuletide fire sharing laughter and joy. If Mary's family was anything like her, he knew the experience of meeting them would be a positive one. In a desperate bid to overcome his indecision, a characteristic he hated in others, he agreed to go with her to Everett.

Wednesday went by quickly as he had two trials to attend and Mary went exploring the shops on her own—meeting for dinner. He was as happy to see her as she was to see him and that night they talked even more of their lives, their work and their acquaintances. Kissing briefly in the darkness of the closet again that night, Oliver realized even more how much he was enjoying Mary's company.

On Thursday, having a day off, he took Mary uptown for breakfast, to a little café near the City Hall; afterwards, they ran into Constable Gray. He told them the escaped prisoner had been recaptured in Port Angeles by a clever US sheriff named Jake Mendell.

"Mendell mentioned the help he'd had from a young man named Oliver Ryan," Harry muttered, raising a puzzled eyebrow and looking squarely at the reporter. "How did you do that, lad? I checked the telegraph office in Fort Street and you didn't send a telegram!"

"I used my supernatural powers," Oliver replied trying to be flippant.

"Aye and pigs can fly!" Harry chuckled moving off down Pandora Street, leaving Mary giggling behind him.

Before they headed over to the railway station on Blanshard Street, Oliver pointed out the large Hudson Bay building a couple of blocks away, towering over nearby buildings.

"It's a shame such a nice-looking building hasn't been completed," he said. "It was almost finished when the depression hit and then the war came along. It's become quite a target for hooligans."

"After the war it will get another chance," said Mary, glad he didn't ask for details because the building ended up having such a long history she didn't want to spoil it for him.

They stopped for lunch at the Royal Oak Hotel, after a train ride on the V & S Railway through the swampy farmland of the Blenkinsop Valley. They were looking out of the window enjoying their meal when Mary laid down her fork, her attention on the little mountain across the valley. The waitress told them it was called Mount Douglas.

"There must be quite a view from up there," she surmised.

"I suppose there would be, I've never been this far out of town before," Oliver replied. "Maybe we should go take a look."

"We can't walk that far," Mary coyly pointed out, "but you could take us there."

He counted out $3.10 to cover their bill, then helped her with her coat and they went outside. "It'll be cold up there," he warned her, as he encircled her waist with one arm. "Close your eyes."

Bone chilling winds whipped around and across the little mountain when they materialized on the craggy summit. Teeth chattering, the wind tore at their clothing as they huddled together and gazed out at the magnificent 360° view. With a thick cloud of black smoke emanating from its smokestack, another train thundered across the valley below, heading toward Victoria. In the distance, they could see the Royal Oak Hotel and the railway station where they'd just been. Turning into the wind, they looked across the waters of Herald Strait.

"I had no idea there were so many islands out there," Mary shouted against the wind.

"The more southerly ones are the San Juan Islands and they belong to the USA. The others," he waved his left arm slightly northward, "are the Gulf Islands and they're Canadian. They all make great hiding places for rum runners! Down there is Gordon Head, remember you were asking Const. Gray where it was?"

"Oh right, it looks like a nice place with lots of waterviews, farmlands and trees, just like home," she exclaimed, as they turned to face the south again. "The mountains are so beautiful and look at the snow—those must be the Olympics near Port Angeles. Brrr, I love it all but I'm freezing, Oliver. Could we go now please? We really need to do this in the summer!"

Sending his thoughts shooting toward the Baltimore Café in Government Street, almost instantly, she felt the fierce wind die away and the noise of streetcars and excited Christmas shoppers returned. He eased her toward the doorway and into the warm, cosy interior. Hot scones and warm coffee soon had the colour returning to their faces. Feeling much better, Mary posed him a new problem—to get him some year 2000-style clothes for their trip to Everett.

Thus, despite his earlier doubts, they now happily made plans for their trip into Mary's world. Linking arms, they left the restaurant and Oliver patiently waited for a break in the traffic so the other pedestrians would move away. Standing at the edge of the sidewalk, he slid his arm around her waist and she looked up at him, closing her eyes. He focussed his mind on the very same spot in the year 2000.

He turned and looked back at the café and now saw there were several shops and a large grey building in that block that hadn't been there before. Verandas had disappeared, all sidewalks and roads were now paved and there was no sign of mud anywhere. Even more amazingly, cars passed along the street with hardly any noise and no smoke!

Across the street, 'W & J Wilson,' beckoned and passersby again stared at him with unmasked suspicion as he walked toward the men's wear store he knew so well. Mary tugged on his sleeve before they entered.

"Oliver, if we don't find what you need in here there are a lot of other stores around," she said in a voice which seemed to be warning him of something.

"It certainly has changed but it looks very nice!" he whispered, stopping with his hand on the door.

"Yes, their reputation is high as a modern-day store and they have prices to match! However, their quality is undisputed. We like to say 'you get what you pay for' these days!" she whispered, pushing him gently forward.

Not having any idea of what she meant, he thought he'd take a look and boldly walked through the store. Looking quickly at the various displays and, not paying particular attention to the prices, he went over to the men's trouser racks. A middle-aged male clerk asked if he could assist them and Mary politely told him they were just browsing and he backed away.

Within 35 minutes, they'd chosen a brown sports jacket, a pair of trousers in a mid-brown tone, two shirts—one surprisingly with blue stripes, a tie, belt and two pair of socks.

"You'll need a coat and shoes as well, Oliver, but we'll go to a different store for those," she said in a low voice.

"Would you like to try on these items, sir?" asked the clerk, appearing at their side.

"That would be a good idea, Oliver," Mary announced, handing the items to the clerk.

The clerk led Oliver to an ample-sized room with an upholstered chair in the corner, hanging the jacket and trousers on a hook.

"I'll take this shirt out of the package and bring it in to you, sir. If there is anything else I can assist you with, my name is John Robinson," he announced, closing the door quietly.

Oliver looked around and whistled under his breath.

"My goodness, this is very comfortable for a changeroom!"

It was ten minutes later when Oliver opened the changeroom door and Mr. Robinson directed him to a large three-way mirror.

Oliver gasped. A modern man of the year 2000 stared back at him.

"Oh Oliver, you look so handsome!" chirped Mary, hurrying to his side. She noted how his cheeks flushed when she gave him the compliment, but he was looking quite pleased with himself.

"It appears the clothes are exactly the correct size," admitted Mr. Robinson, "except we would need to adjust the hems on the trousers, sir. If you'd like to wait for them, it will only take our hemmer ten minutes and you can be on your way."

Receiving a nod, the clerk helped him off with his jacket and Oliver stood looking at his image in the mirror.

"Now that was easy, wasn't it?" Mary commented. "You'll want your shoes back on for the right measurement, honey." As he returned to the changeroom, she followed. "I found some PJs for you."

"PJs?" he asked, screwing up his face in a questioning expression.

She held up the cellophane package with the diagram until his face showed recognition then they both laughed. Although feeling slightly more relaxed, Oliver now realized his new clothes felt somewhat uncomfortable.

"I'm not sure if I have the right sizes, Mary. These trousers feel quite tight and the shirt is too loose, especially at the neck," he admitted.

"It's just the new styles you're not used to," she whispered. "Don't worry, they look great on you and don't appear to be tight. Make sure you can sit down comfortably and you should be fine."

Sitting to put his shoes on he told Mary they were all right even though he still wasn't absolutely sure. Then, he went back to the mirror as Mr. Robinson returned with a supply of pins to deal with his hems.

"There, that's all I need," the clerk announced a few minutes later. "I'll wait while you take them off."

Returning again to the changeroom, Oliver removed his trousers and handed them out to the clerk.

"I'll be back in just a moment," Mr. Robinson announced, leaving briefly. "Were you planning to wear your new clothes, sir?" he asked on his return.

"That's a good idea, Oliver, you won't have to change for dinner!" Mary exclaimed, also thinking it would prevent awkward stares.

"Yes, I suppose you're right," Oliver mumbled from behind the closed door, wondering what else she was planning.

"Is there anything else I can help you with?"

"Yes, there is, Mr. Robinson. I would like to wear my new tie."

"Right you are," he replied. "If you'd like to hand me the items you wish packed up, I'll have Mr. Jordon see to your account."

Oliver handed out his old clothes and his tie arrived soon afterward. While he waited for his pants, he wound the tie around his neck but found he was all thumbs as he attempted to fashion a knot—the width of the tie was different and it was very slippery. Frustrated with the task, he left it and soon heard a tap on the door. True to their word, ten minutes had passed and his trousers were ready. Oliver put them on and came out to meet Mary. Mr. Robinson stopped him, asking if he could assist with the tie which was still hanging around his neck, and quickly had the job done.

"Did you manage to find everything you wanted, sir?" the cashier asked somewhat nervously.

"If you don't tally up this order pretty soon, young man, I'm sure we'll be able to find something else to add to it!" Mary quipped, quite sure the man was wondering if they could afford it.

"Mary, I'm not sure I have enough money to pay for all this," Oliver whispered.

"Stop worrying, I'll use my credit card," she assured him, realizing too late that his raised eyebrows signified he didn't know what she was talking about. She touched his hand and winked. "It's all right."

Beads of sweat appeared on the reporter's brow when he read the itemized account. "They must be mad," he whispered to her, blinking at the total, "they want nearly $1400!"

"It's all right," she whispered back, then turning to the cashier she added, "I think we'll take a sweater as well. I saw a nice brown and blue one that will match your shirts perfectly." Moving back to the sweater display, she left him alone at the counter.

Tom Watson's voice startled the reporter. *Check your billfold, Oliver. Don't you remember, angels are never short of money!*

Squaring his shoulders, his confidence returned and a smile played about his lips. He glanced over to see if the clerk was watching. He wasn't. *Yes, I had forgotten,* he thought. Unable to resist the urge, he held his breath as he took out his billfold noting its thickness. He relaxed and let out his breath. Now feeling much better, when the cashier handed him the adjusted bill, Oliver chuckled to himself. Looking in his billfold, he counted out 15 100-dollar bills. Noting the cashier and Mary's surprised expressions, he raised his eyebrows playfully.

That the young Mr. Jordon was greatly relieved would be an understatement and Oliver thought he did seem rather surprised. He gave Oliver his change and quickly completed folding his purchases, putting them into a large bag with handles. When he came to Oliver's old clothes, he looked at them disdainfully and, handling them gingerly, placed them in a separate bag. Oliver was fascinated by the colourful bags which were certainly not made of paper. He made a mental note to ask Mary about them later.

"There you are, folks. Thank you for shopping at Wilson's and have a great day!" Mr. Jordon said cheerfully, handing the last bag to the customer and watching them move toward the door.

"We should go back to the room with these clothes," Oliver murmured when the door closed behind them.

"It won't be there any more, silly; we're in my time now!" Mary giggled, babbling on as they walked to the crosswalk. "We still need to find you some shoes and a coat; we'll get a suitcase at the mall. Then, we'll take a cab to my hotel room. I'm staying down at ... oh Oliver, be careful! Don't step out like that!" she admonished, grabbing his arm as a car whipped around the corner. You have to wait for the w*alk* light!"

"The w*alk* light?" he asked, confused with all the traffic and looking about for the light she mentioned.

"Yes, see that little lighted sign on the other side of thc street ... the one that has an orange hand on it? Orange means you have to wait for the other one that tells you to go ... the go sign has a little white man on it! You'll get the hang of it." She put her arm through his. "We'll walk over to the Eaton Centre; they'll have everything else we need."

"Is it such a large store?" he asked.

"Just wait, you'll see!" she giggled secretively.

"I could sure use a cup of tea, is ...," Oliver began.

"No problem, we'll just pop into Murchies before we hit the mall," she laughed, walking faster.

"Mall? Murchies? Credit card? And what are these bags made of Mary?" he asked breathlessly, holding up his parcels as they crossed

Government Street. "I know you're enjoying this but I'm so confused and getting quite exhausted."

"So, it's your turn today, is it?" she teased, stopping to point at a building. "Seems I'm getting back at you!"

He stopped and squinted up at the 'E.A. Morris' sign.

"The cigar shop!" he declared. "My goodness it's still here after all these years, amazing."

"I thought you'd recognize it, here we are, this is Murchies," she announced, pushing a door open.

"A tea shop, thank goodness!" he sighed, reading the sign.

As they sat and had a refreshing cup of tea—she had herbal, he had Earl Grey—he asked her all the questions burning in his mind and was both surprised and amazed with the answers.

Half an hour later, they were back out on the street.

"Are you ready for the rest of your shopping trip now?" she asked.

"I suppose we need to do this, don't we?" he asked, hoping her reply would not be the expected one.

"Come on," she prodded, "I promise this will be a real adventure!"

"Don't worry, everything is an adventure," he assured her.

Going outside, she pointed across the street at the huge building labelled 'Eaton Centre.' They crossed at a nearby intersection where he practised with another walk sign. She led him to the side door and they went to find the elevator. As they ascended, he realized the walls of the elevator were glass and he gazed around with astonishment. Reminiscent of a picture he had seen of London's Burlington Arcade, four floors of Christmas decorations and shops were set out before him.

"My word, it's a town all stacked together!" he exclaimed.

Mary giggled. "I guess you could call it that. There are certainly enough stores! Mary chuckled as she thought how her friends would not believe it if she told them she was leading an angel by the hand through a shopping centre.

Acquiring a suitcase from the luggage shop was hardly a problem; the selection was enormous, although Oliver noted with great interest that most of the cases were not made of leather any more. Instead, they were covered by some kind of new material and had extending handles and wheels—a wonderful invention, he marvelled.

They were able to fit all his parcels into the new case and he wheeled it along as they looked for a shoe store. Walking slowly and taking it all in, Oliver was obviously entranced with all the goods, colours and music this modern store had to offer. He asked Mary many questions stopping now and again to look more closely at an item or simply to touch a fabric.

"Let's go up to the Food Court on the Fourth Floor, you've never seen anything like this," she bubbled, leading him over to the escalator.

Stopping short of the first stair, he stepped back and passed Mary the handle of the suitcase.

"Oh no, I'm not dealing with both the case and a moving stairway!" he declared, holding onto the railing for dear life.

Mary, trying not to giggle, took his other arm and stood beside him, until he was safely off at the top. Entering the food floor with its many small restaurants, chairs and tables, was more to the reporter's liking—people watching and eavesdropping was a habit of his occupation. Mary introduced him to a new Canadian fast food dish called poutine, originating in Quebec she explained. They shared a serving while two young men, talking loudly at the next table, discussed a speeding ticket.

Oliver listened with interest. *A hundred thirty miles an hour, that's ridiculous,* he thought to himself, *nothing could go that fast!*

Suddenly, a tiny red dot appeared on the table in front of them. It reminded him of the red light on Mary's camera and he watched it curiously. Slowly moving across the table, it touched his hand and moved up Mary's arm. She suddenly yelped, moving her chair back with a screech.

"That's a laser beam. It's a special light used for lectures that can damage your eyes if not used correctly. Some people think it's fun to play with danger," she said, loud enough for their neighbours to hear.

Oliver frowned. "Where does the light come from?"

"See that young man who's grumbling about the speeding ticket, he has a pen-thingy in his hand. It's actually a laser and somebody should report him!" she said adamantly. Glancing over at Oliver, she saw the intensity in his eyes as he stared at the young man's hand.

Suddenly, a loud pop sounded and the man jumped to his feet shaking his hand and screaming as the laser burst into flames. Dropping it quickly, he stuffed his hand into his glass of pop, looking over at them with a puzzled expression.

"Problem over!" Oliver chuckled under his breath.

Meanwhile, Mary was trying to act as if nothing had happened. Pulling her chair back to the table she put a forkful of food into her mouth to stop from giggling.

Later when they were leaving, she took him down to the Eaton's department store, telling him one could find practically anything here in its four storeys. By the time they reached the door and called a taxi, he had on his new pair of shoes and had to agree with her.

Chapter 9

"My goodness," Oliver exclaimed, leaning back against the seat of the taxi and closing his eyes. "That was some store!"

"Silly, it's not a store, it's about 80 stores in a mall," she reminded him as they drove past the Empress and turned right.

In a few minutes, they pulled up at the side door of Gatsby's. As the driver unloaded their bags, a pleasant young man in a bellhop uniform appeared and asked Mary for her room number. She handed him her key and he went ahead of them with the suitcase. Paying the driver, she continued her chatter as they went up the front stairs and across a wide veranda, passing a restaurant.

"I decided last time I visited Victoria I was going to treat myself. I found out there are some rooms above the restaurant and mine has a wonderful view of the harbour. I had only just checked in that morning when we met." She noticed Oliver was looking all around and apparently not paying any attention to what she was saying as they entered the lobby. *He must be absolutely blown away by all the changes to ... everything!* she thought as the bellhop returned.

"Will you bc joining us for dinner tonight, folks?" he asked, handing back her key as she slipped a tooney into his hand.

"Yes, around 6 o'clock, thank you," she replied, looking at her watch as they continued up the stairs.

When they entered her room, Oliver remembered it and felt more at ease. *This is a room more to my liking,* he thought looking around at the furnishing and noticing the twin beds. Remembering their suitcases at his hotel, he surprised Mary by setting them down on one of the beds. Giggling, she opened hers as he went over to the window and looked out at the harbour. An immense ship was just leaving, almost on their doorstep. He felt her come up beside him.

"It must all seem quite strange and different to you, honey," she commented, following his gaze to the ship. When he didn't answer, she continued, “Nice view from here, isn’t it? This home once belonged to the Pendray family and is now owned by the hotel next door. The Pendrays were an early well-to-do family who came here before the turn of the century. It seems some members of the family owned a great deal of land in this area … Pendray Farm, I believe it was called.”

“The gardens must be lovely in the summer,” said Oliver, hardly hearing her as he continued to look around outside. “The harbour has certainly changed in 84 years!”

“The Port Angeles ferry dock is over to your right, it was the *Coho* ferry you were watching. You’ll get a different view from the dining room and later we can take a walk around the harbour if you feel up to it.”

“Only if I can be relieved of these dang shoes first!” he exclaimed, slumping gratefully into a nearby chair.

“Oh dear, I forgot all about your new shoes. You’ll have to get them broken in quickly but we don’t want you suffering from blisters. Why don’t you leave them off for a while, I’ll sort out these bags.”

Removing his shoes and rubbing his feet for a minute, he lay back in his chair and closed his eyes. He was almost asleep when he felt a cold sensation on the back of his neck.

“Don’t be frightened, Mary,” he murmured, “but there seems to be a ghostly presence in this room.”

“Can you see it?” she asked coming to stand behind him and gripping his shoulders more in excitement than fear.

“I can feel it, it will show itself when the time is right. He or she is no doubt an earthbound spirit … one that is suspended in time and needs help crossing over. I may be able to help.”

It was dark outside when they went downstairs to eat. Once seated, Oliver agreed they had a wonderful view and commented on the amazing number of lights around the harbour and on Belleville Street. Mary surveyed the menu, but he silently stared out into the darkness.

“I’m going to have the roast duck and orange sauce,” she said. “It sounds very good. I can recommend the prime rib from my last visit, it’s a heavenly melt-in-your mouth beef cut,” she informed him, looking at him coyly and giggling.

Oliver looked over at her then, realizing what she was getting at, he smiled. "Then, by all means, I must have it!"

A few minutes later, several more couples took their seats and their waitress returned to take their order. As they waited for the meal, they noticed there were quite a few vehicles going by and Mary guessed that the shops and malls were open late for Christmas shopping.

"What is that building over there?" he asked, pointing to the silhouette of an imposing structure across the street about a block to the east. "The CPR Steamship ticket office used to be on that site. They were all wooden buildings in 1916 when I watched hospital ships come in during the war."

Mary patted his hand then, self-consciously, moved it away. "The present building replaced the original CP terminal back in 1927 and became the Wax Museum in 1971."

"Wax Museum? That sounds intriguing," he mused.

Tom Watson watched his protégé and Mary as they interacted. *These two are perfectly suited for each other, but that boy is so inexperienced he needs a bit more spiritly help. I think I may enjoy this part of our ghostly experiment!*

Their meals arrived and, while eating, Mary told him all about the Wax Museum, interrupting herself to point out an old-fashioned-looking, horse-drawn carriage slowly making its way along the lighted street.

"Isn't that quaint, Oliver? I've often thought a ride in one of those carriages would be such fun."

"I believe it would be much more enjoyable in the summer, my sweet—look they're bundled up to their ears in blankets!" he chuckled, then wondering at his choice of words.

After dinner, they climbed the stairs back to her room so Oliver could rest his feet and change into his more comfortable old Oxfords. Then, putting on their warm coats, they went outside. Walking hand-in-hand, under street lights casting a romantic glow, they made their way toward the Empress.

"My goodness, look at all those lights, there must be thousands of them on the Legislative Building," Oliver declared. "They've had lights as long as I can remember but it seems there are even more now. I also noticed the changes they'd made to the Empress when I first met you there." *Was it really only three days ago? So much has happened.*

They stopped on the causeway to gaze down the length of the harbour and listened to some strolling carollers dressed in turn-of-the-century clothes.

"Gosh, you'd fit right in wearing your old clothes!" Mary quipped squeezing his hand; she sighed and grew more serious. "It's hard to believe Christmas is only a few days away, isn't it?"

"Don't you feel like celebrating Christmas, Mary?" Oliver asked, choosing his words carefully. Perhaps they had more in common than he realized but her answer quickly dispelled that thought.

"Oh yes, I love Christmas, it's always been a special time for me and my family. I told you that my older sister lives in New Zealand so she rarely gets home any more. It's just too expensive and besides she has a husband and three kids. I really miss her though, thank goodness for the internet—I'll show you how it works when we get to Everett. I've been so busy with winding up school and all, then meeting you … Christmas had almost gone out of my head."

Mumbling something incoherently, Oliver continued his history lesson. "The soapworks used to stand over there not far from the Gatsby," he said, pointing to a large modern hotel, "and the paint factory was next door. What does that sign say … 'Laurel Point?' Your modern buildings are something to behold with all those windows!"

Mary laughed, squeezing his hand again. The wind picked up and immediately a cold rain began to fall, sending them scurrying back to the hotel. Fifteen minutes later, they were sitting at the window enjoying the twinkling lights as they drank a hot cup of tea, brewed in their room.

Hearing the sound of a cough behind them, they both instinctively turned to look. On the other side of the room stood the materializing form of a man dressed in a top hat and tails.

Mary grabbed his arm and her fingers dug into Oliver's flesh. She mouthed 'Tom Watson?' and he shook his head.

"Who are you, sir?" he asked.

"I'm William Joseph Pendray and you are in my house!" the apparition replied, his hollow-sounding voice bouncing off the walls. "You, sir, are Oliver Ryan."

Mary's mouth suddenly went dry and she tried to lift her hand to her throat but it felt heavy and fell back onto the arm of her chair. Then something unexpected happened—Oliver suddenly disappeared into thin air. Her eyes grew wide and she wanted to scream; she shivered and a new terror gripped her until a wisp of vapour rose above his chair and Oliver, too, appeared in ghostly form. Stunned, she watched the strange conversation between the spirits, actually feeling somewhat relieved, except something held her immobile.

"I'm searching for my wife and boys," the earthbound spirit said emotionally, "but they've gone and left me."

The apparition began to glow with an eerie blue light and Oliver reached for the man's hand. An instant calming effect settled over Mr. Pendray and, almost immediately, the blue light went away.

"Jane and the boys are waiting for you in that great land of the Hereafter," Oliver said, in a soothing tone. "There are flowers, green pastures and laughter. Come William, I'll help you crossover."

With faces raised, the two misty apparitions faded away.

I've lost him, was Mary's first thought as her mind raced and panic began to set in. Tears welled in her eyes. *He's gone,* she told herself realizing she was now able to control her body again. *No, that's not going to happen,* she thought desperately, closing her eyes and praying fervently, which she hadn't done for many years. Almost immediately, she felt a pair of arms encircle her shoulders.

"I'm sorry, Mary, I had to attend to my angel duties," Oliver murmured, reeling backwards when she leapt wildly into his arms. He held her tightly as she sobbed softly on his shoulder. "It's all right, Mary. I should have warned you this could happen." He gently pulled her away and looked into her tearful eyes. "Hush now, it's all right." He kissed her lightly on the forehead and the nose. "Let's have another cup of tea," he suggested quickly, "it will help our jangled nerves!"

They found plenty to talk about and Oliver became more relaxed than she had ever seen him. She liked this new vibrant and funny side of him and he responded enjoying her laughter. When Mary looked at her watch, she couldn't believe her eyes.

"It's 11 o'clock already. No wonder I'm tired. We were up very early this morning and seem to fit so much into our days."

"You're right, which bed would you like?" he asked.

I'll let you have the one nearest to the bathroom. I don't want you getting lost in the dark!" she teased, feeling suddenly uncomfortable again. She found her shortie PJs in her suitcase and silently groaned. Grabbing her toiletries bag, she mumbled, "I'm in there first!" and disappeared.

Oliver pulled down the covers of his bed and wondered why she had left so quickly. He found his new pajamas in his neatly packed suitcase and tore open the package, laying them on the bed. As he changed, he thought about how different this situation felt from having Mary at his hotel room. He'd never shared a room with anyone before, let alone a woman! Having Bertha and Jane share his apartment had been awkward enough but he had learned to enjoy it.

The door to the bathroom opened and, seeing Oliver's bare back, she practically ran to her bed and jumped in. She wasn't at all prepared for Oliver to see her in her nightclothes, especially these skimpy ones—she wished she'd packed her robe.

"Hand me that remote on top of the TV, please Oliver. I'll introduce you to another marvel of the 20th century," she said hoping a diversion would help the situation.

By now, Oliver had put on his pajama top and was beginning to unbuckle his belt. Mary shut her eyes and prayed that he would go into the bathroom.

"Is this, what did you call it, a remote VT?" he asked, looking around and picking up the small rectangular item from atop a large box-like contraption on the sidetable. He pushed a couple of the buttons. "Dare I ask what is a remote VT?"

"You really should give it to me so I can show you," she giggled.

He did as she suggested and, almost immediately, a bright light flashed in the box beside him and a picture appeared. At the same time, a very loud noise of music and voices emanated from the box causing him to leap onto the bed.

"I'm sorry, it's all right, Oliver. Someone had left the volume up. See that's better," she laughed, going on to explain how the remote worked and what television was.

Oliver silently decided he would investigate this modern electrical contraption in the morning after he'd had some sleep.

Mary was so tired she lay back on the pillows and looked at the ceiling, knowing that Oliver was changing just a few feet away. She did wonder what he was thinking about though and then heard the bathroom door click. She waited until he returned and was in bed before turning off the TV. The room was suddenly dark and quiet except for the sound of their breathing. Mary felt Oliver's hand touch her arm. She took it and whispered 'goodnight.' His touch had such a calming effect on her she soon drifted off to sleep.

Mary Beth Janick's world has been turned upside down since her chance meeting with Oliver Ryan. She thinks she's falling in love with the court reporter but he's giving little indication that she's more than a passing acquaintance. In her dreams that night, her mind repeats one scene over and over until she wakes to find the room in darkness. She hears Oliver's breathing in the other bed and knows he's still asleep—her mind begins to wander.

This is crazy, here I am on holidays with a strange man in my room. He's probably not even bothered by any of this. He's such a gentleman, is this the way men acted back in 1916? I'd like to know what his intensions are—he's acting more like a brother than a date. At my age, I don't particularly want a brother and he's such a nice guy! Perhaps in the morning I'll wake up and find myself alone ... yes, that's it ... it's all just been a silly dream! She turned over and quickly went back to sleep.

In the morning, she had totally forgotten her sleepy thoughts and, over breakfast, they made plans to return to the Eaton Centre to get Oliver another change of clothes. Kathy caught them in the foyer and asked them to sign the visitors' book.

"Mary will sign for both of us," said Oliver.

"Perhaps you both would sign," Kathy gently persisted.

Sensing his reluctance and guessing he had a good reason, Mary pulled the book toward her and wrote across the page, *Mary Beth Janick and Oliver Ryan, Everett and Seattle.*

Mary started toward the cloakroom where they had left their coats but stopped and turned abruptly to face him.

"What's wrong, why didn't you want to sign the book?"

Cocking an eyebrow, he looked around and beckoned her to follow him back into the cloakroom. He reached into his pocket extracting a small piece of paper and Mary's pen, quickly scrawling his signature.

"Watch!" he whispered.

Almost instantly, she clasped her hand over her mouth to stifle her exclamation as a slow spiral of smoke-like vapour lifted from the paper. No flames appeared but the charring spread until he was holding the paper gingerly between his two fingers. It ended abruptly and Mary stared at the charred image left behind.

"The trade mark of an angel!" she murmured in awe.

Crumpling the evidence, he dropped it into the wastebasket. "Let's go, honey, it seems we have things to do."

Mary looked outside and hesitated, suggesting they call a taxi but Oliver put his arm around her and told her to close her eyes. "That was easier," she heard him say and feeling the alternating rush of cold and then warm air she opened her eyes to find they were standing in the men's clothing department in Eaton's. Thankfully, no one else was around. Shopping was easier this time and soon they had another outfit to match the jacket he was wearing. *This should impress my parents,* she thought, as they headed toward the escalator.

"Oh no, not the moving stairway again!" he groaned, standing back and rolling his eyes.

It only took a bit of good-natured coaxing to persuade the man from 1916 to step onto the escalator this time, making it a condition that she hold both his hand and his parcels this time. By the time they reached the bottom floor, they were laughing hysterically.

Making their way out the side door of the mall and back to the harbour, they found the Tourist Information Centre and watched a seaplane zoom in over their heads, making a landing in the centre of the busy waterway. Going inside, Oliver was amazed at the pamphlets he found and realizing they could be there for hours, Mary dragged him away.

"You can come back and visit any time, you know, just not on my time!" she laughed, seeing his disappointed expression. "I wonder what this place looked like in 1900?" she whispered with a hint of devilment on her face.

A light rain was again beginning to fall and only a few people could be seen hurrying about at this end of town. Nearing the Wax Museum, Oliver stopped and put his arms around her.

"Hold onto me, my darling, we're going back to 1900 so my lady can take a look," he said chuckling gleefully, once again hesitating as he realized what he'd called her. *Did I really say that?*

Snowflakes were falling on the old wooden bridge that linked Government Street to James Bay as Mary opened her eyes.

"Cripes," she exclaimed, "no Empress Hotel, it's all water!"

"And that smell!" he declared, wrinkling his nose. "Actually this is James Bay and it's mainly been used as a garbage dump up to now. What else do you smell?" he asked as they followed the harbourside road toward town. Seeing her sniff the air and make a face while facing the harbour, he continued, "It's probably from Pendray's soap factory over there at the corner of Humboldt."

At that moment, a man and woman passing by stopped and scornfully stared at them—the woman obviously taking in their unusual costumes. Before they continued on their way, Mary and Oliver heard her exclaim, "Tourists!"

"It's fun to be where no one knows us, isn't it?" Mary giggled.

"Ignore them, we won't be here long enough to matter. There's the post office," he said indicating a large greystone building on their right at Government and Wharf. Grabbing her hand, they continued along the harbour; she was surprised at his eagerness.

"See, down there is the Harbour Master's office and a Hudson Bay warehouse; they're almost the same in 1916 but look at this tangle of buildings," he exclaimed, indicating a number of shacks and boat landings right on the water below Wharf Street. They kept walking until they could see the area of what she knew as the Johnson Street Bridge. "In 1900 that bridge was the Dunsmuir railway crossing," he explained. "There weren't any cars here yet, so it was only a bridge for the train and the Indians who lived on the other side."

She suddenly realized that in her excitement she hadn't taken notice of what was under her feet—it was a boardwalk and the road was even worse—muddy and pothole strewn, but it hadn't even soiled their shoes. Her eyes moved to the corner where she'd stood at the Tourist Information Centre 100 years in the future. She saw only a rocky bank filled with the squalor of old building materials and a small sailboat-type dinghy tied to a makeshift jetty.

"It's hard to imagine how far a city can progress in a mere hundred years," she said in awe, making mental notes of their surroundings and the mixture of sailing ships and steamships that filled the surprisingly busy harbour.

Engrossed in his own thoughts, Oliver looked back and inspected the wooden structure of the James Bay Bridge. With the sea running underneath through to the swamplands, it was difficult to image that a majestic hotel would stand here in a few short years.

"I'm freezing," he exclaimed putting his arm around her, "have you seen enough, my darling?"

Nodding, Mary looked up at him and smiled. *I wonder what's caused this change in him, calling me honey and darling all of a sudden? I suppose I shouldn't complain, maybe he's changing his mind!* She cuddled closer and smiled inwardly replying to his question. "Yes, it's been fascinating but it is rather cold isn't it, my love? I'm ready."

Landing in exactly the same spot from where they'd left, Oliver's parcels sat waiting on the sidewalk.

"Gosh, I'd forgotten all about them, they may have been stolen in this day and age," she declared.

"Not a chance. Didn't I tell you that time stands still when I'm away?" he reminded her, picking them up.

"That's awfully convenient," she mused, taking his arm.

Because of the cold, they hurried along Belleville Street to the hotel where they gladly sought the warmth of their room. Emptying their shopping bags, Mary repacked his case adding the new items.

"I'd better check my report and get it finished," he muttered, looking around for his briefcase.

"Are you sure you've had time to write one, we've been terribly busy and besides, it's the weekend and Christmas, when is it due?"

"I'm sure I started it, but it seems to have disappeared," Oliver said frowning. "Where the devil can it be?"

"Here it is," she laughed, "you put the suitcase on top of it!"

Taking the papers, he sat down at the small table and began reading when the voice of Tom Watson urgently whispered. *I finished the report for you, Oliver, now read the last page quickly before it's too late.*

Flipping through the pages with fumbling fingers, scattering some of them onto the floor, he found the entry, *"... small boat foundering in high seas off Gonzales Point. Need help!"*

Mary noticed his sudden movement and bent to pick up the papers. It startled her when he uttered a cry of surprise and a warning.

"Don't touch me," he said urgently, his mind already concentrating on Gonzales Point. "I have to do this alone."

About to ask why, she realized he'd already gone as a faint haze floated over his chair. Gathering the papers up, she sat down on the bed and began to put them in order. When the last line on the final page caught her attention, she instantly grasped its implication.

Sighing, her mind became a jumble of feelings and thoughts. Oliver was real and she knew she was falling in love with him. She'd travelled through time, been to new places and seen history in the making, but this was a new twist she hadn't prepared for. Oliver, the angel, could be called from her world at a moment's notice.

Chapter 10

Hovering momentarily over Gonzales Point in Oak Bay where a wild storm raged, Angel Oliver Ryan, peered through the blowing spray and heard the terrified cries of several people coming from a little boat as crashing waves threatened to swamp the helpless craft or toss them onto the rocky coastline.

Getting closer, he saw a woman clutching her two children and, even as he landed on their deck, he spread his arms and around them the gale force wind dropped to a gentle breeze. She watched in frightened fascination as the sea calmed and the boat moved mysteriously without its motor until it reached Oak Bay's sheltered harbour.

Well done, son, complimented his guardian angel.

Fishermen sheltering on the dock stood aghast as the boat with its three occupants slowly floated toward them. They took the children and their mother into eager helping hands and the woman wept with relief and joy. Turning back to offer thanks to the man who had saved them, she stared in astonishment at the empty boat. The stranger had disappeared.

"Mission accomplished," Oliver whispered as he suddenly reappeared in his chair.

Mary sprang to her feet, wrapping her arms around him, her body tense with emotion. Pulse still racing, she pointed at the message Tom Watson's ghostly hand had written—the words were slowly disappearing in a hazy vapour.

"I'll be glad when we get to Everett," she moaned, "and we don't have to worry about Victoria's ghosts."

"It's all right, Mary, you'll get used to it," he said softly, listening to himself with surprise and shaking his head. He continued quickly before Mary had a chance to say anything. "We're going to Seattle first. I have to deliver my court report to Harry at the *Courier*."

"I'm going with you."

"Yes, you are."

Bags packed and ready to go, Oliver sent them ahead to Seattle; they paid the bill and said their 'goodbyes' to Kathy. Outside, they walked down the steps into the garden and stood facing the harbour.

"Hold my hand, sweetheart," he murmured, focussing his mind on his apartment in Seattle, 1916.

Through one of the windows, Kathy saw the young couple holding hands in the garden and sighed with envy. Turning to walk away, she glanced back one more time and blinked. They were gone! Rushing to the door, she checked the street and the walkway, but they were nowhere in sight. At that moment, the faint sweet smell of Mary's perfume caught her sensitive nostrils.

"I know they were here, she assured herself, "it's either magic or I'm asleep on the job!"

"So this is where you live Mr. Ryan." Mary laughed as she opened her eyes to look around the sparsely furnished home of her companion. She noted the half-full coffee mug on the kitchen counter and two shirts draped untidily over a chair.

"Are we staying here tonight?" she murmured.

Watching her closely, he answered, "Yes," and watched her open the door to his bedroom.

"But there's only one bed!" she whispered mischievously.

"Now you just behave yourself, young lady," he scolded with a chuckle. "We shall observe the rules of propriety at all times and I'll sleep on the chesterfield tonight."

"Spoilsport," she teased.

"I'd better change into my normal clothes. I don't want Harry to have anything else to complain about," he commented, going to his closet.

Mary went over to the living room window and looked out at the Seattle skyline. She heard Oliver return and open his briefcase sorting through his papers. It was a little after four and shadows were lengthening after a sunny day in Washington State's capital city. An eerie feeling crept over her body as she thought of how fortunate she was to be able to witness a time in history long gone. *I think I like it without the skyscrapers,* she murmured, then Oliver's voice cut into her thoughts.

"I'm ready, let's go see my editor before he blows his top."

Briefcase in hand and Mary on his arm, Oliver whisked them across the city, his mind concentrating on the foyer of the newspaper office.

Oliver Ryan has a girl on his arm! was the receptionist's surprised reaction as she watched them come through the door.

"Better go straight in," she smirked, "he's not having a good day."

Head jerking up as the door opened, Harry Jenson's cigar ash dropped among the papers littering his desk.

"Where the hell have you been?" he demanded, brushing the ash onto the floor.

Snatching the papers from the reporter's hand, he began flipping through the sheets, grunting as his eyes danced over the text.

"You've forgotten to mention Port Angeles," he snapped, his eyes flicking over Mary and her different style of clothes. "Who's this?" he sneered, "managed to get yourself a girlfriend have you?"

Before Oliver could respond, Mary's own temper exploded.

"You're an ignorant bully, Mr. Jenson," she said tersely. "Has nobody told you yet that manners maketh the man?"

Pushing his chair back, Harry leered at the young couple across his desk. For more than a year he'd been goading Oliver, hoping the reporter would react and give the sadistic copy editor a reason to fire him, and here it was, the opportunity he'd been waiting for.

"Yer fired," he growled, reaching for his pen.

Mary looked over at Oliver but, instead of seeing a fearful expression, a smile played over his lips and his eyes twinkled merrily. He winked at her and nodded down at the desk. Following his gaze, she watched in delight as Harry's pen began to move out of his reach.

"Damn," the editor growled, rising from his chair to catch it before it rolled off the desk.

Stifling a gasp, Mary watched as Oliver moved Harry's chair and, once he caught the pen, he sat in the empty space. Arms flailing, his glasses jumped from his startled face and he disappeared behind the desk with a thud and foul curses.

"Are you drunk, Jenson?" a well-cultured voice asked as the office door sprang open. "Get out of here and don't come back until you're sober!"

All eyes turned to face the man on the floor—winded, speechless, and clutching at his belt which had come apart during the fall, he was having difficulty standing up and was certainly not getting any help from the others. Unable to speak and slobbering uncontrollably, he finally managed to roll over and struggle to his feet, making for the door clutching his pants.

Not quite what we had in mind when we gave you all that power, Oliver, Tom chuckled, *but I'm sure it's given you great satisfaction!*

The smartly dressed older man standing calmly in the doorway glanced over at the giggling Mary and, although amused himself, he did not display it to these strangers.

"You're Oliver Ryan, aren't you?" he murmured. "I read your last column. It was excellent, my boy, keep up the good work."

"Harry was going to give me my next assignment, sir, but now ...." Oliver stopped on purpose, not wanting to admit to the fact Harry had, in fact, fired him.

Albert Lane studied the young couple before him. He was a principal shareholder, member of the board of directors, and a man who wielded great influence at the newspaper office. He appreciated and admired this young man's talent no matter what problem he had with the officious editor whom he had not liked from the day they met.

"Margo!" he called over his shoulder into the corridor.

Reverberating through the hallways, the call of, "Margo, your dad wants you in Harry Jenson's office," bounced from worker to worker, until they heard running feet coming toward them. When the sound stopped a young woman of about 18 with dark, shoulder-length curls ducked under her father's arm and grinned at them.

"This is my daughter, Margo," Lane announced proudly. "Meet Oliver Ryan and ...," he stopped for a moment, looking over his spectacles. "I didn't get your name, my dear."

"Mary Beth Janick," Oliver offered quietly.

"Pleased to meet you folks," Margo grinned hospitably. "So you're the great Oliver Ryan who Jake Mendell is talking about."

"Sheriff Mendell?" Oliver blushed even before he spoke the words, feeling Mary's hand squeeze his fingers in warning.

"Yes, Sheriff Mendell. He's told all the newspapers that you're a hero and that the *Courier* should be proud of you." Margo paused as she turned to Mary and offered her hand, before continuing, "We're just as proud of him here at the *Courier* as you are Mary."

Now it was Mary's turn to blush as the two girls shook hands and their eyes met, welding the beginning of a new friendship.

"He wants a new assignment and Harry's gone home indisposed," her father informed her with a slight roll of his eyes.

"You can go now, Dad," Margo laughed, gently urging her father out of the office. "I've got just the thing for him." Offering them chairs and closing the door, she sat down behind Harry's desk. "Are either of you interested in the supernatural?" she asked leaning forward to speak confidentially across the desk. She waited as they glanced at each other and then both nodded.

"Well, so am I," she confided, "and, over in Oak Bay, that's a suburb of Victoria, there's a woman who says she was rescued from the sea in a howling storm by an angel. Interview her for a post-Christmas story. That's your assignment, Oliver. Maybe we could go ghost hunting together in Everett some time," she whispered secretively.

"Margo!" her father's urgent call came rattling through the building once more.

"I've got to go," she said urgently, grinning as she jumped up from her seat and went to the door. "I'm his right-hand man, woman, or whatever you call it." Her voice trailed off as she dashed away.

Leaving the building, they stepped out and found the street lightly covered with snow. Mary's mind turned wildly with thoughts of Margo Lane. *Here's a name straight out of history ... a woman who became famous for her charitable work during the horrid years of World War Two.*

Eating dinner at a restaurant on Second Avenue, they couldn't help but hear a conversation between a group of uniformed soldiers.

"There's war in the air," Oliver contemplated aloud as they made their way through the bustling shoppers to Pike's Place Market to do their last-minute Christmas shopping before going to Everett.

The noise of shouting vendors made talking impossible and they walked through the market in silence until Oliver found what he wanted. Pushed and jostled by the crowd, he bought embroidered pillowcases for Mary's mother and a pipe for her father while Mary went off and did some shopping of her own. Meeting again an hour later, they escaped onto the waterfront road, walking quickly under the street lights that illuminated the falling snow.

Mary enjoyed her day immensely and was surprised and pleased how attentive Oliver had been. She cooked him dinner from shopping they'd done at the market and he needed no persuading to help with the dishes. When they finished, he took her hand and led her over to the chesterfield pulling her down beside him. Sitting close together, he made an unexpected move and put his arm around her shoulders, drawing her closer.

"Tell me about your Seattle, honey," she whispered happily, nestled in his arms. *TV would certainly be useful about now,* she thought.

Never one for talking very much, in the dim light Oliver realized he felt more comfortable than he thought he ever could with a woman. Feeling quite contented, he began describing, in great detail, the Seattle he knew so well. He told her about some of its prominent characters like Mayor Hiram Gill, on trial for taking bribes in the liquor conflict, and Nellie Cornish whose music school was gaining great fame and recognition due, in part, to her position as Nancy Wilson's pianist.

"We'll stay here for another day so I can take you into town and show you all the wonderfully lit shops, all decked out for Christmas and Saturday we'll ride the Interurban train to Everett. It's actually a fancier electric car somewhat like our trolleys, but larger and very luxurious," he murmured, his words fading as his head began to nod.

"Come on," she insisted, standing up and pulling him to his feet, "we'd better get to bed, I didn't realize it was so late. I'll sleep here tonight, do you have some spare blankets?"

Too tired to argue, he showed her the linen closet and left her to fend for herself. It wasn't long before the apartment was quiet, but tonight, for the first time, he lay awake thinking of Mary. Never having met anyone, especially a girl he liked so much, he wondered why she had become so special to him and what it all meant. On one hand, he could see the possibilities of a relationship with her, yet their difficulties seemed insurmountable. *How much easier it would be,* he thought, *if she were an angel, too.*

Dawn was breaking when he smelled the musty tobacco scent and opened his eyes to watch Tom materialize in the dim light.

I suppose you heard my ramblings last night, Oliver grumbled, speaking to his mentor in thought so Mary didn't hear.

I've let you down, my boy, I made a mistake, the angel's voice quivered in sadness. *I should never have allowed it to happen—it's never happened before.*

You're not making any sense, Oliver pointed out, seeing the frown on Tom's face as light crept into the room.

Well, let me explain to you what has happened, Oliver, he sighed, his mutton-chop whiskers visibly twitching. *You've fallen in love with this girl from the year 2000 and the spirits of Ross Bay are hopping mad!*

Why should it bother them? Oliver asked, although rather interested at how they knew he was in love when he wasn't at all sure about it.

Because angels are supposed to be immune to such personal attachments, Tom explained.

But I'm also a mortal, Oliver argued.

That's my fault, son, I convinced the spirit council it would be fun to make a mortal angel out of you.

You spirits play a game with my life and think it's fun! he declared. *Can't you change me back to normal?*

No, I'm afraid that's not possible.

A smile of satisfaction twisted Oliver's lips. He was used to being an angel now and enjoyed the power it gave him. He really had no desire to return to normal. Suddenly he made up his mind.

Don't worry, Mr. Watson, Oliver's thoughts flashed across the room as he pushed the covers back and came to his feet, *Christmas Eve is not far away and we'll face the Ross Bay internees together. We'll find a solution to this somehow.*

That day, Oliver enjoyed himself even more than when he'd shown Bertha and Jane around town. He had become very comfortable with Mary and was beginning to agree with her—they simply had to find a solution or life would be intolerable.

The next morning, an eager taxi driver loaded their bags and nodded at Oliver's instructions. "Hotel Shirley it is, sir, catching the 11:30 Interurban to Everett, are you?" he chatted pleasantly.

Mary silently watched the city go by outside the taxi window as it wound its way through the slow-morning traffic. Arriving early, they purchased their tickets and went into the hotel's dining room to have breakfast. After giving their order, Mary sat back and smiled across the table.

"You were talking to Tom Watson this morning, weren't you, honey?" she asked.

"You heard?"

"Yes, snatches only, but I could hear you."

"You're right, I was talking to Tom Watson. I'm amazed," he replied. "What did you hear?"

"Why so amazed?" she asked, "you told him tomorrow night was Christmas Eve and you'd face the Ross Bay internees together."

"I'm amazed because, actually we weren't speaking out loud, we were talking in thoughts."

"Don't be silly," she laughed, "I couldn't have heard a thought."

"But you did, my dear, and word for word!"

"That's spooky … oh my gosh, what am I saying?" she hissed. "I'm sitting here with an angel, what could be spookier! Say something right now, I think you're pulling my leg."

I love you, his thoughts whispered, making him cough in surprise.

Mary shook her head in the negative and, with eyes sparkling, she encouraged him. "Try again."

This time Oliver was in complete control of his thoughts. With eyes twinkling, his mind silently shouted the thought across the table.

I think I love you!

"I heard you!" she replied, blushing and looking at him sharply. *Does he really mean it*? "Say something else."

It's 10:45, we should be going, his mind shouted.

"I hear you, I hear you, we'll talk on the train," Mary replied, her voice indicating her excitement as Oliver rose to leave.

They were some of the first passengers to get seated on the Interurban, so Oliver chose the right side of the train, anticipating Mary would have a better view of Lake Washington and the many smaller lakes they would pass as they picked up and dropped off passengers at many of the 30 stops along the way. As they pulled out of the city depot right on time, it picked up speed clanging at intersections.

"Mercer first stop, Mercer first stop. Have your tickets ready," the conductor's voice droned.

"Now let's try it again, say something to me while I look out of the window," Mary whispered, turning to watch Lake Union go by as they crossed the Freemont Bridge. Continuing north past Evanston and Playland, where many people disembarked, they were really enjoying the scenery when Roscoe Harding, the conductor, came back into their car and tapped the reporter's shoulder, holding out his hand for their tickets.

"We're going to Everett," Oliver quietly informed the conductor, placing the dockets in his hand.

"I heard you!" Mary yelped in excitement, swinging around.

The startled conductor took a step backward, blinking at the girl's sudden outburst. "I'm sure you did, Miss," he exclaimed, moving to the next seat.

Mary dropped her head on Oliver's chest and giggled. Across the aisle, the passenger wearing a minister's collar peered over horn-rimmed spectacles at them. On his knee was a bible marked liberally with bookmarks. The men's eyes met and held for a moment while Oliver read his mind.

"So you think we're going to be a noisy nuisance, do you?' said Oliver, not moving his eyes off the man as people around turned to look.

Recovering from her embarrassment, Mary felt her companion's body stiffen a little as she raised her head and looked across the aisle—just in time to see the bookmarks slip out of the bible and onto the floor.

"Want to try again?" she whispered as the train rumbled onward through the Shoreline area. "Oh my, this is Ronald Station. There's the old school with its little bell tower. We used to come here when I was a child. I had no idea there were so many buildings here originally. Some of them are still standing. There's the old saloon and the general store. There was a coal mine here in the late 1800s and they had their share of excitement with strikes and brewing moonshine!" she laughed, obviously pleased with her memory.

As they entered Snohomish County and passed Lake Ballinger, they tried their experiment again with total success when, time after time, she repeated the words she clearly heard in Oliver's thoughts.

As they stopped at the Alderwood Station to take on a young family, she asked, "Can *you* read *my* thoughts?"

"If I concentrate hard enough, I can sometimes read people's thoughts," he replied cautiously, not wanting to admit he had often heard her ramblings.

"But could you hear me, if I stood at the other end of this car?" she persisted.

"I don't know."

"Then let's try it."

"How?"

"You go to the end of the car and listen for my instructions," she ordered, "and then you do what I tell you."

"We're almost there, we don't have time." Oliver objected.

"Go on," Mary insisted, "we still have about half an hour before we reach Everett."

An interruption from the minister across the aisle halted their experiment for a moment, as he rudely made his opinions known.

"Stop this stupid nonsense," snapped Rev. Charles McLough. "I have been listening to your conversation and it's ludicrous to imagine you can hear someone's thoughts."

"Well it would never happen to you, sir," retorted the reporter, "because you'd never be able to mind your own business long enough to listen!"

"Take no notice of him, Oliver," Mary whispered, prodding him to go. "Go on honey, let's try it."

Stunned by the reporter's harsh words, Rev. McLough slumped back in his seat and watched the young man walk away to the end of the train. Oliver turned his back and immediately heard Mary's voice.

Touch your nose with your right hand, she was saying. He could even tell she was giggling. *Now take two steps forward—turn around first and come toward me!* She could see his performance was perfect in every detail.

As they passed the county fairgrounds, looking stark and barren, many people in the carriage began to notice Oliver's antics.

"Is this a game, can I play too, mister?" a young boy asked him.

"Of course you can, son," Oliver chuckled. "Close your eyes and do everything I tell you."

"Three steps forward," he told the boy, "now touch your right ear."

All the way down the aisle, the man and boy gave a flawless performance as they followed Mary's silent instructions.

"Well done, thank you, son!" he complimented the youngster when they reached Mary. "You were a great help to us."

She patted the boy on the head as the passengers laughed and applauded. As the boy returned to his seat, Oliver heard the conductor's announcement. "Everett terminus, all passengers must leave the car!"

"It worked, didn't it?" she asked, grabbing his hand and looking into his smiling face.

"Bunkum and trickery," growled Rev. McLough.

"You think so, do you?" Oliver's voice barely whispered as he nodded downwards. "Your bookmarks, sir!"

Charles McLough glanced down at the bookmarks he had not yet replaced into his bible. His thoughts were to grab them but his hands had become strangely immobile and speech was only a groan in his throat. His Bible snapped open and the bookmarks flew into the air, immediately inserting themselves back into their proper place. Teeth chattering and, eyes staring in terror, his mouth went limp and spittle dribbled down his chin.

Stepping off the train into the city of her birth in olden days gave Mary a peculiar feeling. This was December 23rd, 1916 and here she was staring at living history in the form of the Everett Theatre. She took Oliver's hand and gazed nostalgically at the glorious old building. Next door, the millinery store with a wrought-iron guard fence around its lower-bay window was wonderfully quaint.

"Let's walk and find a hotel," he suggested, collecting their bags. "There should be something close by."

Cold wind and blowing snow had people hurrying along Colby Avenue when Oliver spotted the sign 'Providence Hospital' and pointed to it.

"Oh my gosh, that must have been the original little hospital started by the Sisters of Providence. They purchased the Monte Carlo Hotel and, since then, additions and a modern building have replaced it. She continued to look around for anything familiar—recognizing the Federal Building on the corner, unfinished, but soon to house the downtown post office, its classical columns reaching high above the second-floor windows.

"The high school where I teach is a few block from here," she said, pointing up Colby Avenue. "I'll take you there after Christmas."

Chapter 11

"Oh look, that's the famous Mitchell Hotel—it's a block of apartments now!" Mary's excitement could hardly be contained as they continued walking Everett's streets in 1916. Approaching the large building, Mary could see why its plain solid exterior had become a welcoming sight to weary travellers. "It's not very impressive from the outside but it was supposed to be quite the hotel in its day. At least it should be warm inside," she added with a shiver.

A welcome flush of heat assaulted them when a uniformed doorman swung open the great oak door and motioned them inside. Oliver pushed her ahead of him and they entered the dimly lit, opulent interior of the 1900s first-class hotel. Mary stared up in amazement at the huge, sparkling crystal chandelier, looking like it was recently cleaned for Christmas festivities. As her feet sank deep into the luxurious carpet, his hand steered her toward the reception desk.

"Double room, sir?" the clerk inquired.

"Double room, single beds for two nights."

The reply carried no trace of embarrassment, though a wisp of a smile played around his lips as he watched the desk clerk's eyes stray to Mary's left hand. Although covered by her glove, Oliver read the clerk's thoughts and saw the evil he was thinking.

"Sign here, sir." Frederick Chum, the clerk, said sharply, spinning the register to face the young couple.

At that moment, a rustling noise on the empty staircase drew Mary's attention and her fingers tightened on Oliver's arm.

"It's nothing, folks," assured the clerk, but the tone of his own voice caused Oliver to turn back to face him. The clerk's face and, knuckles gripping the counter, had turned stark white. Frederick Chum's nervousness could well be expected as the sound of a rustling dress on the stairs had become a regular happening of late and it scared him to death. The familiar icy cold sensation touched the hairs on the reporter's neck. He could readily feel the presence of this spirit.

"You have a ghost trapped in here," Oliver whispered.

"Oh no sir, th-th-that's not possible, no, no," the clerk spluttered.

The reporter turned and stretching his arms out toward the sound, a smiling, white-haired old lady materialized on the stairs. Her long black satin and lace skirt rustled as she took the last few steps into the foyer. She was carrying a lovely ornate vase and as she stepped toward them, she reached for Oliver's hand, letting the vase slip from her grasp. It plunged silently toward the uncarpeted floor.

Mary watched spellbound, cringing as she waited for the expected crash, but no sound came and the vase disappeared before hitting the floor. Her pulse beating wildly, Mary tasted blood and realized she'd bitten her lip. From the direction of the front desk, she heard a soft thud as the desk clerk crumpled in a heap behind the counter.

Cold beads of perspiration stood out on Mary's forehead as she watched the scene that defied all logic, unfold. Oliver's angel power was once again at work and although she had now witnessed this phenomenon several times, each situation was so different she felt quite unprepared.

"Why are you here?" Oliver's voice interrupted her thoughts sounding far away.

"I madc my choice to stay here forever," came the eerie reply. "They disturbed my resting place before my Berty came back."

"Who are you?" Oliver asked.

"I'm Alice Jones, wife of Albert Jones, the gold miner. I died of winter fever. My Berty was heart-broken and went back to the Fraser River goldfields. He filled my casket with bags of gold dust, then planted me in the ground, but he never came back to me."

"What was the year you passed over, Alice?"

"Why, that was 1863."

Mary held her breath as the manifestation began to fade. Her fingers bit deeply into Oliver's arm but released him quickly when she heard his reply.

"I can take you to your husband, Alice."

Suddenly, the tension was removed from the room. She felt Oliver's muscles relax, his arm sliding protectively around her.

"She's gone to join her Berty now," he whispered.

"I hope she finds happiness," Mary sighed, "she's had such a long wait."

"They'll be happy," Oliver assured her, "but they might come back to guard their gold."

A noise from behind the counter alerted them that Fred was awakening. As he scrambled to his feet, he peeked nervously over the top of the counter.

"H-has she g-g-gone?" he moaned, his eyes darting about the room before making a wild dash for the door.

Laughing, they checked the register and found the clerk had booked them into Room 23. Their key was still sitting on the counter.

"Well I suppose we can find the room ourselves," said Mary.

Going upstairs, they had no trouble and were soon getting adjusted to their latest temporary home. Going over to the window, they watched as Christmas shoppers below bustled about in the bitter cold on Hewitt Street. Mary's eyes danced across the shopfronts, pointing out the spire of the Methodist church on Broadway.

"I've only seen pictures of this old church—this is amazing. Can we go there Sunday morning?" she asked excitedly. "Oh I forgot, we have to go to my parents."

"Honey, we can do anything you like, remember it's only time in *my* life that stands still. We can go to church and still be at your parents when you need to be there!"

Mary thought about it for a minute. "How amazing, I just can't get used to all this … time travelling. I read about it in novels but I seem to be living it! So I'll be able to worship at a church that's not even there any more, in my world?"

Oliver nodded. "That's right, but for now, let's go explore your city in *my* time, it's still only Friday and we're on holidays!"

A knock at the door interrupted further conversation. Coat and scarf in hand Mary went to the door and opened it revealing a slim, smartly-dressed lady in black.

"Excuse me, sir, I'm Mrs. Helga Lieberman, the housekeeper," she said. "Are you a minister?"

The question had an undertone of anxiety which Oliver noticed immediately.

"No ma'am," he replied politely, "but why do you ask?"

"Oh, it's that fool of a desk clerk. He's just run off, quit his job and says he's leaving town. He said you talked to a ghost in the foyer."

"I talked to Alice Jones, a longtime guest here," he replied, "but she's gone now."

Taking a surprised step back, the housekeeper's face turned ashen.

"W-white hair, b-black skirt—lady on the stairs?" she whispered.

"Yes, you obviously know her."

"And she's gone, you say?"

"Yes ma'am," Oliver replied, "she said her gold would be safe here in the hotel."

"Gold?" Mrs. Lieberman repeated, quickly regaining her composure. "Oh yes, yes, her gold will be quite safe here." Turning quickly, she hurried off down the corridor muttering to herself.

A lacy carpet of snow settled over the streets as Oliver and Mary went outside making a dash across Hewitt between several horse-pulled conveyances. They found an almost empty little diner and went inside. A bell tinkled, signalling their entry.

Finding a seat, Mary whispered, "We must stick out like sore thumbs in this small town. She'll know we're visitors."

The waitress was in her twenties and although very plain-looking, had a friendly smile. When she recommended the beefsteak special, they were quick to order deciding that a large noon meal would go down quite well on this cold winter day.

Soon they were eating the most delicious juicy steaks they had ever tasted. As they ate, they listened to the waitress' chatter, giving them a rundown of some of her city's highlights. When she mentioned a late-afternoon vaudeville show at the theatre, she had Mary's interest. When she finally left them, Mary noticed she had a terrible limp and brought it to Oliver's attention. When she returned, Mary opened the conversation.

"You've hurt your leg, dear," she said sympathetically.

"No ma'am, it's a childhood injury. I hardly know it's there any more."

Oliver smiled at the breezy reply. This girl obviously held no bitterness as she made light of her impediment and his overwhelming urge was to help. "Would you show it to me?" he asked, smiling reassuringly.

"Please let him look," Mary pressed the girl.

Blushing, the young waitress raised her long dress to her knees revealing an ugly, swollen ankle and a twisted shinbone.

"Keep very still for a moment," Oliver whispered. "I promise this won't hurt."

"Is he a doctor, miss?" she asked.

"No dear, he's an angel."

Eyes wide, the girl felt the tingling sensation when Oliver's fingers touched her foot. Mary left her chair and watched as he gently massaged the disfigured bone and the redness paled, bruises began to fade, and the swelling disappeared.

"Oh, that feels wonderful," she exclaimed, without looking down. "You have magic in those hands, sir."

Paying the bill, they left unnoticed as the waitress went to serve new customers. It took a while before she realized the pain in her leg and foot was gone.

"You're awfully quiet, girl," the cook observed. "Who was that man you were talking to?"

"I don't know, Hettie, but he fixed my ankle."

"Don't be silly, Joanie, that ankle will never be right."

Hettie Yackub, the cook, had no illusions about this girl's disability. Having known Joanie from birth, she was aware of the accident that had left her a cripple as an 8-year-old. The ankle, crushed by a log, could never be mended doctors had told her poor widowed mother that fateful day in 1903.

"But it is, Hettie," Joanie whispered. "Look!"

The rotund figure shuffled around the work table as the waitress again hoisted her skirt up to her knees.

"My Lord, child," the cook gasped, clasping her hand to her mouth when she saw the girl's perfectly normal ankle. "It is a miracle! Who did you say this man was?"

"His lady said he was an angel," Joanie murmured innocently, "but angels don't look like people do they, Mrs. Yackub?"

Goose bumps appeared on Hettie's ample arms as a shiver ran down her back. For years, she'd imagined she had psychic inclinations and swore she'd seen the ghosts of Everett's long-dead at the churchyard on more than one occasion. Turning away, she mopped her brow with her work-stained apron.

"You have been blessed, my girl. That man was truly an angel."

Down the street, Mary led Oliver over to the front of the Commerce Building, looking once more up at the towering columns before tugging him through the falling snow to the corner of Hewitt and Wetmore. She stopped and pointed to the metal dragon on the Greenburg building.

The window of Burnett Brothers jewellery store had such a stunning display of precious gems and diamond rings, it drew Mary's interest.

"Let's go in," she coaxed him, pulling on his arm.

Pushing the door open, Oliver heard Tom Watson's ghostly chuckle into his ear. *Careful now son!*

Moving slowly past the counter displays under the watchful eyes of the clerks, she stopped at a tray of sparkling rings. Her eyes full of wonder, she gazed longingly at the beautiful settings.

"Aren't they wonderful?" she whispered.

"If you like, I'll buy you one, honey," he said gently. "It'll be something to remember me by."

"Are you sure, Oliver?" she asked, his comment setting her aback momentarily as she realized the true meaning behind his words. Feeling as if she was taking advantage of their situation, she dropped her head as tears came to her eyes.

Oliver smiled, pretending to be unaware of her discomfort. He nodded at the clerk, pointing to one of the more expensive trays which was moved to the top of the counter. He took Mary's arm and steered her toward it. Mary shyly studied the selection, assisted by Oliver, who encouraged her to try them on. She finally made her choice and handed it to the clerk.

Backing away from the counter, she sighed. She had often thought about having a diamond ring but there had never been that special man in her life and if she wanted to buy a townhouse, she couldn't spend her money on expensive jewellery. Now she was having second thoughts, but Oliver had already paid for it and the clerk was handing him his change. Oliver took the tiny box, put it into his outer coat pocket and, taking her by the arm, they left the store.

Up the street, he found a doorway which would give them some shelter and, taking the box from his pocket, he opened it.

"Wear it for me, honey," he said emotionally, handing it to her.

Mary took the ring from the box and hesitated briefly looking up at him as if to assure herself it was all right. Seeing his smile, she slid it onto the ring finger of her right hand. Self-consciously she kissed him but he surprised her by grasping her shoulders and kissing her passionately.

"I don't want to ever forget you, Mary," he said sadly.

"What are you talking about, Oliver?"

"I have a meeting with the spirits in Victoria tomorrow night," he confessed. "Tom says they aren't very happy with me for being so fond of you."

"Are you fond of me, Oliver?" she asked.

"Yes, I am, Mary," he said sincerely. "I'm very fond of you."

"Well, I'm more than fond of you, Oliver, I'm in love with you and you told me this morning at the restaurant that you thought you were in love with me? Is that true?"

"Well," he began, hesitating so long she interrupted him.

"Well, do you think you are or not?" she asked, becoming more insistent.

"I don't know, Mary. Truthfully, I've never been in love with anyone and, not having parents, I'm afraid it left me quite lacking in that department. I'm also afraid of what the spirits will say or do and I don't want them to vent their anger on you. I also don't know how we could possibly live in two centuries. I care for you deeply but it has all happened so fast. I don't want either of us to regret our decision."

"All right," she said calmly, squeezing his hand as unspoken thoughts ran through her head. "Now I understand better. We'll work this out—we have to. I don't want to lose you, honey. I truly think we're meant for each other."

As they continued their walk arm-in-arm through the streets of Everett, she felt as if she were in a dream. Feeling her ring on her finger, she wished it was an engagement ring instead of merely a friendship ring, then she chastised herself for being unrealistic. Oliver was right, it was all happening too quickly. So, deciding to wait and see what the spirits were going to say and do on Christmas Eve, she tried to put it out of her mind and enjoy their historic walk.

Oliver heard some of her thoughts and silently let his breath out as she began to relax again. They walked past the Spanish-style architecture of the courthouse, then explored Clarke's large department store where Mary bought a few things to show her class. She peeked into the Tontine Saloon and pointed out a large stuffed moose and giggled at the bowler-hatted patrons. Wrinkling her nose, she declined Oliver's invitation to enter the smoky interior.

They noticed daylight was disappearing quickly by the time they found themselves standing in front of the Everett Theatre with its odd-shaped windows rising high on the front façade. Seeing the poster for the vaudeville show, Mary remembered the waitress' comments and they decided they should come back for it.

"It starts in less than an hour," she warned and, realizing how little time they had, Oliver hailed a taxi that was passing on the other side of the street.

The old car swung around in the middle of the street, almost colliding with a streetcar. They got in and told the driver to take them to the high school. The wind had picked up now, blowing snow in all directions. Arriving at their destination, they got out of the taxi and stood looking up at the great arched entrance of this bastion of learning where Mary taught her history lessons 84 years later. The driver didn't want to leave them, but Oliver assured him they could find their way back before dark. As Mary stood gazing up at the school, she felt Oliver's arm go around her.

"I teach behind those walls," she whispered. "You know, I've never thought about it much before—this building has so much history. So many kids and teachers will have walked these halls by the time I teach here."

He was so quiet, she glanced up at him, and was surprised to see the fiery look in his eyes as they focussed on the high parapet wall.

"You have a spirit living in your school," he murmured into her ear, letting go of her and taking a step toward the building.

Mary squinted through the snow searching the high places but only the huge crest balanced on the parapet wall showed any outline against the darkening sky. Fighting her rising excitement, she stared with renewed intensity, desperately hoping to see the form that Oliver was talking about.

"I don't see anything."

"He won't want to be seen by mortals."

"Darn, I really wanted to see him."

"All right, take my hand," he murmured, reaching out to her, "but let go if it becomes too scary."

The moment they touched, she felt the warmth of his body and a faint outline of a male figure came into view leaning against the school crest. Slowly it became brighter and brighter until the luminescent figure showed clearly against the blackening night. "Is he here all the time?" she asked.

"Not likely."

"And nobody can ever see him?"

"I didn't say that," Oliver corrected her, "mortals can only see him when he chooses. Spirits have a habit of appearing when they're least desired or expected!"

"How do you know all that?" she asked.

"He told me, we were talking with our thoughts."

"It's so frustrating," she sighed. "I have only known you for six days and this is utterly fascinating. I want to be part of your world, Oliver. I'm trying my best to understand."

Oliver didn't respond instead, taking her arm, they began the dark walk back to the theatre, leaving their footprints behind them. Mary couldn't get the spirit off her mind. She was surprised how much she seemed to want a ghost to be roaming the halls of Everett High School—a ghost she could become familiar with, not one who remained invisible and anonymous. *I really am becoming comfortable with Oliver's world,* she thought, chuckling to herself. *Or am I?*

Little conversation passed between them as they picked up their speed, enjoying the brisk walk over the four blocks back to Hewitt. They found the area of the theatre well-lit as they joined the end of the queue for the vaudeville show. Choice seats were gone and the only seats left were high in the balcony's upper back row. When they entered, the lights were already dim and an usher led the way in the dark. The music was playing and several dancers were on stage.

"It's real old-time vaudeville," Mary whispered. "Do you know their names?"

"No, this is the first time I've ever been to the theatre."

Surprised with his answer, she was thrilled to see how much he was enjoying the wonderful performance put on by the troupe of singers and dancers, despite having to crane their necks from the worst seats in the house. At the end of the first act, they joined an appreciative audience clapping until their hands hurt.

Intermission gave them the opportunity to stretch cramped muscles and they talked to a gentle old couple a row in front of them. They admitted they were visiting for Christmas and Charlie Evans and his wife, Belle, gave them quite a history lesson about the old theatre.

"We were here before Washington became a state in 1889," 76-year-old Charlie admitted with a hearty laugh. "Not many people can say they're that old!"

Mary listened with growing interest when they talked of Everett's incorporation in 1891, when its roads were mud and sidewalks non-existent or merely rough-cut boards. Belle explained that before Charlie built them a cabin in town, they'd lived in a logging camp deep in the forest. He was a faller and she worked as a cook.

"This is our one big treat of the year," Belle said with a smile. "We watched this theatre being built in 1901!"

"Would you have dinner with us after the show?" Oliver asked as the bell rang for the show to begin and lights started to dim.

"Yes, we will," Charlie replied, getting the nod from his wife, then settling stiffly into his seat and protectively taking her hand.

During the second half, Oliver was aware of the ghostly presence of a young girl sitting among the orchestra members. He could see her clearly, playing the violin, and heard each perfect note.

"Mary," he whispered, taking her hand as the show drew to a close, "look in the orchestra pit in front of the drummer."

"I see her, I see her," Mary gasped, her nails digging into his hand.

Suddenly the lights came on as all the performers filled the stage at the end of the finale. The ghostly apparition stopped playing and stared up into the audience. Oliver and Mary knew, without a doubt, that she was looking right at them. Thunderous applause filled the theatre as the ghost pointed her bow at them, mouthing words that carried no sound.

"Stay a while," Charlie advised from in front of them, "we like to wait until the crowd has gone."

The buzz of voices filled the theatre and shuffling feet stomped down stairways before quiet settled over the building. All of a sudden, the sound of a violin playing a haunting melody was heard.

"Who is that playing?" Mary asked, looking around but seeing nothing.

"We don't know," Charlie whispered, "but it always happens when everybody's gone. Nice, but awfully sad, isn't it?"

Sitting for a few more minutes, they finally joined the crowd out on the street as many waited for cars to pick them up. Charlie suggested a nearby restaurant and Oliver shepherded his three companions along the street to the next block. The wind was blowing along Colby and noisy laughter from taverns was filling the air.

Over a delicious meal of beef stew, Mary posed many questions to the old couple, listening to their answers with great interest and learning more about the early history of the area. Something she could not tell them was that Everett, during the years her parents were growing up, would gain the nickname the "City of Smokestacks" due to the logging industry and the many mills which spouted in the area.

"We live on Cleveland," Belle chuckled, her eyes getting a faraway look as she added, "close to the Jenkins'. When we arrived here in 1892 after working all those years in the logging camp, Everett was heaven to us even though it was the first days of this town. There weren't many houses here yet but we found some land."

"We bought it from Swalwell in 1893—he was one of the partners in the Everett Land Company, with Hewitt and the Rockefellers, who started it all," Charlie took up the story. "We lived in a tent while we built the cabin and Belle helped to raise our two grandchildren while we were doing it. The town was booming and we even had electricity, telephones, and …."

"And streetcars, too!" Belle added excitedly. "I'd take the children for rides while their folks were busy and Charlie was building our house."

"But it all ended that same year," Charlie said sadly, "when The Silver Panic hit and we plunged into a depression with every other city. You folks would know all about that?" He looked over at them as they nodded, then he continued right on. "I lost my job and many people left the area. It was terrible."

"I don't know how we managed but Charlie found enough work to get us through the next six years when things began to turn around and the mills got going again," Belle added.

"Now, we can hardly believe how the area has grown with the Weyerhaeuser mill starting it all off around 1900. Those were bad years for folks, don't want to see that happen again," he added softly.

"Oh my, that must have been hard for you," said Mary.

The old couple glanced at each other across the table. "Hard deary? Yes, it was in a way, but we had the post office at Henderson's Store, and there was a newspaper, the railway, and shops nearby. After living all them years in a logging camp and Charlie risking his life everyday, Everett seemed like heaven. No, that were the easy part," said Belle, watching a grin spread across her husband's face.

It was 8:30 when they said their goodbye's and left the restaurant. Watching the couple trudge away through the snow to their car, Mary looked over at Oliver with misty eyes.

"What lovely people. They've sure experienced life and still have a wonderful attitude despite it all. Are we going back to the hotel?"

"No, we're going back to the theatre."

Chapter 12

Mary's pulse quickened as Oliver led her back to the front of the darkened theatre.

"Evening, folks," the night watchman greeted them from the shadow of the doorway. "Theatre's closed now until the day after Christmas."

"Hold tight," Oliver whispered, concentrating on the theatre stage as they walked past the man and turned to go round the corner.

Eyes bulging, the watchman's pipe slipped from his lips and fell into the snow as the couple disappeared in front of his eyes. Running to the corner of the building, he shook his head, and stared at the footprints in the snow.

"They were there a minute ago," he exclaimed, looking around for someone else to collaborate his thoughts. Fingers fondling the whisky bottle in his pocket, he returned to the doorway. Immediately changing his mind, he went back to look at the footprints, now almost covered by snow. His decision was an instant one, scurrying away mumbling loudly to himself.

When Oliver felt the stageboards beneath his feet, he opened his eyes to total darkness and felt Mary's hand tighten on his arm. He turned on the lights with a flick of his hand and, almost instantly, the ghostly strains of a lonely violin began to play.

Then, as suddenly as it began, the playing stopped and the music stands in the orchestra pit began crashing to the floor, chairs toppled over and drumsticks flew about the area. Mary screamed as the angry spirit wreaked havoc below them and she moved behind Oliver, holding on even tighter.

Eventually, an eerie silence flooded over the destruction. Not a sound was heard and Mary held her breath in anticipation of the next violent outburst. She flinched when the mischievous laughter of a child shattered the stillness.

"Have you finished misbehaving now, Yana?" Mary heard Oliver ask in an unusually disdainful tone.

After a moment of uncomfortable silence, Mary's nerves were again shattered by a resounding scream and Yana materialized in front of them. Her long dark hair hung in disarray, cascading over slim shoulders. Eyes dark and fiery, the beautiful oval face twisted in temper, menacingly raising her violin as if to strike the intruders.

The 14-year-old protégé's career had been abruptly ended in the winter of 1910 when illness and death stole her mortal body. Left behind was an angry and temperamental ghost—a permanent resident of the Everett Theatre.

"Stop that, you little brat," Oliver snapped, "or I'll send you away."

"No, you won't," Yana taunted. "You want me to be friends with your mortal woman!"

"She's reading my mind," Oliver whispered, as the ghostly form began to fade away. Glancing around, he noticed some of the musicians had left instrument cases in the orchestra pit, thankfully untouched by Yana's tantrum. One of them was open and contained a violin.

"Do you happen to play the violin, Mary?" he asked, grinning because he already knew the answer.

"Well, I used to, but I'm not going down there," she replied.

"We'll go together," he assured her and they went to find the stairway to the pit. Mary took the violin from the case and put it in place under her chin nervously touching the bow to the strings.

"Go ahead," he encouraged.

Off-key notes grated on his eardrums as she tentatively tested the strings then, began to play a simple melody with closed eyes. Suddenly another violin began to play along and Yana materialized not far away sending goose bumps rushing over Mary's body. She changed songs and Yana followed, not missing a single beat. Mary began to feel strangely at ease as they picked up the tempo and the theatre filled with their marvellous music.

Outside, the night watchman had returned and was listening at the doorway as people passing to and from the taverns cast surprised glances at the dark theatre.

"Will you take a look inside with me?" the guard begged a passing soldier.

A small crowd was gathered outside the door when the watchman opened it and he and the soldier went inside. Oliver felt their imminent intrusion, snapping his fingers to plunge the theatre into darkness. He sent Mary's violin back to its case and took her hand.

"Hold on," he whispered, "we have to go."

Footsteps sounded in the foyer as unseen forces whisked them outside but not before Yana's haunting words floated after them.

"Please come again; I want to be your friend."

Outside, they watched from the back of the crowd, waiting until the soldier and then the watchman came back outside.

"Everything's in darkness," the soldier shouted as the watchman relocked the door. "Nobody's in there except the ghosts!"

Laughter erupted from the happy crowd and a uniformed seaman yelled, "There's a ghost in every bottle, old man. Try one more drink to wash them away!"

The sound of more noisy revellers spilled out onto the sidewalk filling the night air with drunken laughter as Oliver sent them back to their hotel room. They sat down wearily in the firmly-stuffed chairs and Mary began to chuckle.

"That Yana is quite a girl. I heard her say she wanted to be friends."

"Spirits are often more angry than they were in real life. You're not frightened of her any more?" Oliver chuckled, standing up and resting his hand on her shoulder. "She can become quite violent."

"Yes, I am a bit worried about what could happen, but something seems to be drawing me to her."

"Bedtime, my dear," he replied, taking his pajamas out of the suitcase, "let me think on it."

He went into the bathroom and closed the door. Mary yawned and slowly stood up. She went to the window and looked out into the darkness. She was still standing there when Oliver came up behind her and, gently took her by the shoulders, kissing her on the cheek.

"Come on, honey. Don't worry about Yana, you won't ever have to face her alone."

Climbing into bed, he lay with his eyes closed until he heard Mary get into her bed and she turned off the light. It wasn't long before he heard her breathing deeply in sleep.

Closing his eyes, he sent his thoughts hurtling through space to find Tom. A musty tobacco smell touched his nostrils and he knew the old angel had arrived.

You called me, Oliver?

The old angel's eerie whisper sounded tired and strained as his shadowy figure materialized at the foot of the bed.

Is something wrong? Oliver asked silently. *You sound tired.*

My time is running out, sighed Tom. *I only have two days left.*

Two days to what? Oliver asked, vaguely remembering something his mentor had said earlier.

To the end of my mandate as angel supervisor for the Ross Bay Chapter of Spirits, Tom replied.

Will I lose my angel powers? asked his protégé, concern causing him to sit up in bed.

No son, you're a mortal angel, you're immortal.

You mean I can't die. I'm locked in this world forever? he groaned silently. *What about Mary?*

That's your problem, my boy, Tom replied, beginning to fade away. *You work it out, you're an angel!*

Ghostly chuckling whispered through the room as the apparition disappeared and Oliver heard Tom's parting words, *I'll come for you just before eleven o'clock on Christmas Eve.*

They spent the next day relaxing and trying to stay out of the cold weather, wandering through the stores all dressed up in their Christmas finery, which was quite minimal compared to what Oliver had seen in 2000. Mary purchased a few small souvenirs of the time and they went to bed early. On Sunday they woke as dawn was sending its first streaks of colour through the eastern clouds. Mary shook herself free from her dreams remembering Yana had been playing tricks with her mind all night. Suddenly throwing caution to the wind, she slipped quietly out from under the warmth of her blankets and slid in beside Oliver, nestling up against his warm back. Oliver stirred, turning over and slipping his arms around her.

"It's all right, sweetheart," he murmured sleepily, kissing her forehead. "I'll keep you safe."

Church bells were ringing summoning worshippers to the early service when Mary again awoke finding daylight streaming through the partly pulled curtains.

"Good afternoon, young lady," an already-dressed Oliver teased.

Kicking the blankets off, Mary leapt out of bed, a gleam of devilment in her eyes as she chased him into the corner. Locked in each other's arms Oliver whispered a startling promise.

"Time won't ever separate us, honey, I'll find a way."

"You'd better," she replied, pulling herself away and going to get her clothes, "because I'm not going to give up easily even if you are an angel!"

"Then hurry up, you brazen hussy, and we'll go downstairs and eat before church," he laughed, slapping her backside as she ran to the safety of the bathroom. "What time do you want to arrive at your parents' house?"

"Anytime after three o'clock is fine," she called back.

When she returned 15 minutes later, she found him looking out the window. She walked up to him, encircling him with her arms and hugging him, feeling more content than she could remember. He put an arm around her and pointed to the snowy scene below where slippery roads were causing mayhem and several young boys were throwing snowballs at streetcars and anything else that moved.

"I just need to put on my shoes, we can watch this delightful spectacle as we eat!" she said, going to sit on the bed. "Dressing for this era is very time-consuming and mighty complicated at times, but it sure is fun!" she laughed, buttoning up her 1916-style boots.

Downstairs, they found a window table which provided a perfect view of the bedlam going on outside. Slow-moving, almost-empty streetcars pushing several inches of fresh snow along Hewitt Avenue took their attention and they were surprised to see a horse and rider pass by their window.

Aware that someone was standing beside their table, they looked up. Dressed completely in black, Helga Lieberman appeared stern and foreboding. Her narrow lips attempted a smile before she spoke.

"May I join you?" she inquired.

Without waiting for a reply, she drew out the extra chair and sat down. Mary saw the woman was agitated as she rubbed her hands together, stopping as she noticed Mary watching her. Helga's dark eyes told Oliver she was already planning her next move.

"No, Mrs. Lieberman, we don't know where Albert Jones left his gold," he replied to the housekeeper's unspoken thoughts.

Mouth dropping open, Helga's fingernails bit into her palm. She'd checked the old registers of the Mitchell Hotel back to its opening in 1903 and found no entry in the name of Jones. Greed consumed her every thought and she desperately needed that gold to further her illegal ambitions—running liquor from Vancouver Island in nearby Canada, to the coastal cities, as Washington State headed for prohibition. Drinkers and saloons had returned to Everett after the 1912 referendum vote, but Helga knew the Temperance League was gaining in popularity and state-wide prohibition was imminent.

That gold, Oliver realized after reading her thoughts, *is her stepping stone to a life of luxury and she intends to find it.*

"We have to go now," Mary's voice broke into their thoughts.

"I shall talk to you later," Helga promised, leaving the table.

"She's evil!" Mary commented, bringing a knowing smile to her companion's lips as they went back to their room.

A short time later they returned to the foyer dressed for the outdoors. Oliver went to the desk and told them they would be checking out before four o'clock. As they stepped out into the snow-covered street, he glanced back at the curtained hotel windows and knew the prying eyes of the housekeeper were watching them.

Joining a small group of churchgoers, they walked cautiously down the icy sidewalk to the First Methodist Church. The minister stood braving the cold to greet his flock just inside the open door. Raising an eyebrow at their unfamiliar faces, he shook their hands, welcoming them warmly. As they moved inside, he congratulated himself on his superb performance even though his feet were frozen. Finding a seat in the last row of pews, Oliver and Mary shared whispered observations on the marvellous stained-glass windows, the simple altar, and plain wooden seats.

The organ began to drone as its large pipes warmed up for the first hymn. A small black robed choir, no doubt missing some of its members due to the weather, entered solemnly and took their places as the minister moved behind the large lectern and began his service of worship by reaching out his arms in prayer.

His sermon that morning amazingly coupled the joyous story of Christ's birth with what he called, the demon drink, ranting loud and long on the evils of alcohol. He finally called down the wrath of God on members of his flock who might be temped to stray from the path of righteousness during their Christmas festivities. Then he bade them stand for their song of praise.

Oliver took Mary's hand and her eyes followed his gaze to the heavy wooden rafters. Her singing stopped but her mouth remained open when she saw the host of ghostly apparitions floating like gossamer forms in the shadows.

"Sing, my darling," Oliver whispered reverently, "this is a good place and we're among friends."

Mary looked down at the hymn book for the words of the next verse and when she raised her eyes again, the spirits had vanished.

"Please come again," said the minister, bidding them farewell with a smile and a handshake at the door. His eyes showed surprise when the stranger held onto his hand and a tingle of pain ran up his arm. Unable to escape Oliver's penetrating scrutiny, he stared into his eyes and his knees began to shake. An icy sensation chilled his backbone when hc heard the stranger's whispered words.

"You're a hypocrite, Allen McDuff, heed your own advice and change your ways."

The startled minister could muster no answer as desperate thoughts ran rapidly through his brain. *How could this stranger know, unless ... no it couldn't be true?*

"You knew he was a secret drinker?" Mary murmured.

"Yes," Oliver replied. "Are you hungry yet?"

"Not really but perhaps we had better eat."

"Then we'll go visit Yana."

Locking fingers, they felt the rush of cold air, unaware the minister was still watching.

"Good gracious me, they've gone!" gasped Rev. McDuff, ignoring the line of parishioners waiting for him as he backed away.

Staggering on unsteady legs, he backed across the foyer, unaware his prayer book had clattered to the floor as members of his congregation watched incredulously. Reaching the door to his office, he slammed it closed behind him falling onto his knees screaming in frustrated, silent rage. The secret he'd hidden for years was out and he was petrified of the ramifications.

He'd been so careful to conceal his addiction but now surely others had heard the stranger's comment. Life would become intolerable. There were only two solutions he could think of as he stumbled toward the vestry.

Allen McDuff had not always been a holy man—a sinister past and a need to change his identity had led him into the ministry. Sought by the law in Victoria, he'd assumed the identity of a Scottish minister killed by a streetcar in that city. Claiming kinship to the mortally injured man, Alex Chapman had seized the opportunity. Convincing the mortician, he'd accepted the man's personal affects, stealing the identity of Rev. Allen McDuff and moving to the small town of Everett. For 16 years, he'd lived the lie, gaining respectability while organizing his illegal shipments of liquor from the Canadian mainland.

Keeping well in the background, his cover was a perfect one—no one had ever suspected Rev. McDuff until today. *The secrecy must be maintained,* he thought wildly, *but how?* Who was this studious-looking young man with the penetrating eyes? How could this stranger possibly know he had a drinking problem and why had his handshake given him such an uncomfortable feeling before their disappearing act? It was all too much for him and he began to shake.

"An angel?" he whispered, sloshing more courage into his mouth. "If he's an angel then I'm the devil!"

Chapter 13

Oliver felt the boards of the stage beneath his feet.

"Turn the lights on," Mary urged. "This is frightening me."

An eerie silence consumed the theatre as they listened intently, interrupted only by the occasional creak and groan of the old building.

She's gone, Mary thought with some relief.

"Get the violin, honey," Oliver murmured, "and play me a tune."

Going quickly down to the orchestra pit, she was startled to see the mess from the previous night had been put back to normal. She found the same violin and returned to Oliver's side, the blood beginning to race through her veins. With hands shaking, she drew the bow across the strings—the first phrases rang clearly through the empty theatre and then she abruptly changed to a lively polka. She heard a happy giggle beside her as the ghostly form of Yana materialized, her own bow flashing like magic producing a glorious sound. Perspiration glistened on Mary's forehead by the time the song ended.

"Can we be friends now, Yana?" Mary asked, smiling at the apparition.

"Yes please," the girl replied, gleefully, "you can help me play for an audience again."

"How can I do that?"

"It's easy, you play on the stage and I accompany you!"

"Would that work, Oliver?" Mary asked, her forehead wrinkling. "The theatre wouldn't let me play, would they?"

"He can arrange it," Yana quickly replied.

"Yes, I'm sure I could," Oliver agreed, not wanting to offend the young spirit. "It would be an interesting project—Yana gets to play her music for an audience again while Everett gets a mystery it can't possibly solve!"

All of a sudden, Yana's form glowed with renewed energy and she reached out and touched the school teacher's hand. Mary gasped at the sensation caused when the feather-like touch brushed her skin.

"Do ghosts cry?" Mary whispered, as a tear rolled down her cheek.

"Yes, we do," Yana replied in a faraway voice as her form faded away.

"It's time to go, sweetheart," Oliver urged. "You'd better put the violin back."

It took only a moment to transport them back to the hotel room and Mary pulled him closer wrapping her arms around his waist.

"Oliver Ryan," she murmured, "you're the most exciting thing that ever happened to me. I can't wait to introduce you to mom and dad!"

Downstairs in the foyer, Mrs. Lieberman paced angrily back and forth as she waited to ambush Oliver and Mary as they returned from their outing. They were supposed to be checking out by four o'clock and she'd already been waiting for an hour. Tension was driving her crazy—the clock in the bar had chimed 3:30 over ten minutes ago. *Where the devil are they?* she thought. She had questions to ask them and she felt sure Oliver had the answers she needed.

Steps sounded above on the stairway and when she turned to look she cursed savagely under her breath—they had been in the hotel all the time and she'd missed her chance.

"Let me buy you a drink for Christmas," she whined as they joined her at the bottom of the stairs, hoping to trap them in the bar.

"No, thank you, we must be leaving," Oliver replied, then chuckled as he read her mind, "but I do have some more information for you. I believe Alice Jones buried her gold in your basement."

"How could she," Helga snapped, "it's concrete!"

"Their house was here before the hotel was built," he lied.

An evil light shone in the housekeeper's eyes as Oliver dropped the room keys into her hand. *Old records should be available to give the exact location of the Jones' cabin and the gold will be mine!* she thought gleefully. Consumed by greed, Helga didn't even notice the unusual clothes her guests were wearing.

"It's after 3:30," Mary urged, tugging on Oliver's arm. "Mother is expecting us, honey."

Dark winter clouds hung low over Everett as Oliver hailed a taxi in front of the Mitchell Hotel. Eyes watching from behind the curtains made a note of the driver in case he would be needed later.

"Where to folks?" the cabbie asked cheerily.

"Warren and Tulalip, please," Mary announced.

"But there's nothing there, Miss," he replied."

"It's all right," Oliver intervened, "just drive us there, please. Will this cover the fare?" he asked dropping two silver dollars into the driver's hand.

"Yes, sir, it surely will. I'll have you there in a tick."

Helga felt a peculiar sensation run through her body as she watched the taxi pull away and move slowly into traffic. Her eyes followed its progress down the block, but suddenly, she gasped. Her legs felt like jelly and she reached out to clutch the window frame. The taxi had actually disappeared as if by magic. She looked again, straining her eyes, but no, the car was definitely not there!

As they drove away from the hotel, Oliver decided he was going to have a little fun and focussed his mind on the year 2000. In the blink of an eye, things changed. They were now surrounded by Everett's modern streets and the sounds of the year 2000 as several sleek, colourful cars zipped passed them. Mary recognized her surroundings and smiled when she realized they were a bit overdressed for the present with its warmer weather conditions.

"Don't worry," she whispered as the taxi sped along 33rd, "my parents are going to love you."

"Here we are," said the driver, pulling the car up to the curb. He got out and opened the door for them, then went to take their suitcases from the trunk as if it were a normal day.

"Thank you," said Oliver. "We're fine from here."

The driver tipped his hat and wished them a Merry Christmas as he pocketed the money leaving his passengers at the end of the garden walk leading to an early 1970s house set back from the road. As he walked back to the taxi, he tried desperately to remember where he'd picked up these people. *I must be going senile,* he mumbled. *I'm glad they're my last fare; it's been a long day!*

Reaching into his pocket for the car keys, his fingers felt two large coins. He took them out and stared at them. They were silver dollars.

Even more puzzled, he turned them over and over in his hand. He opened the car door, but hesitated, looking down at the coins again. Noticing the date on one, he looked closer, then checked the other.

"Two 1915s!" he muttered. "Now where in heaven's name did I get these?" Pocketing the coins, he jumped into the car and drove away … as he turned the corner, he returned to 1916 and all memory of his adventure into the future disappeared.

Mary, now beginning to feel quite excited about introducing Oliver to her parents, began walking toward the house pulling her suitcase while Oliver organized the rest of the bags. The door to the house opened as he turned to follow and he saw Mary's mother hurrying toward them. She was an attractive, diminutive woman of middle age, with short dark hair, wearing snug black pants, a bright red Christmas sweatshirt and fluffy red slippers. She tripped and would have fallen in her eagerness to greet her daughter, if Oliver hadn't caught her.

Thanking him, she suspiciously shook his hand and he read her confused thoughts. Obviously, Mary had not told her about him. Hugging her mother, Mary simply announced, "This is Oliver, mother, we'll tell you all about it inside."

"Let them come in Janice, before you catch your death of cold!" a man shouted from the open doorway. "That wind is frigid coming off Gardener Bay today; after all, it is winter you know! Welcome home, honey," he greeted his eldest child with a hug at the bottom of the stairs. Smiling at Oliver, he raised his eyebrows and took Mary's suitcase, carrying it up the stairs.

By the time Oliver stepped into the house, he had already had a taste of the Janick's warm, yet curious, hospitality and their colourful Christmas decorations couldn't help but make him smile. Leaving their coats in the hall closet, they stepped into a roomy and invitingly warm living room where an unusual-looking, enclosed fire burned. It was the first time he had seen one of these fires. He had to drag his eyes away from it to take in the large white Christmas tree, shining brilliantly with a mass of miniature, multi-coloured lights. He should have been surprised by the fact it was white and, obviously artificial, except he had already seen this type of tree at the Eaton Centre.

It's certainly Christmas in this house, he thought, *no wonder Mary has different memories than I do.* He felt her take his arm and she formally introduced him to her parents. A bit embarrassed, he mumbled how lovely their decorations were as they shook hands.

Janice and Gordon were nice people but obviously surprised with her bringing a guest home for the holiday, especially a man. They covered their discomfort well and when Mary mentioned that her father was a year away from retirement at his job as a telephone salesman, Oliver imagined he was a popular employee. Gordon interrupted his thoughts by throwing a few good-natured questions out while Janice, a woman with more of a studious nature, watched Oliver curiously.

"What's wrong, Mom?" Mary asked.

"I have the strangest feeling we should know each other, Oliver," she replied.

"Don't let her worry you, son," Gordon laughed, "she thinks she's psychic, you're probably a face from her past!"

Mary and Oliver glanced at each other trying not to display their surprise. It was 84 years since he had helped Mary's great-grandmother Bertha Bentley and held young Jane in his arms, but Jane was Janice's mother; there was no way she could possibly recognize him.

When her mother went out to the kitchen, Mary followed.

"What can I do to help?" she asked.

"It's mostly under control, dear, but you could check the table and make sure I haven't forgotten anything," Janice replied, standing in the middle of the kitchen. "I wonder why Oliver seems familiar to me?" she asked, more to herself than Mary.

"I was wondering that, too?" Mary commented.

"I'm sure I don't know, this is rather a surprise. You haven't mentioned him before—are you keeping something from us, honey?" she teased. "How long have you known him? What does he do?"

"Well, you don't know all my friends," Mary began. "Oliver is a wonderful, thoughtful guy and he's become very special to me. He's a reporter in Seattle." She moved off to the dining room, hoping her mother would stop asking questions.

"Is dinner going to be long, Janice? Our guests must be famished, I sure am!" called Gordon.

"You poor thing, you can come and sit at the table now," his wife called back.

Mary realized she was safe from her mother's questions for the time being, but what was she going to tell her. *She would freak out if I told her I was in love with an angel!*

With the subject forgotten for the time being, Oliver experienced the true meaning of friendship and family as Mary and her mother brought bowls and plates heaped with food to the table. Not having experienced this type of extravagance before, he felt a bit overwhelmed. *This is a feast fit for royalty,* he sighed.

"It's all right, lad, mother always cooks too much," Gordon joked, "we'll be eating leftovers for a week!"

"And what's wrong with leftovers, Gordon Janick?" Janice scolded her husband. "There won't be many leftovers from this meal, I need the room in the fridge for turkey leftovers tomorrow."

"I'd be happy just with your leftovers, Mrs. Janick," Oliver retorted.

"Thank you, Oliver, and please call us Janice and Gordon," she chuckled, cocking an eye at her husband. "It's nice to have a gentleman in our house at last!"

All through the meal, the banter continued, soon making Oliver feel quite comfortable. *Here's a family who really enjoy each other,* he thought.

Later, retiring to the living room, the men enjoyed conversation and a cup of coffee leaving mother and daughter to wash up. Several times, he caught the sound of laughter coming from the kitchen and knew Mary was having a good visit with her mother.

It was about 7 o'clock when the women came in to join them, refilling their coffees. Half an hour later, Gordon got up and began pulling the furniture back against the walls—explaining it was a family tradition—they always liked to dance on Christmas Eve.

"I can't dance!" the reporter laughed as Mary pulled him from the chair, their bodies melding together. Somehow, his feet knew the steps and he found himself waltzing with such precision that Gordon voiced his envy.

Soon after 10 o'clock, the Janicks said their goodnights, with Janice explaining she would have to be up early to get the turkey ready, and the young people were left alone.

"Tom will be coming for me soon," he reminded her.

"Right, you have that meeting. How long will it take?"

"I don't know, he didn't say."

"Then perhaps we should get our suitcases unpacked, we'll be tired when we get back."

"You're not going with me," he said following her down to the landing where the suitcases had been left.

"Oh yes I am! You might need me."

"I can't imagine why, but I guess there won't be any harm in it," he replied, knowing it would be fruitless to argue. As soon as he said this despair filled his mind, concerned he might be subjecting Mary to danger.

She took him down to the basement, unlike any basement he had ever seen—a lot like the top floor, fully decorated and furnished. She opened the door to a spacious and tastefully decorated guest room, explaining it was her younger sister's old room before she moved away from home. Mary showed him where the bathroom was and left him, going into the next room calling out that he could hang his clothes in the closet.

Ten minutes later, she returned for him. They went back upstairs and he was about to say he had changed his mind when he caught the familiar odour of tobacco. Before he had a chance to warn Mary, a cold draft brushed their skin, bringing goose bumps to her arms. Unsure of what to expect, she watched as the wispy outline of a ghostly figure took shape before them. This was the first time she had seen Tom since the mirror episode, but she recognized him instantly.

"Don't be afraid, Mary," the old angel said gently.

The eerie voice took her off guard as the angel swept the top hat from his head displaying a shoulder-length ponytail. Mary grabbed Oliver's arm even as her mind processed the uncanny thought that this … apparition … possessed an amazing head of silvery hair.

"I'm Tom Watson, Mary, Oliver's guardian angel. The spirits of Ross Bay have sent me to escort you to the council meeting."

"Right now?" she gasped, her knees shaking with excited fear. She began to object but her words trailed off into the inky blackness. She felt the telltale cold wind brush her face and arms and the unfamiliar gates of Ross Bay Cemetery appeared before them.

Oliver slipped his arm protectively about her shoulders shielding her from the cold wind and, hopefully, everything else.

"I'm scared," she whispered. "What's happening?"

"So am I," he admitted, hearing the raging sea pound on the rocky coastline nearby and wondered what they were waiting for.

Mary snuggled in tighter and Oliver felt her body shudder. She whimpered as a loud creaking noise answered their concern. The cemetery gates began to swing slowly open and Mary shivered again, clutching his arm even tighter. A startled night owl flew past, hooting what seemed like a warning. Oliver, noticing Tom had disappeared, coaxed her through the open gateway and into the graveyard, where he had stood twice before.

As they stepped forward, the cemetery filled with warm sunshine, the wind dropped to a gentle breeze, and flowers and colourful shrubbery appeared. Mary relaxed slightly, but tensed again as the spirits of Ross Bay's long dead emerged from nearby graves.

A group of about a dozen smiling apparitions, both male and female, quickly materialized into wispy human forms. Wearing all manner of curious costumes from earlier times and ethnic backgrounds, they moved closer all talking together.

"My word, they're real!" Mary gasped.

"No we're not real," Tom Watson's voice boomed, "we're spirits and angels, ghosts of another time, my dear."

Promptly at eleven o'clock, a trumpet fanfare sounded in the distance and all the ghostly figures fell silent and turned to face southward. Oliver and Mary followed their example.

In the blue southern sky appeared two very bright lights that appeared to be large stars except they were growing larger. At that moment, the lights changed direction and zoomed toward them.

"Our guests from California and Massachusetts have arrived, Oliver," Tom explained. "They're here for your inauguration ceremony. Let me introduce them. This is William Rushmore from Boston," he said, turning to the first form—dressed completely in white and materializing in front of them. Then a smaller form, also in white, materialized. "This is May Brown from San Francisco. They are here because you have caused us a special problem, son, one that must be resolved."

As Tom spoke, William Rushmore took the lady spirit's elbow and steered her toward a large, raised gravestone just off to the left. They floated effortlessly past, seeming to nod at Oliver and Mary—who both felt an extraordinary sense of negative energy emanating from the woman. The vague outlines of the two ghostly faces were almost completely shrouded by white hoods and their bony fingers clasped the hoods tightly closed. Mary's blood ran cold and her eyes flicked nervously over the ghostly gathering as icy beads of perspiration formed on her forehead.

"Send that girl away," a woman's voice rang through the stillness. "She has no standing here!" It was the voice of a very old lady and it belonged to the spirit of May Brown.

As Mary felt her body lifting from the ground, panic welled in her throat and she tried to scream. Desperately, she held onto Oliver, but the force was too strong and even as he applied all his strength they both knew it was useless.

"Leave her alone! Put her down!" he screamed desperately.

"Leave her be, May!" Rushmore growled and the frightened girl's form was lowered to the ground. "She's here as the guest of an angel, you have no right to scorn her. Mr. Watson, read the charges against Oliver Ryan."

"It has been charged," Tom Watson began, "that you, Angel Ryan, have fallen in love with a girl from another time, namely, Mary Janick."

"Take his power away!" a different female voice, declared testily.

Cackling ominously, May Brown nodded her head vigorously in agreement. Her hood eased back on her head revealing a milky-white skull with transparent skin and bedraggled long silvery hair. A hooked nose and broken teeth completed the picture of this grossly ugly apparition and Oliver wondered why she was so important.

Mary winced and buried her face in Oliver's chest.

"You're no angel, madam," the reporter asserted, "have some compassion."

"Don't you dare talk to me like that, you weakling," May screamed rising from her seat, "or I'll change you into a toad or worse! I enjoy scaring the bejabbers out of people!"

"Please be silent, dear lady," Rushmore pleaded, seeming to have some unexplained respect for the lady, until he added, "or I'll banish you to invisibility forever!"

William Rushmore had been the Chief Angel of all the Americas for longer than anyone cared to remember and his words were law in each and every churchyard and burial place in this jurisdiction. He was gentle and kind but the rebellious May Brown was testing his patience to the limit.

"I'll do what I want, you stuffy old party pooper," May retaliated, zooming off into the trees.

Shaking his head, Rushmore raised his arm then slowly brought the pointing finger down to the seat beside him. Kicking and fighting unseen forces, May again appeared beside him, her lips moving but no sound was heard.

"Right, Mr. Watson, let's get on with this," Rushmore continued with a smile. "I'll deal with Mrs. Brown later."

"Well, sir, we made Oliver Ryan into a mortal angel for all eternity. He seemed to be the perfect candidate with no family or friends—a loner with an untouched soul—his emotions had never been tapped. I watched over him closely, sir. He was perfect until he visited the year 2000 and met Mary Beth Janick!"

Mary had been listening closely and, finally with her fears controlled and fighting spirit awakened, she stood confidently with her arms crossed in front of her. She was ready to fight for her man until she felt Oliver's hands on her shoulders.

"Easy honey," he whispered, "let Mr. Watson finish, please."

There was a tenseness in her body that he recognized but she kept silent and a tear rolled down her cheek as he took her hand.

"I won't let them take you from me, I won't!" she muttered defiantly.

Watson shook his head and continued. "You see our dilemma, sir, we cannot part them, they are as one."

"Yes," sighed the Chief Angel, "I can see there's a strong attachment, but we can't have all our plans disturbed by a mere mortal."

"Can we offer suggestions, sir?" a raspy voice called out.

"Hmm that's highly irregular, but I shall permit it in this case."

Dissenting violently, May Brown bounced wildly on her seat as Mary uneasily waited, thankful that Mr. Rushmore was able to hold the maddened spirit under his control.

"We could put her on probation," an eerie voice proffered. "Love, in her time, is a very fickle emotion."

"I vote we give her no special status," the grating tone of a long-dead judge interrupted. "Make Angel Ryan responsible for his own indiscretions."

"And the penalty," Rushmore asked, "if he breaks our laws?"

"Take his powers away and send him back to the mortals."

"Sorry friend, that can't be done, he must always remain an angel. Remember his is a special case."

Oliver sighed with relief, his angel status and powers were safe, it seemed. A tinkle of laughter arose from the gathering and the voice of a child was heard.

"You could banish him to the weather department, if he misbehaves!" the child giggled.

"Yes, yes," many ghostly voices laughingly agreed, "banish him to the weather department, forever!"

"He can help the mortals sort out global warming!" another cried.

"You agree with that proposition, Angel Watson," Rushmore asked with a chuckle. Receiving a confused shrug in reply, he continued, "Then so be it, the matter is closed. Now what about your tenure, Mr. Watson, I believe you requested an extension?"

"Yes, that is correct," replied Oliver's guardian angel.

"I think that's a good idea," said Rushmore, frowning at Oliver and Mary. "I believe they're going to need your guidance for a while longer. You have until mid-January to decide.

Darkness now began to envelop the gathering. A decision had been made and the ghostly figures moved silently back to their resting places beneath marble and granite headstones. The shrouded figures of William Rushmore and May Brown rose into the air and faded slowly away into stars that zoomed toward the heavens. Oliver and Mary were alone with Tom Watson as the darkness became complete.

In the blink of an eye, they found themselves back in the Janick kitchen and Mary quickly sat down, feeling suddenly rather light-headed. Time had indeed stood still—the clock on the wall pointed its hands at 10:45 and steam still rose from their coffee mugs. Mary touched the dampness on her cheek from the tears she'd shed at the cemetery, and knew she hadn't been dreaming.

"How long has your family lived here, Mary?" Oliver asked.

"Over 30 years ago, since mom and dad were married, why?"

Oliver's angel senses were already at work probing deep below the home's foundations. He could feel the potent energy of an angry spirit impatient to be free from the loneliness of its secret burial place.

The spirit belonged to an innocent vagrant murdered by a bullying lawman in 1916 Everett. His grave had been hidden away in shame outside of town on a barren lot—no headstone had ever marked the place, no reverence or pity had ever been displayed for this poor soul and somehow he'd laid buried undisturbed since that time. Now, this mysterious spirit seemed to have a score to settle and tonight it found the presence of an angel a particularly exciting stimulant.

"What are you thinking?" Mary interrupted his thoughts, going to the sink to wash her mug.

"I'm not sure," he murmured, not wanting to alarm her. Coming to his feet, he handed his mug into her outstretched hand.

They went quietly downstairs, whispered their goodnights in the hallway wrapped in each other's arms and went into their rooms.

Oliver went over to the small bedroom window and looked out. Naval ships decorated with Christmas lighting created a scene of peace and tranquillity where lumber mills once stretched along the shoreline. He could feel the pain of the city's ghosts who once lived on the turbulent waterfront where family men fought timber barons for fair pay and others made enemies that lasted a lifetime—bankers became kings and ruled with greed and harshness—and yet Everett survived.

Sleep eluded the young reporter, feeling the strangeness of the firm modern mattress as he stared up at the ceiling, wondering what tomorrow would bring.

All of a sudden, Mary's muffled scream sent a shudder down his spine and he leapt out of bed. Eyes flashing and alert, he hurtled through the wall into her room. Crouching in the corner, her face contorted in fear, she faced a hissing, snarling spirit which looked more like a wild animal than a human. Its fiery energy bounced off the walls and ceiling as its writhing movements were captured in the soft light of the bedside lamp.

Oliver's glowing form began to materialize in the middle of the room and Mary, peeking over arms wrapped tightly around her knees, whimpered as the fight between angel and angry spirit began. Reeling drunkenly, Oliver grabbed the air for support as the spirit struck blow after blow, sending a shower of sparks in its wake, slowly losing energy on Oliver's unflinching form.

"Forgive and rest in peace forever," Oliver whispered.

Mary heard the reporter's whisper and, almost instantly, the spirit's fire fizzled and died, falling as dust at his feet and dissipating.

Fear lingered in Mary's mind as Oliver helped her back into bed, covered her with the blankets, and kissed her tears away. Turning out the light, he touched her brow, swiftly erasing the memory of the last 15 minutes. Listening in the darkness, her soft breathing soon told him sleep had returned.

Chapter 14

Awakened by the clanging of pots and pans, Oliver smiled when he heard the radio cranking out Christmas music. A tap at his door revealed Janice—she held out one of the steaming mugs.

"Good morning, Oliver, and Merry Christmas," she said cheerily.

"How come I don't get that kind of treatment, mother?" her husband called good-naturedly from the stairs.

A door opened and Mary appeared in the hallway loosely draped in a dressing gown and looking quite bedraggled.

"Merry Christmas, Mom!" She gave her mother a quick kiss on the cheek and took the other coffee cup from her hand.

Janice smiled but her eyebrows raised as her daughter moved quickly past her and went to sit on Oliver's bed.

"Mary Beth Janick," she chuckled, "your grandmother would have a fit if she were here!"

"Well, she's not here and this is the year 2000 in case you had forgotten," she winked at Oliver.

"Breakfast's ready!" Gordon called. "Come on, time to stop messing about people. We want to get at those presents, don't we!"

Over breakfast, Mary's folks questioned Oliver's occupation and listened with interest when Mary told them of his latest assignment.

"You're investigating ghost stories?" Janice repeated. "Well, maybe you should start right here, Oliver." She told of the strange happenings which had been going on for years around their home—vases that moved, doors that locked and keys that went missing.

"We've been locked out of the house at least three times," Gordon added with a chuckle, "even the locksmith had a devil of a job opening the door last time."

Careful Mary, Oliver's thoughts shouted. *They mustn't know I'm an angel.* "There's probably a very logical explanation," he said aloud. "The house could be twisting with age and, excuse my bluntness, but you two could be getting a bit forgetful!"

"That's what Kate Reardon said," chuckled Janice. "Kate's a friend of ours who works for the *Everett Daily Journal*."

A lighter note touched the conversation as the breakfast dishes were cleared away and put in the dishwasher before the Janick tradition of opening Christmas presents after breakfast got under way. Mary insisted that her mother open the parcel from Oliver first, handing her the small package.

"They're beautiful!" she gasped, carefully removing the delicately embroidered Hungarian lace pillow cases. "I shall treasure these, thank you, Oliver."

Oliver's turn came next. Untying a brightly wrapped small box from Mary, he stared in wonder at the calculator. "It's just what I needed," he murmured as his mind pondered what this odd-looking contraption with the numbers and buttons could do. Pressing the ON button, he blinked when the digital display lit up, staring in amazement as the numbers changed on the little display panel each time he pressed a button.

To save him embarrassment, Mary reached over and slapped his hand. "You can play with it later," she giggled, handing her father his present from Oliver.

"Well open it, you silly old fool," Janice chastised her husband as he held it up first and rattled it before tearing off the wrapping.

"It's a pipe and case," said Gordon, his voice faltering as he took the objects out of their special box. "This is an antique, lad. They stopped making these in 1915. Where the heck did you find it?"

Realizing he'd bought the presents at the market in Seattle when they were back in 1916, Oliver wasn't quite sure how he should respond. Again, Mary's quick action saved him.

"We found both your presents at the Pike Street Market in Seattle," she explained. "They have amazing stuff there."

"Well, daughter," her father whispered solemnly, "your mother has a surprise for you."

Watching curiously, Oliver noticed the misty dampness of Janice's eyes as she handed her daughter an old-fashioned tea cozy.

"A tea cozy, mother?"

"It was your grandmother's, look inside, dear."

Mary held her breath as she spread the folds of the tea cozy and nestled inside found a plain golden locket. A heavy sigh escaped her lips. "Mother, that's Great-Grandma Bentley's locket!"

"Open it, honey," her mother's voice quivered as she watched Mary fumble with the tiny catch.

Finally, she was able to open it and, for the first time in her life, Mary saw the inside of her grandmother's most treasured possession. Eyes wide, she stared at a picture that could easily have been an image of herself.

"That's your great-grandmother holding my mother," Janice explained, her fingers stopping a tear as it ran down her cheek. "Now look at the other side. That man has never been identified. Your great-grandmother would only say it was the picture of an angel!"

Mary gasped. The man in the picture was none other than Oliver. He was even wearing his glasses.

"Could I see that, please?" The reporter held out his hand and Mary watched him closely as he, too, stared at the image.

"Those pictures could easily be you two," murmured Janice. "The likeness is uncanny."

"It's just a strange coincidence, Mrs. Janick," Oliver laughed. "Here I am investigating ghost stories and you think you've got two of them sitting here in your dining room!"

The mood lightened as the reporter took control of the conversation. Around 10:30, following another family tradition, they put on their coats and left for the Christmas morning church service. Parking the car, the Janicks exchanged Christmas greetings with friends, introducing Oliver as they crossed the snow-covered sidewalk of Hoyt Avenue and climbed the stairs of the modernized Trinity Episcopal Church. It was almost full to capacity but Gordon somehow managed to find four seats in the centre aisle with an unobstructed view of the magnificent stained-glass window.

During the service, Oliver and Mary held hands under the folds of their coats and sang from a single hymn book, their voices blending in harmony and filling the air with the sweetest sounds Trinity Church had ever heard. The congregation around them fell silent as the choirmaster's baton brought the choir down to a gentle murmur.

When only the voices of Oliver and Mary remained, a strange humming sound, keeping perfect tune, seemed to float down from the high rafters. People sank to their knees and prayed aloud as the rector searched his mind for an explanation. Even the organ fell silent and still the wonderful sound filled the church. Only the eyes of Oliver and Mary could see the host of spirits floating overhead in joyful celebration.

"I didn't know you could sing like that," Mary whispered as they completed the hymn and sat down.

"Neither did I," he muttered. "I've never sung an in-tune note in my life!"

"Let us pray," the rector's voice droned.

Snowflakes were everywhere, sticking to cold surfaces, as the eager well-wishers lined the sidewalk leading from the church. Mary was well known to most of them and word was getting around about her guest. She made the introductions presenting an embarrassed Oliver to their many family friends and acquaintances.

Waiting for them by their car, Kate Reardon watched the Janick family approach, her interest peaked. *Who is this studious-looking stranger with the remarkable voice?* she wondered. "Merry Christmas, Mr. and Mrs. Janick," she called as they approached. "Are you going to share this singing stranger with the rest of us, Mary?"

"You have something in common, Kate, Oliver is a newspaper man!" Janice replied, hugging the young woman. "Can you come for lunch? Follow us home then, and Mary will introduce you properly."

A short drive later, the elder Janicks went ahead to start lunch while Mary and Oliver stood talking to Kate out on the sidewalk. Oliver could feel the vibrant, inquisitive nature of the attractive young reporter, her eyes twinkling with laughter as she shot questions at him. Behind those eyes, he was aware of a gentle nature and tenacious drive. Care would have to be taken to guard his secret from this one.

"What's your speciality?" Kate asked, curiosity getting the better of her. "Do you get to interview many important people?"

"No, I'm merely a court reporter," he replied, "unless they're on trial for murder I wouldn't even know them!"

"Oh, boring stuff!" she grimaced, her body shaking in a feigned shiver. "Why are we standing out here freezing?" she asked with a laugh, heading toward the door.

"You *were* just a court reporter, Oliver," Mary reminded him as they trooped up the stairs, "now he's also investigating ghosts."

"Here in Everett?" Kate squealed, stomping her boots on the outside mat before stepping in and removing them. "Can we work together on it?"

"No, to both questions," Oliver laughed. He gently pushed Mary farther into the room and closed the door.

"Thank goodness for that," Janice commented. "I'd be scared to death if I saw one."

"Do you believe in ghosts, Mary?" Kate asked.

"Yes I do, but I believe in angels, too, don't you?"

"Not really."

"Me neither, honey," Gordon piped up behind them. "If there were one around here, it would fix that basement lock for me!"

Mary glanced over at Oliver as they took seats around the table. His impish grin told her he had mischief on his mind as he silently designed a simple demonstration.

"I think you're imagining the door problems, Gordon," he commented. "Think positive for a moment, ask for help and then go try it again."

"There's a test for you, Mr. Janick," Kate giggled, "why don't you try it."

Closing his eyes, Gordon entered into the spirit of the game, thinking hard of his problematic basement door and letting his mind call for help.

"There, that should have done it," he said with a chuckle, opening his eyes again.

"Well, go try it," his wife urged, passing a plate of sandwiches around, then pouring the coffee.

Gordon left the room at the same moment Kate's fingers searched her handbag for her car keys—frowning when she couldn't find them.

"They must be in my coat pocket," she murmured. "Excuse me."

Leaving her chair, she went to the coat closet and searched her pockets. A frown appeared on her face as her search came up empty. Frustrated and, now growing worried, she returned to her seat.

"Hey Janice, come look at this," Gordon called from the basement landing. "The door works perfectly now!"

Winking at Oliver, as her mother scurried off to the basement, Mary watched Kate frantically search through her handbag again, until she had all the items in her lap.

"Darn it, I must have lost them in the snow," she groaned in annoyance.

"Now that's a miracle," Gordon laughed, as he and Janice appeared together in the doorway. "That dang door works perfectly. I guess there is an angel in our house after all!"

Mary, almost choking on her sandwich, kicked Oliver's leg under the table. *That was cute,* her mind whispered, *now what about Kate's keys?*

A worried look was spreading over Kate's face as she returned all the items to her handbag and stood up.

"I'd better go look for them outside," she muttered.

"I'll help you," Gordon offered, going to get their coats.

"Just a minute," said Janice, "why don't *you* try asking an angel for help, Kate?"

"I don't think so," Kate laughed, "that door thing was just a coincidence."

"You're afraid to try it," Mary goaded her.

Always independent and unafraid to take a dare, Kate turned back.

"All right, if it amuses you," she chuckled, "but I'm sure it won't work in this case."

Gordon took over the proceedings as the others watched.

"Close your eyes," he said, "think positively and ask for help in finding your keys."

Closing her eyes, Kate clutched her bag in both hands. As her mind called for help, a gentle feeling of peace came over her.

"Right," Gordon's voice reflected his excitement, "now go check your pockets again."

Smiling as if in a trance, Kate complied, feeling in all the pockets before shaking her head.

"Now your handbag," he insisted.

Going back to her chair, she picked up her handbag. Instantly, a tingling sensation ran though her fingers. Suddenly she was not so sure of herself as she emptied the contents onto her lap—lipstick, wallet, credit cards, cellphone, other items of makeup, followed by pen, notebook, business cards and … her car keys.

"Oh my goodness," Janice gasped, "there really are angels!"

"I must have missed them when I looked before," said Kate finding some moisture on her hand and picking up her napkin.

"No you didn't," Gordon whispered, "those keys are wet, look they're dripping water onto the tablecloth."

Answers to the puzzling questions didn't come easily to the Everett reporter. Lost for words, her training to observe facts and make logical deductions left her nowhere to turn.

"Help me, Oliver," she whispered, "there has to be an explanation."

"Keep an open mind, Kate," he replied grinning, "and believe!"

Driving home later, she smiled to herself as the first lines of a newspaper story ran through her head. Had she really seen a demonstration of the presence of angels or had she been the subject of a wild Christmas prank by the fun-loving Janick family?

Soon Kate's inquisitive mind led her back to Oliver, his assignment and his wonderful singing. There was something strangely peaceful about his soft, gentle voice and warm, steady gaze. She promised herself to check him out on the office computer when she returned to work tomorrow.

Christmas Day, with its glorious dinner referred to as 'turkey and all the trimmings' gave Oliver a good opportunity to get to know Mary and her family better, affording him many new experiences. Feeling part of a family was beginning to grow on the mortal angel and he found he was enjoying every moment. He knew, however, that work beckoned both he and Mary—holidays would soon be over and their problem would surface again.

The weather cleared a bit the next day and sunshine tempered the cold biting wind melting most of the snow on the roads and sidewalks. It was a regular work day for Everett, except schools were still closed, and so they decided to go for a walk. They wandered the streets near Mary's home and Oliver asked questions about modern houses and things they saw in the neighbourhood. Finally, they found themselves at Niles Park. Not a single human footstep disturbed the white carpet as they moved along its pathways.

Suddenly, Oliver stopped. Straining to hear, he heard a distant echo—a cry for help.

"What is it?" Mary asked.

"Hush, you can't hear it."

The cry came louder and Oliver closed his eyes visualizing the figure of Margo Lane in the basement of the newspaper offices in Seattle. She was moving a box containing old framed headline stories of murderers, politicians, and worse, when one of the framed pictures crashed to the floor.

From beneath the broken glass, a wisp of vapour floated upwards as the evil spirit of Captain Jonas Longbow was released. His cackling laughter sent Margo stumbling backwards as a bearded head without a body materialized. With a pipe clasped firmly between blackened teeth, the floating head moved slowly toward her. Chills ran down her spine and freezing cold air swept through the basement as she began to scream.

Taking Mary's hand, he growled, "Hold on, we're needed urgently."

Back at the Janick house, Kate stopped by to visit Mary and Oliver and Janice met her at the door.

"I believe they were going for a walk over toward Niles Park," Janice informed her. "They should be easy enough to find."

"I'll find them," Kate replied, heading back to the car. Speeding around the block, she skidded to a stop at the park entrance where she noticed two sets of footprints in the snow. "Okay, where are you two?" she called, going to follow the tracks. Suddenly, she jerked to a halt—the footprints had disappeared leaving the soft snow undisturbed.

Chapter 15

As Mary and Oliver arrived at the basement of the *Courier,* the free-floating head of Jonas Longbow was screaming a tirade of wild abuse at Margo. Now, with this sudden interruption, Longbow instantly recognized an angel had come to rescue her. Intent on intimidating this female creature who had awakened him from his long sleep, he flew into a distant corner shooting bolts of lightning from his eyes.

Shielded by Oliver, Mary hurried to Margo's assistance, but unable to reach an exit, they daren't move. Huddled under a table, she held the distraught girl tightly as the evil spirit continued its ranting. Both girls flinched at each crash and bang as Oliver and the frightening apparition moved between the shelves in the immense basement. Unlike the sobbing girl, Mary was very conscious of the fact that Oliver was in a fight for his life, but she kept positive thoughts about good defeating evil in her mind, no matter how corny it seemed.

Beneath his feet, Oliver felt the crunch of broken glass. Glancing down, he saw the offending picture staring at him and snatched it up. Sharp glass sliced into his finger splashing drops of blood onto the picture. The effect was immediate and dramatic—no evil spirit can withstand the blood of an angel. Slowly, Jonas Longbow's head lost its substance, the flying lightning bolts stopped and the vile abuse turned into an eerie moaning that faded into the distance. Oliver had won his battle, the evil spirit had retreated to another hiding place and Margo was safe … for now.

Sweating profusely and his blood racing from exertion, Oliver returned to find the girls looking expectantly out from under their hiding place.

"Has he gone?" Mary whispered.

"For now, but I believe I shall meet this Captain Jonas Longbow again. I fear this battle is not over yet."

They took the frightened girl upstairs to her office, away from the inquisitive eyes of passing staff. Sitting down, she wiped her eyes and slowly recovered her composure, ready to ask questions.

"What was that thing? Where did you two come from?"

"I heard your scream for help," Oliver murmured, "and that object was the spirit of an evil man named Captain Jonas Longbow."

"Are you okay, do you think it would be best to go home, Margo?" Mary asked.

"No, I'll be all right but you could call security. I want that basement cleared out today. Would you go with me to the washroom, Mary, I don't feel like going in there alone."

"Certainly I will; come on," Mary replied. As Margo put a cold towel to her face, Mary asked a question she was pretty sure of the answer. "Do you still want to go ghost hunting with Oliver?"

"No! Certainly not!" she declared. "Never, never, never!"

"Better now?" Oliver grinned as the girls returned.

Pale and drawn, Margo nodded uncertainly. Her experience in the basement had petrified her. Wary of being alone, she glanced over at the burly security guard standing guard in the doorway and reached for their hands, thanking them profusely.

"You're both angels," she added with quivering lips.

Mary gave the girl one last hug and, taking Oliver's arm, they turned and walked away down the empty hallway toward the main entrance. Oliver took her arm and looking around, whispered, "We're going home."

When she blinked, the bright sunshine again reflected off the snow in Niles Park. Standing for a moment to watch a squirrel running along a tree branch, they continued walking on through the park and out onto the street. They were almost home when Kate's car pulled up to the sidewalk beside them.

"Jump in you two," she called. "I've something to show you."

Making a u-turn, she drove back to the park and stopped the car where she had seen their footprints. A light dusting of snow had fallen during the time it took to walk to the other side of the park, but their footprints were still clearly visible.

"That's where you both went into the park. These footprints are mine," Kate said, a frown creasing her forehead as she turned to face them, "now please explain this to me."

She followed the footprints toward the trees and pointed to the place where they stopped. Her gloved hand flashed to her mouth stifling her involuntary cry. She looked down at the two sets of fresh footprints. *These are different,* she thought, *they're not covered by snow like the others.* She followed them on through the park, finally arriving at the other sidewalk.

"I'd swear those footprints weren't there half an hour ago," she exclaimed.

"Well, a flying saucer didn't take us away," Mary laughed. "I can assure you of that, so how do you think you missed us?"

Kate was obviously baffled and could find no logical explanation. Had she inadvertently stumbled on the story of the century, where two people could disappear like magic and return to the very same place? *No, no,* Kate reasoned with herself, *the people of Everett would never accept such a story. I'd be the laughing stock of the newspaper world and besides, I know who Mary is.* "Maybe I'm losing it," she said aloud, trying to smile, "but this is very confusing. Can I give you a ride home?"

"No, thanks, we're all right," Oliver replied. "We like to walk."

"Are you sure you're okay?" Mary asked.

Nodding, Kate climbed into her car and slowly drove away, waving before going around a corner. Her brain was still searching for answers as she drove back to the office. She felt sure there was something she'd missed, some important clue. Daylight was fading fast as Kate parked her car and entered the building. Many of the staff had already left and she sat down at her computer. Staring at the screen, she wondered where to begin her investigation.

Mary and Oliver held hands as they walked back to the house for the second time.

"I wonder what poor Kate is thinking?" Mary commented, feeling his fingers stiffen.

"She's thinking of me," he replied, dropping his voice to a whisper as some people approached. "Her mind is talking to an angel!"

Mary looked up at him and grinned. "You never cease to amaze me!"

On her desk, Kate's eyes strayed to a page of copy bearing the next day's headline, 'Canadian Fishermen Lost in Storm.' Fingers flashing over the keyboard, she quickly pulled the article up onto her computer screen—all thoughts of Oliver gone as she read the report.

If there really are angels, she thought, *I sure wish they'd go help these poor men.*

"What is it, darling?" Mary asked, as Oliver stopped dead in his tracks as if listening.

"Fishermen—Kate's calling for an angel. I can hear her thoughts but where are they?" he murmured. "Keep talking, Kate."

Kate continued reading. *"The fishing boat left from Port Moresby with four men aboard."*

"Hold on," Oliver announced, stepping behind a hedge, "we're heading for rough weather."

Rain and sleet lashed their faces as they materialized on the gale-swept dock at Port Moresby. Men with haggard faces stood at the windows of the small harbour building and stared at the mountainous waves pounding the coastline. Corrugated tin sheets rattled wildly above them as the wind tore at their fastenings.

"Wait here," Oliver screamed into her ear, pushing her inside the closest doorway.

Turning as the door banged shut behind her, she realized Oliver had gone.

"Where have you come from lassie? This ain't a good day for being outside," a gnarled old fisherman with a heavy Scottish brogue calmly commented. Not waiting for an answer, he placed a hot, steaming tin mug of black coffee into her hand and invited her to join the group of men who were sitting around an old pot-bellied stove.

Invisible to human eyes, Oliver hovered over the giant waves, searching the dark waters below for the fishing boat. He saw the rescue cutter which kept disappearing as the spray of each huge wave momentarily engulfed it.

Farther out, farther out, he heard Tom's voice tell him. Flying westward, he finally spotted the small red boat with its human cargo of terrified men. Suddenly, his body lit up like a flare hovering over them—a light seen almost two miles away by the coast guard cutter.

"We found them!" the shortwave radio crackled in the harbour shack, and the worried friends cheered. "We've seen their flare."

Half an hour later like a giant, bucking, war horse the coast guard pulled alongside the small boat and took the fishermen safely aboard.

"It's a good job you had that large flare," the coast guard captain shouted, "or we would never have found you."

The men back at the shack on Port Moresby's dock listened carefully as the open radio connection relayed the crackling rescue and ensuing conversation. Looks of amazement passed quickly around the group.

"They didn't have any large flares," one old sailor gruffly commented, kicking the box he was sitting on. "They're still here in this box!"

Suddenly, Oliver burst into the shack, grinning as Mary went to him but not before saying goodbye to the men.

"Come on honey, we're going home," he said, pulling her outside into the wind.

"Where are they going?" gasped one of the seamen, as several of them went to the windows, but they were unable to see anything.

Branches brushed their heads as they arrived back on Warren Avenue. Grinning, Oliver let Mary smooth his hair down before they resumed their walk.

"Is this what the life of an angel is like?" she asked.

"You mean always being interrupted?"

"No, I mean saving people's lives and helping with their problems. I thought you weren't allowed to alter history?"

"I didn't alter history, Mary. We got there before history happened."

A freezing wind was blowing in from the waters of Port Gardener Bay as they reached the house and the warm air welcomed them when Mary opened the door.

"Did Kate find you?" her mother called as they hung up their coats.

"Yes, she did," Mary replied, trying to stifle her giggle.

Later, as they ate a tasty dinner of leftover turkey, Mary smiled to herself. *It seems Oliver has been completely accepted by my family. I wonder if we'll ever be able to tell them that he's an angel?*

When they finished, Gordon invited Oliver into the front room to watch the news. The TV intrigued him. *Things have come a long way from my world,* he thought. Although Mary had done her best to explain the technology, he still found it easier to change the channels with his mind, but he wasn't about to throw any surprises at Gordon.

A newsflash interrupted programming, saying the missing Port Moresby fishermen were rescued just hours before under mysterious circumstances. It gave no other details and announced it would have the full story on the 11 o'clock news.

Kate saw the same newsbrief on the monitor at work as she glanced up from her computer screen, causing an involuntary sigh of relief. She completed another project and then began to search for Oliver through the *Journal*'s archives.

As she typed his name into the search engine and hit enter, she waited, hoping that the dreaded phrase 'not found' wouldn't appear and, this time, it didn't.

This time, many pages of headings appeared … it seemed Oliver Ryan was a popular name. Scanning the first page of entries, she groaned, *this is going to be harder than I imagined.* Then, as a fleeting thought struck her, she added the word *angel* beside his name and hit enter again.

This time, the list changed slightly and as she read an entry near the top of the second page, her eyes widened in disbelief and a chill ran down her back. Quickly scanning the words which read, s*tory by Oliver Ryan, Seattle Courier, January 3, 1917,* she clicked on it. *Could there be another Oliver Ryan that long ago at the Courier?* She sat back in her chair, processing a jumble of thoughts and sighing as she waited for the slow connection.

Oliver has been on my mind all day, she reminded herself. *It was he who said she should keep an open mind when her car keys mysteriously returned and they were definitely his footprints in the park alongside Mary's that had suddenly disappeared—yes, they had both disappeared. Was Mary party to this mystery?*

Biting down on her pencil, her eyes strayed back to the news monitor as she remembered her wishful thought of asking an angel to help her. The pencil snapped when she saw the words, *unusual circumstances surround rescue in Port Moresby.*

Groaning, she spat out the wood splinters into her hand and disposed of them, giving up on that page and trying another idea. Her fingers worked over the keyboard, searching the newspaper's archives for a picture of Oliver this time.

"There must be a picture somewhere," she muttered, her eyes scouring the Oliver Ryan entries, but an hour later, with heavy eyes barely able to focus on the screen, she finally turned off her computer.

Running to her car, she climbed in and slammed the door. Shivering, she found her cold gloves and put them on as she turned the key in the ignition. Icy fingers of frost stretched across her windshield and she turned on the fan at full blast. Watching the wipers grind fiercely to clear her window, she felt the frustration of failure but she knew she couldn't give up … not yet.

Chapter 16

The Janick home had long been in darkness by the time Kate left the newspaper office in the early hours of the morning. Waking to freezing rain hammering on his bedroom window, Oliver listened as another winter storm battered the city.

"You won't be going very far today," Janice said over breakfast. "This weather looks set for the day."

"I could leave for Seattle," he said, "and be in Victoria on Friday."

Disappointment showed on the Janick's faces until their daughter whispered coyly, "No, he's not, we can get into the school today. I'm going to show him the halls of power!" She added quickly, "If I can borrow the car, Dad?"

"I suppose so, honey, but please be careful," Gordon replied. "We have another cold snap forecast and the roads could be treacherous by late afternoon."

"Thanks Dad, now seeing as we have some time, I'm going to show Oliver some of my historical bookmarks on the internet," said Mary beckoning to him.

"What are you talking about?" he asked when they were downstairs.

"Sorry, I had to tell them that to hide the fact you don't know anything about the internet. Think of this as another of your modern adventures, you'll be utterly amazed, trust me!" she replied with a giggle.

Later, as Mary backed the car out of the garage, Oliver asked her to go past the newspaper office. "I'm getting vibes that somebody is searching for me and I'm pretty positive it's Kate."

Crossing the busy junction at California Street, Mary recognized Kate's car in the *Journal*'s car park and pulled into a parking space.

"Are we going to see her?" she asked.

"You're not, honey, I want you to wait here."

"I wish you wouldn't," Mary pleaded, reaching over to touch him, but the passenger seat was empty. Looking desperately outside, she suddenly heard a voice in her head.

I won't be long, it said and she sent her thoughts loudly back to him. *I remember! I can communicate with you like we did on the train.*

Inside the *Journal* offices, Oliver's ghostly form stood behind Kate as she worked on the computer, eyes glued to the screen. He was fascinated but at least he knew what it was after Mary's lesson this morning. He watched her pen busily scribble down some notes then drop it to change to the keyboard. He picked up the pen and put it on the next desk. Still staring at the screen, her fingers searched blindly for it, to no avail.

"Drat," she exclaimed, having to take her eyes off the screen. "Now where has it gone?" Swinging her chair around, she searched the floor and then saw it on the other desk. Obviously puzzled, she reached to get it, passing her arm through Oliver's ghostly form. She gasped as a chill brushed the side of her body.

Grasping the pen, she rolled the chair back to the desk, wincing as the biting cold touched her flesh again. Goose bumps rippled across her shoulders and the hairs on her neck bristled with tension. Kate glanced at the computer and saw a picture had appeared. Her heart almost stopped when she recognized the images of Oliver, Mary and a woman named Margo Lane at the funeral of Margo's father in June of 1926.

Shivering involuntarily, she thought she felt an icy hand on her shoulder and her blood ran cold. Unable to speak, her eyes remained locked on the screen and the picture faded. The text began to pulsate hypnotically. Her body relaxed, releasing a sigh of contentment as the memory of Oliver's secret slipped from her grasp. The pen in Kate's hand tugged her gently to her notebook and wrote, *Angels are real,* on the now-clean page.

Turning to leave, Oliver noticed Kate's earrings and had an idea. Touching each of them, tiny gold angels appeared, sparkling as they dangled from the gold hoops.

My gifts to you, dear girl, he said silently to her. *If you ever need me just touch your earring and I will know.*

Where are you, my darling? Mary's thoughts came screaming at him.

"Right here," he laughed from beside her.

"Did you see Kate?"

"Yes."

Wheels skidded as she pulled the car away from the curb and into traffic making its way up Grand toward 25th. Parking in the back parking lot of the school with a dozen or so other cars, they walked through the slushy snow to the door. Seeing the hard-at-work janitors polishing floors, Mary waved and reminded Oliver to wipe his feet. They climbed the wide stairway to the second floor. Walking along the hallway, she stopped at the second door on the right and opened it.

"Is this where you teach?" he asked, picking up some familiar vibes as he entered the classroom.

Sensing his tension, she moved closer reaching out to him.

"Are you frightened?" he asked, taking her hand.

"No, but if I touch you I'll be able to see what you see, won't I?" she asked.

Oliver looked over at her and, in the silence, she suddenly felt a mixture of excitement and tension as the faintest of odours brushed her nostrils. Somewhere nearby, a door banged in the quiet building and she flinched. Glancing at Oliver, she followed his gaze to a desk in the back row.

"What is it?" she asked, her words tumbling out, yet extracting no reply from her companion.

"Hello Mary!"

The vibrant voice of the PE teacher, Todd Harper, destroyed the moment as he burst into the classroom. His dark flashing eyes had always given Mary an uncomfortable feeling. There was something frightening about this man and she transmitted these thoughts to Oliver. T-shirt bulging with muscle, he reached out his hand to the Seattle reporter, smirking at the bespectacled figure of Mary's studious companion. His recent advances, shunned by Mary, compelled Harper to prove he was superior to this stranger. Confident of his strength, he gripped Oliver's hand before Mary had a chance to introduce them.

"Pleased to meet you," he sneered. Expecting the reporter to wince as he applied more pressure, he soon realized his plan had gone awry. His face turned pale as Oliver returned his powerful grip with one of steel, shooting sharp pains up his arm.

"Easy there, fella," Harper hissed, prying his hand away. "You're going to break my hand!" Released, he quickly backed away, mumbling excuses as he hurried out of the room and disappeared down the hall, glancing furtively over his shoulder.

A door banged shut and they were alone again. Oliver went over and closed Mary's door. Immediately, a hacking cough sounded from the back of the room just feet away. Startled, Mary moved closer to him as they watched a misty shape appear sitting on a desk in the back row. It slowly materializing in the form of a tall, thin boy of about 16-years dressed in a double-breasted black suit with knee-length pants and a white shirt, recognized by both of them as being from mid-to-late 19th century.

"Who are you, son?" Oliver asked softly.

"Don't be stupid, sir," the apparition snapped irritably, "my father's the banker and I am William Butler Junior."

"Why are you here?" Oliver continued, ignoring the boy's attitude.

"I'm always here, you fool. I'm trying to finish my education!"

"Oliver," Mary whispered, "no one likes to sit in that seat. My students say it's drafty and weird."

"You don't need to whisper, Miss Janick," the spirit hissed. "I'm responsible for making it cold and weird. This is *my* seat and no one else's!"

Out in the corridor, a curious Todd Harper cautiously made his way back to Mary's classroom. Hearing another voice, he furtively glanced up and down the empty hallway but saw no one. Moving closer, he pressed his ear against the wood. *Who are they talking to?* he wondered. His curiosity so strong, he slowly turned the doorknob, peeking through the crack. He could barely believe what he saw. Before he had time to think, his eyes met those of the boy and the ghost of William Butler Junior melted into a spiral of mist, shooting up to the ceiling where it hung as a hazy ball.

Harper shivered. What he thought he had witnessed was impossible. He let out his breath, but no sound came. Then he suddenly felt the sensation of being pushed from behind. The door flew open, banging against the wall, and Harper stumbled into the room landing on his knees in front of Mary. She jumped back in surprise.

Oliver had been aware of the intruder and realized the situation called for drastic action. It soon became evident that the effect of his actions, coupled with the strange events, were taking a toll on Harper who now curled into a fetal position. Violently rocking back and forth, he presented a frightening and grotesque picture. His face turned bright red and his eyes were wide with terror—he appeared to be screaming although no sound emanated from his wide open mouth.

Oliver's pointed finger stopped the violent motion and calmed the teacher instantly. Harper's eyes moved around the room and he got to his feet. His face was still red but Oliver had wiped his memory clean. Moving slowly toward the door, he turned and smiled, then said goodbye. There was a previously unknown friendliness in his smile and a new gentleness in his eyes. This Todd Harper was different and Mary watched in wonder as he silently left the room and closed the door quietly behind him.

"You've changed him," she whispered. "I hope it's permanent!"

"He was drowning in his own bitter thoughts," Oliver replied with a chuckle. "He'll be a better man from this day forward. You might even like him now."

"Highly unlikely!"

"And what about me, Angel Ryan?" young Butler's voice crashed through their thoughts, his anger rising again and making pictures on the wall rattle violently. Lights flashed on and off and sheets of paper whirled about the room. "I demand your help!" he continued before a bout of coughing suddenly racked the frail, ghostly body and he materialized again behind Mary's desk.

"All right Butler. I'm willing to help you crossover … your parents are waiting to see you," Oliver replied in a soothing manner. "Would you like to see them?"

"No!" he snarled defiantly. "My father never loved me, just get me away from this place!"

"Step away from me, Mary," Oliver whispered.

Mary felt the room's unusual silence as she watched Oliver disappear, a mere wisp of vapour floating in his place. She was completely alone. She glanced at the clock on the classroom wall, its second hand holding fast at fourteen minutes past eleven. Somehow, Oliver had placed her in a time warp and not a sound penetrated the eerie stillness.

Invisible to Mary, Oliver stood close by, his call to the dead summoning William's parents who floated along the thought waves of his mind sliding silently through the high school walls to appear before the two ghosts.

"You called Angel Ryan?" a hollow male voice rumbled. "You have my son trapped in here."

"No sir, I do not have him trapped, his soul has done that. My job is done now," Oliver replied. "It is you who need to convince the boy that you love him and will take him with you to the Hereafter."

"Oh, my baby, it's been so long!" the lady apparition moaned, reaching out to William. "We've missed you so much, Willie."

"You let death take me!" retorted the boy, pointing angrily at his father.

"No, son," the man's voice rumbled sadly, "it was a terrible day when you left us. Not one day has passed that we haven't thought of you. I had no control over your leaving."

"You lie!"

"Lying is only for the weak, my boy," his father's voice retorted abrasively, "and I was never weak!"

Mr. Butler's harsh logic struck hard at his son's bitter memory. Alone in the Afterworld, he had sought a measure of contentment and attached himself to the high school passing the time learning and watching the living deal with their ordinary lives. Although often bored due to their inferiority, in an effort to forget his bitterness he had discovered ways to amuse himself. Still, decades passed as he waited, not realizing his parents grieved over their separation.

"Please come with us Willie, we love you," pleaded his mother.

Oliver sighed with relief when the two adult figures held out their hands to the boy and he took them. Melded into one, they moved off through the wall. He could still hear the faint call of a thankful mother as the Afterworld swallowed the Butler family forever.

A rustle of papers suddenly lifting off the floor and neatly stacking themselves back on the bookcase, distracted Mary's attention as she patiently waited for Oliver to return. Picture frames again rattled as they returned to their positions. Then silence. Her heart leapt when the wall clock began to tick loudly and the ordinary sounds of the school filled the air once again. She closed her eyes and waited until she felt Oliver's arms encircle her waist.

"I'm back, honey," he whispered.

"Has William gone?" she asked.

"Yes, his parents came for him."

"Oh, I'm so relieved for the poor boy and it will be nice to have that desk back!" she exclaimed. "Now it's time to show you the rest of our school."

It was after three before they emerged from the building, returning to the car in sunshine but it was cold and the slushy sidewalk was freezing again making for difficult walking.

"Look at this lovely blue sky, are you sure you aren't able to control the weather?" she teased.

"I'm sure, in the Afterworld, being a weatherman appears to summon the most pity from my ghostly peers! Come on, take me to Pier One," he said taking her arm to traverse the icy driveway. "I'll show you some more history."

"No, thank you, Mr. Ryan, I've had enough excitement for one day. We're leaving tomorrow and I'd like to take mom and dad out for dinner tonight," she announced, pulling out of the parking lot.

"*We* aren't going anywhere; we both have to get back to work in a few days and I thought you said you had a lesson to prepare for Monday!"

"Are you forgetting about New Year's? We don't have to go to work until Tuesday and I'm going with you this weekend!" she declared.

"Watch out!" he yelled.

Mary turned her attention back to the road and screamed as the oncoming vehicle began to slide toward her. She tried to remember what to do on icy surfaces, desperately hoping there was a way to avoid the collision. Then, she too was skidding and she braced for the unavoidable crash. Mind-bending terror filled her brain as the car came close enough to see the fearful face of the other driver.

Oliver's eyes glowed and the screeching vehicles shuddered to a halt, inches away from a disastrous impact.

Sighing, Mary dropped her head onto the steering wheel and offered a silent prayer of thanks.

"You're very welcome, my love," he whispered.

Smiling weakly as realization struck, Mary held out her hand and Oliver kissed her fingers. A tapping on the window revealed a traffic patrolman, bringing her back to reality. He asked if they were all right and advised extreme caution then went to check on the other car.

"They're back!" Gordon shouted, peering outside and seeing the headlights turn into their driveway.

Nodding, Janice turned the oven up a notch, relieved they were home safely. There was no way she would be venturing from the warmth of her home after listening to the warning on the local radio station. Over the last hour, it had been giving a long list of accidents and fender-benders taking place on the highway and Everett's streets.

"We're home, Mom," Mary called from the back door.

"We were worried about you two, the radio says the roads are treacherous," Janice called.

"They're right and we're glad to be home," she agreed as they came into the kitchen. "Oh you've started dinner already, I was going to suggest we go out but probably better to stay home the way the roads are."

Later, Gordon offered to drive Oliver to Seattle the next morning but Janice breathed a sigh of relief when he wouldn't accept.

"Thanks, Dad, but we'll go by bus," Mary chuckled, "that way we can snuggle up together!"

"Behave yourself, Mary," Janice rebuked her daughter. "You're embarrassing Oliver. Where are you going, I thought you wanted to get ready for school, dear?"

Blushing, Oliver looked at the happy faces around him. He enjoyed the teasing and laughter and was becoming quite comfortable being around Mary's family. They were certainly making him feel welcome. Mary set about helping her mother dish up dinner while the men went to sit at the table.

"Mom, I'm going back to Seattle with Oliver for the weekend." She waited for her mother's reaction, and when there was none, she continued. "I think I'm in love with him, Mom. I've never felt this way about anyone before, it's really strange and I'm not sure what to do about it."

"Oliver seems to be a genuine guy, honey. We like him much more than any of your other boyfriends. Just give yourself time, dear. Get to know him. You have your whole life ahead of you."

"But that's just it, Mom, I don't. I'm almost 30 and my biological clock is ticking so fast it makes me frantic! I really do want to have kids and not when I'm too old to run after them!"

Her dad's voice asking about dinner interrupted their thoughts and her mother gave her a quick hug and kiss.

"You're a sensible girl, Mary, and we trust you to do the right thing. We want you to be happy and maybe Oliver is the right person for you—just enjoy each other and take your time. Now let's get dinner on the table before those men come out here to see what's holding it up!"

The next morning was clear and cold and, after a relaxed breakfast, Oliver said his goodbyes and thanks to the Janicks. Mary told them she'd be back Sunday night and they went out to their taxi.

"I just have to get my own apartment," she told Oliver as they walked to the car. "This arrangement with mom and dad is very convenient but life is getting far too complicated!"

"I thought you wanted a townhouse?" he replied.

"Well, I certainly need something," she muttered.

Fifteen minutes later, the taxi dropped them off at the Greyhound Bus ticket counter.

"Oliver, let's go straight to Victoria," she urged. "If we go back to your time we get to have Christmas again."

"Honey, no matter when we go back to my time, we will still have another Christmas because time is waiting for us and I don't go to work until Tuesday, whenever it comes! When you're ready to go home, we simply make it the day you need."

"This is all so confusing … whatever! I'm ready," she sighed, taking his arm. The cold breath of time brushed her face and they opened their eyes to 1916 Langley Street as dusk was falling.

She shivered as a Model T went by with its huge headlights and canvas roof, thinking how cold its passengers must be, then her attention was drawn to the wind-reddened face of a drayman urging his horses through traffic. She heard the roar of a steam engine over on Johnson Street and her eyes followed the sooty black smoke as it curled into the cold morning air from behind the low buildings.

Clothes, she thought frantically. *We're not dressed correctly!*

Glancing down, she was surprised to see she was wearing the clothes from her suitcase … her black-laced boots, black wool dress that brushed her ankles, and the winter coat they had purchased on her first visit. She looked at her image in a shop window and smiled at herself.

"Surprised?" Oliver asked. "I'm getting more used to this angel business, so I just added the right dress code. It didn't take much guessing; it was all in your suitcase!"

"I-I'm astounded," Mary stammered. "Your power seems to be unlimited … doesn't leave much to the imagination when you can dress me, too!"

"I don't know about that," he admitted, blushing. "I believe I'm still merely an amateur—I have much to learn!" Changing the subject quickly, he suggested they take their bags to the room and go uptown before the stores closed in an hour. He picked up his suitcase and started walking toward the hotel, stopping abruptly when Mary began to giggle. "Now what's so funny?"

"Why don't you save your energy and just send the bags to the hotel?" she said, shaking her head and putting her suitcase beside his.

"I'd forgotten," he said sheepishly.

Glancing up at the Temperance Hotel, he visualized his room and sent his thought waves hurtling at the bags.

"See they've gone!" Mary laughed. "I knew you could do it!"

"Don't get too excited yet," he replied, "I want to try another experiment. I'm going to transport you so you can check on them."

"Don't you dare lose me again like the time I walked back into the year 2000?"

"I didn't lose you, I just got the time mixed up a bit!"

A sudden rush of anxiety washed through her body. *If he loses me, will I wander through time like a ghostly entity, belonging nowhere, neither mortal nor part of the Afterworld?* "I'm not sure we should do this," she said aloud, but it was too late.

Clutching her handbag, she suddenly felt weightless and realized she was in the room and their luggage was right beside her.

"You've done it!" she cried. *Now bring me back, please Oliver,* her mind screamed. Standing with bated breath she waited, unaware that Constable Gray was talking to Oliver in the street below. She looked frantically outside but couldn't see him.

Oh, please take me back, Oliver! her mind shouted.

Five minutes ticked by, an eternity to the school teacher who paced the floor and continually checked the window. Finally, Harry walked off toward the police station and Oliver whisked her back to his side. He felt her tension as she hugged him.

"I couldn't bring you back sooner, honey," he whispered. "Harry Gray stopped to talk to me."

"Oh, is that what happened, you sure had me worried."

"Faith, my dear, you must have faith," Oliver chuckled.

For the next three days, with stores, many restaurants and pubs closed, they did a lot of walking and talking, celebrating a quieter Christmas this time around. Finding daytime activities became quite the winter challenge but Mary found a few historical places she could use in her classroom and she was able to teach Oliver a thing or two. Time went fairly quickly but by Wednesday, they were most eager for a change of pace. A noisy, jostling crowd met them when they appeared at the closed courthouse door on Wednesday morning.

Holding his arm, Mary stayed close beside him as he pushed through the crowd of soldiers, sailors, striking miners, and heavily perfumed ladies of doubtful profession. His press card gained them entry into the smoke-filled courtroom where local reporters grudgingly made space on the bench seat.

Glancing around, his gaze settled on a familiar face in the crowd of observers. The devilish evil spirit of Jonas Longbow had materialized in Victoria, grinning as he ducked out of sight.

"He's here," Oliver whispered, getting ready to take notes.

"Who is?"

"Jonas Longbow … all of him," he hissed.

"Oh no," Mary groaned, moving closer and shutting her eyes.

A bell rang and everyone rose as the court proceedings began. Taking his place, the judge scowled menacingly at the black-robed lawyers awaiting his pleasure.

"Bring in the prisoners," the court clerk called to the bailiff who opened the door beside him.

"Hang 'em all!" a voice shouted from the public benches.

The judge looked upward and two inky black dots under bushy eyebrows scoured the courtroom as an ominous silence prevailed.

"Bring in the prisoners," the bailiff's harsh voice repeated, his voice echoing through the empty corridors.

Dragged into the courtroom by uniformed guards, two young Indian boys moaned in terror as strong arms forced them into the prisoner's box. They took a crouched position keeping close—a vain attempt to hide from the unfriendly faces surrounding them.

"Stand up and be quiet, you heathens!" one of the guards growled. Apparently, knowing some English, the boys went quiet but remained clinging to each other.

The bespectacled clerk who made little effort to look at the accused, read the charges in a monotonous tone. Oliver's eyes, however, focussed unwaveringly on the dark, terrified faces peering from behind their confinement.

"How do you plead?" the voice droned on.

A disinterested court-appointed lawyer named Grimwold muttered, "Not guilty," half rising from his seat.

The charge was murder, a hanging offence, only supported by a constable who caught the young natives stealing boots from the body.

The real story of the murder of this Russian sailor was quite different—he'd been stabbed to death by a lone, drunken miner on Wharf Street in the shadows of the Hudson Bay dock. Trains shunting their carriages at the Johnson Street station had covered the noise of the fight and the murderer simply fled.

"Damning evidence," the prosecutor claimed, as the evil spirit of Jonas Longbow cast his wicked influence over the trial.

With no defence offered and their lawyer making no attempt to address the Court, Oliver decided to take a hand in the proceedings. Mary watched the wisp of vapour float upwards as the angel left Oliver's body and hovered over the shoulder of the boy's lawyer. She tried not to smile when she saw his white wig suddenly move.

Lawyer Grimwold swung around to face his attacker and, finding no one there, a look of startled surprise appeared on his face.

"Question the policeman," Oliver hissed into his ear.

Fixing his wig, he glanced nervously around again before facing the glowering judge.

"Well Mr. Grimwold, you have something to say?" the judge demanded.

"N-no, no sir," the lawyer stammered, as Oliver's unseen hand pushed his spectacles from his nose.

"Question the policeman!" Oliver shouted into his ear.

His brain jarred by the voice in his head, Archibald Grimwold began to shake uncontrollably. "That is … Q-question t-the policeman."

"Objection, My Lord," the prosecution shouted.

"Overruled!" The judge's eyebrows jerked upward, his voice rattling off the walls as his gavel crashed onto the block.

"Constable Bowers is recalled," the call rang through the corridors.

Grimwold tapped nervously on the desk as he waited. He was normally a paper tiger with no stomach for courtroom arguments, this case was supposed to be a mere formality. So far, it was anything but ordinary and, feeling quite out of his depth, his blood ran cold.

As the policeman took the stand, Grimwold heard the ghostly voice once again and his facial muscles twitched violently.

"T-the knife, constable," Grimwold repeated Oliver's words. "You found the knife?"

"No, sir."

"You looked for it?"

"No, sir, the water was close by."

"Was the body stiff and cold or was it warm?"

"Cold, sir."

Judge Harvey listened with growing interest. He almost lost his grim expression in a moment of amusement as the policeman squirmed under Grimwold's surprising line of questioning. He knew this lawyer and marvelled at his new confidence. He liked it.

Mary felt Oliver's elbow jab her ribs and knew he'd returned.

"Get on with it, man!" the judge rasped. "Make your point."

"Tell me, constable," asked Grimwold, trying to hear the voice in his head, but it seemed to have gone. He swallowed hard and continued, "D-do murderers normally wait for a body to go cold before stealing boots?"

Trapped by the question and unsure of an answer, Constable Bower's eyes searched the prosecutor's face for help.

"Answer the question!" snarled the judge.

"I-I don't know, sir."

"Then, Your Honour," Grimwold replied, feeling a new sense of power as he turned to face the judge, "these charges are frivolous nonsense and should be dismissed!"

A few people gasped, but then the courtroom went inordinately quiet as all eyes turned to the judge and waited expectantly. A movement over by the window took Oliver's attention and relief flashed through Mary's body as they heard the fading scream of defeat from the evil spirit of Jonas Longbow.

The judge smashed his gavel on its block. "Case dismissed!"

Chapter 17

Two brown faces stared through the rails of the prisoner's box, whimpering as they misunderstood the proceedings.

"Turn those boys free," the judge growled in a rare moment of compassion, before turning to leave the courtroom. "And you, Grimwold," he flung over his shoulder, "see me in my chambers."

Following the grumbling crowd, cheated of their amusement and pointing at the empty gallows as they left Bastion Street, Mary searched for the two young natives.

"They're still inside," Oliver muttered, reading her thoughts. "They need our help."

Tugging her along behind him, they pushed their way back through the crowd. Turning the corner, they saw a young constable guarding the open back door of the courthouse. From inside, came the pitiful sounds of the young native boys wailing a traditional death chant.

"I'll take those boys home now," the reporter told the jailor.

"On whose authority?" the jailor asked.

"They were acquitted of all charges," Oliver persisted, "you have no right to hold them."

Stepping inside, they heard the jailor's laughter behind them as the heavy steel door clanged shut trapping them in the cell block. Two other uniformed men taunted the boys through the bars.

Mary felt Oliver's fingers tighten on her arm and she looked up to see the blazing light in his eyes as he pointed a finger at the guards. The laugher and taunting stopped as all three guards became rigid. An almost imperceptible nod of his head caused the jailers and the prisoners to change places. Jabbering excitedly, the two brown faces looked up at them and their eyes grew wide.

"Take them to the bridge, Mary," Oliver whispered, "and send them home."

"What are you going to do?" she asked.

"I'm going to stay right here and talk to these heartless creatures."

Suspicious eyes watched the Everett school teacher as she reached out to the boys and shepherded them down the corridor.

"Don't be afraid," she told them, smiling reassuringly, unsure what English they could understand. "I won't hurt you. You're going home and I'm going to help you."

Leaving by the back door, she pulled it almost shut behind her, and told the boys to show her the way to the bridge. They moved cautiously down the yard, hugging the shadows of Court Alley and going between buildings until they reached Yates Street. Pressing tightly to the wall, they peered around the corner before making a dash for the safety of Waddington Alley coming out on Johnson Street.

Making sure no one was following them, Mary pointed to the bridge and hissed, "Go!"

She watched them dash across the street toward the bridge, passing a loudly puffing railway engine sitting at the station. They turned back to look at her just before the train sent a cloud of smoke into the air, hiding them from view.

Wasting no time after Mary and the boys left, Oliver went back to see the jailers.

"Gentlemen, would you like me to let you out of there?"

"Compassion guv'nor," one jailer pleaded. "I don't know how we got in here."

"You want me to feel sorry for you," Oliver laughed, "but you had no sympathy for those poor young boys."

"We were just funning, sir, we meant no harm."

"But you made the ghost angry and he locked you up."

"Ghost, sir?" the jailer's chorused.

"Yes, the Bastion Ghost."

Oliver's voice had an eerie hollow tone that sent icy shivers down their spines. Trapped in the small cell where they often taunted prisoners for amusement, their imaginations now ran wild. One man's nerve suddenly snapped and he dropped to his knees shaking uncontrollably and begging for mercy.

"Sorry," Oliver retorted, "I must leave now."

"Don't go, sir," the terror-filled voices pleaded hopelessly as Oliver disappeared.

Out of sight, Oliver watched Mary come toward him and realized how relieved he was.

"What's happening in there?" she asked.

He motioned with his finger to come closer and, even from the doorway, she could hear the muffled cries and cursing coming from the cells. Suddenly, Oliver's whistle startled her as he got the attention of a Chinaman pulling a small cart heaped with laundry. The man slowed and cautiously peered at them from under his coolie hat.

"You sell me a bedsheet?" Oliver asked the little man.

"Nineteen cent, sir," the Chinaman replied.

"Puzzled?" Oliver turned to Mary after handing the man the coins and taking the folded white sheet.

She nodded.

"Well, my dear, I'm creating a ghost that those jail keepers can recognize."

"You're going to wear that sheet?" Mary giggled.

"No … you are!"

"I am not!" she retorted as he took her hand and led her behind the building.

"Put it over your head …," he began.

"But I won't be able to see," she declared.

"It won't matter, no one is going to be able to see us either! I'll help you, you're going to teach those jailers a lesson."

"I'm a ghost?" she asked, chuckling as she now realized the possibilities.

Making them both invisible, he took her hand and led her back to the courthouse, her white sheet seemingly floating along by itself causing some odd looks from a few passersby. Entering the jailhouse, they could still hear the pitiful moaning of the jailers.

"You have a visitor," Oliver shouted in warning. "The Bastion Ghost wants to meet you."

"No, no, don't let it near us!" they screamed, moving to the far corner of the cell and huddling together.

Slipping past the reporter, Mary moved slowly along the passageway. As she came into their view, she decided she was going to enjoy this role.

"What do you want from us?" one terrified voice whined.

"You're cruel and evil men," Mary's ghost-like voice exclaimed using her long-forgotten thespian skills to the fullest, "and should be hung from your own gallows!"

Out of sight, Oliver covered his mouth to hide his mirth as Mary's performance became even more convincing. Its effect on the jailers was instantaneous as, wailing loudly, they collapsed onto the floor.

"That's enough," said Oliver. "I think we've achieved our object."

Mary went back to the door out of sight and removed the sheet.

"Now what?" she asked, shivering as a cold wind blew through the door. "Am I visible again?"

"Yes, but I've one more thing to do," he said. "Wait here."

Watching him go back toward the cells, she wondered what else he was going to do to the poor men.

"There, that's done," he sighed, returning seconds later. "They're all sleeping peacefully now and I've put this nightmare into their dreams. They'll wake up wondering if it really happened."

"They'll be kinder to the prisoners?" Mary asked.

"Oh yes, they're going to be perfect gentlemen whenever they feel the urge to be horrible!" Oliver snickered.

"You're an angel, honey," she giggled, "but all this has made me awfully hungry."

"You were the perfect ghost, love, where did you learn to be such a thesbian?" he laughed, taking her hand. He led her up Chancery Lane and across Yates to the Northern Hotel.

Later, as they finished eating, Mary suddenly winced with pain, her fingers delicately exploring her jaw.

"Toothache?" he asked in concern.

"Yes, a broken tooth I think; I can feel a rough edge."

"Then let's find a dentist, there's one just up the street."

She nodded, her tongue exploring the damaged tooth as Oliver called for the bill.

Tiny snowflakes swirled about as they went up Yates and found Edwin Tait's dental office at 626. They groaned at the notice plastered across his shingle in the doorway—'Closed for the Holiday' it read in bold black ink. Continuing up Yates, they spotted another dentist—William Russell's upstairs window displayed a sign which said 'Open.' A streetcar rattled by as they climbed the rough wooden stairs to the second floor. The door was slightly ajar, looking cold and uninviting but they pushed it open.

Seeing the dentist, Mary almost screamed. To top it off, he was the most distasteful yet humorous-looking dentist she had ever seen. He wore a horrifically blood-splattered apron which covered his long white smock, heavy wire-framed spectacles covered eyes rimmed by bushy eyebrows, and his bulbous, red nose protruded over a bristling moustache. When he spoke, a deep, commanding voice growled a welcome from between thin tight lips.

"Trouble, my dear?" he asked, pointing to a large swivel chair.

Settling into the hard leather seat, Mary's eyes fastened on the instruments of torture laid neatly side-by-side on a nearby table. Second thoughts suddenly tore through her mind when she realized this was dentistry in 1916, but already prepared, the dentist's hand held her down as she struggled.

"No, no," she yelped. "I've changed my mind! Oliver!"

Well used to unwilling patients, William Russell held Mary firmly in the chair as his free hand picked up a wicked-looking tooth extractor and held it under her nose.

"This won't hurt," he lied, as the school teacher's scream reverberated through the room.

"Stop!" Oliver shouted. "Set her free, man."

Moving quickly to Mary's assistance, Oliver removed the dentist's hand and helped her from the chair. Terror-stricken, she clung to him.

"Please let's leave, Oliver," she pleaded through her tears.

"I have laudanum or opium," Russell growled snootily.

The offer fell on deaf ears as Mary made her escape down the stairs, leaving Oliver to deal with the irate dentist while she waited on the street. A small fee and a limp shake of hands was all that remained before the reporter raced down the stairs after her.

"Now what are you going to do?" he asked, not able to hold back his smile.

"Can't you fix it for me? It doesn't need to be pulled, for heaven's sake, he didn't even look at it!" she pouted.

"I'm an angel, not a dentist, Mary."

"You don't even know—you could do it if you really wanted to."

Oliver's eyes ranged over the signs farther along Yates. "There's a drugstore at the next corner," he said. "Let's go ask, they may be able to help."

Central Drug Store at 702 Yates thankfully exuded a friendly warmth when they entered. The musical jingle of its doorbell and the female clerk's homely greeting soon settled Mary's shattered nerves.

"Toothache?" she asked, noticing Mary's actions. "Why deary, you need oil of cloves."

The cure sounded much more humane than the wicked-looking instruments at the dentist and Mary nodded gratefully. After all, her grandmother always used nature's remedies. Given a mirror, she dabbed the offending tooth with the oil and grimaced. Its nasty taste and harsh burning sensation sent her scurrying for the bathroom and a drink of water.

"Better now?" Oliver asked, struggling to keep a straight face when she returned.

"As if you care!" she snapped, moving her jaw and realizing some of the pain had gone.

The clerk gushed sympathy quietly chatting as she watched Mary apply another application.

"It's really gone!" Mary exclaimed. "I can't thank you enough."

"It's too late for visiting Oak Bay today," Oliver muttered as they returned to the street.

"Oak Bay?" asked Mary. "Why do you want to go to Oak Bay?"

"I have that assignment to do for Margo, remember? I need to find that lady who was rescued in the storm."

"You mean that time Tom wrote the message on your report?" Mary asked. Without thinking, he nodded. "That was about a week ago," she pointed out. "Wouldn't it be simpler to visit the newspaper office?"

"You know, you're right."

"But they're closed now, it's after five o'clock."

"That won't stop us," Oliver grinned mischievously, taking her hand and leading her across Douglas Street.

Pulling their coats about them as the wind whipped up the street from the harbour, they picked their way carefully between the tram tracks partly hidden by fresh snow. Turning down Fort Street, they easily found the newspaper office—a faint glow of light showing behind shuttered windows.

"Hold on, we're going in," Oliver announced.

"Where do we start looking?" she asked, finding they were standing by a desk littered with paper and newspaper clippings.

"Look for newspapers from last week. It will give me the lady's name and address and make finding her easier."

"But Oliver, look at this mess," she cried. "We'll never be able to find anything."

She had no sooner said it when the desktop suddenly cleared, completely.

"Sit," he ordered, grinning at her expression, "we'll check each front page from before the 21st. I wish I could remember what date that was."

Newspapers mysteriously floated by in front of her, disappearing abruptly when she checked each day and pushed them aside.

"Here's something," she whispered, reading the headline. "It's dated Thursday, December the 21st.

"Read me the headline, does it give any information about her?" he asked with pencil poised over his writing pad.

"This can't be the same woman," Mary declared. "I remember now, you rescued that woman and her children in the year 2000. Margo has to be referring to an incident in 1916 and, coincidentally, this story is about 1916!"

"By gosh you're right, we were staying at the Gatsby. This may be the one we need, but I certainly don't remember it. Read it to me."

"No need for that, son, I'll tell you about it," Tom Watson's voice interrupted them. "It was I who rescued that woman."

Mary shivered as a slight chill ran down her spine and she watched Tom materialize a few feet away. She still wasn't used to his sudden appearances.

"She's an actress, a lady of the stage," Tom continued. "She was admired for her talent but shunned by society's highborn women. She was staying alone at the Old Charming Inn in Oak Bay that fateful day."

"And you heard her cry for help?" Oliver asked.

"No, son, I was with her," Tom sighed. "I'm *her* guardian angel, too!"

"Who is she?" Mary whispered.

"Agnes Millington is her name."

"Early suffragette and vaudeville star," added Mary, proud of herself for remembering.

"Would you like to meet her?" the old angel asked.

Oliver's arm slipped around Mary's shoulder, pulling her closer as Tom removed his hat and placed it on the desk. Holding out his hand, they immediately heard the sound of tinkling laughter and a ghostly form began to materialize. The wispy outline of a heavy figure with short hair and a happy, rounded face began to fill out; her misty blue eyes were full of amusement as she smiled at Mary.

"Hello Agnes, can you tell me what happened when you first met Mr. Watson?" Oliver asked, picking up his pencil and notepad.

"Forgive him, Agnes," Tom chuckled, "you have to remember he's a newspaper reporter, always wanting to ask questions."

"Ah hell, don't apologize," laughed Agnes, "I always loved talking and that hasn't changed. Well, son it was like this. My stage career was at rock bottom and the establishment had chased me out of Seattle when …."

"Who chased you out?" Oliver asked, his interest increasing.

"The mayor and saloon keepers, you should know, you live there."

"I don't frequent the bars any more," Oliver replied, glancing over at Mary, "and I haven't seen a newspaper in weeks."

"I was killed in a Seattle night club, shot by a drunken gangster," Agnes sighed. Her voice almost faded away as recent memories flooded into her mind. "But," she smiled, "my death did more for the cause than if I'd lived to be a hundred. It was worth it."

"You saved her life, then let her die?" the reporter's accusing tone addressed their guardian angel.

"Yes, I let her down, son, it happened too fast and, like I told you, we can't change history," Tom explained.

"Stop yer bellyaching, lad," Agnes brashly interceded. "I passed quickly and there wasn't much pain. I'm happier now than I've ever been and I love my new job."

"What is your job?" Mary asked, now totally immersed in the story.

"Why deary," Agnes giggled, "I'm steering the fortunes of Nellie Cornish of Seattle and Nancy Wilson of Victoria. Now there's two independent gals for you!"

"The Cornish School of Arts," Mary commented thoughtfully. "That's a famous Seattle institution."

Casting his mind back a few months, Oliver remembered the redheaded singer, Nancy Wilson, and her friend, Gus Jorgensen.

"I met Nancy," he said. "She's often referred to as Seattle's sweetheart of song and sings regularly at the James Moore Theatre."

"We've heard her name somewhere else," added Mary.

"From the policeman, Harry Gray," Agnes interrupted, "when you were chasing that Egger boy!"

"Now I remember, he said Nancy had a fast boat," Oliver added.

"That's right, she and Danny own the *Stockholm*," Agnes replied, her voice softening momentarily, "but that's another story."

"But you said …?" began Mary.

"Hold it, Agnes," Tom growled cocking his head to listen. "Somebody's calling me, we have to go."

Before leaving, Agnes silently planted a thought into Oliver's mind—to meet her at The Charming Inn in Oak Bay the next day.

Disappointed at their quick disappearance, Mary was surprised to hear Agnes' fading voice call to her. "We'll meet again, Mary."

"This is going to take some getting used to," she sighed. "Can we go back to something familiar now, Oliver?"

In moments, Oliver had returned the room to the state they had found it, newspapers stacked themselves untidily on desks and the lights dimmed. He slipped his arm around Mary's waist and set them lightly on the sidewalk outside the building.

"Are you ready for something to eat?" he asked, pulling her closer and kissing her before letting her go.

"Where have all these people come from?" she asked, watching as small silent groups of people, mainly women, walked past them.

Oliver's answer was interrupted by the loud toot of a ship's whistle in the harbour and, already quite sure what it was, he suggested they follow the crowd. By the time they reached Wharf Street, there was a line of motor vehicles and army trucks extending down to Belleville Street and he explained that one of the hospital ships was docking. When they reached the dimly lit bridge opposite the Empress, Mary was shocked to see the number of people who had gathered. Solemn-faced, the crowd moved toward the entrance of the CPR wharf. She could feel the despair as wives and families prepared for the heart-wrenching sight of their sick and wounded men arriving home.

Over the next hour, they watched mesmerized as a parade of stretchers carrying bandaged, moaning and, often extremely badly injured men, moved toward the waiting trucks and ambulances. Dozens more, their confused expressions seemingly unaware of the frigid weather and falling snow, filled the sidewalk under the lights; some on crutches and others missing limbs, were quickly led away to the waiting vehicles by those more able.

Watching the crowd reaction was heartbreaking as women, many with young children, no doubt looking for their husbands, would move forward and speak with one of the soldiers. Receiving little or no reaction, the women bravely retreated, huddling with their children or crying pitifully.

Overcome, Mary lay her head on Oliver's chest and wept—the evilness of war and its consequences branded forever in her memory.

Chapter 18

"I think we need to get away from this sad place. It's been snowing and we haven't even noticed how cold it is. You look quite a sight, my dear," said Oliver, attempting to lighten the mood. "You have a rather grotesque-looking snow figure atop your hat."

Mary looked up at him, trying to smile despite her tears.

"You have one that looks like a dragon out of Harry Potter."

"Harry Potter, who is he?"

"Oh I forgot, you wouldn't know about him. He's a very modern character from a famous kids' book out of England. It seems to have taken the world by storm."

"You never mention reading books, Mary. What do you read?"

"Well actually, I have a new favourite author who lives in Victoria. I picked up his first book at a little farmers' market in James Bay last summer. It's history, of course, set in London and is about a delightful girl named Lizzie. I wish my students were more like her."

"Who is the author?"

"His name is J. Robert Whittle. Oliver, I wonder, would it be possible to go forward in time and see if he has written more books?"

"Yes, I suppose we could do that," he replied, grinning as his thoughts took over. "Let's wait until we get back to the room."

"No," she begged, "can't you do it right now?"

"Oh all right," he sighed, "he must have really impressed you! Hold tight!"

When she opened her eyes, she was surprised to find they were standing in a narrow alley between two older buildings. The area had a slightly familiar look about it, but it wasn't winter any more, the sun was shining and it was quite warm and very busy with people—many of them dressed in summer clothes and carrying cameras. There seemed to be an outdoor fair or market set up in the nearby courtyard.

"Where are we?" she asked.

"You wanted to find your favourite author … well, this is Bastion Street in 2007, they call it Bastion Square now and apparently this is the Bastion Square Public Market where your J. Robert Whittle now sells his books. Come on, I'll show you," he announced, taking her hand.

Suddenly noticing what Oliver was wearing, she looked down at herself and laughed. Oliver almost had it right as they were wearing summer clothes for a change, even though they were more like 1916 summer clothes. *It's all right,* she assured herself, *styles are even more varied in 2007 than in 2000 by the looks of these people. We should fit right in!*

As they walked through the happy crowds, they stopped to look briefly at the tables full of different wares. Besides books, there were paintings, wooden products, hats, clothes, pottery, all types of jewellery imaginable and more. They crossed a street and Oliver asked if she recognized it.

"Yes, this is Langley Street," she said thoughtfully, "your hotel was … oh my gosh it's still there. Look, there's a pub on the other corner now where the lawyers had their offices."

"Your author is just up there near Government Street, opposite the old Bank of Montreal."

"It wasn't a bank, it was a clothing store," she insisted.

"It was a bank in 1916, but it seems we're both wrong … it's the Irish Times Pub now, my goodness, how fast things change and listen to that different music," Oliver chuckled as they passed more market vendors.

"Look, look Oliver, there he is. Look at all his books! Thank goodness, he kept writing! Let's go talk to him, I could get one of his books now," she begged.

"I think we should leave well enough alone, Mary. Look at all the people around him. He's rather busy and you don't want him to lose his customers and, besides, we can come back anytime." In his mind, Tom warned him that this man was particularly astute and a very knowledgeable historian.

Better to be cautious, were the angel's words.

Mary pulled him closer so they could both study the two large posters in the author's display. Taking mental note of the numerous books and their titles, she was thrilled to see that the Lizzie book she'd purchased in 1999 had grown to four books. She backed away and watched—Robert was still as vibrant as she remembered him. She realized he must be in his seventies by now. She couldn't wait to plan her next summer trip to Victoria. Then suddenly, Robert saw her and reached out with one of his handouts.

She took it and stepped back to read it. *Oh great, this has his website!* she thought. Feeling Oliver's arm around her waist, she allowed him to lead her up the street to a wide doorway where he pulled her into the shadows.

"We're going back to the cold, Mary," he warned, enfolding her in his arms. As he bent to kiss her, they disappeared and a young man nearby did a double take, looking apprehensively at his cigarette.

Arriving back to the cold darkness was quite a shock after their brief visit to the summer's day. They found themselves in exactly the same spot and immediately began walking toward town.

"Victoria has suffered so much from this horrible war," she commented. "I think I'm glad to be living in 2000, Oliver; in modern times, Victoria is a lovely haven from the troubles of the world."

"What about Everett, are you ready to go home yet?"

"No, I want to be with you," she replied adamantly. "Don't get me wrong, I love Everett, it's a lot like Victoria in so many ways, but with the modern terrorist issues and …."

"Terrorist issues?" he asked, stopping to look at her. "What do you mean?"

"You'll find out soon enough, my love," she replied evasively.

"Well, I don't think I want to know any too soon, let's go eat."

"Sounds good to me," she replied, squeezing his arm as they increased their stride.

On the way, they were surprised at finding both the Brown Jug Saloon and the Windsor Hotel quiet, devoid of the usual loudly playing music, as even hardened drinkers showed their respect for the returning soldiers.

An empty streetcar lumbered by as they entered the Manitoba Hotel on Yates, instantly feeling its welcome warmth and friendly interior. Thick carpets muffled their footsteps as they passed through the elegant foyer. Hearing the sound of a woman's sobbing, they looked around, but seeing no one, continued to the dining room.

Hearing the crying again, they realized it was coming from a nearby corner where a young woman, with a small boy of about two-years-old on her lap, was sitting in the shadows. Not wanting to interfere, they accepted their table from a tired-looking waitress who handed them menus.

"Shall I ask her to be quiet?" she asked.

"No, certainly not!" Oliver snapped uncharacteristically.

"Can we help her?" Mary whispered.

Sighing, the waitress came closer and murmured confidentially. "She lost her soldier husband today; he died of his wounds on the hospital ship that docked this afternoon."

Instantly Mary reached for Oliver's arm.

"Shall we try the salmon?" he suggested, ignoring her.

Mary nodded her agreement and the waitress began to move off, then stopped again. "Would you like tea or coffee?"

"Coffee please, for both of us," Oliver replied.

Mary's eyes never left the sad figures and her fingers dug into Oliver's arm. "Can't you help her, Oliver?" she begged.

"How can I help in a situation like this?" he retorted, looking over at them helplessly.

His reply distressed Mary and her eyes glazed over as she watched him remove his steamed-up glasses and wipe them on his cloth napkin. Cups and saucers clinked as the waitress returned with a tray of china, a pot of coffee, and a plate of small raison scones, setting them down quickly and leaving. Mary felt a chilling sensation and, turning back to Oliver, she gasped in surprise, he'd disappeared.

Talk to them, Mary, she heard him whisper. *I'll be back soon.*

Choosing one of the scones, she walked toward the door. Under the dim lights, she saw that the woman was much younger than she had initially thought; her eyes were terribly red and swollen and Mary's heart went out to her.

As she approached, the woman looked at her suspiciously, sliding farther away on the bench. "W-who are you?" she asked, stumbling on her words as she wiped her eyes.

"My name is Mary and I'm a friend who wants to help you. May I give your son this scone?" she asked, sitting down on the bench.

"I-I suppose so, but do I know you?" Gertrude Tuttle asked.

"No dear, you don't. I'm very sorry to hear of your loss," Mary began, handing the little boy the scone and watching as he hungrily took a bite.

"But how did you …?" asked the woman.

"The waitress told us, dear," Mary explained, "such a dreadful way to hear you have lost your husband."

"John joined the army because he was out of work; it was the only way to get a regular pay cheque. He tried so hard to look after us … and now he's gone," she said, beginning to cry again. But she stopped suddenly and gathered her composure, clutching her son even tighter. "I don't know what I'm going to do. We have no money and I fear I will lose our little farm. We worked so hard to look after it."

Mary, ask her if she would like to say goodbye to her husband? Oliver asked her.

When Mary conveyed Oliver's request, Gertrude looked at her in disbelief and wiped her eyes again. She kissed her son on the forehead as she took her time to consider the question.

"Oh, if that were only possible … to be able to see John one last time," she murmured, her eyes closing as memories flooded her mind.

Take the boy, Mary, came the almost inaudible order. *I'm going to put him to sleep.*

Gertrude watched as Mary gently persuaded the boy to come to her. Having finished his scone, he went willingly laying his head on her shoulder. Mary stood up and gently rocked the boy and he fell asleep instantly. Gertrude felt an unusual closeness with this young woman and she now felt a strange feeling of peace envelop her body.

"Hello sweetheart," the voice of Gertrude's husband whispered as both Oliver and John materialized in front of the women.

There was no fear in Gertrude's eyes, only surprise and joy as she smiled tearfully at the ghost of her husband. John moved toward her, sitting down on the bench.

"How can this be, John …?" Gertrude began.

"Shh, we don't have long I'm told," John whispered, speaking quickly but gently. "This man is an angel, Gertie, and he wants to help us … help you. You're going to be all right, things are going to work out. I can't tell you how or when, but you have to trust us."

"I do trust you, oh John, I miss you so much already," she sobbed, her words tumbling over each other.

Even as he took her in his arms, she could see she was losing him.

"I'll be waiting for you one day, Gert. Look after that lad of ours, honey, he'll make you proud," he said, kissing her quickly before his image faded away.

"I don't know how you did that," said Gertrude, after taking a couple of minutes to compose herself again. Wiping her eyes, she looked up at Oliver and Mary, "I can only thank you from the bottom of my heart."

"Your plea was heard by the angels, Gertrude, and I'm merely a messenger," Oliver explained.

When the waitress returned with their dinner, she was surprised to find their seats empty and then noticed the group in the corner. Going toward them, she heard the end of their conversation.

"… tonight I surely met an angel," said Gertrude, finally smiling as she took her sleeping son from Mary.

"An angel in this hotel?" quipped the waitress, raising her eyebrows. "I think that's highly unlikely, ma'am. Enjoy your meals, folks, they're on the table."

Gertrude quickly excused herself but not before saying 'thank you' one final time over her shoulder before going out the door.

"Will she be all right now?" Mary asked as they went back to their table.

"Yes, she's going to be fine once she finds the $20 bill and the note in her pocket."

"Ah … and a note about?"

"It tells her of a tin full of money hidden in her barn and of the three injured soldiers who will call at her house looking for work. They'll clear her land, plant the crops and help her take care of the place. Yes Mary, she's going to be all right."

The aroma of baked salmon drifted under their noses as they sat down and their eyes met.

"What is it, honey?" he asked, a forkful almost to his lips.

"Oh nothing," Mary said, smiling coyly. "I just wanted to say that I love you."

"Mary Janick," Oliver blushed, "somebody will hear you!"

"I know, you did," she giggled, then leaning toward him she kissed his cheek and whispered. "In my time, we tell this to special people in our lives!"

"Well, I still think you're a hussy," he whispered back, grinning. "Although I think I could get used to your time quite nicely!"

Back out on the street, the last army trucks slowly made their way up Government Street. Gertrude boarded her streetcar and as she sat down, her son woke up.

"Hello darling," she said softly. "Mommy's going to try and stop crying now and we're going to start our new lives because we know daddy still loves us very much."

"Is daddy coming home?"

"No honey, he's not, but he'll be in our hearts and someday you'll understand," she assured him, kissing his cheek and hugging him tightly as the streetcar took them home.

An hour later, Oliver and Mary also left the hotel and were walking toward Bastion Street when a noisy group of people spilled out of the Majestic Theatre farther down the block. Then Oliver noticed an even larger crowd leaving the Columbia Theatre down on Government Street.

"The picture theatres have finished their first show," he announced. "Would you like to go to one?"

"To a silent movie?"

"Yes," he said, taking her arm, "I've only been a couple times, it's not quite like the VT at your mother's."

"You mean the TV, silly. Let's see what's on," she suggested, going to look at the posters in front of the Majestic. "Oh my, it's an early Pickford movie. I haven't heard of *Pride of the Clan*."

"You've heard of Mary Pickford?" he asked.

"Oh sure, she became a really famous actress and director."

"A woman director? My goodness, I can't imagine," Oliver replied, looking rather doubtful. "Let's go see what's on at the Columbia."

"Well, believe it honey, in the 20th century women are beginning to take over the world," she laughed, "but I'm not so sure that's a good thing either, we need a good compromise."

"The way men get us into these wars, it might be worth a try!" he declared, making a face.

Arriving at the Columbia Theatre a few minutes later, Mary indicated that the Charlie Chaplin movie featured here was okay with her. He led her over to the end of the short queue.

"I suppose he became famous, too!" Oliver teased.

"How'd you guess!" she laughed. "I think this movie will be more your speed somehow."

"More my speed, is that another one of your sayings … oh, how much?" Oliver asked the man behind the glass window.

"Ten cents each," was the growled reply, accepting Oliver's coins. "You can sit where ya like."

Fewer than 40 people filled the seats when a piano began to play the introduction, lights dimmed, and *The Rink* began to roll. Mary coughed at the choking atmosphere of tobacco smoke swirling upward through the projector light.

The actors jerkily made their movements across the screen, words appeared like sub-titles and about halfway through the one-hour show, everything went haywire when the movie film broke. There was a loud screech and a whirling sound from the direction of the projcction room before the lights came on. The pianist made a quick apology, playing a popular tune until the repair work was finished; the lights went off again and the movie resumed.

Oliver's arm went around Mary's shoulders pulling her closer when the lights went out. Their lips had no sooner met than a spotlight illuminated their faces and the squeaking voice of a young usher yelled from the aisle.

"Hey there, none of that in here you two!"

Mary giggled, covering her face with her hands. "Behave yourself, Mr. Ryan!" she whispered, as thoughts of modern-day movie theatres came to mind. *Cripes, things have sure changed!*

Settling down again, they continued to watch the incredibly zany antics of Charlie Chaplin roller skating his way into movie history.

"He must be an expert on roller skates to do those kinds of tricks," laughed Mary as they left the theatre.

"Or he's broken his neck by now!"

This sent her into another fit of laughter. *How is he to know that Chaplin lived to a ripe old age and became the master of silent comedy?*

They stood for a moment under the theatre's canopy to button their coats, twist scarves around their necks and reaffix their hats before facing the weather. Rain had completely replaced the snow in typical Victoria fashion and the streets were now a slushy mess.

"It's been a long day, let's go back to the hotel," she suggested.

Oliver agreed and they laughed as they made a dash for Yates Street, past the Palace Saloon on the corner and crossed the street into Langley. Dim street lights illuminated a crowd of noisy miners outside the Bank Exchange Saloon. Already heated tempers were getting out of hand and obscenities exchanged through the open door.

All of a sudden, the sound of breaking glass caught their attention and two baton-swinging policemen appeared, quickly moving in. Stepping into a darkened doorway and pressing their backs against a door which read 'Victoria Sign Works,' Oliver and Mary sheltered from the rain and watched the commotion.

Mary noticed a particularly suspicious figure moving around behind the crowd. "Look," she hissed, elbowing Oliver. "See the man skulking around behind the one with the cap pulled down over his eyes ... at the back."

There was a sudden flash of steel and Mary gasped, even as Oliver sent a tiny, hissing ball of fire toward the weapon.

"Hell!" Jack Blakey yelled, his knife crashing to the floor and alerting the men around him.

"Harry Gray's over there," Oliver told her, pointing out the police officer. "Go tell him, Mary."

Held by several of the angry miners, Jack Blakey, the well-known waterfront thief, kicked and protested. When that didn't work, he changed his approach to one of pleading.

"Let me be, boys, ah meant nobody any harm," he whined.

"An ah suppose this were meant ta scratch me back with!" retorted the man who had apparently been Jack's target, picking up the dangerous-looking hunting knife from the ground.

By the time Mary returned with Harry Gray, the earlier commotion had been forgotten and men now turned their anger toward Blakey and the policeman restraining him. Several of the miners called for lynching as they sought to overpower the policeman who had Blakey in hand—now realizing he was outnumbered and calling for assistance. Oliver pointed his finger at Blakey and the officer causing the miners to shrink back in fear as the pair disappeared.

"I ain't stayin here," one of the men shouted, backing away. "That were the work of the devil."

More men followed, their eyes cautiously searching the shadows as someone yelled, "The devil's loose in Langley Street!"

Curious drinkers now streamed out of the saloon, beer tankards in hand. Hearing the new cry, they bolted for safety. Oliver brought the two men back as Harry appeared with Mary.

"We'll need you as a witness, Ryan," Harry yelled as they headed toward the provincial lockup with Blakey in hand.

Oliver raised his arm in reply and taking Mary by the elbow steered her across the street to follow the officers. Hurrying through the rain, they were close behind the group as they entered the police station. The prisoner, dumped unceremoniously onto a chair, glanced furtively around, his eyes searching for a chance to escape.

"What happened out there, Oliver?" Constable Gray inquired.

"He," Oliver pointed at Jack Blakey, "was about to stab a man in the back."

"That's right," Mary agreed. "I saw it, too."

"And just how did you manage to stop him, young lady?" the sarcastic growl of Station Sergeant Duncan McTavish interceded from the doorway of a small office.

Anger welled up inside Oliver as he turned to face the bad-tempered sergeant whom he'd seen in action before. "Divine intervention," he snapped, surprising the group of policemen who had gathered. "A hot spark burned his hand and he dropped the knife."

"In a rainstorm?" retorted McTavish.

Seeing his chance, Jack Blakey whined his objections, pleading for consideration. "They're trying to make trouble for me, sir. I'm an upright citizen of this city."

"Check his hand," Oliver said calmly.

"Show me your hands," the constable ordered the prisoner who had his hands clenched together although not handcuffed. "Not the front man, the back!" he snapped angrily as Jack ignored him and moved his hands behind his back. "Which hand, miss?"

"The right one."

Grabbing the prisoner by the shoulders, two policemen forced him to bring his right hand forward. "It seems to be burned, sir," Constable Gray announced with amazement as they examined it. "She's right!"

"Ah did that two days ago!" the prisoner argued.

"Let me see that," Sergeant McTavish ordered, his heavy boots stomping across the room. "That's a fresh burn, just look at that blister." Rubbing his chin, the sergeant swung his eyes between Oliver and Mary, squinting in thought. "Who did you say intervened?"

"An angel," Oliver replied.

"An angel?" McTavish repeated, shaking his head in frustration. "And did that angel give you any more information about this purported crime?"

"Yes, he did. He indicated this man is carrying Russian money in his billfold."

"Russian money! What might be the significance of that?"

"Sir, this morning in court," Oliver began, "you tried to convict two innocent boys of murdering a Russian sailor." He paused for a moment watching as the sergeant's brow wrinkled into a frown. "I'd say this man is your real culprit and this is your evidence."

"I'll decide that ... search him!" McTavish barked.

Struggling wildly as the two officers searched him thoroughly, the prisoner screamed abuse at Oliver.

"He's right again," Harry Gray announced, holding up a man's billfold and opening it. "This appears to belong to the Russian, it still contains his seaman's papers."

"Ah found it on the street," Blakey wailed.

"Book him!" the sergeant hissed. "He'll swing for this one."

Ignoring the prisoner's objections as they dragged him away, Sgt. McTavish turned back to the young couple. There was something compelling about them, especially the man who talked of angels. In his many years as a provincial policeman, he had never met anyone quite like Oliver Ryan; he knew he had seen him before in the press area at the courthouse but this was different.

"It's rather late," McTavish announced, "but would you join me for a coffee?"

Oliver looked over at Mary who merely raised her eyebrows.

"Certainly, we'd welcome a hot drink," Oliver replied, feeling Mary's hand on his arm.

Going to the doorway, McTavish hollered for three coffees then returned to his desk. Indicating the wooden chairs to his guests, he made small talk until the coffee arrived. Setting it down in front of them on the desk, a young constable retreated, closing the office door as he left.

"Cream and sugar?" asked McTavish and receiving nods of agreement, he brought a tray from behind him and also placed it on the desk. Sitting down, he smiled at Mary as he vigorously stirred the black liquid in his cup with a pencil.

"Now, son," he said softly, "tell me about this angel fella."

"You wouldn't believe me, sir," said Oliver, taking a casual sip of his coffee.

"Try me."

"Well, let me introduce myself, I'm Oliver Ryan and this lovely lady is Mary. We're Americans, and you, sir, are Sergeant Duncan Alexander McTavish, a 16-year veteran of the British Columbia Provincial Police Force."

"I know who you are and I certainly know who I am!" McTavish snapped as a recent phone conversation suddenly came to mind. "Jake Mendell, a sheriff in Port Angeles told me a tall tale last week about two people who sound an awful lot like you."

"Do you believe in angels, sir?" Mary asked.

"No, my dear, I deal in facts, evidence and lunatics, but keep talking, this should be interesting, *you* may be able to convince me," he sneered.

"And why would we want to do that?" Oliver asked. "You've caught your murderer."

"It doesn't explain how that man's hand got burned in a rainstorm," the sergeant muttered.

An uneasy silence settled over the room. Oliver came to his feet and Mary followed, taking his hand. The sergeant realized that no further explanation would be forthcoming from these people and he had no reason to hold them. He set his coffee cup down and tipped his chair back. Nodding to his guests, they turned and left, knowing his eyes were watching their every move.

"Angels!" he mumbled, shaking his head. His chair bounced back onto the floor and he picked up his pencil.

Running through the rain laughing, they headed across the street to their hotel. Mary's fingers gripped tightly to his hand as they climbed the dark stairs and moved along the dimly lit corridor. Her body flinched as they heard a loud bang outside.

"It's probably just a shutter blowing in the wind, relax honey."

Their cold room was even less inviting than she remembered but worse was yet to come as rolling thunder and a flash of lightning ruptured the electricity supply plunging the strcet into darkness. A sliver of moonlight found its way through the clouds, sending grotesque shadows dancing off the walls.

Chapter 19

The next morning, they were up early and made their way to the warmth of the Occidental Café, one of the only restaurants open so early and ordered toast and coffee. The room was almost full and abuzz with talk of the storm and the power outage. Mary soon realized that many buildings in the area did have electricity, unlike Oliver's old hotel.

Amused by the particularly loud conversations of night workers from the railway sheds and rice mill on Store Street, they listened to a conversation at a nearby table where one of the men had a strong opinion on a new conscription law, soon to be implemented.

"I haven't heard that before," Oliver whispered, "though I know there are a lot of strong feelings in Seattle about this war."

Mary nodded, she knew the date that history books had recorded America's entry into the war was April 6th, 1917 but should she tell him. *No need,* she thought to herself when his mouth showed a trace of a smile, *he's heard me!*

"Seeing as I have a day off, let's go and watch dawn break," he suggested paying the cashier, "it's looking promising out there."

Silvery-orange streaks of a new day tinted the clouds in the eastern sky as they strolled along Wharf Street watching the noisy gulls fight for food scraps from the waterfront docks and ships. They heard the rattle of iron-rimmed wheels on a firewood seller's handcart and turned to see a turbaned East Indian vendor making his first delivery of the day.

Hissing steam engines clanked in the railyard as the blackness of night slipped away. Even the shouted commands from a freighter moving slowly down the harbour could be heard as the ship headed for the open sea. Motor vehicles burst into life as shadowy figures loaded goods from the Hudson Bay warehouse and carthorses snorted angrily as drivers coaxed their drays toward the docks.

"There's sure a lot of activity around here," Mary commented.

"Life goes on, animals need to be fed and fishermen need their supplies. Several of the businesses work 24 hour shifts and they probably work on Saturday, too. I noticed that stores are open every day in your time."

"Yes, but that developed over a long time and Sundays, in particular, were not a popular working day when they began opening. Too many churchgoers thought it should remain a day of rest but modern times outweighed them it seems," she explained. "Now some stores are even open 24 hours a day."

"You never cease to amaze me, honey," he declared, looking at her adoringly.

"It's only history, silly," she laughed. "That's my speciality, remember?"

In the early morning mist, they stopped to look down at the Brown and Wilson waterfront office and Mary's attention was taken by an odd-looking ship floating alongside the dock.

"That ship looks transparent," she said, a puzzled note in her voice. "What causes it to look like that? I can just make out the name, it's the *Belfast*."

A passing workman heard Mary's comment and stopped briefly to join them, his voice softening as he stared at the ghostly form.

"It's the ghost ship, Miss," he murmured, "greatest whaler on the West Coast—she's been gone a few years but we see her on these foggy mornings standing at her old moorage."

"She was sunk?" Mary asked, but the man had continued on his way.

"No," Oliver replied continuing the story, "her owners were the Joyce brothers. They sailed her home to Newfoundland just before the start of the war. They were popular old geezers. I think I heard they went through the new Panama Canal and made it safely home."

"That far … do ships have souls, Oliver?" Mary's unusual question brought a smile to his face as he pulled her closer.

"Everything has a soul, honey," he whispered. "Ships, hotels, houses, even rocks …."

"You're making fun of me."

"Never!" he chuckled. "We're going to Oak Bay this afternoon. I have an appointment with Agnes."

"You're full of surprises, Mr. Ryan," she declared, but didn't ask any details. Turning to look back at the dock, she watched the fog lift and the image of the *Belfast* faded away. They returned to the hotel to change quickly realizing it was already lunchtime. Walking up Government Street, they followed the streetcar tracks that turned onto Fort Street then called in at the Edinburgh Café at Blanshard and ate a hearty meal of wild duck.

Before they left, a gentleman at the next table gave them detailed directions to Oak Bay's harbour. They caught the streetcar soon afterwards, asking the conductor to let them off at the Newport and Windsor stop. Then, they settled into their seats to watch the fancy houses roll by as the streetcar rumbled up the hill past Craigdarroch Castle to the junction of Fort and Oak Bay.

At the fork, the tram turned to the right onto the tree-lined avenue that led to the sea. It was ten minutes past three when they rattled past the municipal hall at Hampshire Road and Mary waved as a police constable saluted them.

"Terminus!" the conductor's voice shouted after several more stops. "This is Newport Street, folks; the last car back to Victoria leaves here at 9:25."

They waved their thanks and the streetcar continued on its way.

Across the road stood a lonely boathouse at the edge of the surf-lashed coastline and huge boulders lined the natural harbour which had a small island guarding its entrance.

"Some day this will be a popular place," Oliver predicted.

"I suspect it's popular now, but I know what you mean and, trust me, you're right!" she laughed.

"The Old Charming Inn has good meals!" shouted the conductor, hanging from the streetcar's top step as it completed its turn and passed them.

"Brr, it's cold here, but this Old Charming Inn certainly looks inviting. Why don't we stay here tonight?" she suggested, pulling her collar up against the bitter wind. "I don't want to go back to that depressing place of yours."

"Depressing? You're just too spoiled by your modern life, my dear," he teased, "but all right, I suppose we could do that. Come here, I think we have a visitor." Having received the expected message from Agnes Millington, he took her hand and led Mary to the beachfront. "Imagine how beautiful this must be in the summer."

"Are you trying to make me forget how cold I am?" she asked, shivering so violently Oliver put his arms around her.

Suddenly, he felt her body tense and followed her gaze. Walking nonchalantly along the sand was a young woman in light summer clothes. She kept stopping and peering out at the sea, shading her eyes as if she were searching for something.

"What … Oliver, i-i-is she a spirit … what is she looking for?" Mary asked, watching the woman in fascination.

"It's Agnes, honey. She's come to meet us so I can complete my interview." Seeing Mary's startled expression, he thought she didn't remember. "We were at the *Victoria Times* office with her and Tom."

"Yes, I remember, it's just that she's younger now, and when did you make the appointment? Oh, you're doing it to me again, aren't you? I suppose it's a *spiritual* thing!" she laughed.

"Yes smartie, I guess that's it! Listen," Oliver whispered, as they heard the sound of laughter coming from the beach. "She's returned to the place of a happier moment, contented spirits do that."

"Will she see us?"

"Of course she will," Oliver replied, "if she looks this way, but she'll find an appropriate place to visit us, so be prepared."

There was no sound as the apparition climbed over some logs and arrived at the edge of the loose gravel road, seemingly happy and oblivious to them. Following a distance behind, they watched until she reached the porch of the Old Charming Inn and disappeared.

Mary had to remind herself she was in another world, one with ghosts and other mysterious happenings. She stared up at the historical building she'd only seen in pictures. Her eyes wandered across the front windows, the railed veranda, bulging dormers, high-peaked roof and back to the beautifully painted sign.

"It was built in 1905," Oliver murmured, "in just 19 days and was originally called the Oak Bay Hotel."

"You're kidding me, I never read that!" she declared. "They couldn't build this magnificent building in 19 days." A movement pulled her eyes to an upper dormer window where the face of an older woman watched.

"I know," the reporter chuckled. "Agnes is waiting for us."

"But she's not the same woman we saw on the beach. Oh my gosh, can spirits change their age, too?"

"You'll have to ask her, I guess," he replied with that mischievous twinkle in his eye. "I'm still a baby angel and I have much to learn!"

Climbing the seven steps up to the veranda, she noticed the stack of wrought-iron furniture under a canvas cover in the corner and imagined sitting here on a warm summer's day and enjoying the beautiful view. Oliver opened the highly polished door and they stepped into the carpeted foyer. A crystal chandelier took her attention while he spoke with the middle-aged woman at the reception desk, booking a room overlooking the sea.

"Any luggage, sir?" she asked, glancing over at Mary and obviously looking at her left hand. Phoebe Kitson had been the hotel's receptionist for many years and had gained a reputation for too often sticking her nose in where it didn't belong.

"It's in town, we're staying the night on impulse," he explained, trying to be casual. "This is a lovely location."

Joining him at the reception desk, Mary watched as he pulled the register toward him and, with a flourish, produced his ballpoint pen and wrote their names.

"You devil," she hissed in his ear as he picked up the key and walked toward the stairway. Out of the corner of their eyes, they watched the puzzled look on the woman's face as she examined the empty page.

"I'm sorry, sir, your pen requires some ink," Phoebe called after them, turning the book around and reaching for her inkwell. Suddenly, she let out an exclamation of surprise and leaned over the book, her eyes widening as a thin wisp of smoke appeared.

Oliver took Mary's arm and they made their escape, continuing up the wide stairway. Covered by thick carpets, the sound of creaking timbers was almost non-existent as they went up to the second floor.

The door to their room was slightly ajar and a faint trace of perfume lingered in the air.

"Is she in there?" Mary whispered, stepping behind Oliver.

He pushed the door open and flipped on the light switch. She peeked around him into the well-lit room, her eyes taking in the two easy chairs, sideboard with lamp, and huge four-poster bed with canopy. In fascination, she pushed past him, dropping her handbag on the bed and looking all around.

"There's no one here," she murmured sounding relieved.

Oliver followed her, reaching for her arm just before Agnes' form materialized. Taken by surprise, Mary covered her mouth to hide the expletive that bubbled in her throat. Her heart began pounding and her hand flew to her chest.

"Forgive me for startling you, Mary, but it's lovely to see you again," Agnes apologized, taking a seat in one of the easy chairs by the window. "I'd forgotten you're only a mortal."

"Hello Agnes nice to see you again. I'm afraid this is all just a bit overwhelming ... Agnes, you're always wearing different clothes and changing ages. How do you do that?" she asked.

"Oh Mary, you must know how it is. I'm still a woman and I always loved clothes. I believe even spirits should be able to change their wardrobe; it's just that most don't think of it! As far as age goes, it gives me such enjoyment to take on the person I used to be rather than being stuck here in the age I was when I passed on. You'll understand some day."

Mary began to laugh hysterically and had to sit down on the bed as the possibilities of her own immortality raced through her mind.

"Why don't you just stay there while Agnes and I talk? Let's get you more comfortable," he suggested.

"It's all right, darling, I can do it, you two go ahead," she laughed, as he plumped up the pillows behind her.

He went over to the window and sat in the chair opposite Agnes. Taking out his notepad and ballpoint pen, he glanced up at the actress and told her to begin from where she'd left off the day before.

"Well, Mr. Ryan," Agnes began, "after leaving Seattle in the early years, I came to Victoria and found a job with the theatre group at the splendid Royal Theatre."

"What year was that?" he asked.

"October 1915. They gave me a part in a play opposite a leading citizen that was," Agnes chuckled at the memory, "sort of … risqué!"

Mary's ears perked up. Now, lying back on the pillows covered with the quilt, she was totally relaxed and engrossed in Agnes' story.

"What happened?" she prodded eagerly.

"Well, to tell the truth, deary, we sort of became attached." Another chuckle escaped Agnes's lips. "We tried it for real one night."

"On stage?" Mary gasped.

"Oh no, but we might as well have been," she confessed, her eyes sparkling with mischief as she lowered her voice, "because his wife caught us!"

"Where?" Mary's curiosity was getting the better of her and she felt a desperate desire to fish for the sordid details.

"Right here!" Agnes burst into laughter at the shocked look on the school teacher's face. "Right here in this very room!"

"And that's how you met Tom Watson?" Oliver's pen hovered over his notes.

"Well, it wasn't quite that simple, dear."

"Then how?" Mary asked, swinging her legs off the bed and sliding closer to them.

"Well," Agnes laughed, "remember I'm an actress, so I thought I'd do something really dramatic and drown myself."

"Oh my, you must have been very distressed," said Mary.

"Bless your heart, dear. No, it was more to get some attention and damned stupid too, I might add."

Oliver's pen was writing furiously as Agnes answered Mary's questions. He now glanced up waiting for the saga to continue.

"The row that followed was a fierce one," Agnes related. "The hotel asked me to leave, so I did."

By now, both Mary and Oliver were listening intently and there was not a sound in the room.

"I stole the hotel rowboat and rowed out into a gale," Agnes murmured, her voice growing softer with each word. "It really scared me, so I prayed for help and that's when I met Mr. Watson."

A knock on the door interrupted the interview.

"Just to let you know dinner is served at six, ma'am," the maid politely informed Mary when she opened the door. "Shall we reserve a table for you and your … husband?"

"Thank you, yes," Mary replied, shutting the door quickly and covering her mouth so the girl didn't hear her giggle. She turned and realized Agnes had left them. "Has she gone forever now?" she asked, going to sit where Agnes had been. "Will we see her again?"

Laying his notes and pen down, he slipped off his glasses, resting them on the arm of his chair.

"Do you want to see her again?"

"I would have liked to know how she came to get shot."

"But you already know that."

"I only know what history books say about her," Mary smiled impishly, "and we both know that's not always correct!"

"Do you want me to bring her back?"

The faint sound of a dinner gong delayed her answer and she just sat silent for a moment. Then, she suddenly got up and plopped herself on Oliver's lap. Their eyes met in a moment of gentle sadness as her arms enfolded him and he returned her embrace.

"Oh, Oliver," she whispered, "whatever will become of us?"

"It's an impossible situation, I'm afraid my love," he sighed. Lightly kissing her on the forehead, they looked into each other's eyes. "I think we'd better go downstairs," he said breaking away first. "We'll talk about this later. I promise."

But the interlude had been long enough for Mary to see his confusion. Afraid to think of what it meant, she shook herself and stood up. Going to the mirror in the bathroom, she took a minute to fix her hair and apply some lipstick. Then she stopped and looked at herself. *You have to stay calm, Mary. You know that Oliver cares for you and you're just going to have to have patience and see what happens. Falling in love with an angel from another century may be exciting but it certainly isn't very practical, girl!* She turned and left the bathroom, smiling bravely as she passed Oliver at the open door.

He followed her down the carpeted corridor watching the movement of her body. His mind was in a confused state again as he struggled with the problem of loving this remarkable girl from the future. Unaware of the assistance he was already receiving from his guardian angel, he silently pleaded to him. *I could really use your help on this one Tom!*

Taking a deep breath and putting on her best smile, Mary reached for his hand as they entered the small but luxurious dining room. Tables set with shining silver and glass on snowy white linen, greeted them. From the high decorative ceiling, several crystal chandeliers with dozens of tiny sparkling cluster lights threw a soft mellow glow over the room, and blue velvet drapes hung from high windows.

"This way please," the deep, melodious voice of the maitre d' murmured as he led the way to their table, unsmiling as he sat them. "Your waitress will be with you momentarily." Then he was gone.

"Wow," Mary whispered, "it's like stepping back in time."

"You are," Oliver chuckled softly, "remember?"

A uniformed waitress appeared, offering menus and asking if they would like an apéritif.

Oliver felt his heart begin to beat wildly. *Apéritif?* he thought in desperation, raising his eyebrows and looking over at Mary. *What do I know about apéritifs?*

Mary quickly came to his rescue.

"Red wine, please," she said confidently, pretty sure there wouldn't be the choice that existed in her time.

"And for you, sir?" asked the waitress.

"The same," said Oliver, breathing a sigh of relief when the woman left them. "Whew … thanks!"

"Look at these prices," Mary whispered. "$3.90 for prime rib, $2.10 for baked salmon, and lamb for only $1.90! You wouldn't believe how much these would cost in an exclusive restaurant."

She realized Oliver's attention had been taken as a handsome, well-dressed couple arrived and were shown to a nearby table. Oliver recognized Gus Jorgensen from Seattle and vaguely remembered the lady as being with him at Nancy's concert, although he hadn't met her. When Gus sat down and looked around, he instantly recognized Oliver and raised his hand.

"Hello Oliver, how nice to see you again," the shipping magnate announced in his jovial voice, getting back on his feet and coming to talk to them.

Oliver stood up and they shook hands like old friends.

"How are your glasses, son?" Gus asked, grasping his shoulder. "I believe you have already met my wife. Beth, this is the young man who broke his glasses when Peter knocked him down in the snow."

"Oh yes, I remember," she said smiling, "I'm glad to see you have recovered, Oliver. Did you and your friends enjoy Nancy's concert? That was a sweet little girl you had with you that night."

"Yes ma'am, she is," Oliver blushed, thinking quickly. "They're friends who have started a new life in Seattle. They needed some cheering up that night. Oh, please excuse me," he declared looking over at Mary and suddenly making a decision. "I'd like you to meet my fiancée, Mary Beth Janick from Everett."

Mary cocked her head and for the briefest of moments, looked stunned, but she recovered quickly and smiled at the Jorgensens. Under the table, her fingers searched for her ring and she almost laughed aloud when she found it on the other hand.

I imagine you have a good reason for this, Oliver! her thoughts shouted.

I certainly do, he replied, trying to pay attention to what Gus was saying.

They exchanged greetings, with Gus commenting on the similarity of the woman's names, then he surprised them further with a suggestion.

"It's so nice to see some friendly faces, would you mind if we joined you?" he asked, turning to Mary.

"Gus!" Beth hissed, "these young people might want to be alone."

"Oh, please do," Mary pleaded, "we would love your company."

"Only if you allow this cheeky old devil to pay the bill," Beth insisted.

With his colour rising, Oliver nodded, moving around the table to sit next to Mary as the waitress appeared with a bottle of red wine and two glasses.

"Double that order!" Gus' voice boomed, getting the waitress' attention as he went to assist his wife to their new table.

The maitre d' moved quickly to his side on his way to greet some new arrivals. "Excuse me, sir!" he whispered sternly. "Please don't shout, this is Oak Bay!"

The shipping magnate raised his eyebrows and a mischievous light twinkled in his eyes. "Oak Bay!" he chuckled, as the maitre d' got out of earshot, causing Mary to giggle but the waitress returned and filled four wine glasses with the rich-coloured red liquid.

After discussing the menu items, reminded by Beth that Gus was paying and to have what they liked, they gave the waitress their selection. Making a toast to the future of alcohol as the US and Canada moved closer to prohibition, Gus started a fascinating discussion ranging from the mills in Mary's hometown to the liquor shortage in Seattle.

"Agnes Millington and the anti-saloon league certainly kicked up a storm in the city," Gus said, "but they should never have shot her, that was despicable. I wish she had been on our side."

"Victoria will declare prohibition first," Oliver predicted, "this year, if the rumours are correct."

As the meal continued and Gus insisted on ordering dessert for them, Mary was eager to turn the conversation onto the night they had met her grandmothers at the concert. When dessert arrived, without warning, Oliver changed the subject onto the Nancy Wilson concerts.

"That girl's an angel," Beth sighed. "She's become like a daughter to us."

"Have you ever heard her sing?" Gus asked Mary.

"No, but I'd certainly like to."

"Then, just a minute," he said, putting his hand into his inner jacket pocket and producing some tickets. "I just happen to have two tickets for the January concert. Please come as our guests."

"Where is the concert?" Mary asked.

"They're always at the James Moore Theatre in Seattle and this one is on Friday, the 26th of January."

"Will you take me, Oliver?" Mary asked. "I'd love to meet her."

"Of course he will," Beth assured her, "but you don't need to wait dear. Nancy's a Victorian and lives at Gordon Head, only a few miles away. They're expecting us to drop in after dinner, why don't you both come with us?"

"Hm, it's twenty minutes past eight," Oliver murmured, looking at his pocket watch, then at Mary. "It's a little late to surprise them with extra guests, don't you think?"

Disappointment crossed Mary's face and, that was all the encouragement Gus needed. Jumping to his feet, he appeared fired with enthusiasm. "We won't take no for an answer. The time won't matter to them at all, they love company and are expecting us anyway. Go get your coats and let's go," he urged. "I'll meet you at the car. Beth you wait inside where it's warm, dear. Go, quickly now!"

Chapter 20

Overwhelmed by the Jorgensen's enthusiasm and generosity, Oliver and Mary hurried upstairs for their coats. After paying the bill, Gus went outside and, almost immediately, the green Dodge Tourer burst into life. When the others arrived, he opened the doors for them and, as Mary scrambled in, she gasped at the luxurious interior.

The car pulled quickly away from the inn and they settled into the soft leather seats, entertained by Gus' easy banter. The Dodge moved along quietly until he put it into first gear and they thundered through intersections with Mary trying to read the street signs in the dark. She knew they were heading toward town at first but then they turned right and passed the Jubilee Hospital.

They made a couple more turns and the surface of the road changed. Gus stepped on the gas and commented that this new section of Shelbourne was recently completed. A few minutes later, they were back to the bumps and ruts, slowing to make a right turn onto Ash Road.

"Slow down, Gus," Beth ordered her husband, "and please watch out for animals. You never know what you're going to meet in farm country!"

Turning into the drive of Cunningham Manor the gate suddenly swung open and Oliver grinned in the dark, patting Mary's hand.

"That's strange," Beth muttered, "it usually needs pushing open."

Even in the limited light from the headlights, one got the sense that the property was large and recently cleared, and then the house appeared.

That's a huge house, thought Mary, *these people must be quite wealthy for this day and age*.

The car swept up the drive and its headlights reflected off a small vehicle near the trees.

"Look Mary, they have a blue Model T Ford truck!" declared Oliver. "You don't see many of those around."

The inky blackness hid any trace of the clifftop and a twinkling porch light welcomed them as Gus parked the car. They all tumbled out and Beth led the way to the door. She tapped loudly and it opened to a squeal of delight from the most beautiful young woman Mary had ever seen. She was tall, slim, and her hair—the most glorious shade of red—hung in long curls about her shoulders. Beth addressed the elderly man beside her as Jebediah, giving him a hug. Mary watched the noisy greetings but her eyes were riveted on the young woman whom she assumed to be Nancy.

Jebediah must be her father, she thought as they moved inside. *I'll need to do some research on this family, no doubt they'll make another great story to tell my students!*

Once the door was closed, Gus took care of the introductions and Mary particularly noted he didn't call them family.

"Oliver and Mary are fans of yours," she heard Beth say to Nancy as they went into the living room. "We met them having dinner in Oak Bay, but you met Oliver before at the theatre."

"Yes, I do remember you, Mr. Ryan," Nancy agreed. "You're the newspaper reporter who broke his glasses in Seattle. You were looking after a war widow and her young daughter. What happened to them, are they all right?"

Mary was pleased at the genuine concern in Nancy's voice.

"They're doing well," Oliver replied, "and my crystal ball tells me they're going to have a good life."

"You can see into the future?" Meg giggled, as Jebediah cocked a sceptical eyebrow. "Well then, tell me young man, where did I leave my knitting?"

Amid the laughter, Oliver stared into Meg's eyes. He reached for her hand, making a show of tracing the lines on her palm as he stalled for time.

"Well, tell her, lad," Jebediah chuckled.

"It's under the cushion you're sitting on, sir," the reporter predicted.

"If you've been hiding my knitting again, Jebediah …," Meg threatened, "I'll scalp you!" Everyone watched as Meg pulled Jeb from the chair and lifted the cushion. "You old trickster," she squealed, retrieving up her knitting needles and wool, "you were hiding them all the time!"

Amid hearty laughter, Meg chased Jeb out to the kitchen. Dabbing tears of laughter from her eyes, Beth turned serious, catching Nancy up on the news of their boys. Mary heard the name of someone named Danny, knowing she should remember why it was familiar. The time went quickly and when Gus interrupted to suggest it was time to go, they all objected.

"We have to have these two back 'around 11' I was told at the hotel or they'd lock them out!" he explained with a chuckle.

Mary looked at her watch and couldn't believe the time. It was almost 10:30. She had certainly enjoyed their unplanned evening.

"Thanks for coming," Nancy called from the porch as they hurried to the car, shouting their thanks.

On the way back to the hotel, Oliver remembered his assignment on Nancy and asked the Jorgensens when Nancy had come to Victoria. They were obviously happy to talk about the girl whom they had met on a trip to Victoria several years before.

"That girl has come through a lot in her young life," said Gus, "losing her parents and growing up in an orphanage was pretty hard on her but she seems destined to succeed."

"Jebediah is not her father then?" asked Mary.

"Oh no," Beth joined in, her voice sounding emotional. "Danny is the closest to kin Nancy has and he's fighting in Europe, as are our two dear sons."

"Oh my," Mary replied softly, suddenly feeling they were prying.

It was almost 11 when the Jorgensens left them back at the inn after promising to meet again at Nancy's concert in January.

"Nice couple," Beth murmured, as they watched them enter the building and wave. "Oliver said they were engaged, didn't he?"

"Yes, dear, he did," Gus chuckled.

"I hope they have a long and happy life together … like we do, darling," his wife sighed, sliding a bit closer to him.

Back at the inn, the creaking front door sent a shudder up Mary's spine and she tightened her fingers on Oliver's hand. No one seemed to be around and their footsteps made no sound on the carpet as they went over to the stairs, barely aided by the light from a small lamp.

"This is spooky," she whispered as a stair tread creaked under their feet. "How are we going to find our room, it's terribly dark up there?"

"Like this," he whispered, sending his mind racing ahead … a door swung open and a light shone into the passageway.

"Bathroom's mine," she hissed, dashing ahead.

Oliver chuckled as she came to a sudden stop just inside the door, staring at the cases they'd left at the Temperance. Then her eyes moved to take in the two single beds.

"You are such a chivalrous gentleman, Oliver," she exclaimed, taking her suitcase to one of the beds. "In my time, we complain that chivalry and good manners are dead and buried. Oh, and by the way, you haven't explained your actions tonight," she said coyly, seeing his mystified expression and holding out her left hand palm down.

"My actions … oh, the ring you mean … yes, well I thought it would save trying to make explanations."

"Yes, that's no doubt true, but unless we're getting married I would rather you switch it back."

"I really think we should wait until we leave here tomorrow, that nosy woman will probably be back in the morning." Seeing her nod, he suddenly turned and went into the bathroom.

As Mary got into bed she felt the ring on her left finger trying to pull it off. It wouldn't budge. She played with it … it seemed normal, but it just wouldn't slide off her finger. She heard Oliver leave the bathroom but he surprised her by coming and sitting on the edge of her bed. Silently he took her into his arms and kissed her.

"Do you want me to move it back now?" he asked.

"I want to know how you truly feel?" she replied.

"That's easy, Mary. I love you and want to be with you forever … but we have a slight problem, we aren't in control here."

Unable to contain herself, she began to weep softly and he held her closer. "Please don't cry honey, Tom should have an answer for us soon and, in the meantime …." He hesitated, but in that split second, he made a momentous decision. "We're going to do what we want!"

"Are you kidding?" she asked, tearing herself away from him. "Won't that anger them … these spirits, even more?"

"You heard them at the meeting, I believe Tom has more control over me than they have. So, my darling, if you would like to get married, let's consider this a trial … isn't that what an engagement is? I want you to be happy and I just have a feeling things are going to work out soon," he said, kissing her hand.

"All right, let's do it and to heck with them all! Oh darling, I really do love you. I hope this doesn't get you into more trouble," she sighed, then squeezed his hand and giggled. "We wouldn't want them to banish you to the weather department!"

They laughed as they held each other for a minute longer, then Mary yawned and they kissed goodnight, both of them silently hating to part. He knew she would soon be asleep and, as he lay in the dark listening to her uneven breathing only a few feet away, he reviewed the evening's events. When her breathing changed to a slow rhythmic pattern, he sighed with relief. *Now's the time,* and his mind whisked him to the gates of Ross Bay Cemetery.

Tom, I need your advice, his thoughts pleaded, straining his eyes and ears for a sound or a sign. He walked over to Tom's grave and stroked the cold marble surface. Still no one appeared and his doubts began to consume him and rejection laid its cold hand on his soul. Had he dreamt all the things he thought had happened? Was Mary Janick merely a figment of his drunken imagination?

Searching frantically in his mind, he rose in frustration, kicking the shadows as he walked back along the dark pathway. Suddenly he realized he was in his pajamas and yet, felt quite warm—an eerie silence remained where crashing waves should have been. Turning back, a misty figure rose from Tom's grave.

"There was doubt in your mind, son!" the angel admonished him.

"Y-yes, sir," Oliver stammered. "I just wasn't sure any more."

"Come, let me refresh your memory." Reaching for Oliver's arm, Tom took him upwards into the clouds and a garden seat appeared. "Sit down and let's take a look at your accomplishments."

A picture began to form on the clouds and Oliver saw an old man bouncing a laughing young boy on his knee. "That's the old man you rescued from court with your compassion. Now look at the faces of

Bertha Bentley and Jane, where you experienced love for the first time. Remember how sad you were when they left. And then there were the times you protected Margo Lane and the two native boys. Don't you see the good you are doing, son?"

Tom went on with his dissertation. "Remember Rev. McLough on the train to Everett? Well, son, you taught him humility and now he's a believer. And here is young Joanie, you gave her trust when you healed her ankle." The picture faded and, in its place, Oliver saw the wild raging sea and the dock at Port Moresby. "That was another of your triumphs, Oliver," Tom stated, "but you stirred up a hornet's nest with Kate Reardon. You've a lot of work to do there yet."

"But, sir," Oliver muttered, "you haven't mentioned …."

"I know, son, I know," the angel sighed. "You found your true love and got yourself in a pickle."

"Can I stay with her?"

"It's impossible."

"I won't let her go!" he said adamantly.

Scratching his head, Tom knew this problem was not going to go away and Oliver's act of defiance showed a new side of his protégé. After a long minute, he spoke. "I suppose we could ask the council to allow you to live in each other's time."

"Live two lives at the same time?" Oliver gasped.

"I don't see why not," Tom retorted. "We often let people meet again, in another lifetime."

"We could be married twice," said the reporter, feeling suddenly quite giddy. "It sounds like an arrangement made in heaven and I think it would very well suit Mary!"

"Steady lad, I'll talk to the council and let you know what ruling they make."

Chapter 21

Light snow was falling as daylight woke the guests at the Old Charming Inn. Dressing quickly, Oliver shaved and packed his bag, humming a catchy little tune as he got ready.

Now what's going on in that head of his? Mary wondered.

When they were ready to go, he sent their luggage back to the Temperance. He returned the room to normal and they put their coats over their arms and went downstairs.

"Good morning, I'll hang your coats in our closet for you. Sit where you like, folks," the waitress announced, going to the bottom of the steps and tapping the meal gong with an odd-looking hammer.

"That's what I heard before dinner last night," Mary exclaimed. "I wondered what it was."

"It's an English tradition we have at the Old Charming Inn, ma'am," the girl replied, taking them to a table beside the window.

Once given, their order was quick in coming, and they watched the lightly falling snow and rolling white-capped waves charging into the bay as they ate. Glancing over at the reception desk, Mary caught her breath when she noticed a beautifully dressed woman checking into the hotel. On her head was the most fascinating hat Mary had ever seen. It had a narrow brim and was decorated with rolled-up ribbons which spilled over the sides and a large black, plumed feather jutted upward from one side.

"Quick," she whispered, "give me your pen and notepad, I must sketch that hat!"

"Goodness, you're able to draw, too?" Oliver commented as he watched her hurriedly sketch a remarkable likeness of the hat.

"I took some art classes a few years ago," she admitted, as the waitress came to refill their coffee.

"Can you draw me?" Oliver asked when she'd gone.

"Of course," Mary replied, smiling coyly.

She turned to a clean page, studied her subject intently—trying not to smile—then, in less than five minutes, deftly sketched an amazing likeness of Oliver's face.

"There you are!" she said triumphantly, pushing it across the table.

"Aren't you the woman of many talents?" he declared, studying the picture.

"It's just something I have fun with once in a while," she replied, then remembering something else, her tone changed and she looked at him seriously. "Where did you go last night?"

"How do you know I went anywhere?"

"You woke me."

"I did … how?"

"I heard you shout 'I won't let her go' and when I turned on the light, you were gone."

"Did it frighten you?"

"Of course not, I have faith, my darling," she replied with a straight face, though her eyes were sparkling. "I know you'll come back for me!"

Oliver reached across the table and took her hand. For a minute, they were lost in their own thoughts and didn't notice the waitress move silently across the carpet to stand in front of them.

"Excuse me," she began, speaking tentatively. "Is there anything more I can bring for you, ma'am … sir?"

Awaiting their decision, the girl, though disapproving, felt a twinge of envy at the affection being displayed. Her eyes flicked to Mary's left hand and briefly saw her engagement ring. Then suddenly, an almost imperceptible flash caused her to look again. Her hand flew to her mouth, eyes wide with surprise—a sparkling gold, wedding band now appeared on the young woman's finger. Shaking her head in disbelief, she tried to keep her composure as Mary, unaware of what had happened, looked up at her.

"No, thank you, dear," Mary replied, smiling at the gawking young woman, "that will be all."

Stumbling as she backed away, Judy mumbled incoherently as she returned to the reception desk.

Now all alone in the dining room, Oliver looked over at Mary as the familiar cold effect passed over him. Mary felt it, too, and grasped his hand. By the window, a ghostly form began to take shape. Moving to sit at the table next to them, Tom Watson removed his hat and placed it on the table.

"Children," he addressed them smiling, despite his tiredness, "I'm here to tell you that your request has been granted."

"What request?" Mary asked.

"We're married," Oliver interrupted emotionally. "Look at your finger, Mary!"

"But how?" she gasped, seeing the sparkling, yet unfamiliar, gold band on her left hand next to her engagement ring. Looking at it from all angles and touching it, she tried to pull it off.

"It won't come off, my dear," Tom chuckled. "It's your eternal link to Oliver. This is what you both wanted, is it not?"

Incredulously, Mary looked back and forth between the two angels. Many strange things had happened since her first meeting with Oliver. It was true, she had often imagined what it would be like to be married to him, after all, she was very sure she did love this unusual man. *Perhaps my mortal thoughts are not always realistic,* she reminded herself, *but I do know what I feel.*

But marriage meant a church service, a shopping trip for a wedding gown and invitations to her friends, not just a statement from an angel that it had happened. For the first time since meeting him, she experienced some doubt. *This is happening way too fast!* she agreed with Oliver's earlier concerns. *We've experienced so much but it's only been two weeks.* All she had known and learned was now in question.

Momentarily, she felt like a fraud and tears came to her eyes, and then her mind cleared. *What am I thinking? Of course, I know my own mind. I'm almost 30 years old for heaven's sake and, I know I'm in love with Oliver, but marriage ... so suddenly? Can the angels really control this as Tom said? There would have to be documents, yes, documents to prove we're married.* And then an even more important thought clouded her mind. *Cripes, how on earth am I going to tell mom and dad?*

"You're right, Mary," Tom broke into her thoughts. "I understand your concerns—you should know I'm able to read your thoughts, just like Oliver—check your handbag, my dear."

At the reception desk, the waitress was pointing to their table as she animatedly talked with the receptionist. "There's something very strange going on at that table, Phoebe." She told her about the ring and then noticed something else. "Look, who are they talking to?"

Straining to see, Phoebe watched Mary open her handbag and withdraw two neatly folded pages, spreading them out on the table.

"I'll go take a look," she muttered, her stern expression focussed on the couple as she moved purposely toward their table.

Mary, meanwhile, was trying to keep her composure as she read the papers and realized they were indeed copies of a marriage certificate with their names and today's date.

"Mr. Watson, if I have anything to say in this matter, I have a request," she stated firmly. When neither of her companions objected, she continued. "I don't appreciate that you spirits can read my mind, hear everything I think …," she began.

"But Mary, I don't …," Oliver replied, planning to defend himself.

"Shh, here comes trouble," Mary hissed, noticing the woman out of the corner of her eye and seeing the determined look on her face.

"She can't see me," Tom assured them nonchalantly, "unless," he added with a twinkle in his eye, "I want her to!"

Interrupting their laughter, Mrs. Kitson stormed over to their table.

"Excuse me, madam," she snapped, her reputation for being pompous and authoritative shining through. "Do you require some assistance?"

"I hardly think so," Mary bristled defensively, folding the papers and putting them back into her handbag.

"You're talking to an empty chair, madam … nobody is sitting there. Are you sure you're all right?"

Tom could see his protégé was getting agitated and, with good reason, so he decided to pay this meddlesome mortal a lesson of his own. Jamming the top hat onto his head, he instantly materialized.

"So, I'm a nobody, am I, Mrs. Kitson?" he demanded. "Well, you are an ill-mannered mortal!"

Phoebe Kitson's terror-filled scream shattered the quiet of the dining room as she ran from the room and Judy, having caught a glimpse of the ghostly figure before covering her eyes, hid behind the reception desk, shaking with disbelief.

"Time to leave this place," Tom chuckled, his physical form becoming a wisp of vapour as his voice faded. "Let them try explaining that to their mortal friends!"

"We should go, too," Oliver whispered, "but I'll pay the bill first. That should add to their confusion." Stacking ten silver dollars on top of the bill, he took Mary's hand and they quickly went to get their coats from the hall closet aware that the frightened women had disappeared. Not bothering to put them on, he directed his thoughts to downtown Victoria.

"My goodness, it's cold here today," she retorted with a shiver when they arrived on the sidewalk outside his hotel.

"It might help if you put your coat on, Mrs. Ryan," he suggested, assisting her as they ran to the door.

Without waiting for him, she ran up the stairs. Stopping on the first landing, she called out to him. "It would have saved us this fuss if you had simply brought us back *inside* the hotel. Can we go back to Seattle now?"

"No, not yet, my darling!" came his voice from above on the next landing.

Sighing, she moved toward him. "And why not? You got your interview with Agnes, Tom Watson says we're married and I'm so cold I feel like icicles are growing on me … I want a nice warm room!"

Reaching the third floor, a chuckling Oliver took her into his arms and kissed her. In an instant, they were inside his room and the heat had been turned up, making it a balmy 75 degrees. Feeling her shiver, he held her briefly before helping her off with her coat.

"We'll be back in Seattle for dinner," he promised, "but first would you like to see what is going on over at the Old Charming Inn?"

"I don't want to go back there," she confessed grimacing, "but I'd sure like to see what happened after we left."

"I think I can arrange that, why don't you make yourself comfortable," he chuckled, patting the bed. "Watch the wall."

Doing as he said, she gasped, then laughed. "It's a movie of the restaurant … amazing; I'm not even touching you! But I really shouldn't be amazed any more, should I?"

"We must be connected by your wedding ring," Oliver muttered as she moved closer to him kissing him quickly on the cheek. "Shh, listen."

"No, sir, I didn't imagine it," Mrs. Kitson was saying to the owner. "There was a ghost sitting in that chair! He was wearing a black top hat and had long silver-coloured hair."

"How do you know it was a ghost, Mrs. Kitson?" he asked.

"He-he appeared in a wisp of-of smoke and talked to me, then he disappeared again!" she exclaimed haltingly, her voice becoming louder and more shrill as she relived the still unbelievable experience.

"Stop it!" the man shouted angrily. "This is ridiculous, this hotel is relatively new. We don't have ghosts at the Old Charming Inn!"

Phoebe looked at Judy for confirmation of her story, but the girl was standing silently behind the reception desk. Eyes bulging, her white knuckles still clutched the counter and she looked ready to have a nervous breakdown.

Striding over to the table in question, the frustrated owner pointed at the ten silver dollars stacked neatly on top of the bill.

"And I suppose ghosts pay their bills with real money?" he hissed sarcastically, picking up the coins and examining them.

"N-no, sir," Mrs. Kitson continued in a whimper. "The ghost didn't pay the bill, Mr. Ryan paid it!"

"Dammit girl, I've had about enough of this silly conversation. I should fire both of you," he threatened then, thinking of something pertinent, he asked, "Did you see Mr. and Mrs. Ryan leave?"

Tom Watson smiled as he watched from the corner of the room. The old angel was aware how bad Mary felt about scaring these women.

"Please don't make them suffer any more," she pleaded.

Pointing his finger at the wall Oliver stopped time, inwardly cheering at Mary's compassion. *I could wipe their memories away,* he thought, *but then they would still be their nasty selves. No,* he concluded, *I shall leave a bit of doubt in their minds and every time they feel grouchy or nosy, they'll see a vision of Tom in his top hat!*

Watching him carefully as he reversed time, Mary saw the picture on the wall run backwards, stopping at the moment before Tom's ghostly appearance.

Wow, she thought, *Oliver's using his mind like a video camera yet he lives in the era of silent movies!*

"Stop!" Tom barked from the shadows. "You must not change the facts. I told you before, you can't change history, Oliver."

Mary was so startled, her body flinched and she almost screamed.

"I'm not," Oliver argued taking her hand, "but we left a problem behind us and I'm about to put it right."

"They deserved it," quipped the old angel.

Smiling, Oliver ignored his guardian and started time again. First, he adjusted Judy, the nosy waitress' reaction to Mary's conversation with an empty chair. As the picture moved on, she heard Tom chuckling with satisfaction when Judy responded, "Why Mrs. Kitson, I talk to myself all the time, I find I get less argument that way."

He stopped time again, taking a moment to think it out carefully as Mary applied pressure to his arm. Flicking his hand again, time moved on and the images on the wall played a new scene.

Phoebe appeared behind her reception desk with a rarely seen smile on her face as she glanced up and saw Tom's ghostly figure appear in the chair. No surge of fear charged through her brain this time. Oliver's adjustment was working and she rose from her desk eager to be of service to the strange old gentleman that had suddenly appeared.

"You must be a ghost," she laughed. "I never saw you arrive. May I gct you something, sir?"

"Well done, lad," Tom whispered, fading away with the picture.

"Is that what they'll remember?" Mary whispered, seeing Oliver's grin of satisfaction. "Oliver, I'm so proud of you and I'm very happy to be your wife."

"Are you sure? Wouldn't you like to complete that unfinished conversation we had back at the inn … about my hearing your thoughts?" he asked slyly.

"Yes, I would, it's a dreadful problem for a girl to have someone able to read her mind!"

"Tom! Are you still there?" called Oliver.

"Yes," came the chuckle as the old angel materialized in front of them. "You've given me time to consider this situation, Mary, and here's my suggestion. Would it be more acceptable if, when you wanted Oliver to hear your thoughts, you simply use his name at the beginning of the sentence?"

"Can you really do that, Tom?" asked Mary.

"He can do almost anything he wants, my love—he can also let you try it out for a while to see if it works for you!" Oliver chuckled. "Isn't that true?"

"Yes, it's true. Do you like my solution, Mary?"

"I do like it and if I can try it out for a while, that's even better," she agreed, taking Oliver's hand. "Thank you, to both of you."

"Now go make your plans and enjoy yourselves, children," Tom commanded, fading quickly away.

Going over to the window, Oliver looked at the slushy surfaces below and his mind began planning their journey home to Seattle. Suddenly, he heard a sound and realized Mary was sitting on the bed giggling. Sitting down in the chair opposite her, he asked what was so funny.

"I guess I'm just a bit giddy with happiness," she admitted. "How are we going to explain this to mom, dad and Kate?

"We'll figure out something," he began, before his new wife jumped up from the bed and landed on his lap wrapping her arms around his neck and kissing him. "Hmm," he murmured. "I really think this confirmed bachelor is going to like his new life," he admitted, picking her up in his arms.

Oliver, I love you! her thoughts whispered as her arms tightened around his neck again.

"I heard that!" he reported as their lips met.

"Wouldn't it be nice, if we could take mom and dad to Nancy's concert?" she commented as they tended to their packing a bit later.

"Hmm, I wonder how I could manage that?" he murmured. "You'll have to give me some time to think about it."

Knowing they needed to have some lunch soon, Mary suggested they go over to Rogers' to get some chocolates to take home, receiving only a murmur from Oliver who was busily writing. When they left the hotel, she noticed he was still very quiet.

"It's possible," he suddenly said aloud, "but it would take some planning."

"What would take some planning?" she asked.

"I've been thinking about your request for your parents to see the concert."

"Oh, is that why you're so quiet. What are you thinking?"

"We already have two tickets so we need two more."

"That shouldn't be a problem for an angel!"

"I can't just counterfeit them you know!" he declared, chuckling at his wife's confidence in his abilities.

She tugged him toward the doorway of Rogers' Chocolate Shop.

"I must take some home for mom," she declared, pulling him inside. "Oh look, they've got a new flavour, let's try one."

"Mary Janick!" he teased, as the door banged behind them, "don't you go blaming your mother, it's you who wants the chocolates!"

She turned to face him with as serious an expression as she could muster and pulled off her glove, showing him her hand with the ring sparkling on her finger. "Janick?" she asked sternly, "see this ring, I'm Mrs. Ryan now and don't you forget it!"

"Sorry teacher, a momentary lapse of memory," he said, pouting.

From behind the counter, Mrs. Rogers couldn't help but hear their banter and smiled as she went to serve them.

A few minutes later, they left the store and were greeted by huge wet snowflakes. Taking his arm, she whispered in his ear, "Let's stay one more night at the Gatsby and stop this awful snow. It's so wet!"

"You know I can't change the weather, Mary."

"You can if we go back to my time, there was no snow in the forecast there!" she laughed, her eyes twinkling.

"I thought you wanted to go back to Everett?"

"A girl can change her mind, can't she? Have you heard of a woman's prerogative?"

"Sounds like I have more to learn about women than I thought," he declared, pretending to look frustrated. Agreeing that it seemed a good idea, he willed them back to December 29th, 2000 where a morning of crisp winter sunshine and the modern world welcomed them again.

"If only I could show my students how things have changed, it would make history classes so much more interesting," she declared.

"It should be easy to make your classes more interesting, Mary. You've seen the differences in our times, paint them a picture in words and they can't help but believe it! People will assume you get your knowledge from a history book; you know differently! Your students will love it."

She thanked him with a kiss, saying she would try it. She was beginning to enjoy this quick marriage, maybe it was right for her after all, they complimented each other so well. She'd been looking for that special guy for years and as soon as she'd stopped thinking about it, it was quite amazing what happened. She gave his hand a squeeze as they set out toward the harbour.

He remembered now just how much he enjoyed Mary's time although he still couldn't get used to the designs of the new buildings. Aloud he told her he couldn't wait to visit 21st century Seattle. She began chattering, and in no time, they were at the Gatsby. Before going inside, he brought their luggage from the Temperance and Kathy was there to welcome them.

"Well hello, Mary and Oliver," the girl bubbled from behind the reception desk. "Are you coming back to stay with us again?"

"Just for one night, you do have the room available don't you?" she asked hopefully, suddenly realizing they hadn't made any reservations.

Spinning the register, Kathy offered her a pen. "Will Oliver sign?"

"Certainly not," Mary chuckled, "but I will."

Kathy and Oliver both watched with interest as Mary printed bold and clear, Mr. and Mrs. Oliver Ryan. Blushing at first, then leaping back in alarm, Oliver watched as the squealing girl dashed around the counter to hug Mary.

"Congratulations," she yelped. "I'll give you a different room this time!" she whispered mischievously to Mary handing her a key. "This one's the honeymoon suite and it has a queen-size bed!"

Upstairs, Oliver surprised her by picking her up and carrying her into the room, closing the door with his heel and transferring the luggage by thought. She returned his kiss as the voice of Tom Watson whispered, *Remember children, this is not for one lifetime, it's for all of eternity.*

"Go away, Mr. Watson," she whispered, suddenly feeling quite giddy, "these newlyweds wish to be alone!"

Chapter 22

They had a late lunch at the Gatsby and were pleased to see the clouds disappear and the sun come out. Feeling happier than she had in days and, noticing that Oliver seemed to be more relaxed, Mary suggested they take a cab to Chinatown and visit the museum.

"Why don't we leave the museum for another time," he suggested as they waited for the taxi.

"You're probably right we should try to relax a bit. We have the New Year to celebrate in two days though. You've never mentioned any friends, Oliver, isn't there someone you'd like to celebrate with?"

"Only you, my girl, but we'll be able to celebrate both 1917 and 2001! They might come a few days apart though."

"Oh right, what a hoot! You're becoming a 21st century man, Oliver, because 2001 is the beginning of the 21st, did you know that?"

"Can't say that I ever gave it any thought," he replied as they climbed into the back seat of the taxicab.

"We'll have to give it some thought now because our 84-year celebration is the day after tomorrow night! Do you realize we haven't even talked about living arrangements and that sort of thing? We'll need to get an apartment in Everett, will you come home every night or stay in Seattle?" Mary whispered excitedly as they drove to town, telling the driver to stop at Fisgard Street.

After paying the driver, Oliver grabbed her hand.

"Slow down, honey! We don't have to plan it all in one afternoon, you know. However, I do think we should live some of our lives separate during the week … for now. It will give us both a chance to adjust. We can visit easily enough if we want to see each other. All you have to do is call me!"

"I guess the phone system won't work between 84 years, will it?" she laughed. "We'll just have to use our thoughts."

For the next two hours, they wandered through Chinatown, peering down narrow passageways once the home of hundreds of Chinese families, and looking in quaint stores where you could find trinkets of every shape and kind. They found other interesting gift shops and soon realized it was beginning to get dark and they were hungry again. Glad of the chance to sit down, they stopped at a harbourside restaurant with a view of the illuminated legislative buildings.

They listened with interest to a group of young people at the next table who said they were going to UVic and a lecture on extrasensory perception and faith-healing. Mary translated for him saying it was the University of Victoria. The heated discussion proved they were a divided group—three thought it was impossible and had no intention of being convinced, but the fourth member of their party, a girl with a noticeable speech impediment and sad eyes, caught Mary's interest.

"What is it, darling?" Oliver whispered. "I can't hear you but I sense you'd like to go to the lecture, true?"

"Yes, I really would," she said with only a slight hesitation.

"Excuse me," he said, turning to get the attention of one of the young people. "We couldn't help overhearing some of your conversation. How far away is the university? Is it possible we could attend the lecture?"

"Sure," one of the young men laughed, "five dollars will get you a good laugh at all the fools who believe in this rubbish. You could ride with the stutterer, I'm sure Ruth would be glad of your company."

The bespectacled girl bit her lip in obvious embarrassment as she turned sad eyes toward them.

"That was cruel," Mary snapped, "and totally uncalled for, young man."

"Th-th-th-that's a-a-all right," Ruth struggled to say, "I-I-I'm u-u-used to i-it."

"We're Oliver and Mary, would you mind if we drove with you, Ruth?" Oliver asked the girl as she wiped a tear away.

Being glad of the company, they walked toward the Broughton Street parkade keeping behind Ruth's snickering companions. They could feel the girl's embarrassment and Oliver's temper was rising, his angel powers straining to be unleashed on her tormentors. Mary squeezed his hand in an effort to calm him.

"You sit in the front," he told Mary, when Ruth led them to her small battered car and unlocked the door.

As they got in, he brushed the dented door with his eyes making it new, hinges suddenly lost their squeaks and the paintwork shone with a freshly polished lustre.

Ruth struggled with the gear lever and apologized for the grinding.

"I-I-I have t-t-trouble w-with m-my g-g-gears," she explained.

"Don't you worry, my dear," Oliver consoled her, "from this moment on everything will be fine."

Glancing over at Ruth, Mary saw Oliver put his hand on her shoulder and knew angel power was at work. Making casual conversation, she hoped Ruth would answer and find her stuttering impediment was gone. Would she also notice the gear box grinding had disappeared or that the engine now purred? Ruth, however, remained silent.

Suddenly, as the car turned onto Mackenzie from Quadra, she did speak.

"Oh dear," she murmured, "I left my gloves at the restaurant."

Oliver's mind flashed back to the place they'd eaten dinner and in the blink of an eye, he located the gloves and was back.

"Are these your gloves?" he asked, handing them between the seats.

"How did they get there?" she asked. "I was sure I left them in the restaurant." Suddenly, her voice faded. "My words … I'm not stammering!" she screamed, slamming on the brake.

Lurching sideways, the car skidded wildly. Mary reached instinctively for the dashboard to brace herself, but the belt held firm.

"Faith my darling!" Oliver chuckled in her ear, as the car came to a safe stop.

Attempting to calm herself, Ruth bubbled with enthusiasm. The unbelievable had happened.

"Do you know what's happened?" she asked with a nervous laugh.

"Yes, we know, dear," Mary replied smiling at her. "You've been touched by an angel."

The girl looked at Mary and then back at Oliver.

"You're joshing me," she replied, watching them both smile.

Taking a deep breath, she turned around and started the car again, commenting on the gears being better. She chattered incessantly, loving the sound of her own words and her new, perfect voice. They were turning into the parking lot at the university when she admitted, "I really didn't have faith in this healing thing," she said, "but I hoped like heck somebody would be able to help me." She paused as her eyes searched for an empty space. "Do you think an angel will find me a parking space?" she giggled.

"Sure he will," Oliver chuckled. "Try the row closest to the door, I think there's an empty space just waiting for you."

The space was there just as Oliver had predicted. Ruth locked the car so quickly she didn't notice its exterior changes and they quickly made their way up the steps to the auditorium entrance. Her friends were waiting.

"Did she drive you mad with her stuttering," Brian Dalby, the tall skinny boy, laughed.

"No, I did not," Ruth answered fluently. "I'm cured. Mary says I've been touched by an angel."

"And I suppose Mary is an authority on angels!" Brian sneered, not yet realizing her stutter was absent.

"No, she's not, but I am," Oliver interrupted, "and you're about to learn about compassion my friend."

"W-w-why w-would I w-want t-t-to kn-kn-know a-bout c-c-compassion?" Brian replied scornfully, struggling with his words.

Ruth's other two friends, Betty and Peter, stared at Brian in stunned amazement. Heard by passing students, he quickly became the focus of their laughter and cruel jokes.

"Don't listen to them, Brian," Ruth rushed to defend him. "I know how it feels."

Hardly daring to speak, Brian hung his head as they joined the lineup for tickets—not daring to speak again. These people were supposed to be his friends and instead they were making fun of him. He was beginning to understand this man's point but who was he?

Inside the auditorium, Ruth went to sit with her friends while Oliver and Mary sat in the row behind them. The lecture was about to begin and on the podium, the lecturer stared out at the sea of eager faces.

His first few sentences quickly alerted Oliver to his real intention for when he began speaking of ghosts and spirits he discredited their existence.

"There's no such thing," he shouted from the podium, "ghosts are merely a figment of an over-active imagination."

"And what about angels?" Ruth called from her seat.

"There's no scientific evidence at all," his voice boomed through the speakers. "It's merely the power of one's mind."

"I was cured of a stutter tonight, sir," Ruth persisted.

Smiling at the girl's tenacity, Oliver felt Mary's fingers tighten on his hand. *Oliver, teach him a lesson, sweetheart,* she prodded. He looked at Mary out of the corner of his eye and winked.

"Oh come now, young lady," the speakers crackled, "I think you're exaggerating things."

"N-n-no sh-sh-she's not!" Brian leapt to his seat. "Sh-sh-she was cu-cu-cured t-to-night b-but it was g-g-given to me."

"Then I suggest this angel cure you, too," the quick-thinking lecturer sneered.

"I-I-I w-w-wish the angel w-w-would g-give you a st-st-stammer, y-y-you f-fool!" Brian spat out angrily.

"Tha-tha-that's n-not v-very l-l-likely!" the lecturer exclaimed.

Reaching over, Oliver touched Brian, coaxing him to sit down. "You've learned your lesson, son, you're cured," he whispered, pointing his finger at the lecturer.

An ominous silence filled the auditorium as the man's stuttering voice faded away. With his hands tightly gripping the podium, his eyes grew large and, with shocked amazement, searched the audience.

All of a sudden, Ruth broke the stillness yelling at the top of her voice. "I believe in angels!"

"Time to go," Oliver whispered, as an uproar of discussion filled the auditorium and he whisked them back to Victoria.

When Ruth turned to speak with Oliver and Mary, she gasped. Seeing the empty seats, she realized the truth. She *had* been in the company of an angel, perhaps even two of them.

In the years to follow, she would become a reputable lecturer at this same university and, when she stood at the podium, she often looked out at the seats and remembered this chance meeting which changed her life.

The welcoming, warm interior of the Gatsby enveloped them as they slipped silently into their room. Later, talking in whispers as they lay in each other's arms just before going to sleep, Mary was startled when she heard a faint yet familiar voice calling her name.

"Oliver, is that Kate's voice?" she asked.

"Yes, she's actually rubbing her earring, something must be wrong." They sat up and listened.

Kate, shoulders bowed with fatigue and worry, paced the corridor at the hospital in Everett, her fingers gently rubbing the tiny angel on her earring.

"Where are you, Mary?" her mind silently screamed. "Your father needs you, he's had a heart attack!"

In the room at the end of the corridor, Gordon Janick was fighting for his life. Barely breathing, doctors worked frantically to keep him alive. In the waiting room, comforted by a nurse, Janice was also fighting her own fears.

"I'll be right back," Oliver snapped, sending his spirit body to Gordon's hospital bed and stopping time, then immediately returning to Mary. Taking his wife in his arms, he explained what he had done and the few details he knew about the situation.

"There has to be something we … you can do, Oliver. Please help my dad," she begged, shivering involuntarily and beginning to cry.

Oliver dressed quickly and tried to console his wife.

"Mary you have to keep your wits about you. Come on, get dressed, you can go with me. I only have things under control for a brief time. Hurry … now!"

Oliver's harsh order jerked her into action and she was dressed and ready to go in five minutes. As they were about to leave, Tom Watson appeared, sternly wagging his finger at his protégé.

"You can't change what's already happened, Oliver."

"Don't worry, old friend, you taught me well. I know the rules."

Mary, begging Tom to let them go, locked arms with Oliver. A biting cold wind touched her face as they were transported to Providence Everett Medical Center.

"Oh no," she groaned, her imagination running wild as they pushed through the big doorway. "Nobody's moving, they're all like statues!"

"It's all right, I've stopped time for a while."

Following the long corridor, Mary searched the faces for someone familiar. Oliver's senses now picked up the vibrations from Kate's earrings.

"We'll find them," he snapped, tugging Mary through the maze of silent corridors until, rounding a corner, they found Kate standing statue-like in a waiting area. A sparkling tear set in time hung on her cheek and her fingers still touched her earring.

"Quiet now," Oliver whispered. "I'm going to release her spirit and let her lead us to your father."

Mary watched spellbound as Kate's spirit slipped out of her mortal form, materializing into a perfect duplicate of her living body. No sound came from Kate's feet as she strode along the corridor toward the waiting room where they found Mary's mother.

"Hold tight," Oliver warned as he released her mother's spirit. "Janice, take us to Gordon."

Dreamlike, Janice led them through the surgical wing to a room where the still, pale form of her husband lay on an operating table as if in the middle of a surgery. Three surgeons hovered motionless over him.

"Don't move," Oliver ordered as she saw her father's spirit rise from the table.

Mary saw the fire in Oliver's eyes and the light that slowly swept over her father's human form. She felt the intensity of her husband's effort and knew the power vested in him would be helping her father.

"Are you ready to leave, honey," he whispered wearily. "I have to send the spirits back and start time again."

"Wait," Mary insisted, "perhaps we should leave some proof that we were here."

"All right, hang your locket around your mother's neck and I'll take one of Kate's angels, but hurry."

Mary quickly did as Oliver said.

"It's time, Mary," he insisted, nodding and the spirits disappeared. Pointing his finger, time began once again and they returned to the Gatsby. Collapsing into Oliver's arms, Mary sobbed with relief. Picking her up and laying her on the bed, he covered her with the quilt and handed her the TV remote. Not wanting her to know he was going back to the hospital, he slipped into the bathroom hoping she would be occupied and not miss his short absence.

Back at the hospital, he watched the frantic actions of the surgical team as they finished the operation. He chuckled silently when they looked at each other with puzzled expressions.

"This man's heart is as healthy as mine!" declared one of the surgeons. "Who diagnosed this as cardiac? I believe this was a minor, a minor digestive upset! Give this man some meds, get rid of that smell and monitor him closely, very closely overnight!"

Looking into the future, Oliver knew that the next day, the Janicks would be told there had been a misdiagnosis—Gordon hadn't had a heart attack after all, ending his frightening adventure which had brought him to the brink of the Afterworld. In the meantime, Oliver transported himself back to the Gatsby where he felt Tom's presence and knew he was in trouble.

"You cheated fate tonight, my boy," his ghostly voice rattled through the room as his protégé came out of the bathroom, "it has caused quite a stir in the Afterworld you know."

"I stayed within the rules, sir."

"The angel of death had everything ready for Gordon Janick's soul."

"Let him wait!"

Her eyes red from crying and voice quivering with emotion, Mary sat up in bed and turned to face Oliver's guardian angel.

"Please, don't let them take my dad yet, Mr. Watson," she pleaded.

"Oh, your father will be fine for many more years, Mary, Oliver has his mark on him," the angel chuckled. "That was really smart thinking to stop time, my boy. You're forbidden to change history but all you did was change the situation before it happened, very clever! I commend you, you've learned your lessons well."

In an instant, he was gone and Mary dropped her head into her hands and began to laugh.

"Are you laughing? What's so funny?" asked Oliver, sitting down beside her.

"I was so scared and now I'm so tired but Tom arrives at the darndest times! One day he's going to embarrass himself," she giggled.

"More than likely it will only embarrass us, honey," he assured her, kissing her tenderly. "Now how about both of us getting some sleep."

Sleeping in, they woke curled up beside each other and listened to the sound of the Sunday church bells. Dressing quickly and packing their bags, they presented themselves at the reception desk.

"Not staying for breakfast, Mr. and Mrs. Ryan?" Kathy asked. "The *Coho* doesn't leave until 10:30."

"Oh, we have other arrangements," Oliver replied vaguely, taking out his billfold.

They must be flying, Kathy thought to herself as she finished checking them out and Oliver paid the bill in cash. *I haven't heard any planes in the harbour this morning though, due to the fog.* Glancing up from her desk as she heard the door bang behind them, she waited for them to pass the window, but no one appeared.

"We can eat here," Oliver announced as they materialized in front of a ramshackle diner on the Seattle waterfront. "That's strange," he muttered, "it appears to be closed."

"Read the notice, silly," Mary laughed, "it's due for demolition. This is the year 2000, Oliver; did you intend it to be 1916?"

Oliver stared at the front of his favourite eating place, its dirty windows, peeling paint and the door with its broken latch. *Not everything changes for the better,* he thought. Passersby cast inquisitive glances at them as Oliver pushed the door open and pulled Mary into the cold, dank interior.

"Close your eyes," he whispered, taking her hand and rolling his mind back through the years to 1916. "That's better!"

Mary opened her eyes to find the café had reverted to a bustling, popular restaurant.

"Hi Mr. Ryan, sit anywhere you like," called Alice. "I'll be with you in a tick."

Finding a booth, the waitress brought them two cups of hot coffee and menus. Taking a sip, the steam clouded the reporter's glasses and he slipped them from his face, cleaning them with the paper napkin.

"I'd better go take my report into the office," he announced with a rueful smile. "Do you mind if I leave you for a little while?"

"No, I'll be fine, honey. I'll order for both of us."

Two coffee cups rattled noisily on her tray as the waitress swished between the tables. A puzzled frown crossed her face when she saw Mary sitting alone.

"Has he left already, deary," she chirruped brightly. "Maybe you'd like a newspaper."

"Yes, that would be nice, I'll order in a minute. He'll be back by the time our order comes."

Quickly producing the well-thumbed copy of today's *Courier*, the waitress dropped it on the table. "What can I get ya?" she asked.

Mary ordered two orders of ham, eggs and toast, then sipping her coffee, read the headline on the paper. 'WAR LOOMING OVER AMERICA,' it said in bold letters. It went on to give details of the many army camps now under construction and the training programs and recruiting drives that would be happening all across the country. The inside pages vent fury on leaders that allowed the German government to go unpunished after sinking American merchant ships and the passenger liner *Lusitania* in May of 1915.

"Scary stuff," Mary muttered turning to the inside pages. 'Prohibition Needed To Clean Up City,' she read as the article went on to predict that Canada was about to declare its own anti-liquor law.

"Have you eaten, yet?" Oliver's voice burst into her thoughts, as he rejoined her.

"Of course not, you were too fast … this is history," Mary sighed, showing him the paper. "Can I take this with me? I'd like a couple of these articles for class study."

"It's all right, we'll find you a new copy."

"Can we get one with the *Lusitania* sinking in it, too?"

"That was back in May of 1915."

"Yes, I know. It was sunk on the seventh."

"We'll have to get that from Margo," he laughed, "too bad I didn't know you wanted it when I was just there."

"Here you are, folks," the waitress interrupted, emptying her tray on their table. "Let me know if you need anything else."

Eating slowly, they listened to the hubbub of conversations—opinions on prohibition, the looming war, and the upcoming political race for the mayor of Seattle.

One dockworker shouted, "Hiram Gill has more faces than the City Hall clock. He'll say anything to get elected!"

Tempers flared and chairs crashed over as a number of men came to their feet arguing loudly, obviously prepared to do battle. Mary remembered that history claimed this as the beginning of the violent, formative years of Seattle's greatness.

Oliver paid their $3 bill, leaving a 10-cent tip and they went outside.

"Are you going to take me home now?" she asked, linking his arm and closing her eyes. She expected the street noises to stop, but nothing happened and, hearing him laugh, she opened them again.

"So what's the hold up?" she asked. "Aren't we going to Everett?"

"Of course we are."

"Well, when?"

"After we get your papers!"

Chapter 23

Arriving at the *Courier* office, Oliver nodded to the security guard and went to speak with the new weekend receptionist.

"Is Margo in Harry Jenson's office?" he asked.

"Mr. Jenson is no longer with us, sir," she replied. "If you'll wait, I'll see if Miss Lane is available."

"That's all right, we know our way," he said, heading toward the copy editor's office. *Harry gone?* thought Oliver, looking over at Mary. "That's welcome news, but I wonder what happened to my report?" he whispered.

"Hello Oliver, Mary!" Margo called from behind them. "Oliver, your report on Agnes Millington was brilliant. She proved to be a very interesting subject, just as I thought. I don't know how you do it but you certainly make her story believable."

"Thank you," he murmured. *Well, I guess someone found it on Harry's desk!* "What happened to Harry?"

"He had a row with my father and it seemed it was the excuse we needed to fire the obnoxious man. It's so nice around here without him and I'm getting a lot more responsibility."

"Margo," Mary interrupted, "I'm interested in getting a copy of the newspaper from the 8th of May, 1915. Is that possible?"

"And a copy of today's paper as well," Oliver interjected.

Cocking an eyebrow, Margo thought for a moment and beckoned them to follow her, their hurrying steps echoing in the wide corridors.

"You have a special use for this 1915 copy, Mary?" Margo asked.

"I'm a school teacher at Everett High. I want my class to study the sinking of the *Lusitania*."

"Well done, the kids should know this was a terrible act. It's going to bring America into the war," she said, continuing to give her views on the probability of war until they reached a door labelled, 'Archives.'

When they returned to Margo's office with the papers in hand, they stopped in her office momentarily. As they talked, Mary noticed a number of Nancy Wilson concert tickets on Margo's desk.

"Could we buy two of those tickets, Margo?" she asked.

"I'm sorry, you can't," the girl replied thoughtfully, looking from one to the other. She smiled coyly. "I will make a deal with you, though. If Oliver will write Nancy's story, I'll give you the two tickets."

"What kind of a story?" Oliver asked suspiciously.

"Facts, Oliver, the facts. We know Nancy is a Canadian from Victoria and sings like an angel, there's got to be a good story in there somewhere."

"You'll print whatever I write?" he asked, trying to be casual.

"No guarantees," Margo chuckled, "but she's got thousands of fans in Seattle and it would certainly sell newspapers."

"You've got a deal, now give Mary those tickets, we have to catch the Interurban."

Rain had turned to snow again as they left the *Courier* office going straight for the Interurban terminal. After purchasing tickets, they boarded the 11:30 to Everett and settled into a window seat to watch the familiar scenery roll by the windows.

"What will you write about Nancy Wilson?" Mary asked. "You won't tell her secrets to the world will you, dear?"

"Maybe she doesn't have any."

"Oh, we all have a little something."

"And you, my sweet?" he grinned. "What's your deep dark secret?"

"You are. Do you think anyone would believe me if I told them I was married to an angel!"

It was after one o'clock when they stepped from the trolley and Oliver took them to the year 2000. Looking around, he was greatly surprised to see the Everett Station still existed, now as a medical building. A third floor had been added to the old brick building and, surprisingly, the dispatcher's cupola remained. Mary told him the Interurban had ceased operation in 1939 as better roads encouraged the use of automobiles—nothing had replaced it so far.

"Now the public are demanding a monorail and, with the concern about pollution and getting cars off the busy highways .... oh goodness, here I go again," she laughed. "You don't know what the heck I'm babbling about. I'm sorry, sweetie. We'll have to take this slowly, you're not going to believe what has happened to this area!"

The streets were almost deserted but they easily found a taxi which came quickly when hailed. The frowning driver got out and casually came around to load their luggage in the trunk.

"Very slow, you're only my second fare today," he grumbled, when asked how business was today.

"Drive us past the *Herald* first, then on to Warren Avenue," Oliver ordered. "I just want to check and see if Kate's car is there, honey."

The driver glanced at them through his mirror but made no comment thinking it quite a coincidence that both his fares of the morning went to the same street, the other coming from the hospital.

At the Janick home, Kate paced the floor until Janice poured some tea. She and Gordon had only arrived home from the hospital a short while before and Kate had come over soon after hoping Mary would arrive home early.

Gordon, who had been looking out of the window, began to mumble. "I wonder where she is, the bus must have been late. I hope she's coming home today. Well, I'll be a monkey's uncle, they're here ...," he declared in an obviously relieved tone, "just pulled up in a taxi!"

"You were right, Kate is here!" Mary squealed, seeing her car. Leaving Oliver to pay the driver and bring the bags, she hurried up the path.

"Hi Mom," she called, flinging the door open. "Where's dad? Hi Kate, Oliver thought you might be here!"

"I'm in here," Gordon called from the living room. "You've left that young man of yours to bring all the bags in on his own. I'll go help him."

"No, you won't," she declared, going to hug him. "You sit down and rest. I thought the cab driver would help him."

Her mother glanced over at Kate. *Does she know?* she silently asked Kate, making a face as she went to hug her daughter.

Kate made a face and shrugged.

"Big help you are, girl," Oliver teased from the doorway as Kate went to help him into the house with the luggage.

"Nice to see you, Oliver," Gordon greeted the reporter. "I see you haven't tamed that girl of ours yet!"

"Oh yes he has," Mary giggled, waving her left hand under their noses.

"You're married!" her mother gasped, covering her mouth with her hand as tears sprung to her eyes. "It's a lovely surprise but couldn't you have waited so we could have been there! Oh my, well we want to hear all about it anyway," she continued, trying to hide her disappointment.

"Glad to have you in the family, lad," exclaimed Gordon, pumping his son-in-law's hand. "Ignore her, she'll get over it when she realizes how much money we've saved!"

"It's all right, mom. It wasn't planned, sort of spur-of-the-moment, you might say. We can have a church ceremony or a reception here if you'd like. We'll talk about it next year, okay?" Mary giggled, wrapping her arms around her mum.

It wasn't long before Janice was laughing along with the others. Kate congratulated them, elated at their announcement although feeling a touch of envy. She reached instinctively for her angel earring, frowning when she remembered it was missing yesterday at the hospital.

"You'll stay for lunch, Kate, won't you, dear?" asked Janice.

As the women prepared a simple lunch of soup and sandwiches, they teased Mary mercilessly, plying her with questions that became complicated to answer as she tried to work out how much she dared tell them.

Gordon and Oliver talked quietly in the living room chuckling at the women's chatter. Then Gordon suddenly grew serious describing his health scare of the day before.

"It was very strange," he ended, a faraway look in his eyes.

"Well, we're mighty glad it was all a false alarm," Oliver replied as Mary came to the door and told them lunch was ready. "Mary, did they tell you about your dad's health scare yesterday?"

"Yes, Mom and Kate were just telling me," said Mary going over to put her arms around her father. "I'm so glad you're all right, Dad, are you going to take it a bit easier now?"

"Soup is getting cold!" called her mother.

Over lunch, Janice and Gordon gave them some unexpected news.

"Your mother has convinced me we need to enjoy what years we have left," Gordon began, "so we've both decided it's time to retire and do some travelling. She's been bugging me long enough about it!"

Everyone was commenting on their decision when Kate yelped as she took a spoonful of soup, holding it up to look at it. "My missing earring!" she squealed, squinting at the tiny angel floating among the vegetables. Gingerly, she picked it out, putting it on her napkin.

"It must have fallen in when you were making lunch," Gordon laughed.

"No, it didn't," Kate insisted. "I lost it at the hospital yesterday."

Oliver and Mary's eyes danced with mischief as they glanced at each other, their fingers locking together under the table.

"If you think that's strange," Janice sighed, "look at this. My grandmother's lockct is back around my neck and I don't know how it got there. I gave it to Mary for Christmas!"

"Maybe it came back to you, Mom," Mary whispered reverently. "Did you call for help from an angel?"

"Don't start that again," Kate moaned. "I'm still trying to find a logical explanation for my car keys turning up at Christmas."

"Gordon," Janice laughed, "show them your shoulder."

"For goodness sake, Janice, no!"

"Gordon, show them!" his wife insisted.

"Oh all right, but it's only a tiny burn," he grumbled as he peeled off one arm of his sweater. Janice went to help him, pulling aside his undershirt.

"Look at this, tell us that isn't strange."

Mary got up and went closer to look. "It's similar to a tattoo and, oh my gosh, it looks like an angel! You know that TV show—it looks like you've been touched by an angel, just like they say," she said, trying to be casual.

"More likely it's something they did at the hospital," Gordon grumbled. "I certainly didn't feel anything." Quickly putting his arm back in his sweater, Gordon looked over at Kate who was sitting pensively with her elbows on the table and her chin resting in her hands as she watched them.

"This is crazy," she whispered, "but I'm almost ready to believe in angels."

"Almost?" Oliver asked quietly. "Almost, Kate?"

"I believe," Janice interrupted, "although I'm not too sure if I remembered to ask for help last night when dad was sick."

"It could have been me," Kate whispered. "I once dreamt an angel gave me these earrings and I couldn't bear to take them off."

"OK, that's enough," Gordon rapped the table with his knuckles, "it's time you changed the subject now. Let's play some cards."

"That's a good idea, unless you young people have plans for tonight?" Janice asked, waiting until they all agreed. "All right, you and Oliver go watch the news while we clean up the dishes, Gordon."

"Gosh, I think we almost forgot about the New Year with all our excitement and travelling. We can introduce Oliver to Mad Rummy," said Mary, looking quite excited about it.

KIRO News had Oliver's complete attention as stories of the year 2000, from all around the world, flashed across the screen. When the local weatherman came on showing the weather map and temperature patterns for the cities in Washington State, he leaned forward in his chair but Gordon misconstrued his interest.

"Don't worry, son," Gordon replied blandly, "They have no idea what they're talking about, mainly they're just guessing like the rest of us!"

In the kitchen, Mary was showing her mother and Kate the 1917 newspaper she told them she had found in Seattle.

"Wow, that's cool," Kate whooped, "look at that headline!" She pointed excitedly to the front page. "That's the First World War they're talking about." She eagerly flipped the page over and pointed to the editorial on prohibition. "I want to read that," she laughed, "this is real history." But she turned the page quickly to the entertainment section and perused the vaudeville shows instead. There were names she'd only seen in books or on TV—legends of the old music hall days. Then, her finger found the ad for the James Moore Theatre and she read it aloud.

SEATTLE'S SWEETHEART OF SONG
NANCY WILSON
Sings to the music of the Seattle Symphony
Accompanied by Seattle pianist, Nellie Cornish
January 26, 1917 at 7:30 p.m.

"Oh, how I wish I could have been there," Kate sighed. "My grandfather played a violin in the orchestra and told me all about her. He called her an angel. He said she gave all the money she made to Canadian soldiers' widows and families. What a lady!"

"Oliver!" Mary called. "Can you come in here for a minute?"

"What is it, honey?" he asked, appearing in the doorway.

"Kate wishes she could have heard Nancy Wilson sing," she said loudly, cocking her eyebrow at her husband.

"An angel could arrange that," he replied, just as loudly, "but then she doesn't believe in them!"

"Don't be silly," Kate giggled. "I'd have to go back in time 80 years and I know that's not possible."

"Group regression!" Oliver replied, frowning. "I could hypnotize everyone and see what happens."

"You can't hypnotize me," Kate said haughtily, "I went to a show once and he couldn't hypnotize me worth a darn."

"Hey Dad," Mary shouted, "come and watch this, Oliver's going to try to hypnotize Kate."

"OK, buddy," Kate's eyes twinkled. "Go ahead and make a fool of yourself, I'm ready."

Oliver, please be careful, don't frighten her, Oliver heard Mary silently plead.

Gordon arrived as Oliver was setting out the rules of the experiment.

"First we find out what you'd like to see," he said as they sat facing each other across the table. "And, of course, you know I shall go with you."

"You're serious, aren't you?" Kate said softly. "This is getting scary."

"Well, maybe we shouldn't try it if it makes you nervous," Oliver replied, flicking his eyes over at Mary.

"No, I'm intrigued," Janice added. "This is exciting."

"I'd like to see the sinking of that ship," Kate stated, as if summoning all of her courage. Without hesitation, she pointed to the picture of the *Lusitania* on the front page of the newspaper.

Oliver no, thought Mary, *don't you dare take her there!*

"Goodness Kate," Gordon growled, "can't you find something more pleasant to see? If I were going back in time," he paused, as all eyes turned his way, "I'd want to go to a vaudeville show. Remember Janny, like we did on our first date?"

"You old softy," his wife murmured blowing him a kiss.

"Right then," Kate laughed, "show me an old-time newspaper office."

"Here in Everett?" asked Oliver.

"No, that one," she said, pointing at the newspaper on the table.

"*The Seattle Courier*? What year?"

"Oh it's only a game, you pick the year."

"Now we can begin, Kate," Oliver said sitting down opposite her. "Lay your hands on the table with your fingers just touching mine and look into my eyes."

Oliver, you're quite a showman, thought Mary, raising her eyebrows at him. *Say hello to Margo for me.*

Behave yourself! his thoughts answered as he slowly willed Kate to sleep, raising her spirit from her physical body, and taking her back to 1916 Seattle. They materialized in front of the *Courier*'s main door.

Sitting at the Janick table, Kate's eyes blinked open. Unseeing, they stared straight ahead as her voice began to speak.

"Tell me what you see," Oliver's mortal form prompted.

"We're in Seattle, it's snowing and windy. We're outside the *Courier* office," Kate's voice droned sleepily.

Mesmerized by the result of the experiment, Gordon and his wife listened in amazement to Kate's commentary while Mary furiously wrote the words her friend was speaking in her notebook.

"We're going inside now," Kate's voice continued. "Oh, it's warmer now. Oliver's leading me past the receptionist, she mustn't be able to see us. We're going down a long corridor; he's knocking on a door that says 'Editing.' We're inside the office and Oliver's introducing me to a woman named Margo Lane.

Only Kate and Mary heard Oliver's silent order to stop her commentary and her mortal body now appeared to be sleeping.

At the *Courier* office, Margo showed Kate the new *Noiseless* typewriters—metal models with funny round keys and a hooked return bar—recently acquired for their staff. In conversation, she also mentioned that Oliver was their star reporter. When a sudden message called her away, Oliver told her they would be leaving and took the opportunity to slip Kate and himself back into their mortal bodies, also erasing Kate's memory of some pertinent information.

Only Mary was aware that their spirits had returned and whispered to her parents, "They're waking up."

Hardly able to contain their excitement, the Janicks bubbled with a multitude of questions as Oliver and Kate blinked and appeared to return to normal.

"Did it work?" Janice asked eagerly. "It just looked like you both went to sleep."

"I think so," the girl replied tentatively. "It was very real."

"You talked to us in your sleep," Gordon said, frowning doubtfully. "It was spooky."

"What did I say?"

"Here," said Mary, pushing the writing pad toward her. "Look for yourself, I wrote it all down."

Kate's finger tapped the page excitedly. "I noticed the calendar in the editor's office," she muttered, "8th of January, 1917 it said. It was also snowing. I can easily check that on the office computer and that editor's name was Margo Lane, that's easy to check, too."

Jumping up from her seat, Kate headed for the door, grinning back at her startled friends when she stopped to retrieve her coat. "You're very tricky, Oliver Ryan, but I'm sure there's a logical explanation for this. I'm going down to the office to check this out."

"But it's Sunday, Kate," Gordon reminded her, "they're closed and besides it's New Year's Eve. Aren't you going to party with us?"

"A newspaper never sleeps, Mr. Janick, I have a key and I'll be back to party with you later!" Kate's voice trailed off as she picked up her handbag, waved coyly and left. Almost immediately, the door opened again. "If I don't get back, Happy New Year everyone!" she called and the door closed again.

"Well, are we going to play cards or not?" asked Gordon, obviously eager to do so.

"I haven't played cards in a long time," admitted Oliver, "but I'm willing to learn if you have the patience."

"Piece of cake!" quipped Mary. "You'll probably have beginner's luck. It's a challenging game and it can be a real hoot."

As the afternoon progressed, Oliver found he was totally enjoying himself. As anticipated, Gordon again raised the issue of Oliver's performance as a hypnotist.

"Do you do this hypnotism thing very often?" he asked.

"Once in a while, you might say it's a hobby of mine," Oliver replied, winking at Mary.

"Could you do it to anyone?" asked Janice.

"One of these days," Oliver replied, "we'll all try it together."

"I've a day off on January 26th. It's a Friday," Mary suggested, tuning into her husband's thoughts. "We could do it then."

"We should get Kate in on this, too," Gordon suggested. "She's already experienced!"

"I wonder what on earth she's doing, I thought we'd have heard from her by now," Mary mused.

"Perhaps she's gone back to 1917 again through that computer of hers and can't figure out how to get home!" Gordon snorted.

Over at the newspaper office, Kate was glued to her computer monitor. Leaning back momentarily, she stretched her arms into the air and groaned. Then her fingers quickly returned to the keyboard as she continued her search through long lists of archived material.

"Jeepers, I sure wish we had all this material on the internet. It would make searching through these files so much easier. I suppose one day it will happen. Let's see … at least I've proven the weather was right, now let's see if we can find Margo Lane!" she mused aloud, her fingers flying over the keys.

At the Janick home, the card game was over and Janice was the winner. They had a late dinner and went to watch the New Year's Eve shows that were already starting on TV. They wouldn't have guessed that Kate was still at her office, having only gone out briefly for a bite to eat. When ten o'clock arrived, the elder Janicks said goodnight and Mary popped some popcorn in the microwave, totally surprising Oliver. He told her how he popped popcorn in a long-handled basket on the top of the stove and she remembered her grandmother having one of those baskets when she was a kid.

They went back to the living room and cuddled up together on the chesterfield under a warm blanket. Mary flipped through the channels, finally settling on Dave Clark's New Year's Eve Show featuring bands and popular performers recorded hours before at Times Square in New York City.

"My word, your modern technology is truly amazing," Oliver quipped.

"Almost makes you want to stay in 2000 with me, doesn't it, honey?" she teased.

He looked at her and slowly shook his head, his eyes seeming to penetrate her very soul. "Mary, if I had a choice, I wouldn't want to miss a minute being by your side. You're the best thing that has ever happened to me and I love you so much I can't describe it."

He gently caressed her face with his fingertips and when she looked up again, he kissed her with such passion it took her breath away, and television was forgotten.

At midnight, Kate was listening to the local radio station as the music stopped and the local DJ wished everyone a 'Happy 21st Century' as noisemakers and laughter sounded in the background.

Determined to begin the new century with the story of a lifetime, Kate sat at the large table in the archives vault of the *Everett Journal*. With its floor-to-ceiling array of filing cabinets and shelves containing boxes of old newspapers dating back into the 1800s, she looked around and sighed heavily. Fascinated, her eyes swept over some of the crudely typed notations.

Duwamish Valley News (Seattle) 1912-1965
The Commonwealth (Everett) 1911-1914
Truth (Tacoma) 1913
The Socialist Worker (Tacoma) 1914
The Post-Intelligencer (Seattle, Wash) 1914-1921
The Agitator (Home) 1910-1912
Green Lake Northend Reporter (Seattle) 1917?-1935
The Everett Daily Herald (Everett) 1897-1963 (see *Everett Herald*)
The Independent (Tacoma) 1892-1935

Her eyes stopped and read the last two again. "Holy Smokes, I had no idea there were such old newspapers around here. I wonder how they get these old copies. I sure wish I had time to look at them. Well back to work, girl!"

Taking a box labelled '*Seattle Courier (Seattle) 1925-1926'* off the shelf, she placed it on the table and opened it.

It was almost two in the morning when flipping the page over to the next day's issue, her eyes widened as they gravitated to the one familiar face on the page. It was the June 1st, 1926 issue and her tired eyes skimmed over the heading above the woman's picture, NEW OWNER FOR SEATTLE COURIER.

"That's her!" she gasped, standing up in her excitement and wincing as a pain seared through her lower back. "That's the woman I met under hypnosis!" With one hand on her back and the other gravitating to her angel earring, she whispered, "Or was it hypnosis?"

Quickly jotting down some notes, filing the papers back in the box and heaving it onto the shelf, she ran back upstairs to her computer and entered, *margo lane owner seattle courier* in the search engine.

"Bloody amazing!" she exclaimed, as a list of entries appeared. "Now why the heck didn't that one come up before?" Her eyes stopped on an entry listing Margo, near the bottom of the page. "I sure hope they can improve on these search engines in the near future, this is ridiculous!" As the printer churned out the new information, complete with pictures, she sat back and sighed, touching her earring.

Eyes blinking open in the darkness, Mary's breathing told Oliver she was asleep. His senses now alert, he heard Kate's thoughts as her fingers toyed with the tiny angel. As there was no disturbance of blankets or rustle of sheets, Mary didn't even stir as Oliver's spirit moved out of his mortal body, going to Kate at the newspaper office.

Unaware of his presence, Kate felt a shiver run down her back when his cold hand touched her shoulder. Instantly, Oliver took over her computer bringing Margo's image onto the screen—the same image she'd seen in the old newspaper.

Kate shook herself and stared at the screen.

"You came to see me today, Kate."

The female-sounding voice seemed to be coming from her computer and she leaned forward staring at the image.

"This is ridiculous," she whispered. "It isn't possible."

"You sought the truth, Kate. Three times you were touched by an angel … think and believe," said the voice.

Oliver could hear Kate's mind struggling with her logic.

A rush of air escaped her lips and her body began to tremble. "I think I need some sleep!" she declared. "This just isn't happening!"

She quickly switched off the computer, put on her coat, grabbed her handbag and hurried out of the office.

Chapter 24

On Tuesday January 2nd, 2001, an early breakfast found the Janicks excitedly speculating on what would happen if they took part in Oliver's planned experiment.

"I think we should all do it," Mary repeated her earlier suggestion, "but we can talk about it later, Mom, I need to quickly run over my new history lesson."

"And just what will you be teaching today?" her father asked as Mary rose and pushed her chair in.

"I'm going to start with the 1915 newspaper. I've decided to try something different with Washington State's history—starting with the events leading up to prohibition and World War One."

"How are you getting to school?" Gordon asked.

"Can you take me, Mom?"

"Certainly, and what about you, Oliver?" asked Janice. "What are you up to today?"

"I'll go with you, if that's all right. I do need to go to Seattle for a few days but I can catch a bus from the school."

When they left the house at 8 o'clock, the fond handshake from Gordon pleased Oliver and he longed to stay here with Mary. When Janice pulled the car up in front of the school, Oliver leaned over the back seat and gave her a quick kiss on the cheek before joining Mary on the sidewalk.

"You'll be back for the weekend?" Mary asked, feeling the sting of tears as she kissed him quickly goodbye, to the accompaniment of a few wolf whistles from a group of senior boys walking by. This was no normal parting of husband and wife, their work was almost a century apart. Brushing the tears quickly away and not looking back, she headed for the staff room.

Unknown to Mary, Oliver did not leave. Walking down the block and standing behind a tree, he waited for the street to clear of witnesses and then whisked himself into Mary's classroom, completely forgetting he had left his suitcase behind. Watching Mary at work fascinated him and her teaching skills amazed him. Her description of early 20th century events and what the people had experienced in those challenging times was amazing and definitely enthralled her class. The details she supplied to her students' questions gave many of them an eerie feeling that their teacher could have been there.

"How much did a restaurant meal cost back then, Miss … er, Mrs. Ryan?" one inquisitive young man asked with a giggle, causing Oliver to smile.

Mary's memory flashed back to the dockside restaurant and she tried to visualize the menu.

"I think we paid $1.60 for steak and $1.40 for a meal of salmon, Colin," she said, "and, in those days, coffee and pie came as part of the meal."

"*We* paid, Mrs. Ryan?" a girl called from the back. "It sounds like you were there."

"Yes, I was there, Sharon," she replied, trying to look casual at her slip. "I went back in time and so can you; just use your imagination and your knowledge."

Oliver suddenly thought of his suitcase, missing Mary's clever answer as he returned to the sidewalk. His fear was realized—it was gone! *I'm an angel, my possessions can't be stolen!* he thought. *Whoever you are, you're in for a mighty big shock.*

Two blocks away on a quiet street, a battered old half-ton truck stopped and the two teens inside decided to examine their booty. One of the boys went to get the black, expensive-looking suitcase he had put in the back.

Come back to me, Oliver whispered.

"It's alive!" the boy gasped, as his friend joined him and they watched in disbelief as the suitcase began to lift into the air. Startled, they grabbed for it, cursing as it wriggled out of their grasp landing upright on the sidewalk.

"Get it, you fool!" the older boy snapped.

"I ain't touching it," his friend whimpered. "That thing's alive!"

As they watched, the suitcase handle popped up with a click and the case slowly moved off along the sidewalk as if someone was pulling it. Curiously, the boys began to follow.

An old couple walking on the other side of the street stopped to watch the strange behaviour of the youths and noticed the suitcase.

"It's probably radio-controlled, like that silly ad on TV," the man explained to his wife as they also turned and began to follow it.

Surprised motorists stopped traffic as the little cavalcade made its way across the street, the suitcase always just out of their reach. The gathering onlookers attracted a passing police car.

"I ain't telling the office about this one," the policeman chuckled, following at a safe distance. "They'll think I'm on something!"

"Got ya!" one of the boys yelped as the case suddenly stopped and he grabbed for the handle, not noticing Oliver's feet.

"Is that your case, sir? Was it stolen?" asked the policeman through the open window.

"Yes, yes, I was most concerned when it went missing," Oliver replied.

"Is it remote-controlled?" the policeman continued his line of questioning as he got out of his car.

"Yes, it's experimental," Oliver replied. "A.N.G.E.L. Technology constable. Highly secret, I'm sure you understand."

"Yes sir, I do understand. Do you want me to charge these two?"

"That's only necessary if they won't agree to a penalty imposed by you."

"By me, sir? I don't understand."

"If they agree," Oliver chuckled, "to carry suitcases for passengers at the bus station for a month, you won't need to charge them."

"Okay, okay, we'll do it," the boys agreed reluctantly, realizing they were getting off easy.

"Right then, lads," the policeman growled sternly, "into the car, you're starting right now."

"That was a very good decision, constable," Oliver praised him. "You're quite a statesman, I shall see to it your superiors hear of this."

The constable scratched his head as he climbed back into his squad car and drove away. *Who was that man?* he wondered. *It sounds like a legit organization ... but ANGEL? That's a new one!*

Oliver left 2000 and went to the *Courier* office in 1916 Seattle, remembering that in his time it was still the end of December. Sending his suitcase to his apartment, he proceeded into the building to face the expected sarcastic comments of the receptionist. Saved instead from her biting humour by a phone call, the reporter made his way along the corridor to the copy editor's office.

"Margo's day off," the shirt-sleeved young man behind the desk apologized. "You're Oliver Ryan, aren't you? She left you this," holding the small sealed envelope between two fingers, he cocked an eyebrow. "Perhaps it's a secret assignment!"

"And just who are you?" Oliver asked.

"Ben Smith, a wannabe from the layout room."

"A wannabe what?"

"Reporter."

"Well, lots of luck to you, buddy, it ain't all it's cracked up to be."

Oliver turned to leave but the young man stopped him.

"Aren't you going to open it, sir?"

"In due time," he chuckled, stuffing the letter into his pocket and leaving.

Finding a table in the coffee shop across the street, Oliver took the time to clean his glasses before tearing open Margo's envelope.

Meet me at Second and Pike at noon. There's going to be an Anti-Saloon League march to City Hall, likely to be a riot. I have inside info that the Wobblies are going to stop them. Margo.

Drinking his coffee, he checked the clock on the wall before calling for a refill; he knew about the radical group, *The Industrial Workers of the World* and his mind wondered what the reaction would be from the police and city authorities. *Surely, they know that violence could erupt, it certainly did in Everett.*

Finding Margo in the crowd proved to be quite a chore as people spilled out into the street from saloons and taverns as they heard the rumours. Streetcars, unable to move, became silent as the mass of protesters formed up in the street, but he finally spotted her and managed to get her attention.

"The two factions should meet at Madison," she yelled, running toward him.

Keeping ahead of the crowd, they were able to secure a vantage point offered by a linen shop owner who was hammering the last board across his large front window. They hurried inside with him, locking the door securely. He took them to a third-storey window which provided a perfect view of the junction. Thanking him profusely, he told them he'd be nearby when they were ready to leave. Shaking his head sadly, he left them. Opening the small window, they gasped as the biting cold air attacked their faces.

Their excitement now obvious, with pencils and notebooks ready, they listened expectantly as the chanting anti-saloon league marchers came closer. From the other direction, a new sound grew in intensity as drinking men, dockworkers and hundreds of WWI striking union members marched toward a confrontation. Heavy boots beating on pavement send a cold thrill through Margo's body warning her she was about to witness a day of infamy in Seattle's history.

Unbeknownst to Margo, Oliver left his mortal body and travelled across town to city hall and the Mayor's office.

"Who the hell are you?" Mayor Hiram Gill spluttered, as the reporter appeared in front of him. "How'd you get past the guards, boy?"

"I advise you to call out the police and militia, sir, or you're going to have a blood bath at Second and Madison," Oliver advised with some urgency.

Leaping to his feet, Mayor Gill charged angrily at Oliver. "Who do you think you are to tell me how to run my city?" His face contorted with dismay as his punch missed its target, seeming to pass right through the stranger's body. He gasped and collapsed into a chair.

"Stay there!" Oliver commanded, pointing his finger at the slumping figure.

Aware of his surroundings but, somehow immobile, the mayor's eyes darted around the room—the mysterious interloper has disappeared. His unblinking stare noticed a movement on his desk and he watched as the telephone receiver appeared to rise into the air and he heard the sound of his own voice. It gave the order for emergency services to be deployed and he was helpless to intervene. He slumped back in the chair and cursed.

"Wow, here comes the cavalry," Margo yelped, as minutes later as soldiers and police arrived en masse converging on the junction below. "Mayor Gill must have had a change of heart; he'll be a hero for putting a stop to this fiasco."

Suddenly, the sound of breaking glass was heard below as marchers armed with axe handles and other weapons vented their fury on nearby shops. However, almost immediately they realize the futility of their actions when faced with the immovable forces of shoulder to shoulder militia and police. Shouts of abuse and violent cursing led to a few isolated arrests before the crowd began to disperse and soon vehicles were again moving along Second Street.

Well done, Oliver! said the voice of Agnes Millington in Oliver's ear.

"I dreamt about you last night," said Margo as they pushed their way through the crowd on the street. "I'm frozen, let's go find a hot cup of coffee and I'll tell you about it."

Some shops were already re-opening as they hurried toward a popular and already crowded diner. Talking quietly, while waiting in line for a seat, Margo told him of her strange dream.

"I dreamt you met me at the newspaper office," she whispered, "but I didn't actually see you. I just knew you were there."

"What newspaper, the *Courier*?"

"No, it didn't seem to be ours, the woman's name was Kate."

"What woman?" Oliver asked, trying to look confused. "You're not making any sense."

Before she could answer, the line-up moved and they were next to be seated. A table soon became available and a harassed waitress showed them unceremoniously to a seat by the window.

Two steaming mugs of coffee banged onto the table as the waitress tiredly demanded, "Want the special, folks? It's feathers, Murphys, and two veg!"

Grinning, Oliver nodded, watching his companion's puzzled expression.

"You ordered that, what on earth is it?" Margo asked.

"Chicken, potatoes and two vegetables."

"That's not what she said, is it?"

"Yes, actually it is. You just have to know how to decipher the language. Now tell me about that dream," Oliver prodded but Margo wasn't paying attention.

The next time the waitress went by their table, she swung round to look at Margo. "Well, are ya eatin' or not?"

"Yes please, I'll have the special."

She left without another word and Oliver reminded Margo again.

"Oh yes, well it seems as though I'm in touch with an angel. I think it started that day in the basement when you and Mary rescued me from that thing," she whispered. "Last night I dreamt the angel sent me to convince Kate that there really are angels." Margo looked at him and pursed her lips. "Oh, don't look so serious, Oliver, it was only a dream."

He silently breathed a sigh of relief and soon their meal arrived.

Picking delicately at her chicken leg with knife and fork, Margo's eyes sparkled mischievously. "Maybe I'm an angel, too!"

"Oh sure," he laughed, "does an angel drink coffee and complain of the cold when they hang out of a window to report the news? Yes, I'm sure you're an angel, Margo!"

All week they joked about their silly conversation and each time he landed in the editor's office, she had a new angel story for him.

On Friday morning, while finishing his last assignment, he felt Mary's thoughts trying to pull him back to Everett although there was no actual message—he suspected she was touching her wedding ring.

I'll meet you at the door after school was his message back to her.

He was packing when he looked out of his apartment window at the gathering clouds in the West. "This awful weather just doesn't want to quit; hopefully it will be better in Everett. I think it's time to go," he muttered, glancing at his pocket watch and seeing it was 3 o'clock. Reaching for his suitcase, he directed his thoughts on Everett High School.

Sunshine was barely filtering through the clouds above Everett when he materialized among the milling students and searched for Mary. Settling in to wait, he focussed his attention on a teenaged girl wearing wire-framed spectacles; standing near the doorway, she appeared to be agitated about something. Studying the situation, he noticed a boy on a bicycle behind her, bumping her legs with the tire of his bike.

Ah ha, a bully at work, time to hand out a lesson, he thought gleefully, glad for something constructive to do.

"What is it, Oliver?" Mary whispered coming up beside him. "Who are you so interested in?"

"That boy on the bicycle in the red jacket."

"Oh that's Jason, he can be quite a pest."

"I see that. Call the girl he's annoying to come over here."

"Elizabeth," Mary called, "may I have a word with you?"

Looking up and blinking repeatedly to focus her eyes, 16-year-old Elizabeth Button felt a surge of relief as she recognized the history teacher's voice. Grateful for the chance to escape Jason's tormenting attention, she complied.

"Why don't you walk away from him when he annoys you, dear?" Mary asked.

"I can't see very well and, my eyes are hurting; besides, he'd find a way to keep bugging me, he always does," she explained matter-of-factly.

"Can I see your glasses, Elizabeth?" Oliver asked.

"I guess so, sir," she replied hesitantly, "but please don't break them, I can't see a thing without them."

"I'll be very careful," he assured her.

Slipping her arm around the girl's shoulder, Mary watched as Oliver slowly ran his finger around the frames, handing them back to the girl as a blue car pulled into the busy pick-up area.

"Come on, Elizabeth, we're almost late for your appointment at the optician's," her mother called urgently, causing the girl to hurry over to the car.

"Did you fix her glasses?" Mary asked as she took Oliver's arm and moved as close as she dared knowing students were watching. "Have you a little time for me now, Mr. Ryan."

"No dear, not just yet. Watch Jason!"

Riding away his surly scowl aimed at the history teacher, Jason's bicycle suddenly began acting strangely, racing straight for an oncoming, yet slow-moving, police car. Leaping onto the hood, the bike drove all the way across the roof and down the other side with

Jason still riding and many onlookers gawking. Landing back on the road, he applied all his power to the pedals and tore away up the street, now chased by the angry policeman who was yelling at him through the open window of the police car.

"There," Oliver chuckled, "that should fix your bully boy for a while."

"Perhaps for a few hours," she giggled, taking his arm. "Okay, Mr. Ryan, it's time you paid me some attention; I haven't seen you in four days. Let's walk home, do you have room for my books in there?"

Putting her books into the outside pocket of his suitcase, they walked arm-in-arm up Hoyt Street to town. Daylight was fading as Mary's conversation returned to the subject of Elizabeth.

"I'm glad you fixed her glasses, honey," she murmured, "that was a nice gesture."

"I didn't fix her glasses," chuckled Oliver. "I fixed her eyes. Her optician is going to get quite a surprise when he finds she now has perfect vision!"

"Want a ride home?" a female voice called as Kate pulled up alongside them.

Just as Oliver had predicted Dr. Isacks, Elizabeth's optician, was dumbfounded when he made his examination.

"This is ridiculous," he snorted, "there's no way to explain this Mrs. Button, but Elizabeth will not require glasses any more."

Astounded, Mrs. Button looked at him.

"But how?" she asked.

"I'm afraid, I don't have an explanation. It's very puzzling, I've never seen anything like this before," he replied.

"Perhaps it's time to believe in miracles," she said calmly, taking her daughter's hand. "Thank you, doctor."

As they rode home, Mrs. Button turned the doctor's words over and over in her head, and began to question her daughter.

"Did you meet any strangers today, dear?" she gently prodded.

"Only Miss Janick's new husband."

"Your history teacher? Is he a minister?"

"No Mom, he's a newspaper reporter, but he looked at my glasses. I was afraid he might break them."

"Why would he want to look at your glasses?"

"I don't know, but he noticed I was crying because Jason was teasing me again. Miss Janick, I mean Mrs. Ryan, called me over to talk to them."

"And this man, her husband you said, stopped him?"

"No, once I moved I was okay. We just talked, then you came."

"This has me beat, honey," her mother replied. "At any rate, all I can say is God bless the angel, if that's what it was, who has helped you see better again."

"Are you coming in?" Mary asked, as they got out of Kate's car.

"Yes, I want to talk to Oliver about another trip into the past."

Oliver, she knows, Mary's thoughts jumped into Oliver's mind.

No, she doesn't, she thinks it's hypnotism, he replied, watching his wife's eyes sparkle with amusement.

"Coffee's ready," Gordon announced meeting them at the door. His daughter kissed him, then scooted past to hug her mother in the kitchen.

"Did I hear Kate's voice?" Janice inquired, looking past her daughter.

"She drove us partway home; she's talking to dad and Oliver."

Eager to join the conversation, Janice hurried in with the coffee tray, arriving as Kate made her astounding proposal.

"Can you hypnotize all of us at the same time?" she asked. "I'd like to see if we can all land in the same place."

"No, no, he can't do that, Kate," Janice interrupted, frowning as the phone rang. "Answer that would you please, Kate, it's there by your elbow."

"Janick residence," Kate announced when she picked up the receiver. "Mary, yes, can I tell her who's calling? Mrs. Button, Elizabeth's mother, just a moment." She handed the phone to Mary.

"Hello Mrs. Button," Mary murmured into the phone, blushing at the comments the woman was making. "All he did was look at her glasses, but thank you. Goodnight, Mrs. Button."

"Trouble, dear?" Oliver prodded his wife.

"No, she thinks Elizabeth has been blessed by an angel, me!"

"Why?" Kate's voice rang with curiosity.

"She said Elizabeth's eyesight has suddenly been corrected and they found out the boy who has been tormenting her was arrested."

"And you're to blame?" her father chuckled. "Go on, Kate, there's a story for you … our Mary's an angel!" He paused grinning. "Her mother and I have known that for a long time."

"Don't you laugh too loud, Mr. Janick," Kate chided, "there's something strange going on and I intend to find out what it is."

Oh you do, do you? thought Oliver. *This should be interesting.*

"How are you going to do that?" Mary asked her friend.

"With his help," Kate announced, turning to Oliver. "He can use his hypnotism and send me to meet an angel."

"Not today he won't, it's dinnertime," Janice giggled. "Let's leave it until tomorrow, you come for dinner and we'll get Oliver to try it—if that's all right with Oliver, of course."

"You have a deal, Mrs. Janick," Kate replied, pulling on her coat as Oliver nodded his agreement. "I'll be here at six, goodnight all!"

Snow was again in the forecast and a cold wind was blowing in from Possession Bay. With a fire in the hearth, the front room was a cosy place to be, as the young couple listened to the old folks reminisce, asking them questions that often puzzled the Janicks. It was midnight when the last light went out in the house and the newlyweds lay happily in each other's arms talking. Tom Watson's voice came through the darkness.

"Listen well, children, I've come to make you an offer."

They sat up quickly, watching as the old angel materialized at the foot of the bed. Mary felt no fear this time, as first the top hat and cape became visible and then his round, happy face which tonight had a mischievous smile. As he talked, his fuzzy, mutton-chop whiskers danced about his face, almost making her giggle.

"Now you've experienced love and happiness, Oliver, you must make a choice. You can take Mary back to 1917 and live your life out together in those troubled years or you can bring your mortal body here and belong to the year 2000. The choice is yours and you'll need to make this decision carefully and wisely."

Mary took Oliver's hand. The offer sounded quite simple to her and her anticipation rose. They would be able to live as a normal couple after all, to raise a family and live their lives together.

"I would still be an angel?" Oliver asked.

"You'll always be an angel but we have decided to give you a chance to pick the years in which you'll live. Your responsibility is enormous. I can give you until the last day of the month, then you must make a decision."

Before they had a chance to reply, Tom's image disappeared but not before he had pushed them into slumber.

Chapter 25

Morning brought another dull, grey day to Everett as Oliver and Mary separately contemplated their dreams. They had a choice to make, a choice that would last a lifetime.

"I'm going shopping with mother this afternoon," she told him. "I think dad wants to take you to his club and introduce you to some of his friends."

"I need a haircut, too," Oliver announced.

"Oh, dad will take you to his barber. Jack's quite a character, never stops talking and knows many local stories. You'll enjoy him."

Spending the afternoon walking from store to store gave Mary some time to think and she wondered what life would be like in 1917. She'd read the history of those times and knew the danger—the war, prohibition, and the wildest times of Seattle's past. *No,* she thought, *we must stay here in 2000.*

"What's the matter, honey?" her mother asked. "Are you talking to yourself? Anything I can help with?"

"Well, yes and no, Mom. If you had the choice, would you rather have lived in 1917 or now?"

"Now, without a doubt, they were heathens back then."

"What do you mean, heathens?"

"That's what your grandma called the likes of gangsters, crooked politicians, and rum runners," Janice explained. "Some of the police weren't any better!"

Cripes Mom, do you realize what you're saying? thought Mary. *If you think we live in better times now, you mustn't watch the news!*

Down the street in a tiny barber's shop, Oliver sat in the chair listening to old Jack Thornton expounding his own strong opinions on politicians, sports and the weather. Eventually, Oliver saw his opportunity to turn the conversation onto the history of Washington State in 1917.

"I was born in 1928," the barber reminisced as his scissors briefly stopped snipping. My father was an Irish immigrant who came to Seattle with the O'Reilly gang."

"He was a gangster!" Gordon exclaimed, eager for more details.

"Shut up, Gordie," the barber grouched. "I've never told anyone this story before." Laying down his scissors the old man sighed heavily before continuing. "I was only four-years-old when my dad was killed." His eyes clouded as he stretched his memory back 68 years. "It happened just down the coast from here."

Oliver honed in on the old man's thoughts and felt the cry of terror from a child, as the old man's soul relived the memory.

"You don't have to tell us any more, Mr. Thornton," the reporter murmured. "Maybe those kind of memories are best left trapped inside your heart."

"Don't stop now, Jack," Gordon urged, his interest peaked by morbid curiosity.

"The way my mother told it was strange," Jack whispered, "she said an angel told her to move to Everett."

"Come on Jack," Gordon interrupted, "you don't really believe that, do you?"

Oliver smiled as he watched the barber cock an eyebrow at his old friend. He had more to tell and no amount of sarcasm from Gordon Janick was going to stop him now.

"My sister was younger than me, just a baby. We were destitute." His voice quickened with excitement. "The angel came back again and this time we all saw him."

Wide-eyed Gordon was now on the edge of his seat, hardly daring to breathe as he waited for Jack to continue.

"He was just like a figure built out of smoky vapour," Jack babbled. "He told my mother where dad hid his money."

"Then what?"

"She found it," Jack said flatly, turning his attention to Oliver as he swung the chair back into its normal position and finished cutting his hair.

"That's it?" Gordon gasped in frustration, trading places with Oliver.

"Ain't no more to tell, except I always knew angels were watching over us back in those days."

Watching his father-in-law's image through the mirror, Oliver grinned to himself as the barber's revelations sent his mind racing with possibilities. Everyone was quiet for a while listening to the soft snip-snip of Jack's scissors, lost in his own thoughts.

"I know this sounds silly," Oliver said finally, choosing his words carefully as Jack got out the clippers, "but if you know an angel, Jack, why don't you ask for the state lottery numbers and win a fortune."

The loud buzzing of the clippers caused another lull in the conversation until they were turned off again.

"There you are, that looks better now," the barber whispered, brushing the loose hair from the back of Gordon's neck and removing the cape.

"What about it, Jack?" snickered Gordon. "Haven't you figured out a way to beat the lottery with these angels of yours?"

Jack slowly turned around to face his old friend.

"Don't laugh, you old goat," he muttered. "Some day you may be in desperate need and wish an angel would visit you."

Instinctively, Gordon's fingers reached for his shoulder, touching his angel tattoo. As they left the barber shop, he felt a strange twinge of conscience flash through his mind. Oliver was watching him carefully as they made their way back to the car, knowing what he was thinking.

"Kate's coming for dinner," Gordon reminded him as they drove home. The temperature had dropped making driving precarious. Gordon picked his way carefully through the traffic, skidding a little on the incline when he turned into Warren Street.

They were soon back in the warmth of the house listening to the noisy laughter of mother and daughter as they talked about their shopping trip and began making dinner.

Across town at the *Journal* office, Kate was staring at her computer screen knowing it was almost time to leave for the Janick's. Hypnosis, regression and angels all boggled her mind as page after page of information flipped across her view. She was frustrated and quickly went over the events of the past few weeks for possibly the 50th time.

A joke could easily have been played on her when her keys were mysteriously returned … coincidence could have brought Mary and Oliver to her side when she needed them, but what in the world could explain the disappearing footprints? And the hospital … had she alerted Oliver by touching her angel earring? She promised herself that tonight she was going to solve this mystery once and for all.

Reaching for her handbag, she shut the computer down and applied fresh lipstick, her eyes flicking to the dark screen as she rose to her feet. In disbelief she stopped, her eyes holding fast to the monitor, as a wispy figure appeared.

"Kate, it's six o'clock."

The voice of the janitor startled her, bringing her back to reality.

"Yes, I know. Did you happen to notice anything on my screen?"

"Nope," he replied, continuing to pick up garbage.

"I must be daydreaming," she muttered.

Arriving at the Janick's, she consciously made sure the car keys dropped into her bag before cautiously climbing the slippery stairs to the front door and ringing the bell.

She heard Janice telling her to come in and opened the door.

"Hi Kate, dinner's nearly ready," Mary called from the kitchen. "Make yourself at home."

"A glass of wine with dinner, Kate?" asked Gordon.

"No thanks, Mr. Janick, coffee will be fine tonight."

"I'll get it," Oliver offered, getting up and heading into the kitchen, "just a splash of cream and half a spoon of sugar?"

"That's right but how did you know?"

"Observations … I'm a reporter, remember?" he replied winking.

"Don't you people get too settled in there," Janice called, "dinner's going on the table right now. Bring your drinks with you."

Conversation over the meal was light and jovial as Mary related some of the sights she'd seen in Victoria, adding little details of history that kept their attention riveted. She found she had to be very careful not to give anything away.

"How do you know all that historical stuff?" Kate asked.

"Oliver knows all about Victoria's history."

"Hey, wait a minute," Gordon interrupted, "Jack Thornton told me and Oliver a weird story today. He said he'd seen an angel."

"Was he sober?" Janice asked.

"Yes, and deadly serious!"

"Well, what did he tell you?" Mary urged.

"He said after his dad got killed, an angel told his mother where Jack's dad had hidden his money."

"And you believed him?" Janice laughed. "He's pulling your leg!"

Mary's foot tapped Oliver's under the table.

I know, his mind answered, *Kate's making mental notes. She's already planning to interview Jack Thornton.*

"A childhood fantasy," said Kate, "that's grown with the years. Why, last year I interviewed a man who said he'd seen a ghost."

"Who was that?" Gordon asked eagerly.

"I'm not allowed to say, he told me in confidence."

"Then tell us about the ghost," said Mary.

"I've never been able to make any sense of it," she continued. "He said one foggy night he saw a man staring out into the water at the bottom of Hewitt and when he spoke, the man disappeared."

"Sounds fishy to me," Gordon chuckled.

The women groaned but Oliver looked serious.

"Did he describe him?" he asked.

"Yes, a dapper man of medium height, dark suit, hat, thin pencil moustache and a white handkerchief in his breast pocket." Kate looked up to the ceiling as she reached back into her memory. "Oh yes, and spats on his boots."

"What year was he from?"

"How the devil would I know?" she laughed. "I'm not sure he even existed."

"Stretch your memory," Oliver persisted, "I'll bet he told you more than you think you remember."

Mary and her parents watched with heightened curiosity as Oliver pulled bits and pieces of the story from Kate's memory.

"I have all the notes I made," she whispered, "they're in my office."

"No, just think hard," he said as he gently sent her spirit back to the day of the interview. "You'll see them."

"Yes, yes I remember, he said he heard the clinking of bottles."

"Tell us, Oliver," Janice asked, getting up to clear the table. "Who was it? Was it really a ghost?"

"I'll help you, Janice, then I'll answer your question!"

Grateful for the delay, Mary directed her thoughts at her husband. *Oliver, who was it, darling?* she asked and his mind answered as he took an armload of dishes to the kitchen.

Someone we both know.

Oliver ... who?

Jack Marquette, the former-policeman turned gentleman rum runner.

"I'll bring some more coffee," Janice called from the kitchen. "I don't want to miss anything, this is so exciting."

"All right, Mr. Ryan," Kate began again when they resumed their seats, "you've given us the dramatics; now tell us who you think it was."

"Did you check your newspaper files on rum runners?"

"No, I didn't take the story seriously and I would never have thought of rum runners."

"Bottles, my dear, that's the clue. They shipped liquor bottles in gunny sacks."

"Really, and the man was?" she prodded.

"A perfect description of Jack Marquette."

"Dare I ask how you know all this, Mr. Ryan?"

"I did a story on him, too."

"I shall check you know," Kate reminded him.

Mary's parents listened with rapt attention to this unusual conversation. Their son-in-law was proving to be a most intriguing young man.

Oliver showed no emotion even as he heard the urgent warning from Mary.

Oliver careful, you did that interview in 1916; can you alter the date on the article?

No, he replied, *it seems we have a problem. That's history now and I can't change it.*

"Are you going to hypnotize us now?" Janice's voice cut into their thoughts.

"All right, we'll give it a try," he said, his mind pondering the new problem he'd caused. "Hands on the table everyone, fingers all touching in a circle so we're connected."

"Can I run my tape recorder?" Kate asked eagerly.

"Of course."

Oliver's too-quick reply sent Mary's thoughts racing as Kate set the tiny recorder on the table. She knew he had no idea what a tape recorder was or that it produced a perfect reproduction of voices. Kate would have tangible evidence of her trip back in time.

Oliver, please don't do this, she pleaded desperately.

Worried to the point of distraction and hearing no reply from him, her hands shook as she placed them on the table with the others, connecting the circle.

"What's the matter, Mary?" Kate murmured warily as her fingers touched those of her friend. "Your hand is shaking."

Ignoring her and pressing on, Oliver told them to close their eyes and he whisked them back in time to January 26th, 1917 and they materialized across the street from the opulent Seattle theatre.

"Where are we?" Gordon asked, looking around at the others and then down at himself—they were now wearing appropriate evening clothes, although Oliver would later erase this from their memory.

"How did you manage this, Oliver?" asked Kate.

"It's a trade secret," Oliver quipped. "That's the James Moore Theatre, Gordon; we need to hurry."

As they crossed between the traffic, Gordon was mesmerized by the old cars and well-dressed patrons milling about the ticket booth. Kate, uncharacteristically speechless, caught sight of a vaguely familiar-looking woman as she came through the crowd toward them.

"Hello Oliver, I'm so glad I found you. My father has taken ill and can't attend tonight," she exclaimed. "Can you use an extra ticket?"

"I'm sorry to hear about your father, Margo, but thank you, yes, we can use an extra ticket. Let me introduce you to these people."

"You don't need to, you must be Mary's mom and dad, so nice to meet you, and ... Kate Reardon, right? You and I have met before. Enjoy the show folks, I must get back to my mother." Hurrying away,

Margo quickly disappeared in the crowd leaving explanations to Oliver and Mary.

Oliver that was awfully lucky, Mary commented. *I wondered how you were going to get a ticket for Kate.*

He just grinned over at her and Kate looked like she was going to ask for an explanation, Oliver silenced her with a nod.

"May I direct you to your seats, sir," an usher, with his hand out, accosted Oliver as they entered the sumptuously decorated foyer.

Showing their tickets, he pointed in the direction of an usher who would take them to the Jorgensen box—they soon found themselves seated in luxurious seats. Only a few minutes passed before a waiter arrived, handing Oliver a tray full of drinks.

"We didn't order any drinks, young man," said Gordon.

"Compliments of Mr. Jorgensen, sir."

Oliver took the tray and tipped the boy while the others watched suspiciously. The drinks all looked the same except for one which was lighter in colour. He passed three drinks across to the Janicks and Mary. They sniffed them cautiously.

"Mine's all right," Gordon chuckled, winking at his wife. "I'll pretend it's Everett beer!"

"They're lemonade?" Janice asked, taking a tentative sip. "Gordon can't have alcohol because of his pills. This is amazing."

"Well Mr. Smarty-Pants Ryan," Kate exclaimed with a playful frown, "you won't have mine right because this should be gin with a hint of ginger."

"Try it, Kate," Mary suggested, as Oliver passed her the lighter coloured glass.

Taking a sip, Kate's face broke into a surprised grin. "It's perfect!" she whispered, "how the heck did you do that?"

"They must have a heavenly bartender," he replied as Mary's elbow nudged his arm.

Chapter 26

As the sound of musical instruments alerted them that the show would soon begin, the Jorgensens arrived and introductions were made. Oliver whispered something into Gus' ear and the shipping magnate smiled and waved him off, pointing to an empty seat in the box. Mary knew they were talking about the fact one of them was sitting in the wrong section with Margo's ticket. Looking around she noted that the theatre was almost full to capacity and a few latecomers were still arriving.

Minutes later, the lights dimmed and in the orchestra pit, the face of one of the violinists was momentarily illuminated as the conductor appeared.

"Oh my gosh, that's my grandfather!" Kate gasped, her fingers squeezing Oliver's arm. "It's him, it's really him!"

"Shh," someone behind them hissed as James Moore, looking resplendent in a bright blue oriental-silk dinner jacket and white cravat, strode out to centre stage. Addressing the now silent audience, he gave his usual passionate plea.

"You all know," he began, "that Nancy's performance not only gives us an extreme amount of joy but also brings us the opportunity to help her Widows and Orphans Fund. Every dime we collect eases the suffering of another Victoria-area family so tragically touched by the war in Europe. I know you will be generous, my friends."

"She gives all the money away?" Janice muttered.

"Yes, she does," Mary whispered. "She's a real angel."

Everyone waited expectantly as the great velvet curtain slowly began to rise and the introduction to the first song began. Spotlights danced across the shiny black grand piano at centre stage revealing Nellie Cornish playing along with the orchestra.

As soon as Nancy stepped onto the stage, the noise was tumultuous. Mary heard several of the women near her gasp as the singer stepped into the spotlight—her fiery red hair cascading over milky white shoulders contrasted with her ankle-length emerald green satin gown. She was a sight to behold and the audience clapped and cheered wildly. Finally, raising her hands in gratitude, she moved closer to the piano and the concert began.

Hands locked, Gordon and Janice enjoyed the show immensely, but they were particularly fascinated to watch Kate sitting bolt upright in her seat holding her small tape recorder—no doubt mentally noting every detail as history replayed itself.

Nancy's emotion-filled singing brought tears to many eyes and hearing Mary's sniffles, Oliver secretively passed her his handkerchief.

I'd better not tell her that Nancy's emotions are very real as she hasn't had word from her brother in Europe for some months, he thought.

At the end of the concert, Oliver whisked his group back to Everett then went to speak to the Jorgensens, making excuses for his party's hurried exit. Returning to the Janick's, he found them all sitting in their places at the table.

"Don't wake them yet, Oliver, I need to talk to you," Mary whispered. "But first I want to give you a hug. That was one of the most wonderful experiences I've ever had. Thank you, darling. Now, you have a problem, that little machine Kate has is a recording device and she's recorded the whole trip to Seattle."

"No fears, my darling, I'll figure out something, but thanks for the warning. Quiet now." With that, Oliver woke them.

Blinking, Janice touched her face and felt the wetness of her own tears. "It was real," she sniffled, running for the bathroom.

"How did you do that, son, changing our clothes and all?" asked Gordon. "That was pretty amazing."

No one answered him but Kate's brain was struggling to find a logical explanation. Then she remembered her tape recorder and located it in the pocket of her jacket.

"Now we'll find out the truth," she muttered with a glint in her eyes as she put the recorder on the table.

Arriving back at the table as the tape was rewinding, Janice waited with bated breath.

"Sit down, Mom," Mary whispered, her mind screaming at Oliver. *Oliver, don't let her run that tape, she'll expose you!*

It's all right, I have everything under control, he assured her.

Sitting tensely, Mary waited as the tape completed its rewind and Kate pushed the play button. Everyone's face lit up as immediately the sounds of an orchestra and a vocalist were heard.

"That's Nancy Wilson," Janice gasped. "It *was* real!"

Suddenly, the recorder went quiet and everyone gasped looking at each other. After a while, when still no sound was heard, Kate scowled, reaching for it, but before her hand could touch the recorder, a loud hissing noise startled them. Then, an eerie whisper emanated from the machine and they all leaned forward holding their breath as they strained to hear the words.

"Believe … angels are real!" whispered the voice and then nothing.

They all looked at each other in disbelief.

"Did that thing say what I think it said?" Kate asked, looking around the table.

Ask Kate to run it again, honey, Oliver prompted.

"Play it again, Kate," Mary suggested nervously.

The reporter's hand dithered as she rewound the tape again and pushed the play button. Leaning closer, they all waited for the expected result but there was only silence.

"There's nothing on there at all," said Gordon in a disappointed voice. "Maybe wc dreamt the whole thing."

"I heard that girl singing," Janice stated emphatically. "We were all at the theatre, we were!"

"But were we really there?" Kate asked, smiling coldly as she looked from one to the other, "or were we merely tricked into believing it was so?"

"I think you've hit the nail on the head, Kate," Mary's father chuckled. "I don't see how we could possibly have been there unless it was pretty powerful magic."

Listening to the discussion with growing interest, Mary felt like screaming at them to tell them that it was real, but she curbed the inclination as Oliver laid a soothing hand on her arm.

"Well folks, do you think we should try it again?" he asked.

"Yes, please," Janice replied.

Oliver, you're not! Mary's thoughts yelled at her husband. *That's quite enough for one night.*

Resting her elbows on the table, Kate clasped her hands and supported her chin, studying Oliver intently before she spoke.

"I don't know where Mary found you, Oliver Ryan, but I'm glad she did. In the short time I've known you, you've stretched my imagination to bursting point and left me a string of mysteries to solve … my car keys, footsteps in the snow, and Gordon's heart attack that turned into a false alarm. Oh and after all your talk of angels, yes I begged for their help that night at the hospital."

"Bless you, Kate," Janice whispered.

"Yes I did, but this has me so confused I can't think straight and I don't like it at all. My brain screams logic and my heart wants to believe in angels."

"That's the life of a reporter," Oliver laughed. "You'll have to sort it out for yourself, Kate."

"How long did our trip to the theatre take?" Gordon yawned. "It must be close to bedtime.

Oliver, look at the clock! Mary's mind shouted excitedly. *We started this experiment after dinner. I remember looking at the clock as we sat down. It was 7:15 and it's only 7:25 now.*

I know, remember time stops for us when we change dates.

"Oh it must have been about three hours," Janice sighed, "I'm feeling tired, too."

Glancing at her watch and then to the big burl clock on the wall, Kate squealed. "It's only 7:30," she giggled. "We were only hypnotized for a few minutes. We haven't been anywhere, that rascal played a trick on our minds."

"Well, he had me believing it," Janice whispered wearily.

"Me, too," Gordon yawned again. "I think I'll go have a shower and get ready for bed."

"We'll wash up, Mom," Mary volunteered. "You and the boys can have the night off!"

Mary watched her folks disappear into their room and Oliver turned on the TV. She and Kate tidied up putting the dishes into the dishwasher as they chatted. By the time they finished and joined Oliver in the living room, her parents had decided to retire and said they'd watch TV in their room. Mary sat down beside Oliver and noticed he was reading one of her father's books.

"What have you found?" she asked.

"A book on old Seattle, it's very interesting."

"More ideas for your hypnosis game?" Kate asked.

"No, I'm trying to think which would be the better time to live in, 1917 or now. It's an idea I have for an article," he added, "which reminds me I had better start on that story about Nancy."

"You could send me there to check out 1917 for you," Kate suggested.

"Have you ever been to Victoria?" he asked.

"Yes, of course, but not in 1917."

"Then go take a look!" Oliver exclaimed, waving his hand.

"No!" Mary screamed, clamping her hand over her mouth as her friend disappeared right in front of her eyes. "Bring her back right now, Oliver!" she cried in desperation.

An icy cold blast of air suddenly filled the room. Mary cringed, wrapping her arms around herself, trying to hold back the tears as she watched Oliver. He stood up and silently came over and put his arm around her as Tom materialized.

"Blast it, lad, that was a bad mistake—the worst!" the old angel sighed, shaking his head. "Now you'll have to go find that girl or she'll be trapped in 1917 with no way back."

"I'll lock onto her thoughts," said Oliver, standing up and beginning to pace the floor. "She's wearing angel earrings, don't worry, I'll be able to find her when she touches them."

"I should have warned you, lad," Tom moaned, "but you got over-confident."

"Please help Oliver bring her back, Tom," Mary begged.

"We're in trouble, lad," the apparition continued. "You'll have to go find her, you can't leave her there."

"I can't find her yet, she has to touch her earrings," Oliver mumbled as reality began to set in.

"Let's go get her right now," Mary insisted, "she can't have gone far from where you sent her."

"Trouble is I didn't send her to any specific place, honey," he admitted, dropping his head. "All I can be sure of is she's in Victoria in 1917."

"Oh Oliver, it's January and she's only wearing a sweater. She'll be freezing!"

Mary's concern was definitely Kate's reality as the reporter's transport back to 1917 Victoria had indeed been instant. Blinking at her strange new surroundings and seeing the slushy streets, she felt the sharp bite of winter consuming her body and pulled her fleece sweater tighter about her. Looking around, she saw odd-looking old cars lining a street barely illuminated by sparsely placed street lights.

"Oh my gosh," she whispered beginning to shiver, "where am I?"

Up ahead she noticed a noisy crowd entering a well-lit building. *That must be a restaurant or a night club,* she thought as she read 'Hotel St. Francis' above the door. *It'll be warmer inside than out here, that's for sure.*

Shivering violently now, the thought went through her head that her feet felt like they were in a bucket of ice water and she looked down. She tried to scream but no sound would come out—she was only wearing socks! Confused and so cold she could barely think, somehow she knew she had to do something and fast. She willed her body to move toward the door. Just as she reached out to open it, it burst open and three inebriated young men rushed toward her, throwing her against the wall. Barely managing to keep her balance, she tried to gather her wits and only the faint rush of warm air coming from the partly open door gave her the necessary strength.

A noisy piano was playing, much like those portrayed in old Westerns and she had the crazy thought that she was going to see men with cowboy hats sitting at the tables. Instead, her senses were assaulted by musty bar smells; a great cloud of tobacco smoke almost choked her. Realizing this was preferable to freezing, she sank into an empty chair not far from the door. By the time the waitress arrived, she knew she was in trouble.

"Tea ma'am?" asked the waitress. She eyed the nodding girl curiously, noting her unusual dress and bedraggled condition but, without comment, moved off to fill her order.

Where the devil am I? Kate's mind now screamed in confusion as the warmth began to penetrate her body. *And how did I get here? This is crazy. Why can't I remember?* She glanced around the room noting the gas lamps flickering against old-fashioned flowered wallpaper, heavy velvet curtains covering wooden windows and the dark, battered-looking wooden floor.

"Where am I?" she whispered to the waitress upon her return.

"Hotel Francis, ma'am."

"I-in what city?" she asked hesitantly as the waitress put a china cup, saucer and teapot in front of her.

"You're in Victoria, ma'am," the waitress replied, looking at her with a new sense of disbelief.

"How did I get here?"

"You just walked in through that door," the waitress replied, pointing to the door a few feet away. "Have you been smoking opium, ma'am?" Then, without waiting for an answer, she was called away.

"No," Kate replied, unaware she was talking to herself, "but I'm confused … oh, she's gone." She took a sip of the hot tea, burning her lip but not feeling it. She imagined that she felt better.

"That'll be two pence for the tea, ma'am," said the familiar girl when she returned a few minutes later.

"Two pence … oh dear, I've lost my handbag!" Kate muttered, reaching out for it then bending to look on the floor. *She said pence, what's going on?* She looked up at the young girl and whispered aloud, "I don't seem to have any money."

"Don't you move, ma'am, I'll call the manager," the girl replied, sounding somewhat excited as she hurried away.

Tears of frustration welled in Kate's eyes. *With no handbag, money, credit cards or driver's license, how will anyone believe me?* She was struggling to apply logic to the situation when she saw the waitress returning. Behind her was the rotund figure of the man she guessed was the manager and he looked none too happy.

"Now what's all this I hear?" he began sternly. "We're not a charitable organization you know."

Unable to cope any longer, Kate broke into tears, sobbing as she lowered her face into her hands.

Hardened by years in the business, Charley Nivens felt little sympathy for this obviously distressed young woman. He moved closer and waited while she composed herself. Watching her with an experienced eye, the glint of her earring caught his attention.

"Are they gold?" he demanded.

"Are what gold?" Kate sniffled.

"Your earrings?"

Her hand went automatically to her earring as she replied. "No."

"I'll take them anyway," he snapped.

"For a tuppenny cup of tea, Charley?" a nearby voice interrupted. "Here's yer dammed tuppence, now be off with ya. I'll attend to the young lady."

Turning, Kate watched in surprise as two large brown coins jingled onto the table and an older man joined her at the table.

"Can I help, my dear?" he murmured in a deep, gentle voice. "Let me introduce myself. I'm Sam Logan, a newspaper reporter with the *Daily Victorian*."

"Newspaper reporter …," Kate whispered, a memory bursting into her mind. "Yes, yes, I'm a newspaper reporter, I remember now."

"Yes, I'm sure you are," he whispered tolerantly. "Do you have a coat and hat somewhere?"

"I-I don't think so," she replied, shivering violently.

Hovering close by, the waitress heard the conversation and answered for Kate.

"She just walked in off the street, Mr. Logan. No coat or hat, dressed like you see her now. Odd, ain't it, sir?"

"Find me a shawl or a blanket, girl, she's going to get pneumonia." After the waitress left them, Sam began to ask Kate questions and realized she was suffering some sort of amnesia as she didn't even know her name or where she lived. He noticed she wasn't wearing shoes and was relieved when the waitress returned with a heavy wool blanket. Sam helped her stand up, wrapping the blanket around her. He explained he was going to take her home but somehow he thought she was beyond caring. Thankfully, he had parked his automobile just outside the door. He picked her up bodily, growled to the waitress to open the door and carried her outside, barking at a passerby to open the car door. By the time he had cranked the car to start it and joined her inside, Kate had realized she was sitting in the passenger seat of an unusually old car. As the engine warmed up, he carefully tucked the blanket in all around her, as inquisitive eyes watched from the hotel windows and the street.

"What kind of a car is this and where are you taking me?" Kate asked with a shiver.

"This is my prized Model T, ain't she a beaut? Don't you worry none," Sam continued, trying to be casual, "my Molly will soon have you well again."

Oliver slept fitfully while Mary tossed and turned beside him, sometimes stopping to sob quietly as Tom Watson watched from a distance. Over an hour had gone by and except for that almost unnoticed moment when she touched her earring, no other contact had been made.

"You'll have to solve this problem without me, Oliver," snorted Tom, reappearing briefly. "You've turned a spirit loose in Victoria with no direction or purpose, possibly endangering her mortal life."

"Couldn't you give her angel powers to come back on her own?" Mary asked.

"No, that's impossible!" Tom snapped. As he disappeared, his voice trailed off into the distance and the coldness of his spirit left the room making Mary shiver.

"He's gonc," Oliver sighed. "We really need to get some sleep, Mary. We can't do anything until Kate calls us." He put his arm around her feeling her tension.

"I won't sleep a wink," she said obstinately, settling into her husband's embrace, but Oliver lifted the worry from her mind and relaxing sleep came at last.

Chapter 27

Leaving his body nestled beside his wife, Oliver's spirit went hurtling toward 1917 Victoria, his mission to find Kate before morning. The few street lights had been turned off and, with only a sliver of a moon, it was difficult for even an angel to find his way.

Where do I start? he wondered hopelessly turning toward town. Suddenly he felt Kate's call as her fingers touched her earring.

Do it again, Kate! his mind screamed. *Do it again!*

"Do what again?" Kate whispered hesitantly as Sam drove past a clanking streetcar at the crest of Fort Street.

"Hush girl, we'll soon be home," Sam replied.

"But you asked me to do it again," she repeated.

"No, I didn't say a word. You're ill and you must be hearing voices in your head."

Huddled under her blanket, she lapsed back into a confused silence, only vaguely aware of her surroundings as the Model T turned down Oak Bay Avenue. In a few minutes, they turned a corner and Sam stopped the car in front of a modest one-storey house and came around to help her. Wrapping the blanket around her, he helped her to the door. It opened as he reached for the handle.

"Good gracious!" gasped his wife clutching her shawl with one hand and pulling the girl inside with the other. "Was there an accident, Sam? She looks half frozen. Quickly, bring her in here to the fire."

"No, there was no accident," Sam explained breathlessly, steering the girl toward a wooden rocking chair near the fireplace. "She wandered into the St. Francis Hotel. Lost her memory, it seems."

"Don't worry, deary, I'm Sam's wife, Molly, and you'll feel much better after a nice hot cup of tea," she said pleasantly, fussing around Kate. She helped her on with a warm sweater and covered her legs with a heavy patchwork quilt.

"Thank you," Kate murmured, already feeling a bit better. "I-I know who I am," she began.

"Listen Sam, she's beginning to remember," Molly called to her husband who had dozed off in his chair.

"M-my name is Kate Reardon. I live in Everett."

"Where are you staying, Kate?" Molly gently coaxed.

"I was at home, the last thing I remember I was talking to Mary and Oliver." As she warmed up, frustration returned and one hand reached for her earring, gently twisting the tiny angel.

"Got ya!" Oliver yelped, swinging around to face in the direction from which the vibes were coming, startling a passing couple. *I found her Mary, she's in Oak Bay.*

You did? Mary awoke sitting up with a start when she heard Oliver's voice. Looking at the sleeping figure beside her, she began to shake him. Oliver's spirit, now torn between his duty to Mary and finding Kate, returned instantly to his physical body.

"You found her?" Mary asked excitedly as his eyes flicked open. "Did you bring her home?"

"No, he didn't!" snapped Tom Watson, coming back to join them. "You called to his mortal body and he had to return."

"Don't worry, honey, we can go straight back," Oliver assured her.

"To Victoria?"

"Yes."

"Not in my nightie, I can't!" Mary moaned, looking down at her clothes.

"Hush!" he warned, grasping her hand.

Fingers entwined, Oliver sent them speeding back through time. She felt the familiar cold breeze on her face, then the texture of soft soil under her feet.

"Where are we?" she whispered, glancing down and feeling greatly relieved when she realized she was fully dressed and standing in mud which had already coated her shoes.

"Oak Bay Avenue, Victoria 1917."

"Where is Kate?" she asked, looking around and noting that the vehicles parked on the muddy street were collectors' cars in her world.

"She's close by, don't worry."

"Easy for you to say," Mary groaned. "Please find her, Oliver."

Less than half a mile away on Davie Street, Molly was able to persuade Kate that staying the night with them would be no trouble.

The warmth of the blazing fire and a cup of hot tea had worked a miracle on Kate's cold and confused body. Feeling much better and more alert, her inquisitive mind surveyed her surroundings. Her attention was drawn to the colourful tile surrounding the fireplace. The log fire felt so comforting, her eyes began to droop but she forced them open by focussing on a large clock with a pendulum on the far wall. The pendulum was swinging back and forth inside a glass-fronted case and again she felt like closing her eyes.

She turned her gaze to a small table below which had wonderful carved legs and then she noticed the pictures—photos of people dressed in clothes from another era and they watched her from heavy picture frames. Her gaze travelled toward the doorway where, for the first time, she noticed an unusual, ornate calendar. As she read the date, she stifled a gasp. It said '5th Day January, 1917'.

"Is that today's date?" she whispered, reaching from under the blanket to point at the calendar. "Is it really 1917?"

"Why yes," Sam assured her. "Today is Friday the 5th."

Kate's thoughts flashed back to Everett and, for the first time, remembered her conversation with Oliver. *My memory is coming back,* she thought joyously. The last words he had spoken to her flashed across her mind. *Has it happened again? Did he really send me back to 1917?* "It's a trick, isn't it?" she mumbled, looking up at the Logans. She tried to smile. "You must be actors, this can't really be 1917."

"Yes Kate," Molly sighed, looking puzzled and glancing at her husband, "it is 1917, but don't worry, you'll remember it all tomorrow."

Kate tried to focus her mind on the Janick's Warren Street home in Everett then, closing her eyes, she thought of Oliver and Mary and her fingers moved to her earring.

"Quick!" said Oliver, grabbing Mary's hand. He homed in on Kate's thoughts taking them quickly to the Logan's doorstep. At the same time, he learned just who her rescuers were.

"Take care, son," they heard Tom whisper. "This is a very delicate matter now. We have a mortal who's aware she's travelled through time. This is most unusual."

Seeing the lights were still on, Oliver went up to the door and knocked lightly.

"I wonder who that could be at this time of night?" Sam muttered, looking at his wife.

"Well answer it, dear, and find out," his wife suggested.

"Good evening, sir," Oliver greeted him pleasantly as Sam opened the door. "I believe you have found one of my patients."

"A patient?" Sam repeated.

"Yes, a young woman named Kate Reardon who suffers mental delusions and memory loss."

Hidden from their view, Kate recognized Oliver's voice and her heart lifted. Molly, watching her closely, noticed a brief expression of relief in her eyes.

"Identify yourselves!" Sam demanded gruffly feeling very protective of his charge.

"I'm Oliver Ryan and this is my assistant, Mary, we are Kate's … guardians," Oliver explained.

"How'd you know she was here?"

"That was easy, sir. Our information said you had given her assistance, for which we are grateful. Being a well-known figure in Victoria, you were not difficult to locate."

The explanation seemed to satisfy Sam and he opened the door wide enough to allow them to enter.

"My wife," he muttered, indicating Molly. "Please take a seat. I'll need a few particulars from you."

Opening a drawer in a small writing table, he took out some paper and a pencil. Sitting down, he motioned Oliver to the facing chair and Mary, seeing Kate in front of the fire, rushed over and hugged her.

"Thank goodness you found me, Mary. I was scared out of my wits and so confused," Kate whispered clinging to her hand. "The Logans have been so kind."

They barely paid attention to the questions Sam was asking Oliver.

"Who do you work for, lad?"

"The highest authority, sir."

"Another government man! Don't you devils ever get tired of interfering in people's lives?"

"It's late, we really should be taking Kate with us," Oliver replied, looking over at the women.

"I'll need your name and address, sir, and the name of your superior. I'm a newspaper man and Premier Brewster is a friend of mine. I shall check this out."

"A personal friend of the premier? Then tell me, sir, will prohibition become a reality this year?" asked Oliver.

Both Mary and Kate's ears perked up. Oliver was using Sam to research some historical information and divert his questions.

"I think not, young man," Sam replied, obviously getting irritated, "the referendum clearly turned it down."

"And the emancipation of women?" Oliver pressed.

"That's anybody's guess," Sam said with a noticeable sigh, his eyes flicking over to his wife. "I think women should get to vote."

"You're darned tooting we should get the vote," Molly expounded, "but if I had a vote I'd get them to close down all them stinking ale houses!"

Smiling, Mary joined in the conversation, asking quietly, "How many are there in Victoria, Mrs. Logan?"

"Over a hundred," Molly replied sharply, her eyebrows raising as she nodded toward her husband, "and he knows every one of 'em!"

"A hundred?" Mary and Kate chorused.

"Yes, and that doesn't include the opium factory in Government Street, or the rabbit warrens in Chinatown!"

"Hold on a minute," Sam growled, "let's get back to the subject at hand. It's too late to be taking this young lady anywhere tonight. I think she should stay with us, as we told her she could, and you can come back tomorrow. I'll need to know where you're staying so I can contact you in the morning."

"No!" Kate yelped, grasping Mary's hand so hard her nails dug into the skin. "You're not leaving me again!"

"There, there, dear, it's all right," Molly comforted her. "You don't want to go out in the cold again tonight. We'll take good care of you and," she looked over at the others, "they can return after breakfast."

A sudden thought flashed through Oliver's head. *This may be the perfect way to convince Kate that angels are real.*

Oliver! Tom's voice rattled in his head. *This has gone far enough. Take her home, now!*

"Could we talk to her alone for a few minutes?" Oliver asked.

"Yes, of course you can," Molly bubbled. "You can use the spare bedroom."

"I want to go home, Mary," Kate begged, grasping her arm as they followed Molly to a little bedroom at the end of the hall.

Quietly closing the door behind them, Molly returned to her husband in the front room. Glancing up from the notes he was writing, Sam frowned.

"Are you sure you know what you're doing, dear?" he asked.

"She needs help," Molly said flatly, "and you brought her here."

"I couldn't just leave her downtown in that state, could I?"

"Well, what did you expect to do with her?"

"Find a doctor, I suppose. Oh blast it, I don't know!"

Behind the closed door of the bedroom, Oliver's mind soothed Kate's fears away as she continued to cling to Mary. Then suddenly her hand dropped from Mary's arm and a twinkle of amusement sparkled in her eyes.

"Oliver's an angel, isn't he Mary? He sent me to 1917, didn't he?" she whispered.

"Yes, Kate, he did," Mary replied, frowning.

"This defies all logic," Kate sighed.

"But can you see the possibilities yet, Kate?" Oliver asked.

"What possibilities?"

"You could write a history column for the newspaper and be the first to get all the facts right … for a change."

"I could travel through time to anywhere I want?"

"Not quite, but I should be able to help you."

"But you sent me here on my own."

"Yes, he did," Mary agreed, shaking her head, "but believe us, Kate, that wasn't intended. It was a mistake and we're so sorry it caused you so many problems. Oliver acted too quickly and we didn't know where you were so he couldn't bring you back. It scared us too, believe me, but now it's all under control."

"But what if you had lost me?" Kate insisted.

"You'd be stuck in that time forever," said Oliver looking forlorn.

"So, how did you find me?"

"It was your angel earring, Kate, when you touched it, I was able to locate you," Oliver explained.

"That's very cool and rather clever, but I wish there was a way to prove it," Kate sighed again. "It's both exciting and scary. Can I try it?"

"You have tried it, Kate, that's how we found you," Oliver interjected. "but there is a way to prove it to you. Touch your earring and silently ask me a question."

"Like telepathy," said Kate grinning. "All right, here goes." Closing her eyes, she touched her earring and thought of a trip on the Anacortes Ferry to Sidney on a bright summer day. Then she silently told him her mother's maiden name. She opened her eyes.

"Your mother's maiden name is Major," said Oliver, grinning broadly, "and you were thinking of the Anacortes Ferry."

"I heard you, too," Mary laughed. "It's amazing but when I touch him I can hear what he hears. It's as if our souls are linked together—no doubt because we were married by the angels."

"You two are amazing," Kate spluttered shaking her head in disbelief, but she quickly calmed herself. "Okay, I'll go along with you if it might further my career," she paused, "but I would really like to have my bag. Can you send me back to Mary's home so I can get it … and my coat?"

"I can give you my coat, but what's so important in your bag, you don't want to have anything in your possession which could arouse suspicion. Wouldn't Molly have what you need?" Mary asked with concern in her voice.

"Oh cripes, you're right. I can't wear my makeup anyway and I don't dare have my cellphone. I guess we better forget that idea."

"So you're willing to say for a day or two, you could learn a lot about old Victoria," hinted Oliver.

"Is everything all right?" Molly called from outside the door.

"Yes, we'll be right out," Mary called. "Okay, are we in agreement what is happening—we can leave you here until say Sunday night?"

Kate nodded reluctantly.

"Are we ready?" asked Oliver and, seeing the women both nod their heads, he opened the door and they returned to the front room where he explained the new situation. "After speaking with Kate, I realize she is still in a weakened condition and travelling would be undesirable. She would like to stay a couple of days with you, if that meets with your approval. We would return for her at nine o'clock on Sunday evening."

"Oh that will be lovely, won't it Sam?" responded Molly, looking over at her husband who nodded doubtfully.

"Here, take my coat," Mary offered, smiling at her friend before they hugged. "I'm sure Molly will have some things you can use in the meantime."

"Oh certainly, dear, whatever you need, but surely you will need a coat tonight," Molly responded. "It's cold outside, let me …."

"I'll be fine, Mrs. Logan, I have a warm sweater on and we have a blanket in the car," Mary assured her as they went to the door and quickly left.

Sam shivered as he stood on the porch and watched the couple move quickly up the wet path, sharing Oliver's coat as they closed the gate and waved. Blowing a cloud of smoke from his freshly charged pipe, he contemplated the evening's strange events. *A story for the newspaper maybe or a puzzle to be unravelled? Who was Kate Reardon and how the devil had she arrived in Victoria? And who were these two? Blast it, I'm going to find out,* he promised himself, going inside and slamming the door.

Rounding the corner, Mary gasped from the cold as Oliver held her even more tightly.

"Hurry Oliver," she begged, her teeth beginning to chatter.

There was a rush of cold air and then sudden warmth as she found herself in the deserted kitchen of her parent's home.

"It's very late," she yawned, "mom and dad are asleep and Kate's car is still outside. I'd better drive it home so they don't wonder when they get up."

"I could send it there but I don't know where she lives," Oliver murmured, a mischievous smile tugging at his mouth. "We could try another experiment … you could send it!"

"Me?"

"Yes, it's easy," he chuckled. "Hold onto me then just think of the car parked at Kate's. My powers should transfer through you."

"Gee, that's wild," giggled Mary, "but do you really think it would work?"

"Let's try it on the picture box first."

"You mean the TV?" Mary giggled as they went into the front room.

"Yes, hold my hand and concentrate on turning it on."

Fingers entwined, Mary stared at the TV and concentrated, blinking her eyes. Suddenly the TV came alive blaring out the late news.

"Oh my gosh, we're going to wake mom and dad!' she whispered, searching for the remote and frantically turning the volume down.

"You could have turned it down with your mind, you know! Now turn it off."

Thc TV went off.

"You did that," she whispered accusingly.

"I did not, you did it all yourself!"

Blinking again, her thoughts turned the picture back on, then off and on again.

"You're right," she gasped in amazement. "I can do it."

"You don't need to blink, Mary, why are you doing that?"

Mary giggled. "I remembered the TV show, *I Dream of Jeannie* and she performed magic by blinking her eyes!"

"What?" Oliver asked.

"Never mind, honey, it wasn't in your century!"

"All right, are you ready to send the car home now?"

"Y-yes," she replied, suddenly none-too-sure of herself.

"Come on then, let's go to the window and do it."

Kate's car had been sitting at the curb so long it was covered in snow. At that moment, a young man walking home from the pub stopped to light a cigarette, leaning against it for support.

"Oh no, there's a man by the car."

"We'll have a bit of fun with him."

"Don't you dare, you've been in enough trouble tonight! We're going to wait until he leaves," she said adamantly.

Oliver pretended to pout but they waited a minute and the man walked away. Grasping his hand again and focussing her thoughts on Kate's carport, Mary blinked her eyes and the car disappeared.

"I did it," she squealed, "and we didn't give that poor guy a heart attack either, he hasn't even noticed!"

"Okay young lady, it's bed for us, that's quite enough excitement for one day."

Chapter 28

Kate was also climbing into bed in the tiny spare room at the Logan house. The bed seemed so small after the queen-sized bed she had at home and the furnishings were sparse, but it was a relief to know who she was and feel safe again. She pulled the bedding up under her chin, noting how heavy the blankets and quilt felt.

Thinking back to her conversation with Molly and Sam that evening, she knew they had given her a fascinating insight into the early days of Victoria. They explained that the years prior to and, now during the First World War, were exceedingly difficult ones for the troubled city and she longed to know more.

Through the wall, she could hear their muffled voices in the next room and guessed they were discussing her predicament. *I have two days to explore Victoria,* she thought as sleep closed off her mind.

Sleeping in, Mary and Oliver awoke to her mother's soft call and a tapping at their bedroom door.

"Breakfast's ready, you sleepy heads," she announced. "It's almost lunchtime."

"Lunchtime?" Mary groaned, lifting her head from the pillow and trying to focus her eyes on the clock.

"It's only nine o'clock, your mother is having some fun with us," Oliver chuckled, pulling his wife back down beside him and tickling her.

"We'd better get up," Mary giggled, after returning his kiss. "I want to go see what Kate's up to in Victoria."

"You want to spy on her! Give her time, honey, she'll come back with so much news it will take her days to fill you in and even longer to write about it!"

Over breakfast, the elder Janicks chattered enthusiastically about Oliver's experiment, believing firmly that their son-in-law had used hypnotism to induce the illusion of travelling back in time.

Kate was having no such illusion. She awoke to the chill of a winter morning with frost leaving its icy patterns on the inside of the bedroom window; and her breath created a cloud of condensation in front of her when she opened her mouth. As Sam cleaned out the ash in the hearth of their only fireplace, the noise left no doubt in her mind where she was.

"Kindling, Molly!"

She heard him call to his wife as she buried herself under the thick layer of blankets. Falling asleep again, it seemed only a short time before she awoke feeling much warmer and the vapour from her breath had totally disappeared. Braving the cold, she quickly changed out of the long flannelette nightgown Molly had loaned her and dressed in her own clothes. Ready to face the day, she nervously opened the door and peeked out.

"The bathroom is through there, dear," Molly called cheerily from the kitchen.

Looking in the direction of her pointing finger, she remembered having been there the night before. It was only a short hallway and at the end through a partly open door, was the clawfooted bathtub. *I bet my grandparents had one of these,* she thought, going inside and closing the door behind her. With renewed interest, she looked around the small room, smiling at the antique water toilet complete with pull-chain and high suspended water tank dripping condensation. She had used it the night before but somehow it had more significance now.

"Well, here goes," she sighed, as the call of nature forced her to sit down. Surprised that the wooden seat wasn't as cold as she expected, she next focussed her attention on the porcelain sink with a single brass tap.

"Oh no," she whispered, remembering last night, "they only have cold water!" She grimaced as she ran the water and delicately gathered a small amount in her palms and dabbed the icy cold liquid onto her face, drying it quickly with the small towel Molly had put out for her. "I guess I won't be having any bath or shower in 1917!" she whispered in disappointment, surveying the large bathtub.

"Breakfast's ready!" Molly called.

When Kate entered the kitchen, the welcome warmth of the wood-burning stove brought a smile to her face and she sat down on the plain wooden chair Sam motioned to. Letting her eyes move around the room, she noticed an old Welsh cabinet that displayed Molly's meagre, but unique, china collection.

"That's a beautiful cabinet you have, Molly," she exclaimed.

"It's junk!" Sam growled.

"It was my grandma's," Molly sighed, ignoring her husband's comment. "It's been in the family since 1853 and I'm sort of attached to it. I taped grandma's last letter to the back of the cutlery drawer."

"All right, all right," Sam grumbled. "I've things to do. Let's get on with breakfast."

Kate noticed the tear as it moved down Molly's cheek, even before she quickly wiped it away. Glancing down at her plate, she let out her breath and longed for her normal bowl of cereal when she saw the egg and bacon swimming in fat. *I'll bet cold cereals haven't even been invented yet!* Hunger soon drove her to dip her toast into the runny egg yolk, tasting it gingerly.

"Mm," she murmured with surprise, "this is delicious."

"Should be," Sam murmured, wiping a trickle of bacon fat from his chin with the back of his hand, "it's cured at the Prairie Tavern."

"Prairie Tavern? What's that, a beer parlour?" Kate asked, between mouthfuls, eagerly eating the eggs and bacon and mopping her plate with another piece of dry toast.

"The Prairie Tavern, girl, is a historic landmark out in the country northwest of here," Sam informed her. "First one was built by Henry Simpson in 1859. The present one was built in 1893." He paused. "It's a train stop on the V & S Railway line to Sidney."

"Can you drive me there?"

"No, girl, it's too far and gas is dear. You want to see it, you can catch a streetcar down to Blanshard and walk on to the station at Cormorant."

Kate's eyes lit up. Here was a story she could write, a first-hand report of a ride on one of Victoria's early railways.

"Could I borrow a pen and some paper please?" she asked. "I would like to take some notes."

"Notes?" Sam cocked a doubtful eyebrow.

"Yes, sir, notes.

"You're not serious about thinking you're a newspaper reporter are you?" asked Molly, placing a quill pen and a little glass dish with a lid in front of her.

Kate swallowed her next words realizing too late that ballpoint pens hadn't been invented yet.

"Perhaps a pencil would be better please Molly, and yes, I am a reporter in Everett."

"Humour her, Molly, she'll soon get over it and that Doctor Ryan will be back for her tomorrow anyway."

"He's not a doctor," Kate retorted as Molly placed some paper and a pencil beside her plate.

"Then who is he, dear?" Molly asked, gently touching her on the shoulder.

"He's an angel," Kate replied flippantly.

"An angel?" Molly whispered, glancing nervously at her husband who had a surprised expression on his face. "But," she began, staring down at the odd writing in Kate's notes. Fumbling for words, she pointed at them, motioning for Sam to come take a look.

"And what language might that be, young lady?" he growled sternly over her shoulder.

"It's shorthand."

"I mean what country?" he asked, scratching his chin.

"What street did you say that railway station was on, Blanshard and what?"

"Cormorant. Look here, girl," Sam snapped impatiently, "tell me what language that is?"

Kate's pencil stopped in mid-air as she put a serious expression on her face. "Egyptian," was the first name that popped into her head and she had said it even before thinking. *It would be futile trying to explain modern shorthand to Sam,* she decided.

"Egyptian is it?" he grunted in deep thought, "and you think Dr. Ryan is an angel, do you?"

Panic welled up inside Kate's mind as Sam suddenly reached for her hand; he was smiling.

"Would you mind if I wrote some notes of my own?" he asked. "You're a fascinating subject, Kate."

After refilling their tea, Molly sat quietly listening to her husband's skilled interrogation of their visitor.

"Now," he said, "let's start at the beginning. You're an American from Everett?" He watched her nod. "And you don't know how you got here to Victoria?"

"Well, yes I do," she said, then paused when she saw Molly's puzzled expression, "and then again, not really, it's all very confusing."

"How old are you," Sam muttered, his pencil hovering over his paper, "and what's your date of birth? Maybe we can trace you through the birth registry."

"I'm 26 and I was born on the 7th of May, 1974."

"That's impossible!" he replied, looking over at Molly and seeing the colour drain from her face. "That means you haven't been born yet!"

Once more, panic gripped Kate. She wasn't being cautious enough and her wild adventure back in time was not going the way she'd expected. In a moment of desperation, she fingered her earring and let her mind scream for help.

"Kate's calling," Oliver whispered as they stood at the librarian's desk in the Everett Public Library. "Come here, we have to go."

"Mary," the librarian called, "is this the book you're looking for?"

"I'm over here," Mary called instinctively, reaching for her husband's outstretched hand as they moved behind a deserted group of bookshelves.

Rounding the corner, the librarian stopped short.

"She just spoke to me!" she whispered, looking around, but there wasn't a soul in the area. There was, however, a single black leather glove lying on the carpeted floor.

Mmm, I seem to remember Mary carrying a pair similar to these when I spoke with her. I wonder where they went in such a hurry.

The tiny porch that sheltered the Logan's front door did little to stop the cold wind that was blowing along Davie Street that morning.

"Come in, come in," Molly welcomed them, as she quickly ushered Oliver and Mary into the warm kitchen.

"Mary!" cried Kate, leaping from her chair to hug her friend. "Oh golly, am I glad to see you."

"Look here, Dr. Ryan," Sam began, "I'd like to get to the bottom of this situation. Kate thinks she was born in 1974. Now what the devil's going on?"

"Please, sir," Molly whispered, touching Oliver's arm and getting a strange tingling feeling in her hand. "Don't misunderstand us, we really do want to help her."

"Now, what are you going to do, son?"

Oliver heard the unmistakeable voice of Tom Watson as he materialized next to the stove. Standing closer to Mary so they touched, she could now see and hear Tom's ranting. "Let's see how you get yourself out of this mess!"

"Mr. Logan!" Oliver said sharply, trying to ignore his mentor. "Let me remind you, sir, 'twas you who offered your friendship to this unfortunate girl."

"Unfortunate girl, am I?" Kate whispered to Mary with a giggle.

"I gave you no licence to pry into Kate's affairs or her state of mind."

"A man needs to know what he's getting into," Sam mumbled.

"Did you not think about that when you rescued her? No, sir, you were a man of honour and merely offered assistance and protection."

Sam's face went a shade of crimson, fidgeting uncomfortably under Oliver's attack. At the same time, Mary noticed Tom was nodding in agreement, rubbing his hands together gleefully.

Reading Kate's thoughts, Oliver realized the appreciation she had for the Logans and knew she would be happy to stay with them. At that moment, he felt another presence in the room and, following his instincts, located the ghostly face of an old lady smiling at him from the Welsh cabinet. He suspected she was Molly's grandmother and the old woman verified his thoughts immediately.

"Would you like Kate to stay?" Oliver asked Molly.

"Oh yes, sir," Molly replied, looking quite overcome with emotion. "Kate needs help and I want to be her friend."

"All right, we'll leave her with you until Sunday evening as already arranged," announced Oliver, turning to Sam. "But there must be no more questions!" Oliver waited until Sam nodded in reluctant agreement. "Be kind to her, her mind is very fragile and her delusions must not be questioned."

There, his voice whispered in Kate's mind, *I've set the stage for you, enjoy your two days in Victoria.*

A trace of a smile moved across Kate's face as she saw the wink Oliver gave her. She hugged Mary one last time, then turned with a twinkle of devilment in her eyes to Oliver.

"Before you go, could you do one last thing for me, Dr. Ryan?" she asked. "I know you appreciate unusual furniture, could you give Mr. and Mrs. Logan an experienced opinion on their Welsh cabinet."

"Why, it's priceless," Oliver said instantly, noticing the old lady's face had disappeared. "That's a wonderful piece of craftsmanship and it should be kept in the family."

"It's time we were going, Dr. Ryan," Mary urged with a trace of playfulness. "We have a meeting with the Janicks and we don't want to keep them waiting!"

The wind was blowing as Oliver and Mary left the Logan's home. Looking back, they saw Kate waving from the window.

"Dr. Ryan's a good man, Sam," Molly murmured squeezing her husband's hand as they watched their visitors leave. "Maybe Kate's right, he is an angel!"

With their faces to the wind, Oliver and Mary hurried to the corner where Oliver slid his arm around her waist.

"Hold on, my love," he whispered, "let's get out of this wind."

"Oh, there you are!" said the surprised librarian looking up to see the missing couple standing in front of her at the counter. "I thought you'd gone. I looked everywhere. You dropped a glove, Mary, and here's the book you wanted."

Back out on the street, the young couple hurried along Hewitt to a restaurant opposite the Mitchell Apartments chosen by Mary's mother for their luncheon appointment.

"Nuisance weather!" Oliver grumbled. "I'm getting tired of all this snow and it's colder here than it was in Victoria!"

The family car standing by the curb told them Mary's folks were already inside.

Later that morning, Kate decided to take Sam's suggestion and catch the streetcar to town but, at the last minute, Molly talked him into driving her. Gratefully accepting some gloves, slightly oversized boots and a hat from Molly, the three of them went out to the car.

The ride into town was both pleasant and interesting. *This is wonderful,* she thought, watching scenes of old houses and differently dressed young children being pulled about on old-fashioned sleighs despite the meagre dusting of snow. *It's just like watching a movie!*

Finding a parking spot near Government and Yates Streets, the Logans watched curiously as Kate stopped to look in each shop window. Pulling Mary's coat closer to her body to keep warm, Kate shivered but continued her exploration, thinking of the story she would be able to write on her return home.

She stopped at 652 Yates, staring in wonder at the unusual array of items in the cigar shop window. Then, she moved on to look through the large window of the Wilson Hotel, the barber shop next door, the pool hall and the shoeshine. She asked a myriad of questions and Sam filled her in on snippets of local history whenever he could.

Outside 642 Yates, where a sign said 'White Lunch Café,' Molly announced this was one of their favourite eating places.

"We should take Kate for a cup of tea," Sam suggested.

Molly quickly agreed and they gratefully entered the warm room. Removing their coats, Sam hung them on hooks then, a waitress showed them to a window table, calling them by name. Kate accepted the single-paged menu and began to study it.

"My goodness, these are ridiculously low prices!" she declared, a bit too loudly for Sam's liking and he quickly ordered tea and raisin scones with jam.

All afternoon she led the Logans from shop to shop on both sides of Government Street, down Fort to Wharf and, finally, as darkness began to set in, they walked up Bastion Street. Sam, although obviously tired, continued to describe the history of its famous courthouse and businesses of ill-repute.

There seemed no end to Kate's inquisitive energy and, although trying not to overly show her delight, she was thrilled with the knowledge she had gleaned that day.

The next morning, after a restful evening and a better sleep on the soft mattress, Sam broke down and he and Molly took Kate on a tour. First, they drove to town and boarded the V & S Railway to Sidney. Partway there, in the midst of a farming area, they made one of many stops and Sam came to sit beside her.

"Remember I told you that your bacon was cured at the Prairie Tavern, well, this is the place."

"What a quaint little building," she mused as the train blew its horn and they continued on their way.

After a short stop in Sidney, they returned to Victoria and Sam announced they were going to see some of the local sights. They went back to the car and, going through Beacon Hill Park, they went along Dallas Road, passing some wonderful old homes until they reached the Observatory on Gonzales Hill, explaining this was Victoria's weather station.

"Oh, wouldn't you know it," sighed Molly when they drove up the hill to the odd-shaped white building with the rounded top. "This usually has a wonderful view over to Port Angeles, dear, but it's too foggy today."

They went back to town, stopping at the breakwater and the new deep water docks on Dallas Road but here it was too cold to even get out of the car. Returning to the harbour, they watched the heart-breaking scene of a hospital ship off-loading its cargo of wounded soldiers, and then he announced he was treating them to dinner at the Empress Hotel.

"Ooh Sam, isn't that being a bit extravagant?" asked Molly.

"I thought it would be nice for Kate's last night in Victoria and besides, you don't really want to cook, do you, dear?" he teased, knowing he didn't take his wife out often enough although they could certainly afford it. He also knew Molly had become terribly fond of Kate and her bubbling enthusiasm. He had to admit that, despite the strangeness of the situation, he was glad he had befriended her. No matter what his research turned up, he was confident he would be able to turn Kate's story into a rather interesting newspaper column.

Dawdling over dinner, he had to remind them Kate needed to be back at the house for nine o'clock. Barely arriving home in time, Molly was hanging up her coat as the clock chimed the hour. Almost immediately, a knock at the door announced that Kate's visit had come to an end and Sam went to answer the door.

"Are you ready, Kate?" Mary asked her friend as she and Oliver stepped into the Logan's front room.

"Not really," she admitted. "I've had a wonderful time and feel so much better now."

"You know we have no choice, Kate," said Oliver. "We have to take you back."

It was difficult for Kate to express her thanks to this sweet couple who had taken her in so willingly. She turned to Sam who was holding his hand out to her. Ignoring it, she gave him a hug.

Tearfully, Molly took the young woman in her arms. "Kate, I want you to have this," she sniffled, dropping a chain with a tiny cross into the girl's hand. "It belonged to my grandmother."

Squeezing Oliver's fingers, Mary sighed at the touching scene. Then, seeing the old lady's smiling face appear in the cabinet window, she realized that Oliver had made contact with the spirit of Molly's grandmother.

Tell Kate to accept the gift, Angel Ryan, whispered the fading apparition.

"Oh, I couldn't," Kate gasped tearfully, looking at the old necklace. She seemed to hear Oliver's voice telling her it was all right and she took it from Molly, smiling her thanks.

They went outside and Oliver closed the gate behind them. Kate turned and waved one last time. Oliver hooked arms with the girls and, turning the corner, instantly left the year 1917 behind. Arriving back in the year 2000, he found a phone and called a cab, asking the driver to take them to an all-night restaurant.

"Why are we here?" Kate asked when the taxi stopped and they went inside the restaurant. "I want to go home."

"You are at home," Mary whispered, as Oliver directed them to a table by the window which looked out onto the brightly lit parking lot. Mary threw him an inquiringly glance but said nothing.

"You'll feel better with a cup of coffee," Oliver assured her. "It will help relax you and then we'll get you home."

"I would like to know what happens to Molly and Sam."

"All right," said Oliver, "I'm working in Victoria this week and I'll check into it for you. Mary can bring you over on Friday evening. I'll give you my report and we'll show you the modern city of Victoria."

"That's a great idea," Mary agreed.

"Now why don't you get Kate's car so she can drive us home!"

"Me?" asked Mary, looking out at the empty parking lot.

"Yes silly, you know you can do it, look outside, Kate."

Mary giggled as she took Oliver's hand.

"Oh my gosh!" Kate gasped, recoiling as her car appeared under the light outside. "You … you did that Mary? You're an angel, too!"

"No, I'm an angel's wife and that seems to give me some pretty extraordinary powers," she replied, squeezing Oliver's hand.

"I believe you, but that doesn't alter the fact that this whole thing scares me to death."

"Look Kate. There really isn't anything to be scared about. I've given you an opportunity to write about 1917 from first-hand knowledge. Just accept it," Oliver chuckled. "You've been there and you've seen it, now go and write about it … choosing your words wisely, I might add."

Few words were spoken as they went outside and Kate drove them home, whispering 'good night' as they hugged each other in front of the Janick house. Her thoughts were in turmoil.

Angels are real, she kept repeating to herself. She had no doubts about it any more, she had lived a weekend that defied all known logic.

Chapter 29

The next week passed slowly for Kate, although she did talk to Mary several times so they could plan their trip to Victoria. During their conversations, Mary realized Kate was obsessed with learning more about Oliver.

"Didn't he scare you when you first met him?" she asked one day.

"Not really, by the time I knew he was an angel, we were in love."

"Well, how do you get to be an angel?"

"Oh that's a story only Oliver could tell you," Mary replied evasively, changing the subject.

The trip to Victoria was highly anticipated by both girls and they were full of expectation as they boarded the *Clipper* in Seattle late Friday afternoon. Booked into a nearby hotel, they were met on the dock by Oliver in a taxi. He announced he had made dinner reservations at the Empress but directed the driver to the hotel so they could drop off their overnight bags. After a sumptuous dinner at the Bengal Room, they walked up the street to Rogers' Chocolates where Oliver purchased a selection of their famous creams just before closing.

"I don't want you girls eating all of these," he chided as they returned to the street. "I thought we'd take some back to Gordon and Janice. Let's go for a little walk; we can always catch a taxi back to the hotel later."

"This isn't what it used to look like at all," Kate whispered, as she stopped to stare at the rundown front of the Hotel Francis on Yates Street. "The railway tracks are all gone, too."

"I know," Mary chuckled. "Oliver brought me here in 1916, it's all changed and I'm not sure I like it as much, except it sure is quieter!"

"I'm getting tired but it's such a nice evening, let's walk back to the hotel," Kate suggested after strolling the streets for over an hour.

"I know what you mean, Mary. Victoria is a beautiful and interesting city no matter what year you come here! I love all the lights, the old buildings, and it's not very far to walk to the hotel!"

They all laughed and arm-in-arm they headed down the hill following a horse and carriage with a happy couple cuddled under blankets as they listened to the driver give her spiel on Victoria history. They laughed hysterically, going cross-eyed, after Kate suggested they count the thousands of lights on the Legislative Buildings and the girls dragged Oliver around to the back of the immense building to view the lighted fountain. By the time they arrived at the hotel, they were exhausted. Hugging Kate goodnight at her door, they promised to meet at eight o'clock for breakfast.

The next morning they found a restaurant overlooking the harbour and as they waited for breakfast to be served Kate asked a question.

"Could we go visit the Logans this morning, Oliver?"

"Actually, that would be a good idea," Oliver replied.

After breakfast, they caught a taxi to Ross Bay Cemetery and Oliver asked the driver to wait.

"Why have we come here?" Kate asked. "This isn't Davie Street."

"Come, I've something to show you," Oliver urged, leading the way along the well-kept path through an amazing assortment of monuments and gravestones.

He stopped in front of a tiny headstone and bent down to move a few wet leaves aside.

REST IN PEACE
SAM LOGAN 1865-1947
MOLLY LOGAN 1871-1948

Kate groaned, dropping to her knees in the wet grass.

"I should have realized," she sobbed. "They were so kind to me."

Oliver went to stand next to Mary taking her arm as he exerted his mind's power onto the grave. Suddenly Kate gasped, jumping to her feet as a smoky mist oozed from the ground slowly turning into the images of Sam and Molly. They looked older but were smiling and held each other's hands just as Kate remembered.

"Don't be afraid, Kate dear," Molly's ghostlike voice whispered. "We have a message for you."

Speechless and shaking, Kate clutched Oliver's arm but she couldn't take her eyes off the two figures.

"My grandmother's Welsh cabinet urgently needs your attention," Molly explained. "You'll find it at Lund's Auctioneers on Fort Street." Then, the spirits disappeared as suddenly as they had arrived.

"Did I imagine that?" asked Kate, turning to her friends.

"No, you didn't imagine anything, Kate. We must get to Lund's quickly," Oliver replied.

Making their way back to the taxi, a sudden cold wind rushed through the bare trees. As Kate hurried after the others, she could have sworn she heard voices saying goodbye. She looked up into the trees and shivered.

"Lund's on Fort Street," Oliver snapped as they climbed back into the taxi, "and step on it please!"

In less than ten minutes, they were at the front door of the auction house where a flurry of activity was taking place and people were loading antiques and pictures into their vehicles. Oliver paid the driver and they hurried inside. Kate looked around the almost empty room and shook her head in dismay.

"There seems to be another room over there," said Oliver, taking her arm and urging her forward.

"There, there it is!" Kate cried with relief, pointing to the far wall where the Welsh cabinet stood all by itself.

A clerk was working nearby when he noticed them.

"Would you like to purchase that cabinet? Strangely it didn't sell today." He was eager but Oliver ignored him and went over to the dark wooden cabinet easing it away from the wall.

"Yes, please," Kate hurriedly replied.

"How much?" Oliver grunted.

"Forty dollars, sir."

"Can you deliver it to Everett, Washington?"

"Yes, sir, I'll get you a price."

"No, don't bother," Oliver said with some hesitation. "We'll take it with us, just give us a receipt."

Reaching for his billfold, Oliver was about to extract his money when Kate stopped him.

"No Oliver, but thank you," she said gently, "this is mine, I must pay the bill. How much did you say?"

"Forty-five dollars and sixty cents with tax."

Kate handed the young man her credit card.

"I'll just be a minute, thank you Ms Reardon," he said, reading the card and going over to a nearby cash register.

Kate moved quickly, going over to the cabinet and reaching for the drawer.

"Not yet!" Oliver hissed. "Wait until it's legally yours."

"What are you two talking about?" Mary asked.

Before Oliver could answer, the clerk returned with the paperwork. Handing Kate the credit card slip and a pen he told her, "It has to be out of here by noon on Tuesday." After she signed it, he handed back her card and the receipt. "If you need any further assistance, just give me a shout," he said as he walked away.

"Thank you," Kate said weakly, as excitement began to overcome her. Now, wasting no time, she pulled the drawer out of the cabinet and turned it on its end revealing an old envelope, brown with age, still barely glued to the wood.

"What is it?" Mary whispered as Kate gently pulled it free.

"It's the last letter Molly received from her grandmother. She told me about it when I was with them."

Fingers shaking, Kate slowly eased open the flap of the envelope and slipped out two pieces of paper, both yellowed and faded by time yet still able to be deciphered. Eagerly, she read the first sheet.

"It's just a note on their family genealogy," she sighed. "Hold on, these names look familiar." Kate's finger traced down the paper halting at Molly's parents. "MacDonald, Colin Archibald Fergus MacDonald," she whispered. "There couldn't be two people with that exact name, could there? My mother's family tree has a very similar name. This is really getting spooky. Do you think Molly and I could actually be related?"

"I guess you'll solve the mystery when you get home, Kate," said Mary, looking suspiciously over at Oliver.

Carefully folding the sheets, Kate slipped them into her bag. "I can't wait to check, but right now I have to arrange for it to be delivered to Everett."

"Put the drawer back, Kate, and take Mary's hand," Oliver whispered, winking at her. "Now, think of the place in your apartment where you would like it."

"You can move a cabinet to Everett from here?" Kate gasped. "That's impossible! How?"

"Just the same way I sent you back to 1917!"

With all of them holding hands, Oliver locked his mind onto Kate's thoughts as she visualized her apartment.

"There you are," he whispered, as the cabinet disappeared. "It's already there!"

Kate stared at the empty space and shook her head. "What can I say, Oliver," she said, smiling gratefully as they moved her toward the door. "You're a treasure."

"No Kate, he's an angel," Mary whispered fondly, "and I love him dearly."

"I think I do too!" Kate laughed.

A week later when Oliver came to Everett, he asked Mary if she had had time to think about their upcoming decision. Deciding to go out for a walk after dinner, they compared notes, discussing the strange possibilities of living their lives in two different times.

"It's too difficult a decision to make by ourselves, darling," Mary sighed as they stopped to sit on a bench in the park. "I don't want to leave my parents alone as they face the later years of their lives, yet I know you're more comfortable in 1917. What are we to do?"

"I don't know yet, but I have a plan forming in my head and, perhaps with Tom's help, we won't have to make that decision."

"The Ross Bay spirits won't listen to your mortal argument," came the all-too-familiar voice. "You're making it very difficult, Oliver, and I only have a week left before my time is up," ranted Tom Watson, "unless William Rushmore will grant me another extension."

Immediately things began happening, for when the tired old angel sent his thoughts through space calling for the Chief Angel, a bright star came hurtling to his side illuminating the area near the park bench. Mary looked around furtively, hoping no one was watching.

"You're supposed to retire in a few days. Mr. Watson," the Chief Angel's voice rumbled. "What is it that has become so urgent?"

"I need an extension, sir."

"Another extension?" Rushmore's voice boomed. "Why man, you've earned the rest. You've worked over a hundred years as it is!"

"Please, sir, I know," Tom replied, "but I would like to have at least a short extension."

"All I can offer is a 100-year term, you know that, Watson." Seeing the angel nod, Rushmore continued, "Then, so be it, I hereby appoint you for one more term. We will meet to decide the fate of the Ryans on January 27th, one week from tomorrow." With that, the bright light rose into the air taking the Chief Angel with it.

"Right, now we can make plans," Oliver's guardian said jubilantly, his pleasure quite obvious despite his sacrifice. "It's a long time since I was involved in a worthy fight!"

"You're going to help us, Mr. Watson?" Mary whispered.

"Yes, my dear, I surely am!" he chuckled. "Oliver was my creation—the first mortal to be inaugurated as an angel. The experiment has been a complete success, I might add, despite a few challenges! I know Oliver has a plan which won't exactly meet with the council's approval but I think it is fair and just and I shall defend your decision with all my power."

Having been a lawyer in his mortal life, albeit a longtime ago, he was able to give them some valuable clues on how to face their situation and plan a strategy to use against the council—those great angels of the past who wanted to decide their destiny.

One week later, just before midnight on the evening of Saturday, January 27th, Tom appeared again.

"Are you ready my children?" he inquired, talking even before he materialized. Seeing their solemn faces, he clapped his hands and chided them. "Don't you even think about losing this battle, we have to believe we will win and that the angels are watching over us!"

"Oh Tom," Mary laughed nervously, "you and Oliver are the angels!" Grasping her husband's hand, she had a last fleeting vision of the fears she'd been facing for the past month. She shivered at the thought of confronting these great men of the past as they argued their case to an insensitive court, but she whispered, "Let's do it!"

Seeing Oliver nod his agreement, Tom Watson whisked them back through time to Victoria's Bastion Street courtroom.

"What year are we in, Mr. Watson?" Mary asked before two robed and wigged clerks took each of them by the arm and led them away.

"1917," he replied.

Ushered into the prisoner's box together, the door closed behind them. Mary grabbed Oliver's hand as the presiding judge appeared—the tall foreboding-looking figure none other than Judge Mathew Baillie Begbie, often referred to in history as the 'Hanging Judge.' Dressed in wig and long-flowing black robe, he strode with authority toward the stately looking chair at the front of the courtroom and sat down, wrapping his robes around himself with a flourish. Behind him came the solemn historical figures of Justices Henry Crease, David Cameron and John Hamilton Cray who would act as counsel for the prosecution—the spirits.

"Let the proceedings begin," a hollow-voiced clerk sang out, glowering at the defendants and instructing them to sit down.

Mary took her notebook out of her handbag and began to sketch the scene. She was determined to have a record of the trial for history's sake, but a loud command from the judge brought her scribbling to a halt.

"Pay attention, young lady! Your future is at stake here."

Mary jerked to attention, annoyed and surprised to be admonished by the ghostly judge from the past. Her pencil clattered to the floor.

"Take those things away from her," Begbie ordered a guard, "and bring them here."

"No, you will not," Mary cried defiantly.

"Madam!" Judge Begbie's voice made the windows shake, "you will abide by the rules of this court." Glowering under bushy eyebrows, he brought his gavel down with a resounding crash.

"Give them to him, Mary," Oliver whispered, "you really don't want to annoy him, trust me."

"No!" cried Mary as the bearded guard snatched up her notebook, sneering as he glanced at the drawing and offered it to the judge.

Adjusting his spectacles, the notorious Judge Begbie stared at Mary's sketch of himself. Gently straightening a folded corner on the drawing, he scratched at his beard and uncharacteristically smiled.

"Very good, young lady, but you must pay attention. Guard, give this back to her," he added, handing back the notebook.

Mary, utterly shocked by Begbie's reaction, whispered her thanks, accepting the notebook and retrieving her pencil from the floor.

"Read the charges!" Begbie shouted, returning order to the room.

A wigged-and-gowned court officer rose slowly, shuffling his feet nervously as he turned to face the court.

"M-my L-Lord and o-officers of this court," he began hesitantly.

"Get on with it, man!" the judge cried irritably.

"Th-the prisoners are charged with defying the ancient law of time and refuse to choose a time in which to live."

"Objection!" Tom Watson's voice rang through the court, as his white-haired head bobbed up from the defence counsel bench. "The prisoners have broken no law that I am aware of."

"Sit down, Mr. Watson, you'll get your chance."

"But Your Honour, this is highly irregular—there are no charges to answer," Tom Watson objected.

"Damn it, Tom, sit down!" Judge Begbie hissed, banging his gavel and nodding to the prosecution.

"The prisoners come from two different time zones, sir," Judge Henry Crease droned for the prosecution. "The Afterworld Council were coerced into allowing them to marry and they were given a choice of which time they wanted to live in, but refuse to make a decision. Therefore, we ask that the court make a binding ruling."

"Now it's your turn, Mr. Watson," the judge said mischievously.

Tom Watson hopped onto his feet, winking at Mary and Oliver. He stood as tall as his frame would allow and glowered at his audience.

"When you're ready, Watson," Begbie urged impatiently, watching as Mary again began to sketch furiously on her pad.

"Well, sir, as I said previously, these charges have no foundation whatsoever. No laws have been broken."

"You will elaborate, I presume," Begbie added sardonically.

"Oliver Ryan was initiated into the Great Hall of Angels, an experiment as the first mortal angel. His appointment has been confirmed by Chief Rushmore and cannot be rescinded."

"Then remove Mr. Ryan from the prisoner's box immediately!" Begbie cried. "You're wasting my time!"

"Objection!" the prosecution shouted in unison. "Oliver Ryan must be held responsible for his actions," continued Judge David Cameron.

"His actions, sir, are without reproach," Watson said calmly.

"Gentlemen, gentlemen," Begbie's voice thundered. "I shall tolerate no more of these interruptions."

Mary winced at the noise, unable to follow the proceedings between the fierce exchange of words and Judge Begbie's crashing gavel. She put her head on Oliver's shoulder and tried desperately to hold back her tears as she began to tremble.

"Stop!" another voice suddenly broke through the noise. Casting furtive glances at the speaker, the court settled into a subdued silence as everyone anxiously waited.

Sir James Douglas rose to face the court—whiskers bristling as his walking stick tapped irritably on the wooden floor between his square-toed boots.

"Courage children, hold fast to the faith you have in each other," he said with an unusually calm demeanour.

Wiping her tears, Mary squared her shoulders and sat up straighter. Oliver gave her arm a quick squeeze letting it go as he, too, stood up.

"Gentlemen," Oliver's voice rang through the courtroom. "I didn't ask you to interfere in my life, you chose me. It was you who gave me the power to move through time."

"We gave you no permission to fall in love!" shouted the prosecution.

Getting confidently to her feet, Mary frowned as thoughts of modern-day logic coursed through her brain. "This court has no jurisdiction over love!" she declared in as loud a voice as she could muster. "It's a feeling mortals experience, you were all mortals once, did you never love someone special? You are responsible for this problem as you left Oliver with his mortal emotions."

"Bunkum and rot!" the prosecution shouted.

"Shut up, you fools!" Begbie roared. "She's absolutely right. Case dismissed!" He banged the gavel on the desk and sighed, turning to face the mortal couple. “May I offer you my best wishes, Mr. and Mrs. Ryan. You may now live in any time you please!”

Stunned with the speed of the judge’s decision, Mary stared at this great historical figure, unable to move or say anything.

“It’s all right, darling,” Oliver assured her putting his arm around her. “It’s over at last and we’re safe.”

“Please take me home to my time, Oliver,” she whispered, sitting down heavily.

Oliver sat down beside her and, feeling her body begin to tremble, he took her into his arms and held her close. One by one, they watched the Afterworld figures fade from the courtroom, but Tom Watson was not ready to leave just yet. Coming to stand in front of them, he smiled, and raising his thumb to Mary, winked. Then he turned to Oliver.

“You’ve learned your lessons well, my son, and you certainly chose wiscly in a partner for eternity. Now you’re free to seek your life together, in whatever way and time you wish. I’ll try to find some measurc of obscurity to wait out my years, but I’m still your guardian and will be watching over you, although I doubt you will ever have need of me again. With that, he tipped his hat and faded into oblivion.

Oliver felt a deep sadness briefly wash over him as he watched his old mentor leave, then he gathered Mary into his arms again, kissed her tenderly, and directed his thoughts to home.

THE END